D1007098

Also by Roni Loren

THE ONES WHO GOT AWAY
The Ones Who Got Away
The One You Can't Forget
The One You Fight For
The One for You

SAY EVERYTHING
Yes & I Love You
What If You & Me

for you & no one else

RONI LOREN

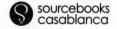
sourcebooks
casablanca

Copyright © 2022 by Roni Loren
Cover and internal design © 2022 by Sourcebooks
Cover illustration by Elizabeth Turner Stokes

Sourcebooks and the colophon are registered trademarks of Sourcebooks.

All rights reserved. No part of this book may be reproduced in any form or by
any electronic or mechanical means including information storage and retrieval
systems—except in the case of brief quotations embodied in critical articles or
reviews—without permission in writing from its publisher, Sourcebooks.

The characters and events portrayed in this book are fictitious or are used fictitiously. Any
similarity to real persons, living or dead, is purely coincidental and not intended by the author.

All brand names and product names used in this book are trademarks, registered trademarks, or trade
names of their respective holders. Sourcebooks is not associated with any product or vendor in this book.

Published by Sourcebooks Casablanca, an imprint of Sourcebooks
P.O. Box 4410, Naperville, Illinois 60567-4410
(630) 961-3900
sourcebooks.com

Library of Congress Cataloging-in-Publication Data

Names: Loren, Roni, author.
Title: For you & no one else / Roni Loren.
Other titles: For you and no one else
Description: Naperville, Illinois: Sourcebooks Casablanca, [2022]
   Series: Say everything; book 3
Identifiers: LCCN 2022004923 (print) | LCCN 2022004924 (ebook)
   (trade paperback) | (epub) | (pdf)
Subjects: LCGFT: Novels.
Classification: LCC PS3612.O764 F67 2022 (print) | LCC PS3612.O764
   (ebook) | DDC 813/.6--dc23/eng/20220204
LC record available at https://lccn.loc.gov/2022004923
LC ebook record available at https://lccn.loc.gov/2022004924

Printed and bound in Canada.
MBP 10 9 8 7 6 5 4 3 2 1

To Donnie, my favorite person ever

For You & No One Else contains frank discussions of mental health, alcohol addiction, the loss of loved ones, escaping a religious cult, and suicidal thoughts.

chapter **one**

MERRY FREAKING CHRISTMAS.

Eliza stared at the ceiling, willing herself to get out of bed, telling herself that she could have gingerbread cookies for breakfast, that she could stay in pajamas for as long as she wanted, that she could binge-watch *The Great British Baking Show* or *Gilmore Girls* all day and no one would be the wiser. She could have a great, rejuvenating day. Do all those self-care activities she talked about on her YouTube wellness channel. But none of her internal pep-talking was working today. Christmas wasn't meant to be a solo holiday, and no mental gymnastics were going to convince her subconscious otherwise. That part of her knew what was up and wanted to pull the blanket back over her head and wait for tomorrow.

Eliza did exactly that for a solid twenty minutes, safe in her blanket tent, but then it started to get humid under there and she had to pee. She groaned at how ridiculous she was being. If her clients could see her now, literally hiding from the world like a little kid, they'd cancel their appointments in a hot second. Therapists weren't supposed to have trouble getting out of bed in the morning. Therapists *also* weren't supposed to wet the bed, so she'd better get herself up before she broke that rule, too.

With a new sense of urgency, she flipped her blanket down

and hurried to the bathroom to take care of the necessities. Once she'd brushed her teeth and washed her face, she felt a little more human, but she plopped back on her bed anyway—on top of the covers, though, so she counted that as progress.

She checked her smartwatch, the screen informing her she'd had a restless night. *You don't say!* She could almost hear its little electronic brain judging her—*Maybe staying up 'til 2:00 a.m. watching sappy Christmas movies and drinking spiked eggnog alone until you're dizzy isn't the best life choice, Eliza.* She winced, her head throbbing from last night's activities—which had seemed like a good idea at the time—and reached for her phone. She grabbed it from the side table and unlocked the screen, making sure she hadn't missed any calls from the answering service.

Zero messages. The ping of disappointment that zipped through Eliza startled her, and she let out a frustrated breath. "*Relief,*" she said aloud, her tone firm. "That's what you're supposed to feel, Eliza. Your clients didn't have any emergencies. That's good news."

But the self-berating didn't help. Knowing she wasn't needed anywhere or by anyone today, even by her clients, made her throat want to close up. Her nose began to burn and her chest tightened. She shook her head. *Nope…nope, nope, nope. Not doing that today.*

She would *not* have a repeat of last Christmas when she'd embodied every open-mouthed sobbing, mascara-streaked GIF on the internet. She'd allowed herself one Ugly Cry Christmas. One. Her parents wouldn't want her to make that a tradition. Her parents would want…

She inhaled a deep breath, trying to suck the energy out of a thought spiral that would lead nowhere good, and quickly opened her YouTube channel to distract herself with the stats on her latest video.

Solo on Christmas?
5 Ways to Make the Holiday Special

232 new likes

Okay. Not bad numbers. And she had a few new comments as well.

> **BreccaBri24:** Love this! My family lives far from me, and I didn't have the funds to travel this year. I was dreading Christmas, but I tried your tip about being open with friends about my solo state and a few have invited me to their family's celebrations. Now I've got more places to go than I can probably fit in!
>
> **GiPesslGi:** I love the idea about volunteering on Christmas! Last year, I helped serve meals at the local women's shelter, and it was the most meaningful holiday I've ever had. This year, I'm going to be helping out at the animal shelter! 🐱 😃

Some of the heaviness in Eliza's chest eased as she scanned through the comments. Even though she was failing spectacularly at taking her own advice today, it gave her some comfort to know her tips had brightened at least a few people's holidays. Plus, good responses to her videos always cheered her. A bigger online platform meant more clients, steadier income, and possibly some online sponsors one day. Maybe something even bigger than that—like a book deal on the relationship book she'd been trying to write for the last year.

Plus, the awkward adolescent version of herself that still lived right beneath the surface, the one who'd had to move to a new school midyear in seventh grade and couldn't have bought popularity with a million-dollar check, still got a little thrill at being *liked*.

Buoyed, she climbed off her bed, vowing to follow her video Tip 5: *Remember, it can be just another day. Remove the pressure.* Her head pounded with a dull thud, and her stomach was considering staging a coup as she made her way back into the bathroom, but the hot shower and putting on a little makeup worked wonders. By the time she was dressed and having her café au lait and a piece of toast on her couch, she felt somewhat human again.

She raised her coffee mug toward her houseplants, which were basking in the meager New Orleans sunshine filtering in through her sliding glass doors. "Merry Christmas, y'all." She'd taken to naming the plants because she'd been posting them on Instagram and felt they needed identities. She set her cup down and took a few quick photos of Hemingway, the pencil cactus with the single red Christmas ornament she'd hung on him Charlie Brown style. She posted the pic with the caption, Happy Holidays from Hemingway! Hope you all have a wonderful day!

A comment instantly popped up from one of her followers. Merry Christmas to you and Hemingway!

Then another. Hemingway looks lonely. You should get a pet!

Eliza frowned at the word *lonely*, the plant suddenly looking sad in the picture instead of festive, and that chest pressure tried to return. She quickly deleted the photo and, for a moment, wished she had a furry companion to post instead. She'd considered adopting a dog a while back, had even filled out the paperwork and gone through all the steps, but the lady who'd done her home visit had seemed very judgy about Eliza's singlehood and busy work schedule. She'd both pissed Eliza off *and* undermined her pet-parent confidence. Maybe she *was* too busy. Maybe she *was* too single. She'd never gone back to the shelter.

She sent a quick text and a GIF of a puppy popping out of a gift box to her friends Andi and Hollyn, puppies on the brain now.

Her friends responded within seconds, each with their own well wishes and accompanying GIF. They had both invited Eliza along to Christmas celebrations with their partners and families, but despite the advice she'd given her YouTube followers, she didn't want to feel like a guest anywhere today, an intruder on other people's family traditions.

Plus, her holiday grief was like a bomb with a hair trigger. She wasn't foisting that liability onto her friends' get-togethers. One minute she might be that fun lady who knew all the words to "Grandma Got Run Over by a Reindeer," and the next she might dissolve into hysterics because someone else's mom *also* likes to make shrimp-and-crabmeat dressing on Christmas. No way. Spending the day alone was the right choice.

Very, very alone.

Eliza closed out her texting screen, and as if on autopilot, her thumb shifted to the bright-magenta square she clicked on way too often—Aligned. Male faces appeared on her screen, and something unlocked in her shoulders, like a nice glass of wine making her muscles relax. Other single people. People like her. Anonymous photos stared back at her. Swipe left. Swipe left. Swipe left. She wondered if any dude on the dating app was sitting alone like her this morning, wishing for his own Hallmark Christmas movie. Not likely.

Most of the guys she met on Aligned were searching for a whole other kind of movie fantasy, one with a mature rating and a one-night expiration date. She'd tried that route for a while but had learned she was too goal-oriented to enjoy hookups that were leading nowhere. Plus, strolling into work the next day to give people advice on how to have a healthy romantic relationship when the guy she'd slept with the night before had called her *sweet thing* because he couldn't remember her name made her feel like a hypocrite.

She didn't begrudge people their hookup lifestyle. She'd just learned it wasn't for her. Her parents had ruined her with their epically romantic relationship. They'd been so devoted to each other that her mom had even given up a tenured professorship so her dad could accept his dream job, and she'd never once seemed bitter about it. His happiness was hers and vice versa.

Watching them, Eliza had seen that real love *could* exist, and now she didn't want to settle for anything else. Sometimes she felt like Veruca Salt, stomping her feet and demanding her own glass elevator, her own Golden Ticket. Maybe she was asking for too much, but setting high standards had worked for her before—straight A's through school, scholarship to college, master's degree by twenty-three. Her own business by twenty-eight. Great friends. So she'd figured, why not with relationships?

The plan had been a good one. Results, though, had been dismal.

Once she'd started telling guys that she didn't go home with anyone on the first date as a rule, she'd quickly learned that she was a woman guys liked to sleep with, not one they wanted to invest any time in. One guy had straight up told her, "No offense, but who would want to date a shrink? I don't want someone trying to get into my head."

On the flip side, she'd had a few dates where the guys wanted free therapy, not a date. Those nights were their own special kind of torture.

She should've ditched the app a long time ago and stuck with imaginary book and movie boyfriends and her vibrator. She'd even tried on occasion to cut the right-swipe habit. But then a few days would pass, hope would spring up like a weed, and she'd find herself opening the app again.

She paused on the photo of a guy with dark hair and what looked to be a confident but kind smile.

ALIGNED Dating Profile

Ryan L.
Age: 32
Location: Metairie
Occupation: Financial planner
Likes: Jazz music, travel, boating, and finding the best
    microbrews in town
Account Status: Open for alignment

The guy was cute, didn't have any red flags that she could tell, and had a steady job. He also was cuddling an adorable dog in one of his photos. You couldn't set a bar much higher than that on a dating app with such limited information. Before she could talk herself out of it, she swiped right.

She let out a breath she hadn't realized she'd been holding. Only then did it hit her that swiping right on Christmas morning would probably look ten kinds of pathetic. Who was on a dating app at this time on this day?

Christmas orphans, that's who. How freaking Dickensian of her. *Please, sir, can you spare a date?*

She quickly closed the app, vowing not to look at it again today. She stared at the screen. Any distraction the app had provided melted away, dragging her back to reality.

Orphan. Orphan. Orphan.

Her phone went dark.

The room hummed with silence.

Her brain flooded with all the thoughts she'd been trying to avoid and pushed the panic button. The tidal wave of emotion that welled inside her was enough to make her audibly choke.

No, no, no. Before the tears broke free, she rushed to her feet, muttering "we are not doing this" under her breath in a white-knuckled pep talk. She'd been wrong to plan a chill, stay-at-home day. She couldn't sit here with nothing to do.

Everything else was closed, but she didn't need to be. WorkAround, the shared workspace where she rented an office, would be empty but open. She could get some filing done, maybe outline a new video. That would make the day go by quickly, occupy her brain. It could just be *Tuesday.* She liked Tuesdays. She poured herself another coffee, this time in her travel mug, and ignored the slight trembling of her hands.

She grabbed her bag and was out the door before she could overthink the plan. The sounds of happy voices and her neighbor's cheery reindeer songs blasted from an open window nearby. She resisted putting her hands over her ears and sped up her pace to get to her car.

Run, run, Rudolph.

....

As expected, the bottom floor of WorkAround was silent as a library when Eliza let herself in around lunchtime. The effect was a little eerie. Normally the place would be a hive of activity with people typing away on their laptops at the rented hot desks, others chatting in the strategically placed groupings of furniture, and the gurgle and whir of drinks being made at the in-house coffee bar. She loved walking in to all those sounds, all that energy.

When she'd first started looking for office space to rent for her therapy practice, she'd been dreading getting stuck in some isolated, soulless office building where no one talked to one another. So when she'd found WorkAround, a concept built on collaboration and start-ups and a constantly rotating corral of creative people, she'd been hooked.

The rent had been a bit of a stretch, but she needed to match the image on her YouTube channel—the successful professional therapist who could afford a nice office. Unfortunately, if her client load didn't increase or she didn't find an additional stream of income, she wouldn't be able to keep renting here long-term.

That grim thought had her even more motivated to get some work done today. She needed to catch up on client notes, outline a new video, and come up with a new thirty-day challenge for January. She did a new wellness challenge each month on her channel. Those videos garnered some of her best numbers. People—herself included—loved a life experiment. This month, the challenge had been about getting better sleep. She'd been an utter fail at it personally, but her followers had seemed to get a lot out of it.

She headed past the closed coffee bar to the elevator and punched the button for the third floor. The hallway was quiet when she stepped out of the elevator, and her lace-up boots moved silently across the gray carpet as she made her way to her office. But when she got closer to her door, she heard the distinct chatter of an old-school *clickety-clack* keyboard. Her eyebrows lifted.

So her too-cool-for-the-room neighbor was working on Christmas, too? It had to be him because she didn't know anyone else on this floor with such a loud keyboard. She'd only heard it a few times before because Beckham Carter almost always kept his door shut tight. She slowed her step as she neared his office. The door was wide open.

She peeked in, planning to greet him since he'd see her pass his door, but he didn't turn his head. His attention was laser-focused on his screen, a pair of noise-canceling headphones over his ears, and his fingers were flying across the obnoxiously loud keyboard. *Ticka, ticka, ticka.*

She let herself take in the view for a moment, her curiosity about her neighbor getting the best of her. If Beckham was stopping in to work before heading to some holiday celebration, it must be a casual get-together. Or maybe he didn't celebrate Christmas. Either way, he was dressed for comfort in a pair of well-worn jeans and a soft-looking green T-shirt with some graphic on the front she couldn't fully see. His arms were inked with artwork and scrawling words she'd never gotten to inspect very closely, and his blond hair, which had a natural loose wave to it and darker roots, was tousled more than normal, like he'd simply rolled out of bed and ran his fingers through it. A little rush of heat went through her at that visual, quickly followed by a *Hell no, don't have that thought.*

She didn't need to be getting any bedroom-related thoughts about her work neighbor—her definitely-too-young-for-her work neighbor. She'd tried to be friendly and welcoming to Beckham when he'd first moved into the office next door, but she'd quickly learned that he had no interest in the neighborly aspects of WorkAround. At least, not with her. She'd seen him interacting with a few of the techie guys from the fourth floor, so she knew he was more than capable of socializing, but his barely there politeness toward her had been all the signal she needed. She wasn't in his "crowd" or "crew," so wasn't worth talking to. Whatever.

Sometimes WorkAround reminded her of middle school with its cliques, and she had no interest in repeating that dynamic—or reliving her adolescent trauma of not being *part* of one of those cliques. If some group didn't want to talk to her, then they weren't people worth knowing. So, since those initial interactions, she and Beckham had kept it to greetings like "hey" and "morning" in the hallway and left it at that. She decided to leave him be right now since he hadn't noticed her, but before she could move out of his doorway, he turned his head.

A startled look crossed his face before he smoothed his expression, a slight frown touching his lips. She lifted a hand in silent greeting.

He pulled off his headphones, looping them around his neck. "Uh, hey."

"Hey," she said, leaning against the doorjamb, trying to look like she'd just casually happened by instead of having stood there for long enough to qualify as creepy. "Sorry to interrupt. I just wanted to let you know I was next door. With the building empty and all, I didn't want you to think there was an intruder out here or something."

"Oh, right," he said, rubbing a hand along his darker stubble, still frowning. "Thanks. I didn't expect anyone else to be here today."

"No problem." She cleared her throat and made an awkward gesture with her thumb. "Well, I better—"

"People have therapy appointments on Christmas Day?" he asked, brows knitting. "Don't you get to set your own hours?"

His question surprised her. Was Mr. Door Always Shut actually going to make small talk? She shrugged. "In theory, I could have emergency appointments, but that's not why I'm here. I have other stuff to work on. Notes. My YouTube stuff."

He cocked his head, a barely there move. "YouTube stuff?"

"I have a mental-health wellness channel," she explained. "I cover different topics, host thirty-day challenges, give tips and tricks for relationships, that kind of thing. It's a way for people to get to know me before choosing me as their therapist—or just to learn things if they're not looking for therapy."

His mouth flattened into a line. "Got it. The influencer thing. We seem to have a lot of those here."

Her lips pursed, her hackles rising and her original suspicions about Beckham having a cooler-than-thou attitude returning. "Well, I don't know if I'd necessarily call myself an influencer at this point. But wow, clearly you have opinions about that job. Some influencer take your favorite spot at the coffee bar or something?"

She expected him to snipe back, but instead he scrubbed a hand through his hair, his blue-green eyes looking tired all of a sudden, and let out a breath. "Sorry. To be honest, I don't *not* have opinions about that job, but you're not here for my op-ed on influencer culture. I didn't mean it personally. I know you're a therapist. I think I've been staring at my screen too long and need more coffee. I'm not fit for other humans yet."

"Don't have Christmas plans?" she asked, regretting it as soon as she let the question slip past her lips. If she asked him that, it'd be fair game for him to ask her the same question. And she didn't want to answer.

He turned his chair fully toward her, the gears squeaking, and hooked an ankle over his knee. Only then did she see that his T-shirt had a vintage-looking Grinch Stole Christmas graphic. "My parents went on a cruise, but I didn't want to use up my vacation time."

Right. Of course. He had family but had chosen not to go. Lucky him, to have that choice. "Oh."

"You?" He asked, glancing downward and taking in her outfit.

She'd thrown on a pair of black skinny jeans and a cranberry-red sweater. Conceivably, she looked like she could be going somewhere festive. She opened her mouth to say, *I have plans later*. But something else came out instead.

"Nope. My parents died in a car crash two years ago so my plan today is to do anything that doesn't remind me of the fact that I have nowhere to be on Christmas."

His jaw slackened.

Oh God. She pressed her fingers to her lips, shocked by what had come out.

A wince of regret crossed his face. "Shit, Eliza, I didn't mean to—"

She shook her head, pressing harder against her lips, forcing the welling emotions back down. "No, you don't have to... I don't know where that came from." She laughed awkwardly, painfully. "Wow. TMI. Sorry about that. I think my lack of sleep has turned off my what's-appropriate-for-casual-conversation filter."

His gaze searched hers, frown deep. All traces of that smug attitude he wore so often were gone, replaced by something quiet and...sad. "I'm sorry about your parents."

The simple words and the way he was looking at her were like a one-two punch right to the stomach, busting through the veneer she'd put on when she left the house. She was half a second away from the dam bursting, all the feelings she'd been fighting all morning swelling up like an overfull balloon. She. Would. Not. Cry. Not in front of a near stranger. Not like this.

This is only a Tuesday, dammit!

"Thanks," she said, forcing a tight smile and swallowing past the lump in her throat. "I'm okay. Holidays just..."

"Suck," he said flatly.

She rolled her lips together and nodded. "Sometimes, yeah."

"And I lied," he said. "My uncle and his husband, who I'd normally spend Christmas with, are on a cruise. My parents aren't. Well, I guess they could be. I'd never know. We don't talk anymore."

She straightened, surprised by his candor. "Oh."

When she was about to ask a follow-up question, he lifted his hand, cutting her off. "And no, I don't want to talk about it. I can see that therapist look in your eye." He gave her a disarming smile, taking some of the sting out of the words. "But you were honest with me, so I figured I'd join you on the TMI train. We can be on Team Christmas Sucks together."

"Right." She stared at him a long moment, recognizing in him the same look she'd seen in her mirror this morning, one that said she wasn't the only one dealing with pain today. He may be playing it off as not a big deal, but whatever the story was with his parents carried a heavy weight. Had he wanted to cry today, too? Was his stomach in knots right now like hers? A weird urge came over her. Before she could stop it, she blurted out, "Do you want to get a puppy with me?"

Beckham blinked like she'd snapped a camera flash in his face. "What?"

What. The. Hell? Her mouth was in full-scale rebellion. A puppy? *Hey, stranger who usually ignores me, do you want to get a puppy with me?* What was wrong with her? "I–I meant…"

A slow smirk rose at the corner of his mouth as she tripped over her words. "We barely know each other, Eliza. Maybe we should start with a plant, possibly a fish—but even those take some work. Who would get it on the weekends? Would we bring it to the office? Who gets to name it?"

She pinched the bridge of her nose, counted to three in her head, and then lowered her arm to her side. The bemused look he was giving her made her cheeks burn. "I meant," she said in her calm, I'm-a-therapist-and-totally-have-my-shit-together voice, "I've decided I might like to adopt a dog. I was considering going to the shelter today. Since we have established that Christmas sucks this year, I thought maybe you would like to come along and look at cute animals with me."

He leaned back in his chair, his eyes narrowed like he was trying to figure her out. "You want me to help you pick out a dog?"

She huffed out a breath. "Sorry, never mind. It's stupid. I just thought maybe since you—"

He rocked forward, bracing his arms on his thighs, his Doc Martens landing heavily against the floor. "You know what? Screw it. I'm in."

She gasped softly, shock echoing through her. "Wait, seriously?"

He stood, rising to his full six feet of lanky height, and it took literally every ounce of willpower she possessed not to let her eyes slide down to take in the full view. The guy looked like he should be in an indie rock band instead of tapping code into a keyboard, which shouldn't work for her but...

He shrugged. "Yeah, why not? I like dogs. And I'm not getting anywhere with this project right now anyway. I could use a break."

He turned and bent over to turn off his computer, his T-shirt riding up a little in the back and showing an expanse of smooth skin and the edge of black boxer briefs.

She gave up trying not to check him out. She had no idea why she was getting so warm everywhere. Beckham was definitely not her type. He probably wasn't a day over twenty-four, for one, and the difference between a guy in his midtwenties and a woman in her early thirties was *real*. Plus, that whole tattooed, always slightly mussed vibe had never been her scene. She liked responsible grown-ups. Men who'd lived some life. Men who owned suits.

But here she was, planning to go puppy shopping with Beckham.

She had no idea how this was happening. How she'd gotten herself here in this moment. And her filter was still on the fritz. "I don't get it. Normally, you barely say a word to me. Why are you saying yes to this?"

"I don't say words to a lot of people. It's nothing personal." He peeked back over his shoulder, his gaze unreadable. "And I'm saying yes because it's the more interesting answer."

"The more interesting answer?"

He turned around, hooking his thumbs in the front pockets of his jeans and shrugging. "Yeah. You play video games?"

"I used to play sometimes when I was a kid but not lately."

"Well, I'm designing one as a side project, and one of the most important parts of game design is offering the player meaningful choices. They're faced with a dilemma, and there are safe choices and risky ones. Sometimes it's obvious, but my favorites are the ones where you can't determine if it's a good idea or bad idea— those are the interesting ones. Picking out a dog with you on Christmas sounds like it could make for an interesting story."

She laughed. "And you don't know if it's a safe move or a risky one?"

His mouth curved. "Of course not. I don't know you. You could be a cold-blooded killer ready to harvest my organs or put me through some demented psychological experiment."

She snorted softly. "You sound like my friend Andi. She's a horror writer and assumes everyone is a murderer until proven otherwise. Rest assured, I'm not in the market for organs or test subjects. Just a second opinion on a dog and"—she let the brightness in her voice fade, too tired for pretense—"maybe a little company on a kind of crappy day."

His expression softened, sympathy there. "Got it. Let's be Team Christmas Sucks and find you a dog."

He swept his hand in front of him, indicating she should head out first, and she turned to walk into the hallway. As he locked up behind her, doubt began to flood in. What was she doing again? She'd obviously guilted her poor coworker into accompanying her. This was completely a pity *yes*. This was her mom getting the neighbor kid to ask Eliza to prom so she wouldn't be dateless. She should shut this down right now. Save herself the humiliation and Beckham the trouble.

Beckham tucked his key card in his back pocket and spun to face her, looking like sin and summer on this gray day. "Ready?"

She swallowed hard, ignoring the pang of want that zipped through her. *No ma'am, mind out of the gutter right this minute.* She started one of her handy mental lists.

Why Beckham Carter Is Not an Appropriate Crush

1. Not my type.
2. Coworker.
3. Too young.
4. Is only going with me out of pity.
5. The attraction is purely physical—don't know him.
6. Usually avoids me.
7. Is probably just a tech bro underneath the indie-rocker disguise.

The list was a good one. A valid one. *A smart one.*

But as they got into her car and pulled away from WorkAround, her mind began to drift to the places it shouldn't. Places that made her skin warm. Lonely people could make bad decisions.

And Beckham Carter suddenly looked like he'd be the perfect bad decision on a cold winter day.

chapter **two**

BECKHAM HAD APPARENTLY LOST HIS EVER-LOVING MIND. *I like the interesting answers?* More like the imbecilic ones. What the hell had he been thinking? One second he'd been fighting with the code for the project he was working on, and the next he was in the passenger seat of Eliza's car on the way to the animal shelter.

Up until this point, he'd managed to avoid dealing with Dr. Sunshine, the nickname he'd given Eliza in his head. He didn't care how good she looked in that pair of jeans, he didn't trust people who were always in a good mood. And he especially didn't need another therapist in his life. He'd had enough of those for a lifetime already. But today, when she'd blurted out an invitation to join her on her dog quest, he'd heard the desperation in her voice, the sharp stab of loneliness. She was dealing with some tough shit today—her normal sunshine was behind a veil of dark clouds—and he didn't have it in him to say no to her. Plus, it wasn't as if he was having a banner Christmas Day either.

Adding dogs couldn't hurt. He just hoped adding *Eliza* wasn't a vast error in judgment.

Eliza pulled out of the parking garage, her fingers wrapped tightly around the wheel and an unreadable expression on her face. He got the sense she was having some kind of internal conversation with herself. She dragged her teeth against her bottom lip in a way that made it hard for him to look away. "I probably should've verified that they're open today."

Her words caught him off guard, and he smirked at her admission. "You don't know?"

She gave him a quick glance as if gauging his reaction. "This wasn't *exactly* a fully thought-out plan."

He stretched his arm along the passenger window, amused to see someone normally so put together looking frazzled. "I'm surprised. You strike me as the planning type."

"I am. To a pretty intense degree, really." She maneuvered her way down a particularly narrow street near the French Quarter, avoiding a horde of well-dressed pedestrians probably heading to a holiday jazz brunch. Then, she turned and headed away from the heart of the city. "But I guess today I'm…taking the day off from my norm. Getting a pet." She peeked over at him. "Kidnapping unsuspecting coworkers and harvesting their organs. You know, traditional Christmas stuff."

He laughed lightly and lifted his hips to grab his phone from his back pocket. He unlocked the screen and did a quick search for the nearest animal shelter. "You're in luck. They're open until three today. And, hey, all Christmas Day adoptions come with a free goody bag."

She lifted a fist in victory. "Score."

He scanned the map. "Take a right at the next stoplight."

She frowned and looked over at him. "I'm pretty sure the shelter is the other way."

"It is." He adjusted his seat belt. "We're making a quick pit stop. Another Christmas tradition awaits."

She gave him a skeptical look. "And that is…"

He lifted a brow. "Hey, lady, you kidnapped me. The least you can do is make sure I'm well fed."

"Oh hell," she said, looking genuinely concerned. "I'm sorry. I didn't even think to ask you if you've had lunch. We'll stop somewhere."

She'd said it like it really *was* her job to make sure he was fed when he'd only been making a joke. But he guessed, at her job, she probably was always the one making sure people had what they needed. "It's not a big deal. Have *you* eaten lunch?"

She shook her head. "No. There was a spiked-eggnog situation last night, and I only managed some toast this morning, but now I'm pretty hungry."

"A spiked-eggnog situation?"

She winced as she pulled up to a stop sign and gave him a look. "Do not recommend. Zero out of five stars."

He laughed. "Well, I've got the perfect hangover food then." He cocked his head toward the street ahead. "Just follow my directions, and I'll make sure you're well taken care of."

"Yeah?" Her gaze darted from his face down his body, before snapping back up—a microsecond of a glance—but he felt as if she'd touched him.

It took a second for him to register what had happened, his body picking up the cue before his brain caught on, but the truth was confirmed when Eliza faced forward again, her throat bobbing with a hard swallow and the honey-gold of her skin darkening a little with a blush. She had checked him out. And he had a sneaking suspicion she'd thought about *exactly* what he could take care of.

A hard kick of desire made his muscles tighten. *Well, shit.* He didn't need to chase that line of thought down the road. Doing anything with Dr. Sunshine would be a really, really bad idea.

He had a keep-it-casual rule for a reason, and Eliza was anything but the casual type. Nothing about her said *laid-back*. She probably had a ten-year plan to discuss and a twenty-page personality test she required before she allowed someone to see her naked. Plus, she was a therapist. Someone who'd want to poke into all his dark corners to see what they could find. He could tell it'd taken a big dose of restraint for her not to ask him more questions about his parents. Hell, no. He didn't need that in his life.

"Turn right up there. Place is on the left," he said, his voice tenser than he wanted it to be. He needed to get all naked Eliza thoughts out of his head. *Puppies.* He was here for puppies. Nothing more.

"You okay?" she asked, giving him a look.

"Yeah, just hungry." He cleared his throat. "Park right over there. This place has the best chicken lo mein you'll find anywhere, and they're always open on holidays."

She smiled, back to normal, polite Dr. Sunshine. "Sounds good."

"I'll just grab us some takeout so we don't risk being too late for you to take your time at the shelter." He reached for the car handle. "You're good with lo mein, or do you want something different?"

"I'm good with that." She grabbed her purse from the floor-board behind him. "Here, let me give you—"

He shook his head. "I got it."

"Beck—"

"Keep your money. It's Chinese food. It's not going to break the bank."

She pressed her lips together like she was going to protest but then nodded. "Thanks. Next time, lunch is on me."

Next time.

He needed to make sure there was no next time.

The animal shelter was decked out in festive red-and-green garland, and they had signs up advertising their holiday adoption event. Eliza waited at the front counter while the receptionist, Beverly, an older Black woman wearing a pair of felt reindeer antlers, looked up Eliza's old application and checked the computer to see if puppies were available. Eliza was trying to stay quiet to let the woman do her job, but the raucous chorus of barking was overwhelming her a bit. She didn't want to think about all of the animals needing families. She'd end up taking home ten of them if she wasn't careful.

Beckham had wandered a few feet away and was sitting on a bench next to a glass-walled room labeled *Cat Play Zone*. There was a couple inside with a little girl who was on the floor, trying to coax one of the cats to play with a little feather on a string.

"I'm afraid we're cleared out of puppies," Beverly said, dragging Eliza's attention back to her. "They're a hot commodity at Christmastime."

Eliza frowned, inwardly cursing. This was why chasing whims didn't work. Had she done her research ahead of time, made a plan... "Oh, no. Well, I mean I guess that's good. That they found homes. But 'oh, no' for me."

Beverly smiled. "Have you considered an adult dog? We have a lot of great ones here that need homes, and they're usually already housebroken. Puppies are a lot of work, and I noticed on your form that you're single and don't work from home. You can't leave a puppy home alone for very long."

Eliza tried not to bristle at the word *single* being used as a reason why she couldn't have what she came here for. That was what had squashed this plan the last time. She didn't think Beverly had meant it that way, but still, it pushed a button that had already been worn out today. She fiddled with the pen she'd used to sign in, contemplating the idea of an older dog. She didn't have anything against a full-grown dog, but she just couldn't bear the thought of bringing home a new family member that only had a few years left. She didn't want to invite another loss into her life. "I—"

"Molly, don't open that!" Beverly said, her voice sharp and her attention no longer on Eliza.

Eliza turned to see what was going on. A young female volunteer in pink scrubs had her hand on the already opened door to the cat room, a startled expression on her face. She moved to shut the door, but a flash of black and white fur darted through the gap before she could and disappeared under the bench where Beckham was sitting.

Beverly groaned and hopped to her feet. "Jesus in a Jeep, here we go again. Trent, *no!*" She pointed at Beckham as she marched over. "Sir, lock the main door for me. Don't let that little escape artist out."

Beckham snapped to it—Beverly's tone channeled school principals and drill sergeants—and he turned the lock on the entryway door so no one could get in or out.

Molly, the volunteer, was standing by the door of the cat room, shifting from foot to foot. "I'm so sorry, Ms. Beverly. I didn't know he was in there."

Beverly sighed a put-upon sigh and flicked a hand. "Never mind, it's not your fault. I told them not to put Trent in there with that family. That little girl wants a cuddly, playful cat, and we know Trent ain't that."

As Beverly walked slowly toward the bench, the cat slipped out between the bench legs and made a beeline for the door, but Beckham was still there. Trent tucked himself into the spot right between Beckham's Doc Martens, punctuating the maneuver with a loud meow.

"Don't move, son," Beverly instructed. "Stay still and keep

him calm so I can catch him. Plus, if you startle him, he'll bite. He's still got a lot of alley cat in him."

Beckham was pressed against the main door, his palms lifted like someone was holding him up at a bank, and he sent a what-the-hell-is-going-on look to Eliza. He looked adorably terrified. She bit her lip, trying not to laugh.

"All right, Trent, you've had your fun, mister," Beverly said in a calm, quiet voice. "Time to go back to your cozy little kennel now."

The cat arched and hissed when she took a step closer.

"Uh, maybe don't come closer just yet." Beckham looked down worriedly and moved his hands from their upright position to protecting his crotch. "I'd rather not be part of Trent's revenge plot."

Beverly paused about five feet from Beckham and Trent. "All right, let's give him a minute and see if he wanders out from that spot."

Eliza crouched down, trying to keep her movements slow. She made a low, kissing sound. "Hey, kitty, why don't you come over here? It's okay. I'm not going to hurt you."

Trent turned his head toward her and gave her the cat version of an eat-shit-and-die look.

Well, then.

"I think I can probably move away," Beckham offered. "These boots are thick if he bites me on the foot."

"Okay, just move slowly," Beverly instructed. "If he darts somewhere else, God knows where he'll end up. Last week he got himself wedged behind the copy machine, and it took us an hour to lure him out."

"Got it." Beckham shifted his weight ever so slowly to one foot, preparing to move, but then froze when Trent meowed loudly and batted at one of Beckham's shoelaces. Beckham took a visible breath, keeping still. "Look, dude. I'm not trying to hurt you, okay? We both just need a little space right now. If you let me…"

Trent yowled again and then slid himself up against Beckham's boot and nuzzled his leg.

Eliza rose up from her crouch, smiling.

"What's he doing?" Beckham asked, looking down and trying to see what was going on without making any sudden movements. "I'm about to lose a testicle, aren't I?"

Eliza laughed and crossed her arms as she watched Trent thread between Beckham's ankles. "No, I think your breakup speech isn't working... I think he's into you."

"What?" Beckham bent a little to see.

Trent wound himself around one of Beckham's legs, purring like a car engine.

"Well, I'll be damned," Beverly said, fist on her hip. "I've never heard that cat purr since he's been here. Looks like he likes you, son."

Beckham frowned. "Don't get any ideas, buddy. I'm not the one here for the adoption."

But Trent was undeterred. He ducked his little black head and rubbed it against Beckham's shoelaces. Eliza bit her lip, the sight too adorable to bear. "Maybe he's adopting *you*."

Beckham's head snapped up, and he gave Eliza a warning look. "Don't even. He's barking—uh, meowing—up the wrong tree. I'm not a cat person." Carefully, he lifted his foot and tried to step away from Trent. He got clear of him and went back to the bench to give Beverly room to grab him, but Trent happily trotted after him. When Beckham sat, Trent hopped up on the bench next to him and started cleaning his paws. As soon as Beverly tried to reach for him, Trent hissed.

Beverly lifted her brows and stepped back. "Now he's a guard cat, apparently. I'm going to go and get help to get him back to the kennel. We might need to use the snare pole."

"The snare pole." Beckham looked down at Trent, brow furrowed. The cat collapsed onto his side against Beckham's thigh and returned to cleaning himself. "Dude, that doesn't sound good. You should let Ms. Beverly take you back to your bed. Doesn't that sound nice? Your bed?"

Beverly headed to the back as Beckham tried to reason with Trent, talking about naps and snacks, painting full-kitty fantasies to tempt him.

Trent yawned and then nuzzled Beckham's hand, angling for some rubbing.

Beckham sighed and scratched Trent's little furry head, inspiring a deep purr from the stubborn cat. "It's like you haven't heard a word I've said."

"I don't think he's buying what you're selling," Eliza said, enormously entertained by Beckham's earnest negotiating. "I think you've been hired as his new employee. Salary nonnegotiable. He's already setting up endless Zoom meetings and is going to call you Beck instead of Beckham because he wants to be a tough but cool boss. Your fate might be sealed, *Beck*."

He gave her a droll look. "I can't adopt a cat, *Eli*."

The nickname made her smile, but she nodded resolutely, indulging him. "Of course not, Beck."

"I'm not a cat person, Eli."

"You've mentioned that."

His eyes narrowed. "Are you using therapy techniques on me? Leading me to my own conclusion? Because it's not going to work. I didn't come here for this and—"

"Here we go," Beverly said as she came back into the lobby with a young guy in scrubs at her side. He was holding a long pole with a loop on the end. "Trent, visiting time is up."

Trent took one look at the pole and then dove behind Beckham's back, squeezing himself between Beckham and the back of the bench. The pitiful sound Trent released could've shattered glass—and hearts.

Well, it worked on at least one heart.

"Goddammit." Beckham raked a hand through his hair, threw Eliza a helpless look, and then leaned his head back against the glass wall. "Get me paperwork to fill out."

....

"This is one hundred percent your fault," Beckham declared as Trent meowed in protest from his carrier in Eliza's back seat.

Eliza rolled her lips together, working really hard not to grin like an idiot. "You *did* say you liked interesting choices. You gotta be careful speaking that stuff into the universe."

"Nice. Throw my words back at me. Really appreciate that."

"And how lucky for you that for hard-to-adopt cases, they let you skip the home visit if you have a reference from someone who already cleared the process." She sent him an innocent look. "I mean, it was really serendipitous that I was there."

"Imagine my luck," he said dryly. "They even gave me free supplies. It's like winning the lottery. Except the prize is a really cantankerous furball who is definitely going to pee on my pillow if I don't bow to his every whim."

She shook her head, dropping the act. "I can't believe you *adopted a cat.*"

He groaned and rubbed the back of his neck. "Well, what else was I supposed to do? Did you hear what they said about him? He's been there for six months. He hates everyone, bites, and is always trying to escape so he's never going to get adopted. But for whatever reason, he doesn't run away from me. If I didn't take him, that cat would be on my conscience. I don't need more things on my conscience."

Trent let out a mournful meow as if on cue.

"Stop the hard sell, cat," Beckham said grumpily. "I'm already taking you home. You've won."

Eliza couldn't hold back her smile anymore. She was already giddy that she'd found a dog—Mabel, a three-year-old lab-collie mix that she'd be able to pick up tomorrow after she purchased all the supplies Mabel needed—but Beckham ending up with a cat was icing on the cake. The man was clearly in love even if he wouldn't admit it out loud. And seeing that side of him had made her realize how greatly she'd misjudged the guy just because he hadn't wanted to have office chitchat. The dude was *kind*. And out of all the things she looked for in friends, kindness flipped her switches more than anything. Well, that and the ability to both wield and understand sarcasm. He was solid there, too.

She looked over at her maligned coworker. "Maybe it was fate. What are the chances you'd end up at a shelter today? Maybe the reason you said yes to me today was because the universe knew you were Trent's last chance."

"There's no such thing as fate." Beckham sighed, his head leaning back against the car seat as he turned to look at her. "I didn't say yes to you because of fate."

She looked back to the road, her buoyant mood flattening. "I know. You said yes because you felt sorry for me."

"No." He shifted in his seat, facing forward again. "This wasn't a pity thing. I'm not that altruistic."

She peeked over at him, wanting to ask questions, but he was staring straight ahead, his jaw flexing, giving every signal that he didn't want to answer more questions.

Trent meowed.

"Not altruistic." She cleared her throat. "Says the guy who just adopted a grumpy cat."

He sniffed derisively. "Maybe I said yes because—"

Her phone chimed from the cup holder with a distinct cartoon-ish sound, and she winced. *Not now. Not. Now.*

Beckham's words cut off, and her phone screen lit with what

Eliza knew would be an animation of two champagne glasses clinking together.

"What kind of notification is that?" Beckham asked, leaning over and eyeing the screen.

"It's rude to look at other people's phones," she said, keeping her focus on the road but reaching for her phone to tilt it downward.

Beckham ignored her comment and picked up her phone. "That animation work is *terrible*."

He turned it toward her, which naturally made her look and the Face ID registered and unlocked her phone, opening the full notification. "Beckham."

He turned the screen back toward him. "I could draw something better than this even if I were drunk and only using my left hand. Trent could draw something better than that using his tail."

"Are you done?"

"Sorry. I couldn't look away." He was outright staring at her phone screen. "This is Aligned? That dating app?"

She tipped her chin up like she was the queen and no one should dare question her choices. "Yes."

"Wow. You'd think an app that so many people use would spend more money on their graphics." He brought the phone closer. "Looks like some dude named Ryan has toasted you or whatever. What's that mean?"

"Oh my God." She glanced his way. "Stop. Reading. My. Phone."

He gave her a pointed look. "I have an entire feline in the car because of you. One who I will have to clothe and feed and water until the end of his natural born life or mine, whoever goes first, so…"

"He's not going to need to be clothed," she groused. "In fact, I think he'd murder you in your sleep if you tried to put him in a sweater."

"Either way, you don't get to be mad at me for being curious." He eyed her screen. "A financial planner? Likes boating? This guy sounds like a tool, Eli."

Eli. Apparently, their little joke about names was going to stick, but this time the nickname hit her in a way that made her stomach flip a little. They'd stumbled into new territory. Coworkers who rarely spoke didn't have nicknames for each other. And they certainly didn't feel comfortable enough to comment on each other's dating choices. But Beckham seemed to be one of those people who once you were past his very high gates and armed guard tower, you were in. A friend. No pretense or games. Even though she was about to throttle him for looking at her phone, she found she didn't mind the shift. "I'm about to pull over and drop you on the side of the road, just so you know."

He chuckled, completely unrepentant. "Ten bucks says that this boat he's posing on is definitely not his."

Blessedly, the parking garage for WorkAround came into view. She pulled in and parked, turning her body toward him. "Are you done now?"

He smiled at her and held up a pic of Ryan like it was Exhibit A in a court trial. "This dog he's cuddling with? Clearly bait." He turned back to the phone, leaning in close to it. "Blink twice, Fluffy. Are you okay? Does the bad man lock you in the basement when he's not taking dating profile photos with you?"

Eliza groaned and grabbed the phone from him. "You're the worst."

He was grinning as he let her retrieve her phone. "Come on. Do you really want to be *toasted* by some dude posing on a boat?"

"I have nothing against boats," she said, her cheeks burning. "And I'm sure if I looked at your dating-app inbox, it'd be full of women with pouty lips and low-cut shirts who claim they're always up for an adventure."

He made a sound in the back of his throat. "I don't do dating apps."

She rolled her eyes. "Of course you don't. Because you're twenty-nothing, look like that, and probably have girls sign up on a list outside your door just for the chance to lick your tattoos."

His brows jumped up.

Every part of her cringed at her outburst. *Aaaand I'll see myself out so I can go die of embarrassment somewhere else.*

"I look like how now?" he asked, his mouth kicking up at one corner, a dimple appearing. "Are you telling me I'm pretty, Eli?"

"Shut up." *Real mature, Eliza.*

"And I'm twenty-five for the record," he said matter-of-factly. "I'd say that's more twentysomething than twenty-nothing."

"Wow. Ancient." Eliza took a breath, trying to regain some shred of her dignity. "All I'm saying is that you shouldn't judge someone for being on a dating app. Meeting people might not be as easy for some as it is for others."

"I'm not judging you," he said, those blue-green eyes locked on her. "I just think you're setting yourself up for a bunch of nonsense. Those apps are advertising campaigns. Smoke and mirrors. Like the rest of social media. I guarantee you ninety percent of those guys on that app are lying about something and mainly just want to get laid."

"And what if I'm just trying to get laid?" she shot back.

He was unfazed. "Are you?"

Trent meowed, like yes, he would indeed like some feline loving if they were inquiring.

She stared at Beckham, chin tipped up, ready for a fight, but then her shoulders sagged. For some reason, she found she didn't have the energy or desire to lie to him. Maybe *he* should've been a therapist. Or maybe all the emotion of the day had shorted out her normal filters. She was dumping all her truths on him today.

"No. I've already been down that road. I'm looking for more than that."

He shrugged and looked away. "Well, then I think you're wasting your time with this stuff."

She unhooked her seat belt and climbed out of the car, irritated and feeling some other emotion she couldn't pinpoint. She lifted Trent's carrier and the bag of supplies from the back seat and then walked around the car to hand them to Beckham. "Duly noted. But until you're a thirty-two-year-old woman who would like to, one day, have a partner and a family and not have to celebrate Christmas alone, you don't get to have an opinion on my dating life. Maybe a financial planner with a boat and dog is exactly what I want."

He took the carrier and bag from her, frowning, his gaze going stormy. "You're right. None of my business."

"Nope."

He stared at her for a moment and then leaned down.

Her heart jumped right into her throat because he looked like he was coming in to kiss her, but before he reached her mouth, he shifted over and pecked her cheek. "Merry Christmas, Eli." He straightened and that devil-may-care look returned. "I hope by next Christmas you've found what you're looking for and don't need to resort to kidnapping coworkers and forcing vicious cats upon them to keep the day interesting."

chapter **three**

A FEW DAYS AFTER NEW YEAR'S, THE PRIVATE SANCTUARY
of Beckham's office was breached at exactly six fifty-five when his
noise-canceling headphones died and the sound of loud, racking
sobs replaced the driving beats of the action-movie score he'd
been listening to. He hit the save command on his work and tried
to ignore the sounds of anguish on the other side of his wall as
he fiddled with his headphones. But jiggling them and peering at
them intently did nothing for the failed electrical bits contained
inside. His hacking skills didn't help him with hardware.

He sighed, tossed the headphones aside, and then tried to
refocus on what he was doing. He'd found two ways into the
medical records of the hospital that had hired him, but he knew
there were probably more. The security on this system wasn't
nearly as robust as it should be for this level of private information, and they'd had multiple breaches over the past few years. He
wanted to find all the holes before going back to them with his
report and recommendations.

He stared at the screen, trying to concentrate, but then a higher-
pitched voice started shouting, the deeper sobbing still going. So it
was the guy crying today. Beckham couldn't understand what was
being said. Eliza used one of those white-noise machines, presumably

to give her clients some privacy, but that didn't stop Beckham from hearing the emotion of it all even if he couldn't decipher the words. He had no idea how Eliza maintained any desire for matrimony after seeing dysfunctional couples all day. Marriage was a bad bet. Hitch yourself to someone and then have to pay a therapist to continually convince you not to leave each other.

Or, go about marriage like his parents did. Quietly seethe and snipe at each other but then put on a smiling, adoring face out in public. *We couldn't be happier. We're so blessed.*

Right. *Blessed.* Either way, marriage was a trap. He'd learned that the hard way, and didn't need to repeat that lesson. But lucky him, he now got to be a sideline observer of other people's screwed-up marriages while he worked.

When the small company he contracted with had decided to move out of their cramped space on the industrial side of town this past summer and into the WorkAround building in downtown New Orleans, he'd been happy to go along with the plan. More room. Better lunch options within walking distance. A private office. He'd volunteered to take the one office that wouldn't be on the fourth floor with the rest of the team. He didn't mind his coworkers, but he liked not being easily accessible. He worked better without interruptions.

What he hadn't anticipated was sharing a wall with a therapist. No, not just a therapist but *Eliza*—the woman he'd had a weird, strangely intimate day with on Christmas. He'd ruined their nicely established arrangement of being polite hallway-passing coworkers. Now there was this *thing* between them.

Not that she seemed to be feeling that.

Sure, they exchanged more words in the hallway now, but they were empty. *How's Trent? How's the new dog?* He'd insulted her that night and now he'd lost access to the real Eliza, the one he'd met on Christmas. She was back in day-planner-toting businesswoman mode. The smart, ambitious, hustling therapist and influencer. His day pass to get beyond the gates had been revoked.

Which was *fine*. He didn't need to get involved with someone like Eliza. It had been an *exceedingly wise* decision *not* to invite her back to his place when she'd mentioned licking his tattoos— even if that visual had assaulted his brain regularly since. Hooking up with her would've been a terrible idea. She saw him as an immature kid. He took issue with that. He'd been through more life than any guy his age should've. But in one respect, he understood that he and Eliza lived in different worlds. She knew what she wanted, and he definitely couldn't provide it.

Things were as they should be.

Beckham shoved thoughts of Eliza out of his head, tried to ignore the crying on the other side of the wall, and went back to the screen with its lines of code. Maybe if he went into the system via—

A sharp knock on his door made his hand jerk and random letters appear on the screen. He let out a frustrated sound, undid the mistake, and rolled his chair backward with a hard shove. Everyone else from the team had left for the day, so he had no idea who'd be knocking on his door at this hour. He'd come in late today after taking Trent to the vet for a checkup, hoping he could get a few uninterrupted hours.

He crossed the small space, the hand-drawn sketches of his game ideas on the whiteboard/corkboard combo next to his computer fluttering in his wake. He grabbed the handle and pulled open the door. A vaguely familiar dark-haired guy in jeans and a blazer was standing there, twirling a pair of sunglasses in his hand.

"Can I help you?" Beckham asked, unable to mask the impatience in his voice.

"Hey, man," the guy said with a half smile, "sorry to bother you, but I wanted to make sure I'm in the right place." He flicked his head to the left. "I'm supposed to be picking up this woman for a date. She told me to wait downstairs and she'd meet me by the coffee bar, but we were supposed to meet fifteen minutes ago. I decided to come up in case I misunderstood. But the door I thought was hers is locked."

"Therapist or fashion designer?" Beckham asked, dread curling through him because he already knew the answer. This was the guy with the fake boat.

"Therapist." He turned his phone screen toward Beckham. "Eliza Catalano."

Beckham glanced at the photo. Eliza's dating profile pic. In it, she was laughing, head slightly tipped to the side, dark hair cascading along her bare arm. Candid and open. The pic had probably been taken by a friend, based on the warm expression on Eliza's face. She looked great, happy. Beckham's gaze scanned down the picture. The hint of cleavage her tank top revealed probably had a long line of swipe rights in her inbox. Beckham looked up—dudes like this tool. A bitter taste crossed his tongue. *Not my business. Not my business.* He braced a hand on the doorknob, ready to close the door. "You have the right office, but I think she has a session running long. I'd wait downstairs."

"All right, cool, cool," the guy said, glancing at Eliza's closed door. He looked back to Beckham with a smirk. "So is she as hot in person as she is in her YouTube videos?"

Beckham frowned at his we're-all-just-bros-here tone.

"You know, the ones where she gives relationship advice?" the guy said. "She wears these tight little skirt suits and…" He gave Beckham a conspiratorial look. "Well, it's hard to concentrate on the advice when a sexy Latina woman is giving it, if you know what I'm saying."

Beckham bristled, jaw tightening, the whole vibe of this guy getting under his skin. "I wouldn't know. I don't use YouTube."

The guy gave him a yeah-right look. "What do you mean, you don't use YouTube?"

Beckham wasn't going to get into an explanation about his analog life choices with this idiot. "I've got to get back to work."

"Oh right, yeah, sure," the guy said.

Beckham was about to close his door when the one next to him opened. A balding man with puffy, post-cry eyes stepped out first. He quickly turned down the hall and a petite woman, presumably his partner, walked out with Eliza by her side. Eliza was murmuring something to her. The woman nodded, a Kleenex held tightly in her fist, and then followed the man out.

Eliza watched them go for a second and then turned toward Beckham's office. A startled look lit her brown eyes. Her gaze jumped to the guy with the sunglasses and then to Beckham. "Oh. Hi. I didn't realize anyone else was out here."

She'd worn her long, black hair down today, the ends curling right above her breasts, and Beckham couldn't help but notice that she was wearing one of those skirted suits the guy had mentioned. Now he wouldn't be able to *un*notice how great that suit hugged her body, how nice her legs looked, how much smooth, tan skin was exposed. He cleared his throat.

"Yeah, this guy was looking for you." Beckham jutted a thumb toward his uninvited guest.

Mr. Fake Boat put out his hand. "Hey. I'm Ryan, but my friends call me Ry, like the bread."

Like the bread? Beckham scoffed. This fucking guy.

Eliza's attention jumped to Ryan, a little line appearing between her brows, then awareness dawned. She took his hand. "Oh my God. Ryan. Right. Is it past seven?"

"It is," Ryan said, releasing the handshake.

Eliza winced and glanced at her smartwatch, clearly flustered.

"I'm so sorry. I'm usually hyperaware of the time in a session, but this one ran long."

"Are you ready to go?" Ryan asked, not giving Eliza any grace with a *No problem, do you need a minute, it's not a big deal.*

Eliza blinked. "I, uh…"

Beckham's dislike of the dude swelled. He needed to shut his door and get back to work. Instead, he found himself saying, "Hey, *Ry*, why don't you go down to the lobby and grab something from the coffee bar? There's a procedure to shut down and lock up offices here, and it takes a minute."

Eliza's gaze snapped to him, confusion there.

Ryan frowned at Eliza. "Yeah, sure. Okay."

Eliza turned back to Ryan, a smile jumping to her face. "That'd be great. I'm so sorry for making you wait. First drink's on me at the restaurant. I promise I'll just be a minute."

Beckham hated the false brightness in her tone, but he kept his mouth shut until Ryan disappeared into the elevator.

Eliza turned back to him, her smile long gone and a defeated look replacing it. "Thanks for that. I need to make a few notes about the session before I forget."

"No problem," he said, meaning it. That guy needed to take a walk. "The dude should've offered you a little time."

"Probably." She leaned back against the wall and rubbed the spot between her eyes, looking tired. "And I probably should've remembered that I had a date tonight."

"You okay?" he asked, unable to stop himself. "Sounded like it got pretty intense in there."

She turned her head, still leaning against the wall, and lowered her arm. "You can hear?"

"Just the crying and raised voices. Not the words." He pointed to his ear. "My headphones stopped working tonight. Normally, I wouldn't hear anything but the music I listen to."

"Sorry about that," she said. "I can't say anything because of confidentiality, but I will say it's been a long day and I really, really need a drink tonight."

"One you'll apparently be buying for yourself," he said, unable to hide his irritation.

She pushed away from the wall and shrugged. "As long as it's strong, I don't care who's paying for it."

He frowned.

"At least Ryan looks like his dating profile, so we're starting off better than some other dates I've been on." She gave him a wan smile. "Well, thanks again for the save. I better get on with my"—she made air quotes—"special operating procedure for locking up so I don't make Ry-like-the-bread wait any longer."

She stepped toward her open office door.

"I'd leave Sourdough waiting down there all night," Beckham said, his mouth taking on a mind of its own tonight.

Shut. Up. Don't get involved.

Eliza turned, bracing a hand on the doorjamb. "What? Why? Are we still on the fact that he might have a fake boat? We've already established you don't get to judge my dating choices."

"I know that." Beckham rubbed the back of his neck, wishing he'd stayed in his office. "But come on. *That guy?*"

Her eyes narrowed. "Sounding judgy..."

Beckham put his hands out at his sides. "His first question for me was if you were as hot in real life as you look on your YouTube channel."

Her lips parted slightly, a startled look on her face. "Oh. That's, uh...forward to ask someone's coworker."

He sniffed. "That's one word for it."

She tilted her head and crossed her arms. "What'd you say?"

"What?"

She shrugged. "What'd you tell him?"

Was she seriously asking him this? He scanned her expression. *Yes, yes she is.*

"I assume you had an answer," she said. "Like a good office mate, did you tell him of course I was and he should definitely be looking forward to the date?"

He gave her a disbelieving look. "I told him I don't use YouTube."

She huffed. "Well, you're not a good liar. Who doesn't use YouTube?"

"I don't," he said, annoyed now. "Or social media or any of that stuff."

Her brows arched. "Wait, seriously?"

"I work in cybersecurity. I know how vulnerable information is online. I try to be analog where I can. Plus, it's the more..."

"Interesting choice," she filled in.

"Something like that."

"Huh." She seemed to be processing the revelation. "Is that what the obnoxiously loud keyboard is about?"

"It's not ob—It's a mechanical keyboard. Better for typing because of the tactile and auditory feedback. It keeps your hands... Never mind." He stopped there. He could feel himself getting defensive and nerdy about his keyboard. Now was not the time. "You're going to be late for your date. And he doesn't seem like a very patient bro."

Her eyes scanned his face. "Wow. You *really* don't like Ryan. You sure he didn't say anything else? Should I be worried or something? I mean, beyond the normal worry a woman has to have going on a date with a stranger?" Her tone had gone serious. "Asking you if I'm hot is one thing. That's mild compared to the crap that gets dropped into my dating app DMs. But if you think he's, like...dangerous, then you need to tell me."

Beckham wanted to say *Yes, don't go*, but what concerns did he really have? The guy seemed like a smarmy asshole, not a serial killer. Why should he care if the dude was going out with Eliza? That *Ry* may end up in her bed tonight? His fist curled against his thigh. Not. His. Business. Nope. Not at all. "No, he didn't say anything else. Just…well, you're a therapist. I'm sure your radar is finely tuned. You don't need me to tell you to be careful."

A little smile touched her lips. "I don't, but I appreciate the heads-up."

"Of course." He gave her a wry look. "You better go. He's probably pacing downstairs watching reruns of your YouTube videos to psych himself up for the big night."

She glanced toward the elevator. "Meh, let him wait." She turned back to him. "But I really do need to make those notes."

Beckham gave a quick nod. "Have a good night, Eli. Hope the boat is real, but if not, save Fluffy from the basement, okay?"

She gave him a look he couldn't read. "Yeah, thanks. Night, Beckham."

He slipped back into his office before he said anything else, before he asked if she'd rather grab a burger with him and to hell with giving Ryan her night. He couldn't offer her the husband and family thing, but he could damn well show her a good time. He closed his door and raked a hand through his hair, frustrated with himself for getting involved and for caring at all.

He needed to stop this. He had no reason to be so annoyed that Eliza was going on a date with that guy. He didn't know her, not really. Maybe Ryan was just her type. Maybe they'd be perfect together. Maybe she liked smarmy and pretentious. Maybe they'd fall in love, get married, and have smarmy, pretentious children named Brioche and Ciabatta. Or maybe she was just going out to have a drink, get laid, and never call the guy again. It wasn't his business.

He plunked back down in his office chair and stared at his sleeping computer screen, but didn't get any work done for the rest of the night.

chapter **four**

ELIZA WATCHED THE DOOR CLOSE AS BECKHAM RETURNED to his office. The pieces of the Beckham puzzle she'd started assembling in her brain after their Christmas together rearranged themselves yet again. She'd put some distance between them because she'd said way too much on Christmas and had felt embarrassed. She didn't blab her drama to strangers. Strangers paid money to blab to her. Plus, he'd been judgy about her dating app. And she may have possibly made some comment about tattoo licking. She'd deny that last part in a court of law, but she'd figured it would be best to reestablish boundaries. Chalk up their adventure to a Christmas Day anomaly of two lonely people connecting when the real world was on pause.

But then tonight he had to go and show...concern? Calling her Eli. Acting like a friend. She didn't know what to do with that, but it was abundantly clear that he did not approve of her date. The therapist part of her wanted to know *why*. Because he saw her as a friend to be worried about? Because he sensed something about Ryan? Or maybe, as usual, she was just overthinking things.

It was probably just residual judgment about the world of online dating. She needed to stop worrying about Beckham and get to her date. She'd already made Ryan wait too long.

She went into her office, typed up a few quick notes from the exhausting therapy session, and then grabbed her purse. An unexpected wave of hesitation washed over her when she reached the door. Maybe she should cancel the date. If Beckham had gotten a bad gut feeling about the guy, maybe that was worth paying attention to? She was a big believer in gut feelings, the intuition. Our brains and bodies picked up so many subtle cues and signals that our conscious minds didn't register. She could go home, order some takeout, and watch a Netflix marathon instead.

But she quickly dismissed the idea. This had been Beckham's read, not hers. She didn't know him well enough to put any stock in his gut feelings. Maybe she was only looking for excuses because she'd had a long day and didn't know if she had the energy to muster enthusiasm on tonight's date. But going home and couch-potatoing it all night would only make her feel worse. Not to mention, it'd be rude to cancel on Ryan when he was already here and waiting. She could manage a meal, and she could definitely use a drink. Plus, Ryan was cute. Any guy who actually looked like his profile picture was already a boon.

She needed to tap into her reserves and get downstairs for the date. If she wanted things to be different in her personal life, she couldn't sit home and wait for life to happen. She had to put herself out there. A soul mate wasn't going to randomly stumble into her lap while she sat on her own couch watching *Friends* reruns. Maybe Ry-like-the-bread was *the* guy. Maybe he'd surprise her. Maybe one day they'd laugh over their anniversary dinner about how she was late for their first date and how he asked her coworker if she was hot.

Eliza smiled to herself, her resolve returning. That was what she needed to keep at the forefront of her mind—maybe this was the first date that would change everything. She couldn't lose that *maybe*. That maybe she'd one day have the kind of love like her parents had for each other. She needed to hold on to that to get her through the exhausting parts of dating. She'd seen what happened to clients when they lost hope for a better future. Without that belief that it could happen for her, she would be left staring down a lifetime of solo Christmases, a lifetime of watching rom-coms, knowing she'd never have that kind of permanent, lasting love in her life. She didn't want to peek down that hallway in her psyche. That path would lead nowhere good.

Dating sucked most of the time, but life rewarded action. She needed to keep swimming, even if it was upstream.

She locked up her office, glanced at Beckham's closed door, and then strode with purpose downstairs for her date, giving herself a little internal pep talk.

Tonight will be a good night.

Tonight will be a good night…

....

Tonight was a terrible mistake.

Eliza sat up straighter in her chair at the restaurant and tried to focus on what Ry was saying, but her head was swimming with all his words—many of which were *I* and *me*. The guy *really* liked to talk about himself.

"I'm the youngest supervisor at my firm."

"I'm about to buy a beach condo in Florida."

"I know it's a bad investment, but I can't resist getting a new Mercedes every two years. There's just something about that new car smell, you know?"

At some point in the last half hour, she'd lost the thread of the conversation and had only been catching snippets while she gulped the cocktails that kept arriving with each new dish and watched other couples at other tables who seemed to be having actual two-way conversations. But this time he'd asked her a direct question. She cleared her throat, downed the newest shot that had been placed before her, and feigned a smile. "Right. Or you could save yourself the money and just buy one of those car air-freshener thingies that smell like new car."

A line appeared between his brows. "That's not the same."

Inwardly, she sighed. Score in the understanding-humor column? Zero out of five stars.

Before she could respond, he was on to another topic. Something about bitcoin. She hardly knew what that was. Beckham would probably know.

But on and on it went. She'd tried to keep an I'm-listening expression on her face, pulling on her therapist skills to look engaged, but her ability had faltered with each new drink she'd downed.

They'd gone to The Stacks, a cool little gastropub near the French Quarter that Ryan's friend owned. The walls were lined with old books, and the whole place had a secret-hideaway vibe. She'd loved it instantly and had thought it was a good omen for the date. *Order whatever you want,* Ry had said confidently when they'd arrived. *Jake and I go way back.*

Jake the owner had insisted on presenting them with a tasting menu so they could get a bit of everything. Deep-fried crab dumplings, creamy artichoke crostini, seafood gumbo in shot glasses, rice balls stuffed with shrimp étouffée, and most recently, for dessert, bread pudding with a salted caramel sauce and mini-beignets. The food had been delicious, but cocktails or shots had been served with each dish. Jake had insisted that they comple-mented the food and would enhance the experience. That the whole concept of The Stacks was pairing each appetizer with the perfect drink.

Both Ryan and Jake had assured her that the food would be enough to absorb the alcohol, that the menu had been planned

that way. But after dessert, her head started to swim in a dangerous way. She was usually careful on dates, keeping her intake to
a minimum, but she'd underestimated the amount of booze in the
drinks. Her chair felt as if it was starting to sway, and Ryan's
words were running together in her head.

Jake the owner walked up. "How we doing over here?"

Eliza narrowed her eyes, trying to focus, and forced a smile.
She gave a thumbs-up. "Great."

But the word sounded weird in her head. *Great. Greeeaatt.*

She focused on her thumb, which looked to be splitting into
two thumbs. *Uh-oh.* She tucked her hand under the table.

Ryan chuckled and gave Jake a look. "I'd say we're doing just
fine, man. You really took care of us. I owe you one."

"Happy to be of service." Jake put his hand out, and they did
some sort of weird handshake-and-snap thing.

Eliza squinted at them, feeling like she was missing something.

Jake put his hand on Ryan's shoulder, patting it, and then gave
Eliza a little smile. "Enjoy the rest of your night, y'all."

"We will," Ryan said with way too much confidence. He
turned back to Eliza. "You ready to get out of here? My place is
just around the corner. We could go there for a little while."

"Your place?"

He leaned forward on his forearms like he was going to tell
her a secret. "Yeah. I could show you that artwork I was telling
you about."

Her stomach lurched a little, the rich food and alcohol clash-
ing, and she flattened her palm against the table to try to keep
herself focused. All she could manage was repeating his words.
"Artwork."

He reached out and traced the back of her hand with his
fingertip. "Yeah. It's really something worth seeing in person."

She slid her hand away from his touch. She had the sinking

feeling the so-called artwork he was going to show her would be in his pants. "Do you have a dog?"

He frowned at where she'd moved her hand. "What?"

"A dog," she repeated, concentrating so she could get the words right. The question suddenly seemed epically important. "Do you have a dog? You had one...in your photos."

He flicked his hand dismissively and leaned back in his chair. "Oh. No, that's my sister's dog. I work too much to have my own."

The dog is bait. Beckham's words drifted back to her. Something sharp and hot started filling her chest.

"So," Ry said. "You ready?"

Her head was full of cotton. She turned to find Jake, who was talking to customers at another table, and then looked back to Ryan, another thought hitting her. "How are you so sober?"

She could hear herself holding her *s*'s too long: *ssso sssober.*

He gave her a smug smile. "High tolerance, I guess."

She gripped the edge of the table, trying to ground herself, get her thoughts together. "You sure your friend wasn't more generous with my drinks than yours?"

He lifted his brows, amusement playing at the corners of his eyes. "Are you being serious? I probably have forty pounds on you, and I ate more. I think you just underestimated how much you could handle." He leaned in again. "But don't worry about it. You're a cute drunk."

His gaze swept down her face to the V-neck of her blouse. She shivered. *Had* he drunk as much as she had? He'd done the shots, but she tried to remember if he'd finished his drinks. She hadn't finished all of hers.

A little alarm bell was going off in her brain.

"I am. Really drunk," she confirmed. "But you're inviting me to your place?"

He shrugged. "Sure. We can watch a movie or something. Let

you sober up a little. All is not lost. We can still have some more fun tonight."

"Right," she said flatly. "Fun."

He reached out and put his hand over hers again, his thumb brushing across her skin. "Yes, lots of fun."

His tone and his touch hit her at all the wrong angles and she pulled her hand free. "You mean sex."

He laughed, obviously pleased. "I like a straightforward girl. I'm not going to lie." His finger tracked up her inner arm. "I've been wanting to get you out of that suit all night. I spent yesterday watching your YouTube videos, and I can't say I was thinking anything about mental wellness. Come on, let's get out of here."

Such confidence. Such assumption. Not a question. A statement.

Like she was a sure thing.

Her gaze went to his spiked-coffee dessert cocktail, the one still half-full, and an awful thought hit her. With more speed than she thought herself capable of, she reached out and grabbed his drink.

"What are you—"

But she was already bringing it to her lips before he could finish his sentence. She took a big gulp, held it in her mouth, rolled along her tongue. And tasted…coffee and cream. None of the burn her matching drink had caused. It took her fuzzy mind an extra beat for reality to sink in.

Virgin. His drink was a fucking virgin.

She spat it back into the glass, so many things rushing up in her that she had to take a second to breathe, long and deep, before she could speak. "There's no booze in this."

Ryan smiled an easy smile, but there was something in his gaze that didn't match. "I don't like dessert cocktails. Jake knows that about me."

She was drunk but not stupid. She'd bet her house that he hadn't had more than two drinks with actual liquor in them. She gripped the edge of the table to steady herself, to try find some kernel of sobriety inside her. "Is this your MO?"

He frowned. "What do you mean?"

"Bring a date to your BFF's restaurant and have him load her up with drinks while you sip on goddamned *mocktails* until she's too shit-faced to say no?"

He scoffed and gave her a patronizing look. "Oh, come on, sweetheart. Don't get crazy. It's not my fault you can't hold your liquor." He softened his tone. "Look, why don't I just take you to my place and we'll let you sober up?"

"*You still want to take me home?*" She could hear her voice getting too loud for the restaurant.

"Of course." He smiled and then put his finger to his lips, shushing her. "But maybe quiet down. Don't want to get arrested for drunk and disorderly before we get there." He took her hand again and squeezed it. "Come on, let's go."

She stared at him in shock. He was still trying to take her to bed. And did he... Had he just *shushed* her?

She yanked her hand away, and a literal roar sounded in her ears—of blood, of disbelief, of all the years of shitty dates and creepy propositions crashing together in one glittering moment of righteous rage.

She launched to her feet, knocking the drink over in the process.

"What the hell?" Ryan grabbed his phone to avoid the spilled drink and shoved his chair back.

"I'm drunk," she announced, holding her hands out at her sides and feeling the room tilt. "Like real drunk."

Heads were turning their way.

"Yeah, I got that," Ryan said, watching her, phone tight in his hand.

"But doesn't matter to you, doss'it? As long as you have a... warm place to park your dick for the night, you're good. I'm just a meal you ordered up on an app. I'm...fucking *takeout*." She could hear that her words weren't coming out totally right, the syllables bumping together, but she couldn't stop.

"Eliza," he said, his tone like a teacher to a misbehaving child. "You need to calm down."

"Shut. The fuck. Up!" she shouted, her fists balling. Red edged her vision. Words started pouring from her mouth without her registering anything she was saying. Something else took over, something deep and buried and primally *pissed*.

She didn't know how long it went on or if people were still staring or if her words were making sense. It was a deluge she couldn't stop until she was emptied of the poison.

She sometimes had clients who said that they could black out with anger and not remember what they'd said in the heat of an argument. She'd never fully believed them. But as she stood outside the pub a while later, high heels in her hands and her legs unsteady, she had to readjust her stance on that topic. She had no idea what she'd said in that restaurant or even how she'd gotten outside. The past few minutes were a big blank spot in her brain. All she knew was she needed to get out of there.

But she'd ridden to dinner with Ryan and was nowhere near home. She fumbled around in her purse, looking for her phone, but before she could find it, a hand landed on her arm. She startled and glanced up to find a dark-haired young woman with deep maroon lipstick and a concerned frown. "Hey, are you okay?"

Eliza blinked, registering that the woman was wearing the black-pants-and-white-shirt uniform of the waitstaff. "I–I think so."

The woman glanced back at the restaurant and then to Eliza

again. "Look, my shift just ended. Do you need a ride? I'm Lien, by the way." She pulled a bottle of water from her shoulder bag. "Here. Take this. It will help."

It took a second for Eliza to process the request as she accepted the water. "You want to give me a ride?"

Lien smiled a little. "Look, I heard what you said in there and I just... I've been there. With the nightmare dates. You said a lot of things I've wanted to say." She sniffed derisively. "And Jake, the owner, he's an asshole. He overserved you. I've heard that spiel about the food absorbing the alcohol. It's a bullshit way to sell the highest-ticket items. And you're not the first date that other guy has brought here."

"Shocked face," Eliza said tiredly, the night breeze clearing her head a little. She took a big swig of water.

Lien gave her a sympathetic look. "I can call you an Uber or call a friend for you, but I'm headed out anyway, so I don't mind giving you a ride if you live nearby. You shouldn't be walking around like this. It's not safe."

The kindness almost undid her. She nodded. "Okay. Thank you. I... Can you take me to the WorkAround building? It's not too far, and there are always people working late. My car's there and they have coffee."

"As long as you promise you won't drive until you can say your ABCs backward?" Lien said with a stern brow lift.

"Not sure I can do that when sober, but I promise."

Lien cocked her head. "Come on. Let's get you out of here before the dickhead comes out to find you."

....

A few minutes later, Lien dropped Eliza at off at the door. "You sure you're okay from here?"

Eliza grabbed her purse and gave Lien a grateful look. "I'll be okay. Thanks so much for doing this. I'm feeling a little better already. The water helped."

Lien smiled. "Go drink all the coffee. A little better than shit-faced is still pretty drunk."

Eliza laughed. "Got it." She climbed out of the car, taking her time since her head spun if she moved too quickly. "Thanks again."

Once Lien had pulled away, Eliza fished her key card from her purse and swiped to get the door to open. She stepped inside, the quiet of the building a relief for her overstimulated senses. She passed a few people who were working at hot desks—desks people could rent for certain hours—but kept her head down and focused on keeping her gait as steady as possible. The last thing she needed was chitchat when she was in this state. She grabbed a cup of black coffee and then headed up to her office.

The hallway was silent when she exited the elevator, but as she neared her office, the door next to hers opened. She startled, almost dropping her coffee, and Beckham stepped out. He had his backpack over his shoulder and his keys in his hand, but when he caught sight of her, he froze. "Eli. Hey."

God. The universe really wasn't giving her any breaks today. She was going to prove every point he'd tried to make the other night about online dating.

"Hi." She lifted a hand in a feeble attempt at a wave, but it threw her off-balance a little and she had to put her palm to the wall to steady herself. Was the floor moving? Her stomach turned.

Beckham's eyebrows lifted. "Uh, you all right?"

"I'm *fine.*" The *f* came out a little too emphatic.

"Okay..." His forehead wrinkled and his gaze swept over her, lingering on her bare feet for a moment, and then moving back up. "Did something happen on the date?" He took a step closer, his jaw tight. "Are you okay? Tell me what's going on."

She moved her hand from the wall and lifted a finger like she was going to explain something important but all that came out was, "I'm drunk."

"Yeah, I can see that," he said impatiently. "But you look... Your buttons aren't done up right, and where are your shoes?"

She closed her eyes, trying to gather her thoughts. "Ry took me to his friend's gustro...*gastro*pub and there were drinks with each course and...a lot of courses and I thought he was drinking with me but..."

"But what?" There was a hard edge in his voice.

"I found out his were virgin. He lied. To get me drunk. To—"

"I know why. That fucking prick."

She winced and opened her eyes, her head spinning. "I can't believe I was so stupid."

"Don't," he said. "Don't you dare take blame."

Her hand slipped along the wall and she quickly reset it, but her stomach flipped over. "I don't feel great."

"Fucking hell." Beckham's warm hand touched her elbow, and the hot coffee was removed from her hand. "Come on, let's get you to the bathroom."

A while later, she walked out of the bathroom with a sheen of sweat on her skin and a burn in her throat, but her head felt a little clearer.

Beckham was leaning against the wall, her coffee still in his hand. "How'd the exorcism go?"

"Violently."

He handed her the cup. "Feel any better?"

"A little." She glanced down the hall where she'd dropped her bag to hustle to the restroom. "I have my office key card in my purse."

"I'd rather keep an eye on you. Come on." She followed him to his office, and he guided her to a dark-blue couch. "Just sit here and drink the coffee. You're going to be hating life in the morning."

She sat on the couch, the cozy feel of it making her want to curl up and lay her head down, but instead she took the coffee from him, the warmth heating her fingers, and drank a tentative sip.

Beckham grabbed his rolling desk chair and turned it to face her before sitting down across from her. He braced his hands on his knees, giving her an evaluating look. "So where's the dickhead now?"

She shrugged as she took another sip of coffee. "Dunno. I got upset and left the restaurant. Got a ride with a waitress."

"You did what? And he let—" Beckham pressed his lips together as if reeling his words in. "Okay, that's not important now. You're here and safe. Keep drinking. The caffeine will help."

She took a few more sips of the coffee, already nearing the bottom of the paper cup.

"I'll be right back," he said.

Beckham returned shortly with a fresh cup of coffee and some saltine crackers. He traded her empty cup for the new one. He sat there patiently, watching her like he was afraid she was going to pass out or something. After a while, she could feel the caffeine kicking in and pushing out some of the fog in her head, though her thoughts still felt slow and her stomach was still rolling. She looked up at Beckham. "You told me he was a jerk. Should've listened."

A muscle in Beckham's cheek twitched. "Apparently, I under-estimated him. This guy is a sociopath. I can't believe he purposely got you plastered and then let you walk out in this state in the city at night. You could've gotten lost or hit by a car or worse. What is *wrong* with people?"

"Not people. *Men.*" She gave him a look. "You're right. I don't know why I bother with these apps. I keep convincing myself that these are actual dates. That someone is going out with me to get to know me. How delusional am I?"

"I—"

"Because it doesn't matter what I do or who I am or what I'm interested in. If I'm the right body type, have no expectations, and am willing to get naked, that's all that counts. Screwable or not, that's it. I could literally have Marshmallow Fluff for brains and believe aliens run our government, and it wouldn't matter."

Beckham cleared his throat and scrubbed a hand over his jaw, his scruff making a scratchy sound. "Right."

"Is that what you think?" She looked up, challenge in her voice.

He laughed softly. "I wouldn't want to sleep with a woman who thinks aliens run our government unless she can lay out a compelling scientific argument to convince me. That could be an interesting conversation."

She snorted. "You're obsessed with interesting."

Beckham sighed. "Look, I'm not going to lie to you and say that most guys aren't highly motivated to get laid. But I promise not all of us are setting the bar as low as...warm and willing. In my opinion, sex is a whole lot more fun when you get to know the person and connect with them on other levels first."

"Uh-huh. Sure, Jan."

"Don't 'sure, Jan' me. I'm being serious. It's why I don't do the dating scene. My hookups tend to be with friends. It's low-key. Everyone knows what's what—no pressure to make it into something it's not—but also, we're friends because we have things in common and get along. So the sex is fun, but then afterward, the hanging-out part is cool, too."

"Friends with benefits." A little smile touched her lips. "You and your friends sound very twenty-five."

He gave her a patient look. "Stop acting like you're ancient, Eli. I don't buy the old lady routine. You and I could friend-with-benefit the hell out of each other."

Her attention snapped upward. "What?"

chapter **five**

HELL. BECKHAM REALIZED HE'D GONE TOO FAR. HE shouldn't be having this kind of conversation with Eliza while she was drunk—or anytime really. *Therapist. Remember? Coworker. Remember? Wants a husband and 2.5 kids. Remember?*

"I know that's not your scene," he added. "You're looking for the boyfriend and happily-ever-after thing. All I'm saying is that you're not having bad luck on dates because there's something wrong with you. You're having a bad time because you're looking for something real in a system set up for show. You're looking for a seven-course meal at a fast-food restaurant."

"But what if there aren't any fine-dining establishments anymore?" she said between sips of coffee. "This is the system we're left with."

"Finding people outside of the online dating world can *be* the fine-dining establishment," he said. "You think I sound young? Well, prepare yourself for my old man, get-off-my-lawn speech."

She gave him a cocked brow like she'd believe it when she saw it.

"Get off your apps, Eli, and go live your life. Meet people in other situations. Non-dating situations. Make friends with dudes. Stop putting so much pressure on yourself. I know you like plans, but sometimes you have to let things happen organically. Guys will get to know you first, and you'll get a chance to know them because sex won't be on the table yet. Well, I don't mean sex on an actual table... You know what I mean." He shrugged. "And if that takes some time and you get in the mood to get laid before you find someone to date seriously, there's always the option for a friends-with-benefits hookup."

"Option," she said flatly. "Are you saying..."

What *was* he saying? No, he knew what he was saying and knew it was an A+ bad idea, but he still wanted to hear her response to it. "I'm saying..."

"Oh God." She gave him a wide-eyed look and set down her coffee.

Yep. She was going to slap him. He deserved it. He'd just proven her theory that all guys think about is sex and only sex.

But instead of slapping him, she put her hand over her mouth and mumbled, "I think I'm going to be sick again."

Shit. He hopped out of his chair like it was on fire and grabbed his trash can from under his desk, shoving it in front of her.

"Oh no." She reached for it with quick hands. "Look away."

She didn't need to worry. Vomit didn't faze him. His dad used to give people a concoction to "get the devil out." He'd seen more retching people than he could count. Instead of turning away, he sat next to her while she bent over the trash can and gathered her hair in his fist. "Go ahead. You'll feel better."

She gagged.

He turned his head, keeping her hair in his hand but trying to give her some semblance of privacy as she let loose. He winced in sympathy. He'd been that drunk more times than he cared to remember in his life and didn't wish that feeling on anyone. Being sober wasn't always easy, but in that moment, he was glad he didn't have to go through this part anymore.

When she was done, he took the trash can into the hall, and then grabbed her some tissues and a bottle of water from his mini-fridge. "Here."

She peered up at him, eyes bloodshot, and took his offerings. "I'm the worst office neighbor ever."

He chuckled at her dramatic tone. "Nope. You don't get that trophy. Daphne, on the other side, regularly has her boyfriend over after hours and they have really loud desk sex right up against my wall."

Eliza's eyes widened, a glimmer of humor surfacing. "Are you serious?"

"One hundred percent. Once they banged against the wall so hard, it knocked that picture off the nail." He pointed at a black-and-white abstract painting.

"Wow," Eliza said, glancing at the artwork. "Go, Daphne."

He chuckled. "Feeling any better?"

She took a tentative sip of water and nodded. "Yeah, a little."

"Good. Getting it out of your system is probably the best thing."

"I can't believe I drank that much." She put a hand to her forehead. "I'm usually careful about stuff like that on dates, but when his friend said the drinks and food were paired purposely, that the meal was paced with that in mind, I thought it'd be fine. And Ryan wasn't getting tipsy, so I figured I was good, too. But right around dessert, it hit me hard."

Beckham frowned and sat in his chair again. "If his friend was pouring the drinks, do you think maybe he slipped something in one of them?"

She looked up sharply. "You think I was drugged?"

He rubbed a hand along his jaw, the possibility making him want to track Ryan down and punch him in the throat. "Just asking the question."

She stared at him for a moment and then blew out a breath. "I don't think anything was slipped into my drink. But I do think he set it up so that I was overserved and he was sober. He told me only his last drink was virgin, but I'm not buying it."

"What a loser," Beckham said, disgusted. "He wanted the hot YouTube therapist and knew she was way the hell out of his league, so he stacked the deck in his favor."

She smirked and dabbed at her mouth. "I *am* out of his league, aren't I?"

He grinned. "Eli, he's not even on the practice squad of your league."

"And you were right, the dog wasn't his."

He snapped his fingers and pointed. "See? I could feel that. No dog would have him. He was definitely holding Fluffy hostage."

She pressed her fingers to the spot between her eyes and shook her head, but a smile lingered on her lips. "Thanks, Beckham. You have an uncanny ability to show up when I'm at my worst and make me feel better. I promise I'm higher functioning than how I've appeared lately. People do pay me to help with their problems."

He clasped his hands between his spread knees. "Who says you always have to be high-functioning?"

She gave him a droll look. "Um, everyone. I'm a therapist. My job depends on people believing I have it together at all times."

He grunted. "Tough job requirement. Not allowed to be human?"

She tucked her hair behind her ear. "Not fully."

"Well, I'll keep your secret." He leaned forward and lowered his voice. "That you're not a robot."

She stared at him for a moment and then gave him a sad smile. "Thanks."

"No problem."

"I'm feeling a little better. I'm going to go and let you get home." She rubbed her palms along her skirt. "But before I do, can I ask you something?"

"Yeah, sure."

She narrowed her eyes like she was concentrating and trying to find the right words. "I'm not sure how much booze I still have in my system and if I'm processing things correctly, but earlier... were you about to offer to be an FWB hookup?"

The question made tension rush through him and he got to his feet. He should say *no*, that she'd misconstrued what he'd said. He could back out now, no harm, no foul. She probably wouldn't even remember half of their conversation tomorrow.

"Never mind." She stood and wobbled a little.

On instinct, he put a hand to her elbow to steady her. Her skin was warm, silky. The truth fell out of him. "I was. I know that's not what you're looking for, but if you ever find the idea of a low-key hookup with a friend...*interesting*, or just want to have a little fun while you're looking for *the* guy, I bet we could figure out some ways to entertain ourselves."

Her brown eyes were more focused than they'd been all night, her gaze calculating, then a playful smile curved her lips. "Would you let me lick your tattoos?"

He laughed at the unexpected question even as heat rushed straight downward at the thought. "You're *definitely* still a little drunk."

"Maybe," she murmured.

"But, Eli"—he bent close to her ear—"I'd let you lick whatever you want...as long as I got the same privilege afforded to me."

She shuddered a little in his grip and exhaled slowly. "I'll... keep that in mind."

He leaned back, shaking his head. No way would she remember this conversation tomorrow.

She cleared her throat and straightened her spine, her attempt at her professional face sliding into place. "I need to get going. Mabel will be worried—and she'll pee all over the carpet."

His gaze swept over her, concern filling him. "You're not ready to drive."

She grabbed her purse. "I know. The room has stopped spinning, though. And I think my graceful renditions of *The Exorcist* helped. I can get an Uber now."

Beckham glanced at the clock by his desk. It was almost midnight. "You don't need to do that. Come on. I'll drive you home."

She shook her head. "No, it's fine. I've wasted enough of your night."

"Can the speech, Eli. I'm driving you home and will deliver you safely to Mabel. I'll feel better knowing you got there." He grabbed his backpack and looped it over his shoulder, then put out his hand to Eliza. "Come on, rock star. Let's get you home so you can sleep it off."

After a moment's hesitation, she grabbed her purse and took his hand. "Thanks."

They walked out together, Eliza surreptitiously holding his arm to keep herself steady. They got a couple of curious looks from the few hot-deskers working a night shift on the bottom floor, but otherwise made it outside without incident.

Once they were in his car, she gave him her address and then closed her eyes. By the time he pulled up to her house, she was fast asleep in the passenger seat. He turned off the car and gave her arm a squeeze to rouse her. When they made it to her front door, the night bugs happily buzzing around the porch light, Mabel's barking greeted them. The smile that lit Eliza's face at the sound was a sight to behold.

She unlocked the door, and Mabel—the brown-and-white

lab-collie mix Eliza had adopted—burst out the door, nearly toppling her owner. Eliza crouched down, murmuring baby talk to the dog and telling her what a good girl she was. Mabel whined like she was about to explode from doggie glee, her tail thumping against the doorjamb. Eliza grinned up at Beckham. "Isn't she the best?"

Seeing Eliza in the gold-edged darkness on her knees in front of him, smiling and disheveled, had him thinking things he shouldn't, had him wanting to invite himself in. He shoved his hands in his pockets and rocked back on his heels. "I'm contractually obligated to state that Trent, the very stubborn cat who insists on sleeping literally on my head every night, is the actual best. Because if he hears otherwise, he's definitely going to gouge my eyes out. But Mabel is pretty freaking adorable."

Eliza stood, Mabel turning circles at her feet, and stepped forward. Before he could register what she was doing, she wrapped her arms around him and hugged him with a fierce hug. "Thanks for tonight. You're a good dude. I'm sorry I vomited in your trash can. I'll buy you a new one."

He'd stiffened at the hug at first, caught off guard, but now he let himself return the hug, forcing himself to keep it brief and friendly. "No problem."

She released him and stepped back. "And I'm going to think about what you said. About the online-dating stuff."

He nodded, noting she hadn't said anything about the other part of that conversation. "Good."

She gave him one last look and then herded Mabel inside. "G'night."

"Night, Eli."

As he headed back to his car, all he could think was *What the hell did I get myself into?* Maybe he *should* hope that Eliza forgot every last thing by the time she woke up in the morning. Because this could get really complicated really quickly. If this were a video game, he'd just gotten blinded by the potential reward—sheet time with his sexy coworker—and ignored the high risk attached to it. He was out on a drawbridge above the snake pit, and the ropes holding it up were burning. But if that meant he got to be in her bed for a little while, maybe it'd be worth the fall.

chapter **six**

ELIZA'S SKULL WASN'T GOING TO HOLD HER BRAIN anymore. That had to be what was happening—the bone was fracturing and everything was just going to leak out, because nothing else could hurt this much. She put a hand to her forehead and forced open an eyelid, the morning sunlight like a knife to her eyeball. She groaned and pressed her face back into the pillow.

I'm never, ever, ever drinking again. Ever.

Her mouth was dry and sour, and her stomach was an empty pit. She rolled onto her back, a fresh wave of regret washing over her. How had she let this happen? She wasn't some nineteen-year-old college kid who got out of hand at dollar-shot night at the bar. She was a grown-ass woman and knew better than this.

Her mind drifted back to the previous night, big blurry spots painted across her memory. She remembered some of the food. There'd definitely been a beignet involved. She remembered Ryan talking and talking and talking and him wanting to go back to his place, and the anger that had flooded her about the drinks. She remembered—*oh God*—vomiting in Beckham's trash can and talking about her online dating life. Them talking about sex with friends.

Everything inside her cringed in mortification. She'd made it *so weird*. He probably thought she was some charity project. He'd have sex with her if she needed it.

Shoot me now.

That was it. She had her new thirty-day challenge. No more drinking.

She dragged herself out of bed to brush her teeth and take care of the necessities before grabbing her phone, letting Mabel outside, and heading to her living room with a giant mug of coffee. She took a sip and picked up her phone, ready to call Andi so she could download her horrible night to her best friend. Andi would somehow make her laugh about it and would promise to write Ryan into one of her horror novels and then kill him off in some embarrassing way. Or maybe she should just text both Andi and her other friend, Hollyn, and see if they wanted to meet up this morning. But when she unlocked her phone, the screen was filled with notification bubbles. Comment. Comment. Comment. Follow. Comment.

Her brain was slow processing the flood of little boxes. She clicked one of the notifications. "What the hell?"

Solo on Christmas?
5 Ways to Make the Holiday Special

3k views
Weekly Wellness with Eliza Catalano
8k Subscribers
132 Comments

> **Avil3372** 15 minutes ago
> This bitch is craaazy
> **Duuude6777A** 32 minutes ago
> Looks like someone needs an intervention.

HunnyBear9G9 41 minutes ago
Wow. Just...wow.
GrrrlllEd21 1 hour ago
Eliza r u ok? Let us know!

The comments were posted on her latest YouTube video. She scrolled through, trying to make sense of the comments. Had she been hacked?

The older comments were ones directly talking about the content of her video, but new comments had started popping up a few hours ago that seemed to be about something else. She skimmed through, and a tight, sinking feeling filled her gut. Some of the comments were straight-up vicious, calling her names and insulting her. Others were some of her regular followers checking on her. Then she came across one that came in during the middle of the night.

AlienXDirt 4 hours ago
Ppl pay HER for advice? Better ask for a refund! Check out *this link*.

With heavy dread in her chest, she clicked the link in the comment, hoping it would just bring her to some random porn or spam site, something easily explainable. But instead, she was led to a site she didn't recognize called *Worst. Date. Ever.*

The site was styled like a Reddit page. There were user posts of what looked to be stories and videos that people could comment on. Her attention jumped around, not knowing where to land, but when she scrolled down a bit, the newest video titled *From Serious Bore to Crazy Whore* had her muscles freezing. The screenshot had her own face staring back at her.

"Oh shit," she whispered.

No. *No, no, no, no.*

She recognized the suit, the restaurant, the lighting.

She clicked on the video and turned her phone sideways to expand it, the sound of a busy restaurant filling the silence in her living room. And then she heard her own voice. Angry. Loud. Slurred.

"Shut. The fuck. Up! I can't do this anymore. You hear me? Date after date after date, it's the same blue shit. No, blue shirt. Bull. Shit."

Acid burned the back of her throat as she watched her drunk self stumble over her words. The video was taken from table height, putting her at the most unflattering angle possible, but there was no mistaking who she was or what she was saying.

That sonofabitch Ryan had *filmed her.*

"What are we going to do back at your place? You going to pretend to talk with me, right? Like I'm en-resting. But only long enough to get my clothes off. 'Cause that's all that's really en-resting to you." Video Eliza slapped her hand on the bar table, making the video jump for a moment. *"Well, why don't we just get that outta way right now?"*

Panic went through Eliza as she watched. *No. Please, girl. Don't.*

But Video Eliza was already trucking down that path. She grabbed the top button of her blouse and unhooked it, spreading the shirt open and revealing her lacy black bra. "There. Happy? You paid for dinner and a show, right?"

"Sweetheart...don't." Ryan's voice was patient, patronizing, because that narcissistic sonofabitch knew he was recording. This was entertaining him. "Close your shirt. You're drunk and embarrassing yourself. Let me take you home."

"Screw you." Video Eliza fastened her shirt back together and stood up, going half out of frame but rattling the table as she bumped into it. *"I'm leaving."*

She disappeared from the video, but Ryan's voice filled in the last few seconds, his face conveniently not on-screen. *"And that, ladies and gentleman, is internet dating. All I'd asked her was if she wanted to see a new art piece I'd purchased, and that's the reaction I got. You think you're going on a date with a hot therapist, and you end up with a night of seriously boring conversation and then a whole lot of crazy once the drinks came out. She looked so normal and fun on her YouTube videos, but we know the internet lies. Be careful out there, kids."*

Eliza's teeth were clenched together so hard her jaw started to ache. That *fucking bastard*.

But the anger turned to horror as she scrolled down, reading the comments. Tucked a few down was a comment that read: Found her! This is definitely the same woman.

Next to it was a link to her YouTube and professional web page. Her email dinged.

She opened it up, her fingers numb. The scheduling program she used had sent an update about a new client appointment for this afternoon.

Adam and Olivia Wolfe

Appointment: Canceled
Reason: Other
Rescheduled for: None

She stared at the words, unable to process everything at once. *Other*. No one ever picked *other* from the drop-down menu as an appointment cancellation reason. The canceled appointment was probably a coincidence, but her intuition alarms were going off, calling bullshit on that. They'd canceled because one of them had seen the comments on her YouTube.

The gravity of that hit her. *Anyone* could see this.

She was on the internet. Drunk. Flashing her boobs. And people now knew who she was.

Something dark and heavy seeped through her, making her limbs tingle and her skin hot. Embarrassment. Horror. *Shame.*

She was brought right back to sixth grade when Eric Geiger had called her Werewolf Legs in front of the whole PE class because her mom hadn't allowed her to shave yet. The sound of laughter in her ears was fresh and clear.

These people were laughing at her, too. Not just laughing… *labeling.* Damaging her reputation.

Fear rushed in, bright and cold.

Everything she'd worked so hard for—the business she'd built, the image she'd honed, the life she created—all of it was at risk.

How many people had seen this? How could she get this pulled down?

She hurried into her room to grab her laptop. When she got it booted up, her fingers were trembling, but she managed to get to her YouTube account and switched the settings to disable new comments. Then she went in and deleted the Christmas video altogether, deleting the comments with it. She also made her Instagram and other social media temporarily private. No one could comment on them if they weren't there. There was no way to flag a post on the Worst. Date. Ever. site, though. She clicked around the pages, trying to find any option where she could report it, but if they had a way, it was buried too deep for anyone to find it.

More comments were popping up on the post.

"Goddammit." She tossed her laptop aside. Flashes of the video went through her mind on loop. Her sloppy speech. Her pulling her shirt open in public.

She'd worked so hard to get where she was, to be a respected professional. She could not let some self-involved dude-bro take her down.

She imagined her clients watching that video, imagined them seeing the person they trusted with their most personal secrets, the person they trusted to help with their relationships, their mental health, falling down drunk and losing her shit.

No. No. No. Her heart was racing and she stood up to pace. She fanned her hot face and tried to breathe. She needed to think this through. Having a panic attack wasn't going to help.

The panic attack came anyway.

She grabbed onto her dresser, flattening her hands atop it and focusing on the feel of the solid wood beneath her fingertips. *You're here. You're okay.* She started counting backward from one hundred by twos in her head, making sure to feel the grounding sensations of the dresser against her hands, the floor against her bare feet. Then she breathed, focusing on long exhales. Exhaling activated the parasympathetic nervous system, sending her body the calming signals it would need. She knew how to do this. Walked clients through it all the time. But it took everything she had to make herself go through the process and not crumple into a ball on her bed.

When her heartbeat finally slowed and the tingling in her arms stopped, she opened her eyes. A plan. She needed a plan. How was she going to deal with this?

First, shower.

She couldn't function at full capacity with the funk of a hangover and the horrible night clinging to her. She ran a hot shower and got under the spray. She closed her eyes, letting the water wash away the night, and let her mind go where it wanted. She usually got her best ideas in the shower, and she needed all the help she could get. The mental list started to populate.

Ways to Combat the Narcissistic, Misogynistic, Assholic Actions of Ry the Bread

1. Quit job and escape to a beach cottage in the Bahamas, go by the name Lola.
2. Go to Ryan's social media and tell everyone he does not have a dog, calls his penis artwork, and gets women drunk because no one would sleep with him otherwise.
3. Hunt down Ryan's car and/or boat. Purchase baseball bat. Channel Beyoncé and go *Lemonade* style on all his modes of transportation.
4. Call Andi and Hollyn because they're the smartest people I know and will have advice that will not put me in jail.

Number three was the most tempting, but by the time she was out of the shower and getting dressed, Eliza decided number four was the most prudent. She pulled on black jeans, her favorite green sweater, and her trusty boots. She left her smartwatch on her bedside table because the last thing she needed was her wrist vibrating with more bad news. She let Mabel back inside, put on a little makeup because it felt like body armor on a vulnerable day, and then secured her still-damp hair into a ponytail.

Before tucking her phone in her back pocket, she texted Andi and Hollyn on their group thread with a GIF of a dancing eclair and the message *Emergency Pastry Meeting Needed. Will be there in about 20.*

Both replied within a few seconds. Hollyn replied that she'd procure the cinnamon rolls. Andi said she'd be ready with the coffee and they could meet in her office.

A little of the tension Eliza was carrying in her muscles loosened. No matter what fire was burning in her personal life, her friends would still be there. Having those women in her corner made everything feel more manageable.

She grabbed her bag and hustled out the door. She was halfway to the driveway before she realized there were no car there. A snap of panic went through her. Had it been stolen? But then she remembered that Beckham had dropped her off last night. Her car was still at work.

Dammit.

The wait for an Uber seemed interminable, but the car finally pulled up. As she rode in the back seat, Eliza kept reaching for her phone, but she couldn't scroll through her social media like she'd normally do to distract herself. And she definitely wasn't going to swipe through Aligned. Her hands had nothing to do, and she had to clasp them tight to keep from fidgeting.

The still quiet was uncomfortable and had all the worries rushing back. It felt like every minute that passed was another few thousand people seeing that video. By the time the car pulled up to WorkAround, Eliza was ready to launch out of it like a rocket.

She rushed through the main doors, not bothering to say hello to anyone, and headed upstairs. Andi's door was already open. There was a white pastry box on her desk, and Hollyn was sitting in one of Andi's chairs.

"Hey," Andi waved Eliza in. Her bright-red hair was half-covered with a blue polka-dot head scarf, making her look like she was about to take a trip in a convertible in the 1950s.

Hollyn smiled and tucked her mass of curly blond hair behind her ears. "Pastry has been acquired."

Eliza stepped inside, feeling like she'd run a marathon already. "Thank you."

She hadn't told either of them what was going on yet, but as soon as Andi saw Eliza's face, she got up and hugged her.

"Good lord, girl. You look like you just saw the boogey-man." She leaned back, her hands on Eliza's upper arms, her eyes scanning her face. "What's wrong?"

"All the things," she said, a catch in her voice. "All of them."

"Oh no," Hollyn said in that naturally empathetic way she had, the way that said *I understand on the deepest level and am here for you.* It made Eliza want to cry.

"Shit." Andi frowned and stepped around her to shut the door. "Okay. Sit. Tell us the things."

Eliza settled into the chair closest to Andi's desk. Hollyn immediately grabbed the box of pastries and opened it, offering Eliza a cinnamon roll.

Eliza took one, the sweet cinnamon scent the first thing that hadn't turned her stomach all morning. She shoved a big bite in her mouth. When she'd swallowed it down, she forced the words out. "I had a date last night. From that Aligned app..."

Andi's expression darkened as she sat on the edge of her desk. Eliza had no doubt her horror-writer friend was imagining every single terrifying possibility. She'd never been a fan of the dating apps. She called them serial-killer shopping apps.

Angry tears burned in Eliza's throat, making it hard to talk. "This guy. That...bastard...did a...made a..."

"He did what?" Hollyn asked, leaning forward and putting a hand on her knee. "You're scaring us, Eliza."

"I'm sorry. It's just..." The story poured out, Eliza barely taking a breath. When she was done, she pulled out her phone and handed it to Hollyn with the video pulled up.

Andi stepped behind Hollyn, and Hollyn hit Play. They watched the whole thing with grim looks on their faces. Hollyn had Tourette's syndrome and her nose and cheek twitched, her growing agitation evident. Andi's face got red.

When they were done, Hollyn handed the phone back to Eliza. "I can't even... I don't even know what to say."

Eliza took another harsh bite of cinnamon roll.

"I do," Andi said. "I'm thinking of at least a hundred painful ways I could kill this guy. I'm leaning toward removing his balls and shoving them down his throat. Or maybe just a good ice pick to the asshole."

Eliza snorted, some sound between a laugh and a cry, and almost choked on her pastry. Andi could always be counted on to bring levity to a dark situation, and she was the best at colorful death threats.

"I just don't get it," Hollyn said. "Why would he do this? What's the point?"

Eliza shook her head. "The therapist part of my brain keeps trying to answer that, searching for the motivation. Is it just to get a laugh? Or to make himself feel superior? Maybe he didn't even think about how it could tank my business, because God knows he didn't seem to care about anyone but himself, but this could be really damaging. I've already had a cancellation." She groaned and put the half-eaten cinnamon roll back in the box. "God, I feel sick to my stomach again."

"I'm so sorry, honey," Andi said, sliding her hand along her forehead and pushing her bangs back like this was making her brain hurt. "This is just straight-up sadistic."

Eliza sighed, sagging in the chair, thinking back to what she could remember from the night before, her brain searching for a diagnosis, something that would help her make sense of this. "I think this is just an ego thing."

Andi sat on the edge of her desk again and handed Eliza one of the coffees that had been next to the pastry box.

Eliza took a small sip. "I didn't fall all over him last night— even after he got me drunk—so he's going to make me pay for wounding his precious pride. He can mess with my career, my image. He can shame me."

"Ugh," Hollyn said, her nose wrinkling. "I bet he's really, really bad in bed."

"Oh, no doubt," Eliza said. "Probably only does it in front of a mirror so he can watch himself. *Oh baby, tell me how good I am.*"

Andi snorted. "Probably calls out his own name when he jerks off."

Eliza laughed, almost spilling her coffee, and Hollyn pressed her hand over her mouth, trying not to spit out a bite of cinnamon roll.

"Thanks," Eliza said, looking back and forth between her friends. "Laughing feels better than crying."

"What have you done so far?" Hollyn asked. "Did you try to report the video?"

"I've made my social media private, deleted the post that people were leaving rude comments on, and closed my YouTube to any new comments. But...I'm not really sure where to go from here. I have no access to Ryan's video."

Andi frowned, her fingernails tapping against the desk. "There's got to be a way to get it taken down. Isn't it like defamation or something? If it could damage your career?"

"I don't know." Eliza rubbed the spot between her eyes where her hangover headache was still throbbing. "My guess is pursuing something like that isn't a quick process. I'm going to dig deeper into that site to see if there's a place to report the video, but I don't know how much good it's going to do. Once something is out there, it's like playing Whac-A-Mole. And Ryan could conceivably post it again as soon as I get it taken down. I don't know if playing defense is going to work."

"Right." Andi sat her chin in her hand, a pensive look in her eyes. "So if defense isn't an option, how do we play offense? Also, this is as far as I can follow you on sports-ball analogies. Can we go back to murder plots?"

Eliza smirked. "It always comes back to murder plots. I did

have some really vivid fantasies of taking a baseball bat to his car this morning."

"What if offense is speaking out about it?" Hollyn said, her gaze on Eliza.

"What do you mean? Like putting a comment on the video?" Eliza asked. "Or doing my own response video?"

"No, not that exactly." Hollyn shook her head. "I'm just thinking about how celebrities handle scandals. If this happened to someone famous and I was covering the story, I'd reach out to that person to get a comment. I'd tell them that the media and whoever is on the other side would have control of the narrative if they don't comment."

Eliza nodded, processing her friend's words. Hollyn was a well-respected entertainment reviewer in New Orleans, but her roots were in journalism. "So right now Ryan's controlling the narrative?"

"Exactly. But you have a voice, too," Hollyn said. "You could choose not to accept his narrative. Or the public shaming attached to it."

Eliza wiped her sweaty palms on her jeans, her friend's words sparking something inside her. "Right, and the thing about shaming someone is that it's only effective if that person feels the shame, accepts it. Shaming a sociopath, for instance, wouldn't do anything because they feel no shame." An idea was opening up in her mind, stretching out its petals, blooming. She didn't remember everything about her conversation with Beckham last night, but she did remember him saying, *What, you can't be human?*" "Conceivably, I could...not accept the shame."

Andi grabbed a cinnamon roll for herself. "You shouldn't have to. You didn't do anything wrong. Fuck that guy."

"I could flip it on him," Eliza said, leaning forward, her mind racing ahead. "Women know how guys can be. How horrible dating is these days. What if I just announce that yes, I lost it? I was fed up. I couldn't take one more guy just wanting to get laid instead of having an actual conversation. And yes, I drank more than I should've, but haven't we all a time or two?"

Andi's mouth curved. "*So* many people will identify with all of that."

"Amen," Hollyn said.

"And sure," Eliza said, "some guys may side with him and I may get blackballed on dating apps, but you know what?"

"What?" Andi said with a mouth full of pastry.

Eliza smiled, thinking of the conversation with Beckham again. "I don't think I give a damn anymore. To hell with online dating."

Andi's eyebrows arched.

"I'm opting out," Eliza said, her voice getting more confident. "I can't do this anymore. I can go...analog."

Hollyn sipped her coffee and gave her a skeptical look. "Analog?"

Eliza's heartbeat had picked up speed, this plan of action filling her with something she hadn't felt in way too long. *Control.* She didn't have to opt in to how everyone else did it. There wasn't a rule that dating had to be done that way. The species had coupled up and procreated without apps for millions of years.

Make the more interesting choice. Beckham had shown her that. Dating apps were the convenient choice, the obvious one, the path of least resistance. The more interesting choice was finding another way. She didn't need to put up with men who treated her like this just because she wanted some companionship.

And other women didn't have to either.

Another idea hit her. "I could make this a thing."

Andi was popping chunks of cinnamon roll into her mouth like it was popcorn at the movies. "A thing?"

Eliza's brain was moving too fast now. "A YouTube series or

something. Or, wait, I could write a book. You know how people do those experiments where it's like a year without sugar or booze or they cook all of Julia Child's recipes?"

"Ooh, I love those," Hollyn said, perking up. "Stunt books."

"Exactly. I could document a year of being single in my thirties and opting out of online dating. Or how to find love without the apps. Or something. I don't know. I'd have to brainstorm it."

Andi pointed at her. "A book about that could totally sell."

"For sure. I would've bought that book," Hollyn said. "Before Jasper, of course. Because I definitely didn't have the guts for online dating."

Eliza's brain was racing ahead now, her inner planner going into overdrive. "Maybe that's what I should be writing instead of the relationship book. With the relationship book, I keep getting bored with it because it's so dry. It's all professional knowledge, no personal flavor because I'm not *in* a relationship. But this?" She set her coffee down. "This, I'm in the trenches. I have real feelings about it. Personal horror stories to share. Too many, honestly. And after last night, I definitely have my opening chapter. You know openings are always the rock-bottom chapter."

She laughed and pressed her palms together, touching them to her lips as an idea hit. "Oh my God, wouldn't it be amazing if somehow I got a book deal out of this and I could dedicate the book to Ryan?"

Hollyn laughed. "I love that so hard."

"Me too." Andi lifted her hand and drew a circle in the air around Eliza's face. "And this. How you look right now? I haven't seen that in months. So whatever burst of inspiration this is, from one writer to another, I say chase it. I have no doubt your book will be brilliant."

"Bestseller for sure," Hollyn agreed.

Eliza let out a breath, love for her friends filling her. "Y'all are the best. You know that right? My kick-ass lady soul-mates."

"Back at ya." Hollyn reached out and squeezed Eliza's knee.

"Same, girl, same. But…" Andi lifted her icing-covered finger. "Just one quick question…"

Eliza pulled her ponytail tighter, ready to leap out of her chair and get started. "Yeah?"

Andi tilted her head like a confused puppy. "You have any idea how to do that?"

Eliza frowned. "What?"

Andi wrinkled her nose like she didn't want to say it. "Um, find love without the internet?"

Eliza let out a long breath and looked down at her phone, which was sitting on her lap like a sleeping tiger. She picked it up to unlock it and then found the bright-magenta app. After a brief moment of hesitation, she opened it and changed her account status to inactive. She long-pressed the familiar little square with her thumb, and when it started to wiggle, she dumped the Aligned dating app into a folder she never opened. She looked up at Andi. "Not a freaking clue."

Andi laughed. "Welp, guess you've got your research cut out for you. But I believe in you!"

Hollyn lifted her fists in the air. "Go, Team Eliza!"

"Thank you. I love y'all. And yes, lots of research to do." She glanced toward the door. "But I have to see what I can do in the meantime to minimize the impact of this on my business. A book will take time to write. I need to keep my clients. Bills need to be paid."

"Do you have any ideas on how to do that?" Hollyn asked.

"Not yet, but I think I know someone who might be able to help," she said, hoping that was true.

"Okay," Andi said. "Figure out how to keep the clients. Then…world domination."

"Yes." Eliza got up and hugged each of her friends, giving them an extra tight squeeze. "Thanks for listening and for the cinnamon rolls."

"Of course." Hollyn reached for another cinnamon roll and wrapped it in a napkin. She handed it to Eliza. "For later."

"And I'm on my way out to buy an ice pick." Andi made stabbing motions with her hand. "Right to the balls."

Eliza smirked and grabbed her coffee. "Let's put a pin in the murder plot for now."

Andi stuck her bottom lip out in a pout. "Y'all never let me have any fun."

chapter **seven**

NOTHING.

Come on. Eliza knocked again, louder.

She didn't know Beckham's specific tech expertise, but she had a feeling that even if he didn't know how to help her, he'd know who to point her toward. But his door didn't open. He wasn't there. She should've come here before her client appointments this afternoon instead of after. She must've missed him.

She pressed her head against his door, frustrated and still a little hungover. She'd felt a surge of momentum in Andi's office this morning and wanted to keep moving. She'd been busy this afternoon with appointments, but the minute she'd walked the last client out, the whole thing had hit her all over again. She had two more canceled appointments in her inbox and a call from a client concerned about how Eliza was doing, checking on her. Sweet but not cool. People weren't paying her so that *they* could worry about *her*.

But all of it had just underlined the reality she was living in now. She'd been publicly shamed on the internet. Her drunken, shirt-opening tirade was currently being viewed by God knew who, and Ryan was probably laughing about it with his friends, sending the link around, proudly watching his clicks increase.

She didn't want to think about it. She didn't want to picture it. It would make her go buy a baseball bat or that ice pick Andi had suggested.

"Eliza?"

Beckham's voice drifted over her like a welcome breeze, breaking her from her murderous thoughts.

"Is everything okay?" he asked from somewhere to her right.

She lifted her head. He was standing in the hallway with coffee and a concerned look on his face. Today's vintage shirt was a Beastie Boys "Sabotage" tee.

"Whoa, what's wrong?" he asked, stepping forward.

Great. Apparently she looked as shitty as she felt, based on the concern on his face. She tipped up her chin, trying to look more put together. "You have a minute?"

A deep line had appeared between his brows, but to his credit, he nodded without asking more questions. "Yeah, sure. Door's unlocked. Go on in."

She turned the knob and went straight to his comfy blue couch. For being a therapist, she was sure ending up on *his* couch a lot.

He followed in behind her. "Hey, look, if this is about the stuff I said last night... It was late and I'm sorry if I made it weird. And—"

She peered up at him, amused by his rambling. "Beckham, I barfed in your trash can and drunkenly said embarrassing things to you. I think I win on the making-it-weird part."

He narrowed his eyes, evaluating her. "How much do you remember about last night?"

Her face got warm. She vaguely remembered a mortifying comment about what she'd like to do to his tattoos. She cleared her throat. "Enough. I'm definitely not here to talk about *that*. Let's forget the things I said under the influence."

He nodded, gaze still examining her. "O...kay. Then what's up?"

"I'm sorry to come to you with this. I know you're busy with your own work," she said. "But you're the only person I could think of."

He arched a brow. "Well, with an endorsement like that…"

She opened her mouth to explain, but despite her best efforts not to get emotional, her eyes began to burn again. "Dammit."

"Shit, Eli." He set down his coffee and sat on the couch next to her. "Now you're freaking me out. What's wrong?"

She couldn't get the words out. Instead, she pulled her phone from her purse and brought up the link. She handed it to him, knowing what he'd see, but if he was going to help her, he'd see it anyway. She needed to get this part out of the way. "Just watch."

He gave her a wary look but took her phone and then clicked the link. She turned her head away while he did. Hearing her drunken words again was enough to send a fresh wave of embarrassment through her. She could sense him tense next to her, and then he sucked in a breath. Before the video ended, he was on his feet again.

"*The fuck?*" he said, anger hot in his voice. "He got you drunk and then *filmed* you?"

She looked up, her shoulder muscles tight and her face burning. "And someone recognized me and put my name and links in the thread. I had comments all over my YouTube this morning and some on my Instagram." She inhaled a deep breath. "People are already canceling appointments."

His jaw clenched. "This is…"

"Awful," she filled in. "I know. I've been freaking out most of the morning, but I have a plan to try to turn this around."

"A plan?" He sent her a look. "Does it involve tracking him down at his office and punching him in that smug face of his? Because that seems like a solid plan A. I'm here for plan A."

"Believe me, I'd love to, but adding an assault charge might not be the best way to repair my professional reputation." She watched his fist open and close. "But I do need to stop the video from spreading further if I can. That site doesn't have a takedown procedure or anyone to contact. I thought maybe you or one of the people you work with might know if there's anything else I can do. I've already taken down my YouTube video and closed comments on the rest. I made my social media temporarily private so I don't get more comments on those."

He handed her phone back to her, his face all business. "Good. Don't give any of these trolls a forum to post a comment. Make sure there's no place for comments on your business website, and you may want to check Yelp if your business is on there or if there's a Yelp-like site for rating therapists."

She took her phone, dread moving through her. "Shit, I didn't even think about that."

"And email me the link so I can get to the post on my computer." He grabbed a business card off his desk. "My email's on there."

"Do you know how to get the video down?" she asked, taking the card. "Sites have to have a procedure, right?"

"They're supposed to. That doesn't mean they all do." He pulled out his desk chair and sat down, waking his screen and typing in a long password. "Let me see what I can do."

She quickly forwarded the link to his email.

Beckham closed out the screen he'd worked on last, which looked to be a drawing of an intimidating-looking green-and-gold dragon, and went to his email. He grabbed the link and opened his browser, eyes narrowing at the screen. She chewed at her thumbnail, an old childhood habit, as he clicked through a few pages.

"Sometimes they hide the contact info deep. These types of sites avoid regulation." He kept clicking. "And some just flout the rules and don't have any info at all. This looks like one of those."

"So there's nothing I can do?" she asked, frustration welling again.

"There's nothing *official* we can do." He glanced at her over his shoulder. "But...give me a few minutes." His hands flew over the keyboard, his teeth biting into his bottom lip and the tattoos on his forearms flexing with the motion. "This site is pretty rudimentary. I'm sure I can find a way in."

She tucked her hands between her knees, her eyes on his profile. "A way in?"

He peered over at her. "Hypothetically, how do you feel about some mildly illegal activity?"

Her lips parted. "Uh...how illegal? Hypothetically."

He scratched the back of his head as if gauging whether or not to say more. "Just some light hacking on a site that isn't following the rules anyway."

She straightened. "You know how to do that?"

"I don't *not* know how to do that," he hedged with a little half-tilt smile that made her forget her crisis for a second. "I'm designing a video game because that's what I want to move into eventually, but cybersecurity work is what pays my bills. Companies contract with me to do penetration testing—basically to hack their own systems to find the weak spots."

"Oh." She relaxed a little. "So this is legal?"

"This? No, *this* isn't. I don't have permission from the site but...fuck them," he said, cocking his head toward the screen. "I have zero guilt about screwing with some site that gets its hits from publicly shaming people. Privacy is kind of my thing, and this type of stuff makes me really, really angry." He rocked back in his chair. "I had a good friend who had a sex tape posted of her when we were younger. She... It really messed up things in her life. After that, I learned how to take stuff down, by alternative methods if necessary."

She stared at him, taking that all in, a new picture forming of her neighbor. As chill as Beckham seemed most of the time, the way he'd talked about his friend and the way he'd reacted to Ryan's behavior hinted at a guy who had some intensity bubbling beneath the surface. Some passion. It made her wonder what happened when that kind of passion was directed at other parts of his life.

She did *not* want to examine why that made her start thinking about their conversation from last night again. "Don't go to jail on my behalf."

He gave her an I've-got-this smirk. "I know better than to get caught. And this site wouldn't have a legal leg to stand on anyway."

She wet her lips, glancing at his computer, her paused video taunting her. Her stomach fluttered with nerves. She didn't like the idea of breaking any laws. She'd always been a rule-follower, but... "Do it. Please."

"On it. Now you're officially an accomplice. Hope you like wearing prison orange." He winked and turned back to his computer.

"*Beck.*"

He laughed. "Kidding. I'd never rat you out." His fingers typed at a rapid pace, the screen changing. "Want me to send a nasty virus to Ry's account after I'm done with this?"

She gasped. "Is that possible?"

He glanced over at her, grinning. "I love that you want to say yes to that. I can see it on your face."

She clamped her lips together, *soooo* tempted, but shook her head. "Let's just get the video down for now. Could you do something to his account so that he can't repost the video?"

"Probably. I'll check once I get in." He concentrated on his screen, that clackety keyboard now like music instead of an annoyance.

"Thanks for this. Really. I can't tell you how much I appreciate it." She leaned back and massaged her throbbing temples. "Now I know why you usually avoided talking to me. Apparently, I bring nothing but drama to your doorstep."

He didn't look her way, but he gave a little headshake. "This drama was brought *to* you, not by you. You didn't invite this. Ryan has posted here before, multiple times. Maybe he gets off on getting attention for all his bad dates. I'm glad you left before he could get you into his car."

"God, me too." She shuddered and rubbed her arms, chasing away the goose bumps that had formed. "I'm going to take your advice, you know."

Beckham's hands kept moving, a musician at his instrument. "Yeah? Which advice is that?"

"Getting off the dating apps, trying it analog," she said, twisting the simple gold band she wore on her right ring finger, her mom's wedding ring.

His fingers paused and his gaze went her way again. "Really?"

"Yeah, that's part of my plan to turn this whole incident around." She continued twisting the ring, his focused attention making her self-conscious. "I'm going to write about what happened last night and then document an analog dating experiment. I may blog about it along the way and then put it all together in a book. Like one of those 'Year Without Whatever' books. Maybe it might help other people."

He turned his attention back to the screen, his shoulders hunching. "Right."

The heavy dose of judgment in that one little word had her fingers curling into a fist. "What?"

"What *what*?" he asked innocently.

"Let's not pretend that wasn't laced with sarcasm," she said with a derisive sniff. "I'm taking your advice. What's your issue?"

He stopped typing and exhaled loudly. "Nothing. It just sounds like a...performance."

She bristled. "A performance."

He spun his chair toward her and shrugged. "Look, you do what you need to do. Like I said last night, it's not my business. But if you really want to do something for real, don't you think it will be influenced by knowing you have to write it about it for public consumption afterward? That there will be an element of performance to it?" He flicked his hand in the air like he was trying to grab onto a thought. "It's like that thing when research subjects know they're being watched. It changes their behavior. What's that called?"

She frowned and pulled the random fact from her grad school years. "The Hawthorne effect."

He pointed at her. "Yes. That. Like you'll almost want the date to go badly because it will give you better material. You could sabotage it without knowing it. And what guy is going to want to go on a date knowing the woman is going to blog about him or whatever afterward? I definitely wouldn't." He tipped his head toward the computer screen. "Think about how you feel right now, with this dumbass publicly airing what happened on your date last night. Would you want to do that to someone else?"

"I wouldn't be posting drunken videos," she said with a huff. "And I would keep things anonymous."

"But those guys will know who you are and could easily find out you have an online thing going, so they'll know who you're talking about," he said. "Plus, when you're on the date, you'll be thinking about how you're going to portray it. You won't be in the moment. You'll be thinking about who you're going to tell about it and what they'll think instead of just... experiencing it all, *feeling* it all."

The way he'd said *feeling it all* had her swallowing hard.

"That's why secret relationships turn people on so much—and get people in so much trouble," he said with a shrug. "The privacy of it all feels…intense. And hot. You're in on a secret together. No one else gets a peek."

She grimaced. "Secret relationships land a lot of people in my office with divorce papers. Secrets eat people up from the inside out."

He made a dismissive noise. "I'm not advocating for people cheating on each other or anything. I'm just saying that the more people and opinions you bring into something, especially in the beginning, the less…visceral it's going to feel. The less real it will be. It becomes a show. It becomes those *Look how fantastic our vacation is!* photos on Facebook. When in reality, people are often spending more time worrying about how to get the best picture to post than, you know, actually experiencing the vacation. And you know they're not posting all the bad or boring parts of the vacation. Same goes for posting about relationships." He shook his head. "If you put your whole life on the internet for public opinion, what part is left for just you—and whoever you're with?"

She pressed her lips together. "Maybe people just want to share their happiness."

"Or show off," he said. "Have you ever considered that maybe your dates aren't working out because you're choosing people who would 'appear' right in your curated world instead of people who actually intrigue you?" He cocked his head to the side. "The financial planner with the boat dating the successful therapist would look pretty great on Insta."

She huffed, indignant. "I'm not after some guy's money or status."

"I believe you."

She crossed her arms and gave him her cop-interrogation face. He lifted his hands. "I *do*. Honestly. But I also think there may be part of you that's casting for a role instead of just…being in the world and being open to whoever sparks something in you—curiosity, interest, pants feelings."

She snorted. "Pants feelings?"

"Of course. Those are just as valid as other types of feelings." His lips tipped up at one corner, a playful look in his eyes. "You're familiar with them, I believe. You did ask to lick my tattoos last night."

chapter **eight**

ELIZA GASPED, GRABBED THE THROW PILLOW FROM HIS couch, and tossed it at him. "We said we weren't going to talk about the things I said last night…when I was very, *very* inebriated." She pointed toward his computer screen. "Did you see the video? Clearly, I was out of my mind."

Beckham laughed, catching the pillow before it hit his face. "Don't worry. Remember, I'm into privacy. I'll keep your tattoo kink a secret." He leaned closer, lowering his voice. "And your younger-man fetish."

"Oh, you can go to hell, Beckham Carter," she said, flipping him off. "I'm glad you feel it necessary to make me feel more embarrassed—and *old*—on a day I've already been humiliated. I mean, I've already been called boring and crazy. Let's just add that to the pile."

He gave her a patient look and tossed the pillow next to her on the couch. "Aww, come on. You know none of that stuff is true. You're not boring, crazy, or old. And why be embarrassed about what you said? Nothing wrong with harmless flirting. I said stuff back to you, and I was stone-cold sober. It was all in good fun. I knew not to take you seriously—especially when you were that hammered. I'm surprised you even remember you said it."

"I…" She met his gaze and frowned. "Right."

"But here I am giving you dating advice again. I'll stop." He turned back to his computer, his fingers returning to the keyboard. "Let's get this fire put out."

"Yes, please."

Eliza found herself watching Beckham's profile again, his sea-glass-colored eyes intense, his teeth scraping over his bottom lip as his hands moved with practiced ease, screen after screen of what she assumed was computer code flickering past. A man on a mission. A guy who definitely knew his way around breaking into places he shouldn't be—which should've been concerning to her but somehow felt thrilling instead. The therapist side of her didn't want to examine *that* too closely. But still, she couldn't stop watching.

She didn't know how much time had passed when Beckham stopped typing and glanced over at her with a satisfied smirk. "I'm in."

Her heart leapt. "Seriously?"

He looked back to the screen and did some more clicking. "Yeah, that wasn't even a fun challenge. Their security sucks. Here it is." He rolled his chair back a bit and turned his monitor so she could see his screen fully. "Behold… Bread Man's account."

She bent forward to read the screen, the fresh scent of Beckham's soap or shampoo hitting her nose as she got closer. "Oh my God. His password is RYisFLY69? I'm embarrassed for him."

"Such. A. Tool," Beckham said with an eye roll. "Let's change this for him. Save him from himself." He deleted the password and typed in *ShitForBrains*. "That's better. More accurate." He went through another screen of code, changing a few more things in Ryan's account. Then he clicked into another page, her video coming up. "And…delete."

He hit a button and the video disappeared from the screen.

Beckham clicked into some other icon on his computer. He grabbed a file and dumped it into the upload box. A progress bar appeared. Eliza scooted even closer, their arms nearly touching now, but she was fascinated. They were viewing Ryan's account as if they were him. "What are you doing?"

"Wait for it…" Beckham said, rubbing his palms together with relish.

After a few seconds, the video he'd added loaded and he hit Play. The opening notes of the song "Never Gonna Give You Up" by Rick Astley started playing.

Eliza pressed her fingers to her mouth, grinning. She'd seen this video before, numerous times when searching up random things on YouTube. "This is amazing."

"Ry, my friend, you've officially been Rickrolled." Beckham hit Save to make it official and the main screen came back into view. The thread with her video on it was still there, but the eighties pop song had replaced the content. He'd also deleted the text part of the post and disabled comments, making the old comments not visible to the public.

"It's gone," Eliza said in wonder.

Beckham spun around in his chair, brushing his knees against hers. "And he won't be able to get back into his account because I changed his password and the answers to his security questions, so he won't be able to reset his password. He could start from scratch with a new account, but I'll monitor the site and do this again if the video shows up."

Eliza stared at him for a moment, the pressure that had been pushing on her chest all day easing and finally letting her take a full breath. Before she could think too hard about it, she got up from the couch and hugged Beckham. "Thank you…*thank you, thank you, thank you.*"

He'd gone still for a moment, but after a few seconds he put his arm around her to return the hug. "Happy to help. If you see it pop up anywhere else, just let me know."

She collapsed back onto the couch, her entire being feeling lighter. "I can't believe you made it disappear." She snapped her fingers. "Just like that. This is like...a superpower. How'd you learn to do that?"

He rocked back in his chair, hooking his ankle over his knee. "Too much time on my hands as a teenager. My parents were... very strict and had all kinds of blocks on our computers. If I wanted to get to anything, I had to learn how to break through, get their passwords, that kind of thing." He shrugged. "I found I had a knack for it. Got hooked into some hacker groups online and got better. Eventually got good enough to convince a company to help me go to school for it."

"Wow. Companies do that?" she asked, thinking of the mountain of student loans she was still paying off.

His expression turned slightly chagrined. "I may have broken into their system illegally and then told them if they wanted me to show them how I did it, I wanted a job and some help with school."

Her brows went up. "So, like, blackmail?"

He tipped his head side to side as if he were weighing the word. "Technically, it's called gray-hat hacking. Not legal but not meant maliciously—helpful to the company because they *did* have holes in their system—but also self-serving." He shrugged. "It worked."

"Damn. I should've gone into hacking instead of psychology." She shook her head. "I would've saved a lot of money in student loans."

"I think you're right where you need to be. You're a great therapist."

She picked at a piece of lint on the arm of her sweater. "Thanks, but how would you even know?"

Beckham shrugged. "Because the first day we spent together, you had me confessing shit I never talk about to anyone." His gaze held no jest. "You're easy to talk to."

The comment warmed her and she smiled. "Thanks."

His lips hitched at one corner. "Plus, you somehow got me to adopt an evil genius cat. Your ability to direct someone into a new behavior is impressive. Even if that cat may end up killing me."

She gave him a knowing look. "You know you love Trent. And by the way, let's not ignore the fact that *you've* been trying to direct *me* into new behavior since then, too. Maybe you should've gone to school for therapy instead of hacking."

He gave her a *who me?* look and put a hand to his chest. "I have no idea what you're talking about."

"Uh-huh. But for what it's worth," she said with a sigh, "I think your advice about not going public with my off-line dating experiment is sound."

"Really?"

"Now that the video is down, I think it might be a bad idea to bring attention to it. Hopefully, not too many people who know me saw it, and I can keep comments on my sites closed until this cools down. I don't want people going out and searching—like, *what video is she talking about?* If any clients bring it up in session, I'll deal with it on an individual level." She didn't offer that she wasn't giving up on the book idea. "Plus, maybe it's time I take a step back from not just online dating but the online stuff in general. Going through this, seeing how ugly it can get... I don't know. Maybe a break would be good. I feel really...over it right now."

He considered her, as if gauging how serious she was. "I'm sure your followers would understand if you put up a note about a digital detox or something. That's wellness focused, right? On brand and all that."

"Sure. I've recommended that kind of thing to my clients

before." She made a chagrined sound. "It's more a matter of if I can actually do it. You should've seen me in the Uber this morning with no social media to distract me. I thought I was going to jump out the window. But I *know* that's a sign that I probably need to do a detox. Fear crops up when we're headed toward growth and all that jazz, blah, blah, blah."

He laughed, a sharp bark of a sound. "Therapy, blah, blah, blah. Mental health, blah, blah, blah."

She smiled and wiggled her fingers jazz-hands style. "Healer, heal thyself, blah, blah, blah."

"For what it's worth, it's survivable," he said. "Life without social media. I manage. I still have a social life. And fun fact: meals that you don't take a photo of still taste good."

She sniffed. "You sound like a pretentious asshole."

"When it comes to this, I definitely am," he said unrepentantly. "But what can it hurt to give it a try for a little while? I'm happy to provide pretentious moral support."

"You are?" She gave him a skeptical look. "Why?"

"Mainly because I like to be right. You do this, and I guarantee you're going to feel better...and probably will find guys you actually can enjoy spending time with by the end of it. Then,"—he put his hands out to his sides—"I can gloat about how badass I am at giving advice, and *to a therapist* no less. Big feather in my cap."

She stared at him for a moment and then snort-laughed. "You're a special snowflake, Beckham Carter."

"Yes, my friends tell me that all the time."

She rolled her eyes. "Fine. I'm in. I'll take your bet. Let's say I'll go off social media, dating apps, and my YouTube for six w—"

"Months."

Her eyes widened. "*Months?*"

"You're not going to get any real effect from six weeks," he said. "Too easy to just fall back into old habits."

Panic tried to well up again. She'd planned to take a good chunk of time off of dating apps for the book—but social media, too? What would that even look like? Six months without those connections? "That's a long time."

"Make the big move, Eli. The grand gesture," he said. "Those are the ones that make a difference. You don't tell an alcoholic to just stop drinking for a few weeks."

Ugh, she couldn't argue with that logic. Even though she wouldn't classify this as a true addiction for herself, she needed time to create a new normal to get a real feel for what it would be like. She needed to wipe the slate clean and see where she was at—what was truly adding to her life and what was stealing from it. "Okay. Six months."

He smiled like she'd given him a prize, and he put out his hand. "Shake on it?"

"What happens if I don't make it six months?" she asked. "We should have stakes."

He lowered his hand, a pondering look on his face. "I like how you're thinking, Eli. Let's gamify it. What happens if you fail on your quest?"

"My quest?" She smirked. "You're secretly such a nerd."

He gave her a droll look. "That's definitely not a secret."

No, she guessed not, but when did nerds get so hot? *Focus.* She took a breath. "How about if I can't go six months, I have to delete my YouTube channel and all the videos?"

His brows shot up, and he leaned back in his chair. "Wow. Harsh." Then he grinned. "I like it."

"Stakes aren't really effective unless they're real. I have to have something that would really sting." She rubbed her hands on her thighs, nervous at the thought. "And I'm on that channel giving advice. If I can't take my own advice and follow through on this, then what am I even doing?"

"And if you do make it the six months," he said, "how about *you* get something fun, like a vacation?"

She sighed. "Sounds lovely, but I don't exactly have extra funds for that right now."

He shrugged. "I could help with that. I have a buddy who has a beach house in Florida. I do security for his site at no charge. He'd let you use it for a week if I ask."

"You're serious?"

He put out his hand. "Do we have a deal, Eli?"

She shook her head, amazed at the turn of events, but she put out her hand, taking his. He wrapped his fingers around hers, his skin warm against her palm. A little shiver went through her. "Deal."

"Good. Now, that you've come over to the dark side, I can do this…" He released her hand and leaned over to grab the business card she'd set aside on the couch. He flipped it facedown on his desk, scribbled something on the back, and then handed it back to her.

There was an address in his neat, narrow handwriting and the word *ECHO* in all caps. "What's this?"

"The first part of your quest. That's the address and password for an event next Saturday for people who like to get together without phones getting in the way," he said, twirling his pen between his fingers. "Some are friends of mine, a few coworkers, but I won't know everyone there. It's called a NoPho party, meant to be a mixer and networking thing, but they're usually pretty relaxed and fun. You'll have to give them my name and the password so they know you were invited, since they keep it private. And you have to lock your phone into this little pouch they'll give you. They stay locked up until you leave the party."

Her lips parted and she looked up, meeting his gaze. "You're kidding. You're part of *a secret club with a password?*" She narrowed her eyes. "Is this some kind of kinky sex club?"

He gave her a patient look. "It's not a kinky sex club, much to your disappointment, I'm sure. But it is a place that you could practice some non-dating-app meeting of people. And it feels private because no one can use their phones and everyone agrees not to post anything about the night. So it's a safe zone. Which, honestly, can be good and bad. It was *real bad* on karaoke night. The things people will sing when they know they can't be filmed."

She laughed. "This sounds bizarre but..."

"Interesting?" he offered.

Interesting. This guy and his "interesting." She looked down at the card again, the whole idea completely out of her comfort zone. Unlike going on a date from an app, she couldn't research at all. She'd have to walk into a room full of strangers. She wet her lips. *Fear and growth. Fear and growth.* "Are you going to be there?"

"Plan to. And if you want to bring a friend, you can. I get two invites under my name, and I don't plan on using the other this week."

She took a breath and nodded, knowing that she could bring someone with her making her feel a little braver. "All right. I'll give it a shot."

He nodded, looking pleased. "Cool."

She ran her finger over the address. "What's the dress code?"

"Oh, you leave your clothes at the door when you lock up your phone."

Her head snapped upward.

He was wearing a shit-eating grin. "Kidding. You're making this too easy, Eli. Dressing casual is always safe. It's seventy percent tech or tech-adjacent people."

"Why so many techies?"

"Because we're the ones who know how the digital sausage is made," he said, his tone frank. "We helped build the sites and apps. We know the internet, social media in particular, is designed to be a big dopamine-inducing slot machine. That doesn't mean we don't want to use it, but we know why breaks from it are important."

"I feel like I'm stepping outside of the Matrix or something."

He laughed and then got a serious expression. "What is real, Eliza?"

"Don't you use that creepy Morpheus voice on me," she said, sending him a look of warning. She stood and tucked the card into her pocket, shaking her head. "This has been the weirdest day."

He stood, too, arms crossed but an easy expression on his face. "Weird isn't always bad, right?"

She looked up at him, a wash of gratitude moving through her. Beckham had no reason to help her, no reason to risk himself by getting that video taken down, no reason to offer her assistance with her analog project—but he had. She resisted hugging him again. "Weird isn't always bad. Thanks for what you did with the video and for everything else. Honestly, I feel a hundred times better than I did an hour ago. I owe you."

He tucked his hands in his back pockets. "You don't owe me a thing. I wanted to do this. I'm still trying to talk myself out of sending that idiot a virus."

She bit her lip, tempted all over again, and then shook her head. "Not worth it. I don't want you to get in any trouble on my behalf."

"As if I'd get caught." He gave her a playfully devious look. "One penis enhancement email to his inbox, and I bet he'd click it in a heartbeat."

"Ha. I have no doubt, but you've done more than enough." She headed toward his door and he followed her. "I'll be spending the rest of my day setting up my accounts with detox announcements and cleaning up any more collateral damage from the video. I at least like having a plan."

He gave her a little mock salute when they reached the door. "Godspeed, my friend."

Friend. She put her hand on the doorjamb, meeting his eyes. "I'm glad we get to be friends now."

His gaze softened. "Me too, Eli."

With that, she turned and went into her office, nervous but filled with purpose.

She hadn't lied to Beckham when she told him she wasn't going to document this experiment on a blog, but she *needed* this book. If she was going to last six months without social media, internet dating, and YouTube videos, she needed a project to focus on. She'd learned that having goals to be excited about was vital to her own mental health. A new project was the only thing that had gotten her out of bed again after losing her parents—launching her YouTube wellness channel. Plus, maybe the results of this new goal would eventually help other people, too. She wanted to put something good out into the world.

If Beckham thought that was some kind of performance, oh well. He didn't have to know she was writing the book.

After she closed the door to her office, she found herself gravitating toward her computer. Instead of opening her social media accounts or looking for more comments about Ryan's video, she opened up a blank Word document and began to type.

Untitled Book Because Titles Are Hard
By Eliza Catalano

Chapter 1
The Shame & Blame

Day 1: On Friday morning, I woke up with a hangover and more than a hundred notifications on my phone...

chapter **nine**

BECKHAM UNLOCKED THE DOOR TO HIS CONDO, HIS backpack trying to slide off his shoulder, and stepped inside before the bag could fall to the ground. He set it on the floor and turned off the house alarm. From somewhere behind him, Trent meowed, the sound of tiny padded feet on polished wood following.

When he turned, Trent was heading toward him from the living room. Beckham had heard how aloof cats were, but apparently Trent hadn't gotten that memo. He greeted Beckham when he came home like a dog would. Trent curved around Beckham's leg like he had at the shelter. Beckham crouched down to scratch the cat's head. "Hello to you, too. Tough day at the office?"

Trent nuzzled Beckham's palm, angling to get his ears scratched.

"Yeah, me too," Beckham agreed. "Some jerk-off tried to mess with my friend."

Trent looked at him with half-closed eyes as he leaned into the scratching. Beckham blew out a breath and stood—*my friend.* Somehow *that* had happened. Inviting her to a NoPho party, agreeing to help with her detox plans, all of it brought her deeper into his life than he had planned. But he hadn't been able to stop himself. For so long, he'd been the train wreck, the one people had to help out or deal with. The family fuckup. Knowing that *Eliza*, this smart, put-together therapist, was coming to *him* for help, *and* that he could actually provide her with it, had been a heady rush.

Now he just hoped he could deliver.

He had no doubt Eliza would feel better and calmer going off-line. There was science out there to prove that. He also didn't doubt that she'd be able to meet men who'd be better than what she was finding on dating apps. He could think of a number of guys who'd be at the party this weekend who were decent dudes. No, the part he was worried about was that he enjoyed the playful flirting they'd done a little too much. The images that had flitted through his head when they'd been joking about getting naked or secret fetishes had been potent and impossible to ignore. Eliza was tempting as hell, and he got the sense that under the right circumstances, she'd be into a hookup with him. There was attraction on her end, too.

But then...he'd just be another guy looking to her for a good time. He had nothing else to offer beyond that. He wasn't in the market to be anyone's husband, or boyfriend for that matter. He didn't want kids. If he pursued her, he'd become exactly what she was trying to avoid. The thought that he'd be included in anywhere near the same category as that dickbag Ryan was a grim one. He didn't want to be *that* guy.

He groaned as he headed toward the kitchen. He pulled open the fridge, grabbing a bottle of fizzy water, and took a long swig after popping the cap off. Trent hopped onto one of the chairs by the island, staring at him.

"You're a stalker," he said. "You know that, right?"

Trent flicked his tail but kept staring.

Beckham held out his arms to his sides. "I can rise above this, right? It's just attraction. Nothing special." He leaned back against the counter, taking another swig of seltzer, wondering how he'd become someone who talked things out with his cat. "Maybe it's just been too long since I've hooked up with someone. The only company I've had in my bed lately is you. And no offense, but you're a pillow hog and your breath could use some work."

Trent lifted a back leg high and ducked his head down to lick the unmentionable parts of his anatomy.

Beckham snorted. Yep, that had to be the problem. He wasn't thinking straight because he hadn't slept with anyone since Halloween. The holidays had shut everything down for a while, and then he'd been busy with work stuff. Maybe Eliza wasn't the only one who could get something out of the party this weekend. Megan, one of his hacker friends, usually came to the parties. She had declared boyfriends too much work and too much of a distraction, so was often down for a casual hookup. He'd focus on that. Because at least if he was focusing on that, he wouldn't be obsessing about Eliza.

He looked back to Trent. "Good plan, Trent. Thanks for the talk."

Trent meowed like he understood completely.

....

Later that night, Beckham was getting out of the shower when his phone dinged. He grabbed a towel, knotting it around his waist, and walked over to the bathroom counter. A number he didn't recognize showed on his screen.

He opened up the text.

> **Unknown:** Analog Guru, what does one do at night if not scrolling Instagram, YouTube, or dating apps?

He smiled. *Eliza.* He assigned her name to the contact in his phone and then typed back.

Beckham: You're allowed to stream TV. Or you could read. Practice a new language. Learn to make cheese. Take up the bagpipes.
Eliza: Is that what you're doing? Bagpipes?

Beckham leaned against the counter. He should say yes. Keep it light.

Beckham: No, you caught me getting out of the shower.

There was a long pause. Three dots appeared like she was typing. Then another pause. Finally, the message popped up.

Eliza: Oops! Sorry, I'll leave you alone.
Beckham: It's fine. I wouldn't have replied if I was busy. Just give me a sec. Close your eyes while I change.

She sent the emoji of the monkey with its hands over its eyes, and he laughed.

He set the phone down, went to his walk-in closet, and slipped on a pair of flannel pajama bottoms. Then he headed into his bedroom and stretched out on the bed, propping his pillows up behind him.

Beckham: All right I'm decent. You can look now.
Eliza: 👀 Good choice! I think those Star Wars footie pajamas really suit you.

He smiled and glanced down at his bare chest, highly tempted to snap a shot of what he was wearing. But that'd be crossing a line.

Beckham: Just garden-variety plaid. Sorry to disappoint. I save the Star Wars pj's for Sundays.

When she didn't respond, he sent another message.

Beckham: Any other fallout with the video?

Eliza: I think I'm in the clear. One client messaged me about it and I talked it through with her. She was fine after I explained. And I posted about my digital detox on all my channels this afternoon. People seem supportive. Thanks again for your help.

Beckham: No worries, u good otherwise?

Eliza: *sigh* Yes. This is just harder than I thought it'd be. I keep picking up this damn phone to check things but I deleted all the fun apps. It looks so empty. I think I just saw a tumbleweed roll across my screen.

Beckham: It'll get easier. You'll find other things to do to fill the time.

Eliza: This makes me wonder if that jerk was right about one thing. I've gotten boring. I don't even have a hobby outside of work and my YouTube. I read, watch sappy old movies, and binge-watch the occasional TV show but that's about it.

He frowned.

Beckham: That dipshit was right about nothing but if u want to find some hobbies, put that on your 6-month plan. I have no doubt you'll have one outlined in detail, annotated with sticky notes, and organized in no time.

Eliza: I may have purchased a special notebook for such occasion 🤓

He shook his head in amusement. Of course she did. His thumbs moved quickly over the screen.

> **Beckham:** There you go. Go try some new things, take some classes, join some clubs.
> **Eliza:** Like your secret sex club?
> **Beckham:** I didn't invite you to THAT one. You have to know me longer to get that kind of invitation.

Well, damn. He'd hit Send before evaluating how flirty that sounded. He quickly typed something to offset it.

> **Beckham:** Plus, you'd have to buy your own set of Star Wars footie pj's to get into that one.
> **Eliza:** Oh well. Mine are at the dry cleaners.

He chuckled. He needed to get his shit together. Eliza would be a fun friend to have if he could get his thoughts back into the PG-13 zone when he was around her.

> **Beckham:** I could teach u how to send annoying computer viruses to bad dates. New hobby!!
> **Eliza:** LOL ur evil

He sent the devil emoji.

> **Eliza:** Don't tempt me.

Heh. He could say the same to her.

> **Beckham:** Confession—I did send Ry a phishing email this afternoon.

Beckham: He clicked.

Three dots appeared. Then disappeared. Then reappeared. Then disappeared.

His phone rang.

He laughed and answered. "Uh-oh, am I in trouble?"

"Beck! You didn't," Eliza said, her voice a gasp. "I said you didn't need to do that."

"Didn't *need* to, but you wanted to. You just have a better moral compass than I do. Your conscious can stay clear. I did it on my own, and there won't be any permanent damage."

She groaned. "What exactly did you do?"

He shifted on the bed, sitting up a little higher against the headboard. "Nothing terrible. Him clicking on the phishing link let me into his system. I went in and found your video. Deleted it off his computer, which should sync and delete it off his phone, too, so he won't be able to repost it anywhere."

"Oh my God," she said with a distinct note of glee in her voice. "That's...amazing."

"And I may have slowed his system down *just a little*," he said, trying to land the words gently.

"Beckham!" The word was full of admonishment.

"It won't hurt anything," he assured her. "It'll just be annoying, and any help-desk tech will be able to clean it out if he gets it serviced. *If* he gets it serviced. He'll probably assume he got something from the *vast* amounts of porn he's downloaded and won't tell anyone."

"Vast?" she asked, unable to hide her curiosity.

He smirked, loving that she couldn't help asking. "Yeah, I mean, look, to each his or her own. If it's not hurting anyone and everybody's consenting, people can get off how they want to get off, but he's quite the collector. It took me a while to find your video amongst all the other video files. If he's going to random sites for it, he probably gets computer viruses on the regular."

She let out a breath, the sound soft against his ear. "I can't believe you got into his system."

He could hear the relief in her voice underneath her proper moral objection to breaking and entering, and knowing that he was able to give her that made the risk totally worth it.

"Man," she said after a long pause. "You're kind of a scary genius, Beck. I better stay on your good side."

He frowned. Even though she'd said it with a light tone, he sensed the trepidation underneath it. "Eliza, you don't have to worry. Seriously. Despite what you've seen today, I stick to the ethical hacking side of things." *At least these days.* "I drifted into the gray today only because this guy deserved it. I didn't do him any permanent harm. I simply stole a video he shouldn't have had in the first place."

"I know," she said softly. "And I really do appreciate it. I'm glad it's gone, like really glad. I just get...nervous breaking rules. Probably from all that Catholic school I went to. Nuns could be nice, but they also could be scary as all get-out if you got in trouble."

He'd splayed his hand against his chest, and he could feel his heartbeat pick up speed at the mention of religion. "I get that. I was raised...in a church. Not Catholic so no nuns, but I think in that circumstance, you either get really good at following rules so you escape notice or you feel so smothered, you completely rebel against them."

"I'm guessing you chose the latter."

She had no idea. "I did. But I've reined it in. I don't break rules just to break them anymore."

"The thoughtful rebel," she said, and he could hear the smile in her voice.

"Something like that. I mean, I had to do *something*. I couldn't very well align myself with the Sith," he teased.

She laughed. "Right. Maybe my activity for the night will be starting a rewatch of the Star Wars movies. I haven't watched them in a few years. I'm suddenly in the mood for watching the Rebel Alliance kick some ass."

He glanced at his TV. "Vital question: release order or chronological order? If you answer wrong, we may have to end this friendship now."

She scoffed. "Obviously, release order."

He let out a purposely dramatic breath. "Okay. We can still be friends."

"You're such a nerd," she said, voice warm and the shift of fabric sounding in the background as she apparently adjusted her position.

Was she already in bed, too? He tried to stop himself from picturing that. "We've established this. But now you're letting your nerd flag fly, so don't throw stones, Eli."

"Never." After a pause, she cleared her throat. "Well, I better let you go. Thanks for being my digital-detox sponsor tonight."

He eyed his TV again, an idea niggling him, refusing to leave him alone. "Are you really going to watch Star Wars?"

"Yeah, I think so."

Say good night. Say good night. Say good night. "We could co-watch it, if you want. Stay on text while we both watch?"

"Co-watch it?" she asked, surprise in her voice.

"Yeah. It's been a while for me, too, and I was going to watch something before bed anyway. Trent wanted *The Secret Life of Pets*, but I could probably change his mind."

She was quiet for a few agonizing seconds, and he started to feel like he'd crossed the line again, but then she said, "Yeah, sure. That could be fun."

He sat up and ran his hand through his hair, annoyed at how much he liked that she'd said yes. This didn't need to be *a thing*. He'd do this with a friend. She was having a lonely night. They were going to kinda sorta hang out. No big deal.

"All right, cool," he said. "Go pop your popcorn or whatever you need to do. Meet back on chat in fifteen minutes or so?"

"Sounds good," she said, her voice upbeat. "I'll just go wrap my hair into some Leia buns and I'll be all set."

"Me too."

She laughed. "*Hawt.*"

He rolled his eyes at her tongue-in-cheek response. *See, brain. Harmless flirting between friends. We can do this.* "Get your popcorn, Eli."

They ended the call. Beckham tossed his phone aside and rubbed his hands over his face, blatantly ignoring the half-hard situation in his pants.

Glutton for goddamned punishment. That's what he was.

A group counselor had once suggested that his decision to get so much ink was a sign that he sought out pain. He'd dismissed her observation out of hand. He got ink because he liked how it looked and because it distanced him even further from who he used to be. No one would expect Matthew Joseph Laketon, the kid they'd watched grow up on the reality show *Seven on Sunday*, estranged son of fundamentalist preacher John Laketon, to be some tatted-up hacker living in New Orleans.

But this thing with Eliza... Maybe he was more of a masochist than he thought.

chapter **ten**

"I THINK I LOVE HIM."

Eliza kept her expression smooth even though she was scream-
ing a little on the inside. She was used to this feeling after all these
years—Lake Placid on the outside, Mount Vesuvius on the inside.
She'd had to practice this *I'm listening, not critiquing* look in the
mirror when she was in grad school, after a mentor had mentioned
she had too expressive a face. *"Every one of your emotions is
right there,"* Dr. Geir had told her. *"You'd lose every hand of
poker—and you'll lose your clients' trust. It's okay to feel things—
normal—but you can only show the reactions that will be therapeutic for the client."*

Kinley, the nineteen-year-old client sitting on the couch across
from her, was giving Eliza a lot of practice with her Lake Placid
face. Eliza set her pen down on top of the pad in her lap. "Okay.
You think you love him. Tell me what that means for you."

Kinley smiled a dreamy smile and pulled her legs up onto
the couch to sit crisscross-applesauce style. "I mean, how do you
explain love? I just feel happy when I'm with him, and he makes
me feel like…I'm the only girl on earth. And the sex is like…*whoa*.
Way better than any I've had with other guys."

Eliza narrowed her eyes slightly, just enough to convey *I hear you, but aren't we ignoring some parts of the story?* "But we know you're not the only woman in his life."

Kinley huffed at Eliza's gentle reminder, the move making her thick, dark bangs flutter. "He doesn't love his wife. He's told me that."

Eliza set her notepad aside, empathy for Kinley filling her. This young woman was so smart. She was acing her classes and on the way to a microbiology degree. Yet, she was getting duped ten ways 'til Tuesday by a master manipulator—a thirty-six-year-old English professor who knew how to woo just-old-enough-to-be-legal students with his British accent and some softly whispered Shakespeare.

Eliza didn't doubt that Kinley believed she was in love and that this was the start of something real, so she had to tread carefully. If she came at Kinley directly with the obvious truth, Kinley would stop coming to sessions. But Lord, she wished she had a magic wand that let people step outside themselves and their situations for a minute to see what everyone else could see, to clear the fog that feelings breathed on the glass.

"Has he told you he wants a long-term relationship with you? Or that he's seeking a divorce?" Eliza asked.

Kinley picked at the piping on Eliza's bright-red couch, averting her eyes. "Not exactly. But he's told me he cares for me."

Eliza nodded. "That may be true. That he cares. But that doesn't necessarily mean he's looking to change his situation. He has a wife and child. Leaving them would be a major life change. And going public with a relationship with a student could get him fired. From what you've told me, he's working toward tenure." She tried to catch Kinley's gaze but couldn't. "Tenure is the brass ring for professors. Most would do anything they could to not jeopardize that opportunity."

Kinley watched her own fingers plucking at the sofa piping.

Eliza was trying to appeal to the sharp, scientific part of Kinley's mind. Lay out evidence, let her brain work its way to the most realistic conclusions.

For a moment, she thought she'd gotten through, but then Kinley turned her head and met Eliza's gaze. "Maybe he's just waiting for tenure. Then his job will be secure, and I'll be out of his class, and they won't be able to fire him."

Inside, Eliza deflated. No epiphanies were coming today. Not that she was giving up. Therapy was an exercise in patience, like sculpting stone with a butter knife, gently chipping away little bits over a long period of time to find the best, healthiest version of that person beneath. Kinley may figure out in time that this was a doomed path and that this drunk-on-male-attention feeling was what she was in love with, not the professor. That years of being the awkward, ignored girl in high school, not to mention having major issues with her dad, had set her up for a man like this to take advantage.

Or, she'd get her heart broken. Either way, she'd learn something. Eliza could only be a guide, not a dictator. Sometimes, no matter how she tried to help soften the fall, people had to crash hard to grow.

"Are you protecting yourself from pregnancy and STDs?" Eliza asked, deciding to focus on practical matters and aiming for ways to keep the situation from having longer-term consequences.

Kinley pressed her lips together and nodded. "Yeah, I'm on the pill, and he uses a condom since I know he still…has to sleep with her."

"Good." Eliza gave her a small smile. "Protecting yourself is important. You have big career plans."

"I know. I do." Kinley looked out the window, a pensive look on her face.

Eliza watched her, keeping quiet. Maybe there were a few seeds sinking in. Maybe.

After a few silent moments, Kinley started talking again and spent her last few minutes discussing a tiff she was having with her roommate and actively ignoring the I'm-sleeping-with-my-professor elephant in the room.

Eliza was used to the elephants. Her office got crowded with them daily. She wrapped up Kinley's session and walked her out a few minutes later. She left her door open and went back to her desk to send the bill for the session to Kinley's parents. If they only knew they were paying for their nineteen-year-old daughter to process her feelings about her affair with her much older professor and not the mild depression they'd originally sent her here for, they'd have a fit.

Beckham's words about secret relationships drifted back to her. Kinley was definitely tapping into that forbidden vibe. If she had to actually start dating her thirty-six-year-old professor out in public, the mystique would probably wear off quickly.

Eliza opened another screen on her computer and made her notes about the session.

A light knock had her looking up a few minutes later. Beckham was standing in her doorway, a shoulder against the jamb, looking like he was made to lean casually and smile sardonically. Like that was the purpose God had assigned to him: *lean and look amazing.* "Hey."

For privacy reasons, she minimized her screen, even though her computer didn't face the door. "Hey, yourself."

It'd been almost a week since their Star Wars co-watch, which had been more fun than she would've anticipated and had made a great entry in her secret book project, but since then, they hadn't had much time to chat. They'd exchanged a few texts over the weekend, but once Monday came she'd been slammed with appointments and he was deep into a difficult project.

"How's the penetration testing going?" She wrinkled her nose.

"I literally can't keep a straight face when I say that. Couldn't they name it something else?"

"And miss out on all the dirty jokes about entering back doors and all that? No way," he said. "And it's...going. It's a big network so there's still lots of testing to do. Solid challenge."

"So no time to work on the game?" She'd figured out that though he seemed to be amazing at the hacking thing, the game was his passion project.

He shrugged the shoulder that wasn't pressed up against the doorjamb, making the Commodore 64 graphic on his T-shirt twitch. "Not really. But that's okay. The game is more of an art project than a technical one—designing graphics, creating the story lines. Taking breaks from it helps that creative subconscious stuff to do some work in the background." He cocked his chin toward her computer. "How's your day been?"

"Imagine all the headdesk GIFs, and that will give you some idea."

He winced and stepped inside. "Ouch. Sorry."

"It's fine. Nothing I'm not used to." She reached back and tightened her low ponytail. "A lot of people imagine therapists giving advice all day, but much of my day is spent *not* saying all the things I want to say because I have to guide people to come to the answers themselves. My tongue is sore from all the times I've had to bite it today."

He gripped the back of the chair she used during sessions. "I would make a terrible therapist."

She rolled her desk chair back and crossed her legs, smiling. "You're definitely not one to hold back your opinions or advice. But honestly, neither am I when I'm not in session."

His gaze flicked down, so quickly she almost missed it, but she felt the effect immediately. He'd checked out her legs. She knew that interest wouldn't go anywhere. They were establishing a friendship with some light flirting, and they both knew it was not wise to pursue any of it further than that. But it still gave her a little thrill to know she had some effect on him. He definitely had an effect on her. She crossed her legs the other way, not above a little torture.

Beckham cleared his throat. "I just wanted to check with you to see what you'd decided about the get-together tomorrow night."

"Your secret club? I plan on going," she said, her nerves fluttering at the thought. "My friend Andi is going to come with me."

His fingers flexed against the leather of the chair. "Cool. She's the horror writer?"

"Yep. I suspect she agreed to come because it will be good story fodder—and to make sure I'm not going to get murdered," she said. "She's definitely not coming along to meet guys. She's got a dude she's crazy about."

He put a hand over his heart. "No murder, I promise."

"Excellent. That'd really put a hitch in my meeting-new-people plan." She eyed him as he drummed his fingers along the top of the chair. "Was there something else? I feel like you're debating telling me something."

He winced. "This is the hazard of being friends with a therapist."

She arched her brow in her most intimidating tell-me face. "Spill it, Beck."

He sighed. "Fine. I don't want to scare you off, but a warning seems fair. The parties sometimes have themes and always have activities. People don't have their phones, so they like to have icebreaker-type stuff and things to do."

She crossed her arms, his body language making her nervous. "Like the karaoke you warned me about."

"Right, but this weekend, the theme is...eighties slumber party."

Her lips parted. "Eighties slumber party. Uh...what exactly does that mean?"

He linked his hands behind his neck like this news was slightly painful to him as well. "I don't know the whole plan, but I know the dress code is pajamas. And I expect there will be slumber-party-themed games."

"Like?"

"Well, I wasn't exactly on the slumber-party circuit, but if it's anything like church camp, I'm guessing like Truth or Dare, Would You Rather, that kind of thing. Adult versions."

She bit her lip, trying not to laugh. "You know this sounds ridiculous, right?"

He dipped his head in defeat. "Yes, I'm very aware. I promise that most of the time, these get-togethers are non-cheesy and a good time, but the event planners go a little nuts sometimes. I guess the casino night we had last month wasn't exciting enough for them." He met her gaze. "But I understand if you want to bail and wait 'til next time."

She clasped her hands together in front of her. "And miss the opportunity to see you in your footie pajamas? Not for a million dollars, Beck."

He snorted.

"Seriously. It's fine. I can roll with the silly theme." She lowered her hands. "In fact, that takes a little bit of the pressure off. I was expecting some sophisticated secret society that I wasn't going to fit in with."

He frowned. "I wouldn't put you in that position. The people that attend—at least the ones I know—are a good group. Open and friendly." He leaned forward and waggled his eyebrows. "*Interesting.*"

"Your favorite," she said with a smirk. "No, it's fine. I'm still in. I'll make sure Andi has pajamas to wear, too. This probably makes it even more enticing for her." She shook her head, thinking of her friend's general zest for things. "She's going to love the hell out of this."

"Awesome," he said, looking genuinely relieved. "And if it sucks, I'll take full blame."

"Just as long as they don't make me do a seance," she warned. "When we did one at my friend Heather's tenth birthday party, we *definitely* were visited by the spirit of Jack the Ripper and I definitely called my mom to come pick me up and save me."

He laughed. "No spirits of dead serial killers. You've got yourself a deal."

She gave him a look. "Always making deals with you lately. It's becoming a habit."

"Guess you better hope I'm not the devil." He winked and then turned to head out of the office. "See you tomorrow night, Eli."

chapter **eleven**

"THIS IS GOING TO BE SO RAD!" ANDI DECLARED AS SHE gave Eliza a hug and then leaned back to take in Eliza's fish and chips pajamas. They were the only silly pair Eliza had—teal green and covered with swimming fish, vinegar bottles, and fries. A friend had brought them back from England as a gift last year. "Look how cute we are." Andi turned toward the open doorway, putting her arm around Eliza's shoulders. "Aren't we goddamned adorable?"

Andi was in a white T-shirt with a Camp Crystal Lake counselor graphic on the front and pajama bottoms decorated with Friday the 13th Jason masks. This horror-movie ensemble was undermined by the pink bunny slippers on her feet.

"Downright enchanting." Andi's boyfriend, Hill, was standing inside their doorway with a bemused expression on his face. "Eliza, can I just say I'm glad it's you taking her to this and not me? This event sounds like my personal nightmare."

Eliza laughed. For as outgoing and enthusiastic as Andi was, Hill was her friend's perfect counterbalance. Quiet and steady with a dry sense of humor. Also, really good-looking and could cook like a dream. Eliza was over-the-moon happy for Andi that she'd found her person. "You're welcome. I'm glad she'll be with me. I would say I'm sorry I only had one invite but…"

He lifted a hand. "I'm good. No bunny slippers for me. You two have fun. Just let me know if y'all need a ride afterward."

"Oh, I'm not drinking," Eliza said. She'd certainly had enough of *that* for a while. "I'll be the designated driver."

"Unless she meets some cute guy she wants to take home," Andi added as she stepped forward and wrapped her arms around Hill's neck. She pushed up on her toes and gave him a lingering kiss. "Then I'll give you a call."

Eliza gave her friend a quelling look when Andi turned back around. "I'm taking no one home. Three-date rule, remember?"

Hill crossed his arms, giving Andi an indulgent look. "Either of you need anything, call me. I'll be up late. I have a bread dough recipe I'm in complex negotiations with."

"Sounds tense," Eliza said.

Andi hooked her arm in Eliza's. "You have no idea. The colorful words that were coming out of his mouth last night when he overproved the dough… Well, I think he might've killed the yeast with words alone."

Hill's expression turned grim. "I will conquer it."

"I know you will, babe," Andi said with full confidence. "I'm looking forward to fresh baked bread in the morning. Love you."

"Love you, too. Y'all have fun and don't get into too much trouble," he said.

"Us? Never." Andi leaned her head on Eliza's shoulder.

Hill shook his head, chuckling. "Text me when you're on your way home."

"Will do." Andi tugged Eliza. "Come on, it's slumber-party time!"

·····································

Eliza listened to the formal voice of her GPS guiding her and Andi to the address Beckham had scrawled on the card, her nerves starting to creep in. "Thanks for doing this with me."

"Happy to join," Andi said, flipping the visor down and checking her lipstick. "I'm at a stuck point in the book I'm writing anyway, so I could use a little distraction. Maybe this will provide some inspiration. It kind of sounds like the setup for a locked-room mystery."

Eliza put on her signal and took a left turn. "A locked-room mystery?"

"Yeah, you know, Agatha Christie's *And Then There Were None* style," she said brightly. "A bunch of houseguests show up to a party or a weekend away, and there's no escape for some reason—like a storm blocks them in or it's on an island and boats only run during the day—so no one can come in or out once the guests are there." She snapped the visor closed. "Then, someone's murdered, and everyone knows the murderer has to be one of the guests and now they're stuck with one another."

Eliza glanced her way. "Well, that sounds terrifying. Let's hope that's not what we're doing. No murder, please."

Andi grinned at her in the dark, her teeth standing out against her red lipstick. "I mean, they *are* taking our phones. That's kind of a version of a locked door. A house full of strangers. *No way to call for help.*"

She'd said the last sentence in a deep, ominous voice.

"You're not making me feel any better," Eliza said.

Andi reached over and patted Eliza's thigh. "I'm just messing with you. I'm wearing bunny slippers for God's sake. What could go wrong? Ooh...*bunny slippers.* It'd be hard to run in these. A dead body with bunny slippers could make for a really interesting scene."

"*Andi.*"

"What?" she said, no remorse in her voice. "Inspiration is inspiration. But I'll stop talking about scary stuff. Tell me about the guy who invited you. All I know is that he's in tech and works next door to you. What's the story?"

"Beckham. I'm sure you've seen him around. He's blond, twenty-five, full-sleeve tattoos. Usually wears graphic T-shirts. Tall and lanky but fit. Good shoulders." She glanced over, seeing if any of that was ringing a bell for Andi. "He works in cybersecurity and is designing a video game on the side."

"I think so, but I've never talked to him," she said, frowning like she was disturbed that someone at WorkAround had eluded the Andi Welcoming Committee. "But let's focus on the important part. You obviously think he's hot."

Eliza kept her expression smooth, knowing Andi was probably studying her profile. "I didn't say that."

"Girl," she said with a come-on-now tone. "You've noticed his *shoulders.*"

Eliza kept her eyes on the road, tightening her grip on the wheel. "Fine. He's kind of gorgeous. But too young. We're just friends."

"Too young?" Andi made a dismissive sound. "Please. Twenty-five is in range."

"It's not the number." Eliza took another turn, wondering how far out of the city this thing was. "He's too young in the sense that he's not looking for what I'm looking for. Different stage of life. I'm not looking for hookups. I'm past that."

Andi shifted in her seat. "Ah, yeah, I see your point. That's a bummer."

"It's okay," Eliza said, maybe trying to convince herself as well. "He's helping me, actually—to meet more guys. He's very anti-online dating."

"Amen," Andi said, voice emphatic. "That's just a serial killer menu waiting to happen. Which woman do I want to torture? Like ordering up some takeout."

Eliza rolled her eyes. "It's not the serial killer factor. He's anti-online about a lot of stuff. Probably because he knows how easy it is to break into things and get people's information. His job is basically being a good-guy hacker—or white-hat hacker. I think that's what it's called."

"Ooh, I'm going to file that information away." Andi picked up her phone and typed something into it. "I may need him for a book resource one day. I have a stalker story knocking around my brain that would involve some hacking stuff."

"He'd probably be happy to answer any questions you have," Eliza said. "He's the one that got me thinking about this digital detox thing in the first place. And like I said, he's kind of helping me with this project. But don't tell him it's an official project." She gave Andi a quick glance. "As far as he knows, this is for my personal development only. I want to keep the book thing private for now since I don't know what it might turn into—if it turns into anything at all."

"No problem," Andi said without hesitation. "So if he doesn't realize you're doing this as a project, he's just being helpful for the sake of being helpful?"

"Yeah, that's what this party invite is about. Meeting people off-line and without phones. He said the crowd is a good group. He'll introduce me to some people." She tapped her fingers against the steering wheel, nerves creeping in.

"Huh." Andi shifted in her seat. "That's really nice of him. To help. What's in it for him?"

Headlights from an oncoming car blinded Eliza for a moment on the dark road, the Spanish moss hanging from the cypress trees that lined the street lighting up like electric worms. She slowed down a little. "What?"

"I'm a writer," Andi said. "No one does something without motivation. What's he getting out of helping you?"

Eliza focused on the yellow reflectors on the road, her attention on staying within the lines but her mind wrestling with the question. "I don't know. I think mainly he wants to prove a point. That he's right about his analog lifestyle."

"Hmm."

"What's that noise for?" Eliza asked. The GPS dinged, startling her, and she almost missed the turn. She wrenched the steering wheel.

Andi grabbed onto the dashboard as Eliza made a hard right. "Nothing. I just... Well, I'm looking forward to meeting him."

Eliza sent her friend a look. "He's not a serial killer."

Andi's eyes were as innocent as the bunnies on her slippers. "I didn't say he was."

"Don't give him the third degree," Eliza warned.

Andi made a noise like a properly offended southern lady and put her hand to her chest. "I would *never*."

Eliza shook her head. Yep. Andi definitely was going to interrogate him. Beckham was in trouble and didn't even know it yet. Eliza would have to get to him first to give him a heads-up.

....

Beckham took out his phone and handed it to Jayleigh, who was manning—womaning?—the check-in table for the party tonight. The members of the group rotated door duty.

"Hey, Becks." She smiled up at him, pushing back a long, hot-pink loc that had escaped the large bun she'd twirled the rest of her hair into. "Ready to party like it's 1989?"

"Totally, for sure," he deadpanned as she reached under the table and pulled out one of the phone sleeves. "The slumber-party theme is...an interesting choice."

Jayleigh smiled as she slipped his phone into the sleeve and turned the locking mechanism. "Oh, come on, who doesn't want to see everyone in their pajamas? And Truth or Dare plus alcohol? That's genius. Tell me that's not genius."

He smiled. "So it was your idea?"

She tipped her head slyly. "It wasn't *not* my idea."

"Fair enough." He lifted his palms in surrender. "I'm here and open to the possibilities."

She gave him a nod of concession. "That's all we ask."

"I invited two new people, names are Eliza and Andi," he added. "So if two women show up and give you my name, can you let them know I'm already here?"

"Will do." She handed him back his encased phone. Now he wouldn't be able to get to it without coming back to the front and getting it unlocked. And if he did that, he wasn't allowed back into the party. "Have fun."

"Thanks. You too."

He headed up a set of stairs. Because the house was on the bayou, it sat on stilts. All the living areas were elevated and safe from flooding, and only the small garage was on the bottom level. The place was owned by Alice, one of the founding members of NoPho. She'd made a shit ton of money on an app she'd developed a few years ago and had bought this seventies-era place and renovated it. She lived in a condo in the city during the week, but kept this as a weekend retreat and let the group use it for the monthly parties.

The sound of voices and a Cyndi Lauper song greeted Beckham as he walked through the main door. A few clusters of people were already in the living room, chatting and drinking. The wall of windows that lined the back side of the house provided a view of a long porch that faced the still, dark water of the bayou and the cypress trees that guarded it, but no one was out there. Tonight was a little chilly for New Orleanians. People would probably wander out once they had enough booze to keep them warm.

Beckham went to the bar and got his usual club soda with lime and then caught sight of his friend Will, who was sitting on one of the couches and wearing an LSU tiger-stripe onesie. A lawyer in a onesie. Beckham shook his head, laughing in chagrin. What had he been thinking, inviting Eliza to this? She was going to tease him relentlessly about the ridiculousness of this whole thing.

Will spotted him and lifted a hand, waving him over. Beckham headed that way and greeted his friend with a fist bump before taking the spot next to him on the couch. "Looking sharp, man."

"Hell yeah, I am." Will patted him on the shoulder, his deep voice booming. "Beckham, meet Hannah and Kevin. You already know Khuyen and Trinity." Will waved his drink at the two women and two guys sitting in the semicircle of chairs in front of the couch. "Everybody, Beckham."

Beckham lifted his drink. "Everybody."

He'd chatted with Trinity, a pretty Black woman with a nose ring, at a previous party—a dance instructor if he was remembering right. And Khuyen was a friend who owned a Cajun-Vietnamese-fusion food truck that served ridiculously good gumbo and pho. (Khuyen regularly complained about the NoPho name of the group because he said it sounded like a group against delicious soup.) The other two people—a blond woman in Hannah Montana pajamas (Beckham smiled when the joke hit him, a Hannah in Hannah Montana pajamas) and a stocky, dark-haired white guy with glasses and Christmas pj's—were apparently Will's guests this week.

"So what did I miss?" Beckham asked.

Will took a sip of his drink—whiskey. Beckham still picked up the smell of alcohol like a bloodhound, but thankfully, the pull of it didn't affect him like it used to. Will leaned back against the couch, hooking his ankle over his knee, the ice in his glass rattling. "We've been debating which games we're going to try. They've set up each room with something different."

"What are the options?" Beckham asked.

"I went in one and they were playing Light as a Feather, Stiff as a Board," Trinity said, already shaking her head. "Who in their right mind is going to trust a bunch of hammered people to hold them up in the air? No thanks. I'll end up going to work on Monday with a broken arm."

Hannah made a sound of agreement as she sipped her bright-pink drink. "Yeah, I'm skipping that one. Next they'll be playing Bloody Mary in the bathroom."

"I'm *out*," Trinity said. "That shit scared the hell out of me when I was a kid. I'm not calling forth any spirits out here on the bayou. That's how horror movies start."

"I think Truth or Dare will be fun—once I've got a buzz going, at least," Khuyen said, shaking the ice cubes in his drink. "I might try all of the games. In middle school, I always wanted to be invited to a slumber party. I used to imagine what girls did with each other during those late-night games. So many possibilities..."

He got a goofy, dreamy smile on his face.

Hannah smacked him playfully with a couch pillow. "Ugh. Boys."

"Hey, my parents didn't have cable and the family computer was in the living room," he said with mock woundedness. "I had to get creative."

Trinity snorted. "We weren't kissing at the parties, I can tell you that—much to my disappointment. My young lesbian heart was vastly let down. There was a lot of talk about boys—who was cute and who wasn't. Yawn." She patted her mouth and rolled her eyes in mock boredom. "I'm hoping tonight will be more fun than that."

"You should try Spin the Bottle," Will said as he pushed back the tiger-eared hoodie part of his ensemble and dabbed sweat off his shaved brown head with a cocktail napkin. "I heard that was in one of the rooms."

"That's not a slumber-party game," Hannah replied with a headshake. "That was boy-girl party territory. Along with Seven Minutes in Heaven."

"Well, this *is* a boy-girl slumber party." Kevin adjusted his glasses and cut a shy glance toward Hannah. "Conceivably, it fits. I bet there's Seven Minutes in Heaven somewhere, too."

Hannah smiled. "That could get interesting."

Beckham had been leaning back, enjoying being a passive player in the conversation. Hearing people's stories about their own childhoods always fascinated him. Growing up, there were no boy-girl parties in his world. No spinning of bottles, no minutes in heaven. Just the mere mention of *heaven* for a game like that would've been considered blasphemous. All he'd been left with as a teen were raging hormones and the knowledge that his thoughts about girls were sinful and wrong. Unclean. Impure. Damaged.

He wondered, not for the first time, how different his life would've looked if he had grown up in a world where Spin the Bottle was just a harmless kids' game.

Before he could get lost in his own thoughts, a flash of bright-red hair caught his eye. He leaned over, peering between Trinity and Khuyen, and saw Eliza walking in behind her friend Andi. Eliza's dark hair was in a high ponytail and she was wearing teal patterned pajamas. She seemed a little hesitant as she scanned the room, looking for something. No, *someone*. For him. Tension he hadn't realized he'd been holding released in his shoulders.

"Hey, excuse me a sec," he said, getting up and stepping over Will's legs. "I invited a couple of new people, and they just walked in looking a little overwhelmed."

Trinity turned her head to see where Beckham was looking. "Bring them over if they're scared. We'll make them feel welcome."

"Thanks," Beckham said, meaning it. "I'm sure I'll be back."

He made his way across the great room, dodging a guy carrying a stack of pizza boxes. Eliza turned her head and broke into a relieved smile when she saw him. She lifted her hand in a little wave. Her friend, Andi, spun at the movement and looked his way. She gave him a quick once-over, and then a barely there smile lifted the corners of her mouth.

"Hey," he said when he reached them. "You made it."

He didn't know what to do. His instinct was to hug, but he wasn't sure if they were friends who regularly hugged or kissed on the cheek yet, and shaking hands or a fist bump would be ridiculous. Eliza made the first move, saving him the debate. She stepped forward and gave him a quick, one-armed hug. "Hey."

The scent of her shampoo—something citrusy—filled his nose and her ponytail brushed his arm, sending chill bumps along his skin. The whole thing was over in two seconds, and he fought the urge to pull her back to him and turn it into a full, lingering hug instead.

Eliza tipped her head toward her friend. "This is Andi, the writer friend I told you about. Andi, Beckham."

Andi stuck out her hand and gave his a firm shake—maybe a little too firm—as she eyed him. "Nice to meet you."

"Same," he said. He'd seen Andi at WorkAround, her bright-red hair hard to miss, but they'd never chatted. "Thanks for being willing to come with Eliza. I'm sure it sounded like a weird proposition."

Andi smiled at that. "For what it's worth, I like weird. This whole thing"—she waved her hand, indicating the room of people—"sounds like my kind of good time. But either way, I wouldn't have wanted her to come alone." She arched a brow.

"I don't know you and your people yet. Had to make sure you weren't going to locked-room murder her or have her join a cult."

He tried not to wince at the last part. "Or try to sell her a time share?"

Andi pointed. "Exactly. A fate worse than death."

Eliza let out a half laugh/half groan. "I would like it to be noted that I am capable of going out and about unchaperoned, but I also know bringing Andi to a party will make it that much more fun."

"Plus, I'm totally using this as book research," Andi said. "You've been warned."

Beckham laughed. "As long as names and details are changed to protect the innocent—and the guilty."

"Obviously." Andi's lips hitched at the corner. "Welp. I'm going find us drinks. What're you drinking?"

He lifted his club soda and lime. "I'm good. But I can get y'all something."

"Nope, you two chat while I check out the scenery," Andi said. "Eliza, what'cha drinking, *chica*?"

"I don't know." She wrinkled her nose as if the thought of a drink didn't appeal. "Something fruity and virginal, maybe?"

Beckham nodded toward the bar area. "Sammy, the guy who mans the bar, usually has themed drinks and one's always a mocktail. I bet there's something sweet for slumber-party night."

"On it." Andi whirled around and headed for Sammy.

Eliza turned back to him. "I'm going to end up with something bright pink and topped with cotton candy or sparklers, aren't I?"

"Most definitely. But it'll taste good," he assured her. "Sammy owns a bar downtown and knows what he's doing."

Eliza glanced downward, her lips curving as she read his shirt. *"Wookiee of the Year.* Oh my God." Delight lit her expression. "You weren't lying that you owned Star Wars pajamas!"

His neck warmed and he rubbed a hand along the back of his head. "I feel like there's no right answer to that."

She bit her lip, dark eyes sparkling. "I love it. Though I'm vastly disappointed that they're not footie pajamas."

He looked down at his black pants with small Millennium Falcons all over them. "As am I." He nodded toward her outfit. "I'm digging the British vibe of yours."

"Thanks." She touched the collar. "They were a gift and are the only true pajamas I own. I'm more of a boxers and T-shirt kind of person."

Don't picture it. Don't picture it. Do not picture her in her nightclothes. "Guess footie pajamas will be on both of our Christmas lists this year."

"Absolutely." She glanced past him into the great room, her gaze curious. "So do you know all these people?"

"Not all of them, but a good number of them." Beckham turned and noticed Will was looking their way, flicking his hand like they should come over. "I know the core group that started the parties."

"The guy in a tiger onesie seems to want you to join him," Eliza said. "And *that* is a sentence I never thought I'd utter."

"Get used to it. I have a feeling tonight is going to be weirder than normal. And Tiger Onesie is my friend Will. Believe or not, he's a well-respected lawyer by day." Beckham lifted his finger in the give-me-a-sec gesture to let Will know he'd seen him. For some reason, even though he'd invited Eliza here to introduce her to people, he suddenly felt less than enthused to do so. *He* wanted to be the one to show her around the party.

But when Andi returned with drinks, Beckham knew he needed to stop being territorial and do what he'd agreed to do. This wasn't a date. This was a friend helping another friend meet new people.

Eliza looked at her bright-purple drink warily. "I'm not sure I even want to know what they put in here to achieve this color." She lifted it toward the light. "And is that Nerds candy frozen in the ice cubes?"

Andi laughed. "Don't ask. Just drink. I promise it's virginal. I watched the bartender make it." She looked to Beckham. "So where to first?"

"How about I introduce y'all to some friends?" Beckham reluctantly nodded toward the group he'd left. "They were debating which games to try first."

Beckham led Eliza and Andi to the group, and everyone's heads turned in their direction. "Hey, any more room?" he asked. "This is Eliza and this is Andi. They work in the same building as I do. This is their first NoPho party."

"Absolutely," Trinity said, and smacked Kevin playfully. "Grab these ladies some chairs."

Kevin and Khuyen both got up and procured two extra chairs while Trinity and Hannah introduced themselves. Will patted the spot next to him on the couch, giving Eliza a warm smile. "There's room here, too."

"Thanks," Eliza said.

Will put out his hand. "No problem. Will Langford."

Andi shook his hand first and then Eliza did as well. Beckham noticed that Will's handshake lasted longer with Eliza than was polite and the smile on his face had a spark to it. Beckham knew that look. He groaned inwardly. *Fantastic.* Will, the supersuccessful lawyer, was interested in Eliza. Of course he was. She was beautiful. But Eliza didn't seem to mind the warm welcome either. And why would she? Will would be the perfect kind of guy for what Eliza was looking for—tiger onesie notwithstanding. Will was brilliant, in his thirties, and probably capable of settling down without feeling like a trapped animal.

Beckham forced himself to take the chair Khuyen had vacated instead of blatantly placing himself next to Will on the couch. Eliza took the spot next to Will, and Andi sat on the other side of her.

There. Beckham had done the right thing. The friend thing. He was her wingman tonight, not her date.

Of course he was now sitting right across from her and would have a front-row seat to watch her and Will flirt. This movie would not be fun to watch.

Why had he agreed to do this again?

He was supposed to be helping her find quality dates. Will would be exactly that. Beckham could prove he was right. He *loved* being right.

So why did this feel so goddamned wrong?

chapter **twelve**

WILL WAS FUNNY—AND CUTE. ELIZA LOOKED DOWN AT HER drink, wondering if maybe she'd been served alcohol instead of a mocktail because she found she was actually having a good time on a night out for the first time in longer than she could remember. She'd been laughing so much over the last twenty minutes that she felt almost drunk with it, but no, there was no taste of booze in her drink. Beckham's friends were just a great group—smart, *interesting* people.

Because of course they were. And Beckham had also done her a solid, setting her up to sit next to Will, the handsome lawyer who was *definitely* flirting with her.

Eliza had been afraid that she wouldn't fit in with a group of young techies, but Beckham's friends had much more varied backgrounds than she'd expected. All were obviously sharp but also laid-back in that everyone's-welcome way that made it feel like she'd been part of this group all along. She was able to exhale in a way she hadn't in a while. Maybe this project wouldn't be so hard after all. Maybe she really could meet great guys without the pre-date research, the vague Facebook stalking, and the dating-app profiles. She'd always figured that more information was better. Research was smart. But she hadn't thought about how skewed that research was when applied to online profiles. People only put stuff online they wanted you to see. Those online nuggets weren't real research findings, that was being wooed by a curated advertising campaign.

Silently, she made mental notes about her first no-phone party so that she could jot them down later for the book.

As Andi answered Trinity's question about writing horror, Eliza glanced at Beckham, feeling a little guilty for making mental notes when she'd told him this wouldn't be a public project. His gaze met hers, eyes unreadable. He'd been uncharacteristically quiet since they'd joined the group a while ago. He gave her a quick, barely there smile—a silent exchange between them—but she got the sense he wasn't having as good a time as she was. Or maybe he was the quiet guy of the group. A listener. An observer. The poker player who always kept his cards close.

"So who's game for some games?" Khuyen asked, dragging Eliza's attention back to the group. Khuyen tucked his shoulder-length black hair behind his ears and smiled. "As good as the company is, we didn't come here to be couch warmers, right?"

Will draped his hand across the back of the sofa, being respectful and not touching Eliza, but she could feel the heat of his presence there, the hint of suggestion. "I'm game for anything."

"Me too, but I *really* want to see the scary games," Andi said, rubbing her hands together. "I'm here for the book fodder. Bring on the Bloody Mary chanting and seances!"

Trinity shook her head. "You have fun with that, sugar. I'm O-U-T out."

Eliza looked to Andi, giving her a sheepish look. "Um, you know I love you, but…"

Andi patted her knee. "Oh Lize, I know you're a scaredy-cat. I'll be fine on my own." Her lips twitched into a conspiratorial smile that only Eliza would catch. "You stay here and find the right games for you. Will looks like a scaredy-cat, too."

Oh. Eliza got it then. Andi wasn't really that focused on book research. She was giving Eliza space to flirt.

"Damn straight," Will agreed wholeheartedly. "My grandmother would not appreciate me trying to call forth her spirit in some seance. She never liked her naps interrupted."

Eliza laughed.

Hannah stood. "I'll go with you, Andi. I ain't skerred."

"Awesome." Andi pushed herself up off the couch and grabbed her drink. "Let's go conjure some spirits!"

Trinity gave them a pointed look and made the sign of the cross. "Lord help them for they know not what they do."

Andi grinned and gave Eliza a little wave before heading toward one of the hallways.

"So," Khuyen said, slapping his thighs like he was raring to go. "Since it's hard to pick a game, how about we gamble a little? There are three rooms down that hallway." He pointed to the hallway opposite the one Andi had gone down and then reached out to a bowl of Skittles sitting in the middle of the coffee table. He plucked out a red, an orange, and a green Skittle. "Red means room one, orange room two, green room three. Whichever one we pick, we have to go and play at least one round. Who's in?"

Kevin, who hadn't said much and looked like he'd already had too many drinks, shook his head and stood. "Not me. I need another drink."

"Chicken," Will teased.

Kevin flipped him off with a smile and then headed to the bar.

"I'm cool with that," Trinity said and wiggled her fingers at the candies. "Leave it up to the fates."

"Me too." Will reached out to grab some Skittles to pop into his mouth. "Let's see what the night brings us."

Khuyen nodded and looked to Eliza, arching his eyebrows playfully. "How about you, newbie? Feeling brave?"

She glanced at Beckham, who was sipping his drink but watching for her answer. She didn't know exactly what she was getting herself into, but she felt safe enough that if she found something she didn't want to be a part of, she could say no and walk away without it being a big deal. "Yeah, sure, why not?"

Khuyen smiled and then turned his head. "Beckham?"

Beckham leaned forward, bracing his inked forearms on his thighs, his expression calm and cool. "Sure. Can't be anything more dangerous than listening to you sing Queen on karaoke night."

Khuyen snorted. "Don't even. You know I slayed that shit."

"He's right," Beckham said to Eliza. "You haven't really lived until you've seen an award-winning chef drunkenly sing 'Don't Stop Me Now' complete with dance moves."

"Times when I'm sad these are no-phone parties," Trinity chimed in wistfully. "The blackmail I could've set up…"

"Jealous. All of you. Now stop distracting me." Khuyen smirked and cupped his hands around the candy and shook them up. Then, he held out his hands, still covering the candy, toward Eliza. "Newbie's choice. Close your eyes."

She closed her eyes and reached out, Alice in Wonderland vibes moving through her. *Which one makes you bigger? Which one makes you smaller?* She found his hand, selected a Skittle, and then opened her eyes.

"Red," Khuyen said, taking the candy from her and dumping it with the other two Skittles into an abandoned cup on the table. "Room one it is."

Will set his drink down and stood. He put his hand out to Eliza to help her up. "Let's see what fate awaits us."

Eliza took his hand, but found herself turning to Beckham. He was looking at her and Will's clasped hands.

"What's in room one?" she asked.

Beckham's attention flicked up to her face. He cleared his throat. "I have no idea."

"I do." Trinity groaned as she stood and then reached down to snag a few Skittles. "We all might want to grab some extra candy."

Eliza was going to ask what she meant by that, but Trinity and Khuyen had already passed her and Will was tugging her gently toward the hallway to follow. She let herself be led for a second but then allowed her hand to slip from Will's when she saw Beckham had hesitated and was still a few steps behind. Will released her hand easily, and she slowed her pace. Beckham caught up to her, a wary set to his jaw.

"What's in room one?" she asked. "You look like you know and aren't happy about it."

"I don't know, but I have a theory now," he said as he walked beside her. When they caught up to the group, he pointed toward the bowl of candy sitting on a little table outside of room one. "Yep. Mints."

She frowned. "I don't get it. What slumber-party game has mints?"

He gave her a brace-yourself look. "Apparently, there aren't just slumber-party games. There are boy-girl party games."

Her lips parted and she glanced at the door again. The little paper sign on door number one had lipstick kisses on it. "Oh shit. Are we about to play Seven Minutes in Heaven?"

"Nope," Will announced from in front of them. He turned and smiled, looking enormously pleased. "Spin the Bottle!"

"*Spin the Bottle?*" She turned back to Beckham in mild horror.

Beckham tipped his head back and looked to the ceiling, squinting. "Sure, Beckham, invite your coworker to a party to introduce her to people. That will be great. She won't mind you setting her up to *make out with complete strangers*. That's totally appropriate. Solid move."

Beckham's dramatic regret over the party's theme made a laugh bubble out of Eliza's throat, which chased away some of her initial dismay. She genuinely felt bad for him. "You didn't know this was the theme."

He lowered his head and stared at her. "You don't have to do this. Seriously."

Her initial instinct was to bail. This wouldn't be the first time she'd been surprised by the appearance of this game. And the last time hadn't gone well at all. But…last time she'd been twelve. And had been at a party where she shouldn't have been with kids she couldn't trust.

She glanced toward the door. Will, Khuyen, and Trinity were all looking their way expectantly. These people weren't those kids. They weren't out to tease her or embarrass her. They wouldn't call out *Ewww!* if the bottle landed on her. This was just a silly party game. Pecking a stranger on the lips and laughing about it. All in good fun.

The therapist part of her knew that the butterflies in her stomach were just old childhood scars fluttering up, that this posed no real danger. She didn't want to back out and ruin the fun she'd been having. Plus, this might make for an interesting story in the book. She turned back to Beckham, resolve filling her. "It's fine. It's just a silly game. We agreed to bow to the gods of randomness. Far be it from me to go against that."

Beckham's eyes narrowed. "You sure?"

"Yes. I'm embracing the spirit of the party," she said, hooking her arm with his. "Let's take a spin."

"Yes," Will enthused. "Stop being a party pooper, Carter."

Beckham snorted but let Eliza lead him fully into the hallway. She unhooked her arm from his, and everybody grabbed a mint while they waited for the current group to exit. Will came to stand next to her, leaning his shoulder against the wall, his breath minty fresh. "So how did Beckham sell you on this party? Most people think we're pretentious assholes for acting like we're above phone culture."

"No, I didn't think—"

Beckham sniffed from where he was standing on her other side. "I do recall her calling *me* a pretentious asshole."

"I—" she started in defense but then pressed her lips together and gave Beckham a look. "Okay, I may have called you that. *Once.*"

"That's just a smart woman calling it like she sees it," Will teased. "Carter hasn't met a high horse he doesn't want to saddle."

"Giddyup," Beckham said dryly.

"See?" Will gave her a disarming smile and she laughed.

"For what it's worth, he didn't sell me on the idea. I was complaining to him about the hellscape of online dating, and he suggested I go off-line for a while. These parties came up. The concept sounded..." She glanced over at Beckham with a conspiratorial smile. "*Interesting.*"

His gaze held hers for a moment, the word now their own private joke. His lips twitched in quiet amusement, but something else flickered in his eyes, something she couldn't quite pin down. Her belly tightened.

"Well, however he got you here," Will said, breaking the odd moment with Beckham and bringing her attention back to him, "I'm glad you came."

She smiled, the openness on Will's face putting her at ease. "Same."

"Hopefully you'll still feel that way after playing these games," Beckham said, pointing at the opening door. "Looks like it's our turn."

Trinity turned around and gave them all a droll look. "Let's go, losers. If any of you slip me tongue, it's a knee to the balls for you."

The door opened fully, letting people out, and Eliza followed the group inside once the entrance was clear. Someone waiting inside the dim room handed her a tube of something as she entered—lip balm of some sort—and she got separated from Will as more people came in behind them.

The room had been cleared of furniture but had eight square floor pillows arranged in a circle and a few tall lamps tucked into the corners. The light bulbs had been switched to blue so the whole room glowed with almost a twilight color, and Debbie Gibson's "Lost in Your Eyes" was playing softly in the background. Somehow they'd captured the secretive vibe of the Spin the Bottle game but had elevated the atmosphere and drizzled in some irony. She lifted the lip balm closer to her face and read the label, laughing when she realized what it was. Bonne Bell Lip Smacker, Peach of My Heart flavor. Another eighties touch. Whoever had organized this party had a great eye for detail and had clearly had a lot of fun.

Beckham sidled up next to her, squinting at his tube. "I guess I'm supposed to put this on?"

She leaned over, trying to eye his. "What flavor did you get?"

He flipped the tube to see the other side. "One in a Melon." He popped it open and rubbed it on his lips, the scent of watermelon filling the space between them. He licked his lips. "That's... different."

She laughed and put her peach lip gloss on. "Yours smells better than mine."

"Want to trade?" he asked, offering up his tube.

"You might be trading soon enough," Khuyen said, coming up to them and putting hands on both their shoulders. "A peach-watermelon fusion." He made a kissing sound. "Or y'all will land on me and make some flavored lemonade. I've got You Are the Zest. I'll add some tart to your sweet."

Beckham's gaze flicked away from Eliza's. "I think you're enjoying this a little too much, Khuyen."

"I get that all the time." He walked between them to find his spot on the floor.

A petite woman with pink foam rollers in her hair and *Cobra Kai* pajamas was on her feet outside of the pillow circle and was holding an empty wine bottle. "Welcome, welcome," she said brightly. "For those who don't know me, I'm Dahlia. Take a seat where you can find one. We'll start again in a minute. We run the game for fifteen minutes and then switch groups."

Will walked over to them and put his hand lightly on Eliza's back. "Want to find a place to sit?"

Eliza chose a blue pillow to sit on and Will took the spot next to her. Beckham claimed the green one across the circle from her and next to Khuyen. Trinity looked indecisive and then ended up with the last spot when everyone else filled in. She sniffed her gloss and wrinkled her nose. "Nothing should ever be grapefruit-flavored. Or scented. Grapefruit should just be eradicated altogether."

Khuyen reached over the person sitting between him and Trinity and traded glosses with her.

Dahlia shut the door and then cleared her throat. "All right, y'all. Rules are simple. I'll spin to see who goes first. That person will spin the bottle. They will then kiss the person the bottle points to—regardless of gender."

There was a groan from one guy. Khuyen rolled his eyes at that guy and muttered something that sounded like *there's always one.*

"The next turn goes to the person to the right of whoever the bottle landed on. Also, we're all about consent here, so if you're not comfortable kissing someone, you can opt out and leave the game," Dahlia continued, giving groaning guy a you-can-leave-now-if-you-don't-like-it look. When he didn't move, she went on.

"While you're kissing someone, you will hold hands with that person. If they let go of your hand for any reason at any time, that means stop everything immediately. No pushing anyone past where they want to go." She lifted her brow. "This *No Mercy* line on my shirt isn't just for show. I know karate. Don't make me take you down."

Eliza smiled even though her stomach was now flipping with nerves. She hadn't kissed anyone in a while, and even though the logical part of her knew this was just a silly game, she also was well aware that she was in this circle with more than a bunch of inexperienced preteens. What if this was awkward as hell? What if she embarrassed herself? Maybe she hadn't thought this through fully.

"Does everyone understand?" Dahlia asked crisply.

Eliza found herself nodding, her hands clasped tightly in her lap. *Too late to leave now.*

"Yes, ma'am," Will said, his deep voice resonating over the other yeses.

"Okay then." Dahlia grinned and stepped inside the circle. She placed the bottle on its side in the center. "May the odds be ever in your favor."

She gave the bottle a spin and Eliza rolled her lips together, anticipation fluttering through her. The bottle slowed to a stop and landed on Khuyen.

"And we have a winner!" Dahlia said, making her way out of the circle.

"Hell yes," Khuyen said with delight. He rocked forward onto his knees and leaned over to give the bottle a spin.

Everyone watched the thing turn like it was the most interesting movie they'd ever seen. Soon, the bottle slowed again and pointed toward a woman with bright-blue hair and Transformer pajamas. She waggled her eyebrows at Khuyen with an amused smile. They got up and went to the center of the circle to stand in front of each other. Khuyen reached out and took her hand.

"I think we're supposed to say *ooooohhh* while this is happening," Trinity offered. "If I'm remembering how this works."

Beckham laughed quietly from across the circle, and Eliza couldn't help but smile back at him.

Khuyen leaned down to touch his lips to the woman's, and they all *ooh*ed like middle schoolers. The kiss only lasted a few seconds, and the whole vibe in the room was so light that Eliza felt the tension drain out of her. The guy to the right of the blue-haired woman spun the bottle and a few turns went by. Trinity kept getting picked, and she joked that the universe was against her because she kept having to kiss the guys.

Beckham's turn eventually came up and as he leaned over to spin the bottle, Eliza held her breath, not really knowing if she was scared for it to land on her or not. *Just a game, Eliza.* But she didn't have to worry. The bottle pointed at Khuyen again.

Beckham smirked and got to his feet.

Khuyen looked pleased as punch as he joined him. "Watermelon lemonade, my friend."

Beckham flicked his hand in a bring-it-on motion. "Show me what you got, big talker."

"You can't handle what I've got, but I'll go easy on you." Khuyen didn't grab Beckham's hand like the rules stated. Instead he put his hands on Beckham's face and pressed his mouth to Beckham's with a dramatic flourish, making everyone laugh.

When they broke apart, Beckham was laughing, too. "I can't handle that lip gloss. That's what I can't handle." He puckered his mouth. "Wow, that's sour."

Khuyen licked his lips and winked. "It was good for me, too."

Eliza leaned back on her hands, still grinning. She loved seeing this side of Beckham, that playful ease he had with his friends. She loved that he wasn't like the guy who'd groaned at the any-gender rule. Instead, he was the guy who could kiss his male friend, who Eliza suspected was gay or bi, and it wasn't *a thing*. He didn't have to act macho or defend his straightness or whatever. She smiled at Beckham when he took his seat, and he shook his head, eyes dancing with amusement.

A few more spins went by. The first time it landed on Eliza, it was Trinity who'd been spinning. Trinity raised her hands above her head. "Finally, a lady."

She and Trinity shared a friendly kiss, which got a cheer of approval from some of the guys. Trinity rolled her eyes at Eliza. "Dudes are so predictable."

A few more turns went by, and then it was time for Eliza to spin. She leaned over and gave the wine bottle a good hard spin. That had been a bad idea. It seemed to take *forever* to stop. When it finally started slowing, it looked like it was going to point right back at her—which would mean another spin—but it stopped just short. Right on Will, who somehow hadn't had to kiss anyone yet.

Will glanced over at her and smiled, clearly pleased. "Lucky me."

Eliza's shoulder muscles tightened just a bit. This one had more stakes to it than the kiss with Trinity. Will was someone she could see herself going on a date with. She didn't want to mess this up or be awkward about it. She could squash any chance they had before it started. She swallowed past the constriction in her throat and smiled.

Will got to his feet and offered her his hand to help her up. They went to the middle of the circle, and Eliza ended up with Beckham in her peripheral vision. The earlier amusement on his face had disappeared, and the look he was giving her set her off-balance for a moment. He looked...tense? Annoyed? But before she could put her thoughts together, Will took her other hand.

She looked up, forcing a small smile on her face even though an anxious feeling was filling her. Maybe she shouldn't do this. Maybe this game wasn't as lighthearted as it seemed. But before she knew it, Will had leaned down and gently put his mouth against hers. The scent of strawberries filled her nose, and he kissed her softly, just enough to make it more than a peck but not enough to cross any lines. *This guy would be a good kisser*, she thought, as if from outside herself, like she wasn't part of the kiss and was watching it instead. The circle *ooh*ed.

Before she knew it, Will was pulling back, his gaze holding hers. He squeezed her hands. "Thanks."

She rubbed her lips together, awkwardness filling her. For some reason she felt like she'd zoned out on a conversation and was now trying to respond to things she'd missed. "Same."

They walked back to their spots. Will didn't let go of her hand until they sat on their pillows again, but she was almost too in her head to notice. What the hell was wrong with her? Maybe she'd been more nervous than she'd thought. The guy she'd been flirting with tonight had kissed her. She should've relished the moment. Instead she'd taken some mental trip to la-la land.

Two more turns went by, and Eliza's mind wandered, her brain still turning over what had happened, but when Beckham got up to spin again, she snapped back into the moment. She watched the bottle rotate, *whoosh, whoosh, whoosh*, almost as if it were in slow motion. When it stopped and was pointing straight at her, it took her an extra second to process it.

Beckham's gaze jumped to hers, wary. "Eli."

If she'd had butterflies earlier, pterodactyls had now replaced them. She'd told herself that she'd thought this through. She absolutely *had not*. Being physically attracted to Beckham and knowing they could only be friends was one thing. Kissing that friend was a whole other ball game. Some things couldn't be walked back so easily. She needed to keep this one hundred percent platonic. Just like she had with Trinity. A peck. Nothing more. She couldn't do what she'd done with Will. Even that would be too much.

"Eliza?" Beckham repeated.

"Oh, right," she said, snapping out of her whirling thoughts and getting to her feet. "Sorry."

When she got close, he said quietly, "You don't have to."

Her hands were sweating. She rubbed them on her pajamas pants so he wouldn't grab sweaty palms and nodded. "I know. I'm fine."

He searched her face as if looking for the real answer. He let out a breath. "Okay."

She held out her hand and he took it. He laced his fingers with hers, almost as if he was trying to ground her. The grip helped...a little.

"Ready?" she asked, voice soft. And in that moment, she realized she was. She wanted to see what it was like...to kiss Beckham. Maybe doing that could get this attraction thing out of the way. She could kiss him and see that he was just another guy. Break the tension that hummed between them.

His Adam's apple bobbed, and his gaze held hers. His fingers tightened against hers. She closed her eyes. But as she prepared to feel his mouth against hers, the sound of his voice broke through.

"I don't want to do this," he said, loud enough for the room to hear.

And before she could register the words, his solid grip released her hand, leaving her hanging. Her eyes flew open. He'd backed up a step and looked apologetic.

"I'm sorry," he said to her.

There were a million smart reasons why they shouldn't kiss. Valid reasons. But in that moment, all she felt was the stinging burn of embarrassment and the gut punch of rejection. It was like middle school all over again, the boy she'd liked laughing that no one would want to kiss her.

Beckham had kissed Khuyen with no problem. He wasn't opposed to kissing friends. He was just opposed to kissing *her*. "Oh," she said, feeling stupid. "No, it's okay."

"No problem," Dahlia said brightly. "Consent, consent, consent. But Beckham, you'll have to leave the game."

"That's fine," he said, stepping out of the circle and giving Eliza one last glance before heading out of the room.

Eliza sat back down, cheeks burning.

"Sorry," Will said. "I don't know what's up with him. That was weird."

She cleared her throat. "It's probably because we work together. It could make it awkward."

He smiled and nodded. "Probably. Want to get out of this room? I think I'm over this game."

She gave him a grateful look. "Yeah, me too."

chapter **thirteen**

"AND HE JUST LEFT YOU STANDING THERE?" ANDI ASKED AS she piled a small paper plate with fresh-baked cookies from a platter on the kitchen island.

Eliza grabbed a cookie and took a big bite before responding. "Yeah, it was super awkward. I mean, I get it. We work next door to each other and we're friends, but he could've let me know it was a hard line for him before making me stand up in front of everyone and then just bailing. I know we're having a preteen theme tonight, but I didn't want actual angst to be part of the night."

Andi hummed her assent as she chewed, a line appearing between her brows. After she swallowed, she said, "Maybe he didn't know until that very moment that it was a hard line. Like he thought it wouldn't be a big deal and then realized it might be."

"Oh God," Eliza groaned. "Do you think I looked at him too eagerly or something? Like *oh shit, this woman might have a thing for me?*"

Andi arched her brows. "*Do* you have a thing for him?"

"No," Eliza said defensively. "I told you. Different places in life and all that. But there's some attraction there, sure. I mean, have you seen him? Maybe that showed on my face."

Andi licked chocolate off her thumb. "Maybe he didn't want to kiss you in front of the friend he's trying to set you up with."

Eliza leaned back against the island. "Huh. Maybe. I hadn't thought of that. That could make sense."

Andi shifted to the left to let someone else get to the cookie platter. She and Eliza moved to a quieter corner of the kitchen, both ready for a break from the activities. Eliza had tried a few games after Spin the Bottle to try to shake off the weirdness with Beckham. She'd been a holder for a round of Light as a Feather, Stiff as a Board. Then, she and Will had won a complicated scavenger hunt because they'd been the only ones to figure out how to find a fish that doesn't swim—a Goldfish cracker. But when Will had to leave early, she'd decided she was done with gaming for the night and had found Andi.

"So how was that kiss?" Andi asked.

"With Will?" When Andi nodded, Eliza shrugged. "It was nice."

Andi's nose wrinkled. "Nice?"

"Nice isn't a bad thing. It's not like we could have some passionate kiss in front of a group of strangers. It was appropriately good," she said, even though she barely remembered any detail of the kiss. All she remembered was that Will had been respectful. "And he must've thought it was good, too. He had to leave the party a little early, but he asked for my number, wants to get together for dinner."

"You like him?"

Eliza swallowed another bite of cookie. "I do. Smart. Polite. Nice to look at."

Andi tossed her paper plate in the trash and brushed the crumbs from her hands. "Then, that's great. Mission accomplished. You came to a party without your phone and met a nice guy. *And* kissed him." She lifted her hand. "High five."

Eliza tapped her palm to Andi's. "You're right. I *did* do that. This was a thousand times better than any dating-app date I've had in months. Even with the weird moment with Beckham."

"That's what you need to focus on." Andi glanced over at the wall clock, which was moving toward the single digits. "Are you ready to head out? I've made my way through all the spooky rooms. Pretty cool stuff. They're really into nailing the details here."

"They definitely are. Remind me to tell you about the free Lip Smackers," Eliza said.

Andi looked aghast. "I missed Lip Smackers? I used to love those."

Eliza smirked. "You would've had to kiss strangers."

"Never mind. I'll buy my own." She cocked her head toward the door. "So, shall we make our exit?"

"Yeah, I'm wiped out," Eliza said. "But I should probably find Beckham and at least tell him bye. He *is* the one who invited me here."

"Sure," Andi said. "Have you seen him since he bailed on Spin the Bottle?"

Eliza frowned. "No."

"Hmm. Do you know if he's still here?"

"I don't. And I obviously can't text him without my phone. But I get the feeling he wouldn't leave without at least saying goodbye." Eliza glanced around the kitchen, hoping to spot him. "Plus, I don't want the first time I see him after that awkward moment to be at work. Do you mind if I do a quick round and try to find him?"

"Nope. Not at all," Andi said. "If you give me your phone, I'll go get ours unlocked and meet you downstairs."

Eliza pulled out her packaged phone and handed it to Andi. Then she leaned over and gave Andi a side hug. "I love you. Thanks for coming with me tonight."

"Of course. Love you back." Andi flicked her hand in a shoo motion. "Now go find awkward boy. Tell him I said thanks for the invite, too."

Eliza nodded and then grabbed a napkin to wipe her mouth. She wanted no trace of chocolate from the cookie or Lip Smackers on her face. She left Andi in the kitchen and made her way to the great room. She didn't want to have to check each of the game rooms. Plus, based on the look on Beckham's face when she'd last seen him, he was done with games for the night. She ran across Khuyen in the living room. He was back on the couch with Kevin and a few people she hadn't met yet. She asked him if he'd seen Beckham.

"Not lately, but I know he hasn't left. Maybe check the back porch. He likes to go out there sometimes," Khuyen said.

"Thanks." Eliza headed to the back of the house where the long screened-in porch faced the bayou. She couldn't see outside because the windows just reflected the light of the party back at her. She pushed open the back door and went outside, the cooler air enveloping her and offering relief from the stuffy air inside. It took a second for her eyes to adjust to the low light of the porch. On the far right, there was a small group of people hanging out in rocking chairs and vaping under a dim yellow porch light, but when she turned to look to the other darkened end, she found Beckham.

He was leaning back in an old wooden chair, feet propped up on the lower rung of the porch railing, only the moonlight breaking the darkness. He hadn't seen her come out, and for a moment, she simply watched him. He had a pensive look on his face and seemed to be staring out into the black waters of the bayou. To see someone sitting alone with nothing in their hands—no phone, no book, nothing to take their attention—was an anomaly, but Beckham seemed more than a little occupied by his own thoughts.

Part of her wanted to leave him to it. This was sure to be an awkward conversation, but she couldn't bring herself to take the easy road. They needed to clear the air and move on.

After a fortifying breath—which smelled of all the green things growing in the bayou—she headed his way. When she was about six feet from him, the moonlight sent her shadow over him and he looked up. He dropped his feet to the porch floor and his jaw ticked. "Hey."

"Hey," she said, turning her back to the railing and leaning against it. Mosquitoes buzzed against the screen behind her. "I'd wondered if you'd left."

"Not yet," he said. "I like to stick around in case anyone needs a designated driver."

She glanced at the two glasses next to his chair. She'd assumed he'd been drinking vodka sodas. "Should you be a designated driver?"

"What?" He noticed where she was looking and then shook his head. "Oh, that. It's club soda and lime. I don't drink."

"Oh."

"Anymore." He glanced up, weight in that one word.

Oh. He didn't need to spell it out. She slid that piece into her Beckham puzzle, but there were still too many missing pieces to make sense of anything. "Gotcha."

"Will told me he asked for your number," Beckham said, looking out to the water again.

She was a little thrown by the non sequitur. "He did. He seems nice."

Beckham nodded almost to himself. "He is. Good guy."

"Good." She fiddled with the sleeve of her pajamas. "Guess this experiment worked. I got a date out of your party. You were right."

He smirked and glanced over briefly. "I usually am."

She snorted but was happy to see a glimmer of the normal

Beckham coming through instead of all the awkwardness that had risen up between them. "So..."

"Look, I'm sorry about the Spin the Bottle thing," he said. "I didn't mean to, like, make a scene or whatever."

She tried to read his expression, but he was giving her nothing. "Why did you then?"

"I don't know." He put his hands to his face and rubbed like he was too tired to think.

She crossed her arms. "You don't know."

He dropped his hands into his lap and looked her way. "Yeah. I just...couldn't kiss you."

The words hit her like little shards of glass, cutting deeper than they should. "Right." She forced a tight, no-big-deal smile. "It's fine. You had the right to not want to. That was in the rules."

He frowned, dropping his gaze to the wooden slats of the porch floor.

"To be honest," she went on, unable to stop talking, "it's not the first time in Spin the Bottle a boy realized he didn't want to kiss me. This time was far less traumatic. My seventh-grade crush made gagging sounds when the bottle landed on me. Said he'd rather kiss his dog. So thanks for not doing *that*."

His head turned sharply, his eyes flaring. "*What?*"

Her face burned with the memory. Why the hell was she sharing this? *Shut up.* But she couldn't seem to keep her mouth shut. "Just one of those things. I went through a really awkward phase in middle school. A little too chubby compared to the other girls, a little too hairy, a lot too brown for the lily-white popular group at my Catholic school."

"Jesus," Beckham said, standing up and sounding genuinely angry. "Kids can be such dicks."

She grunted in agreement. "I'm pretty sure middle school is one of the circles of hell. It's a miracle any of us make it out."

"That's the truth." He stepped in front of her, eyes serious. "I'm sorry that happened to you."

She shrugged even though her stomach was tight with the old memory. "You didn't do it."

"No, but if I did anything tonight to remind you of that, I'm sorry." He shook his head and raked a hand through his hair. "I screwed this all up. I should've just kissed you."

She scoffed. "Right. Forcing yourself to kiss me. What every girl wants. A grin-and-bear-it kiss."

He eyes widened like she'd spoken another language, and he made a sound in the back of his throat. "A grin and bea—Is *that* what you think?"

She sighed. "I don't know what I think. I mean, you kissed Khuyen and—"

"Fucking hell," he said, cutting her off and thrusting his palms out toward her. "Give me your hands."

"What?"

He lifted his palms higher. "Hold my hands, Eli."

She put her hands in his, his palms warm and dry. "Beckham…"

He wrapped his fingers around hers, his gaze burning into hers with singular determination. "You let go if you want me to stop."

And then he leaned in and kissed her.

Her breath caught, and her eyelids automatically fell shut. His mouth pressed against hers, warm and soft and gentle at first. A sweet kiss. One that should've ended quickly. But when she found herself kissing him back and squeezing his hands instead of letting go, his mouth became more urgent, the kiss more possessive.

More *everything*.

A rush of heat flooded her skin, and her hands squeezed his tightly—*more, more, more, please*. He groaned against her mouth, and she parted her lips, gasping into the point of connection and tasting watermelon. His tongue brushed hers, sending lightning crackling through her nerve endings, and her knees wobbled. *Oh God.* She must've made some needy sound because he deepened the kiss even more and shifted closer. Her back pressed into the column she'd been leaning against and their bodies touched, their fingers lacing tighter.

She lost all train of thought, the taste of watermelon in her mouth and the scent of Beckham filling her senses. She'd kissed a few people tonight, but in this moment, she felt like she'd never been kissed in her life. Every part of her body was involved, every cell ached. Beckham nipped at her lip and then kissed along her jaw, murmuring her name. *No.* Murmuring *Eli. His* name for her.

For some reason, that only made her burn hotter. He went back to her mouth, their tongues stroking, and he wrapped their linked hands behind him at the small of his back. She had his arms pinned but he had her pinned right back, and she didn't want to be anywhere else.

But when she rocked her hips, lost to the sensation of it all, and bumped up against a newly stiff part of him, her belly dipped in mild panic. The shock of feeling him against her, hard and hot, made her break rhythm for a moment, and one of her hands slipped from his. She hadn't meant for it to be a signal, but Beckham immediately broke the kiss and let her go.

When he stepped back, he was breathing hard, eyes black, and his pajamas were doing nothing to hide his obvious interest. "Fuck." He lowered his head, lacing his fingers behind his neck, and exhaled. "*That's* why."

Eliza felt drunk and dazed, though she hadn't had a drop of booze tonight. She braced a hand on the column and tried to find her voice. "That's why, what?"

She sounded like she'd run a goddamned marathon.

He lifted his head, met her gaze. "That's why I didn't kiss

you." He swept a hand in front of him. "I can kiss Khuyen. I don't want to sleep with Khuyen."

Oh. The thrill of his words rippled through her with hot promise. She licked her lips, tasting the lip gloss there. If Beckham kissed like that, she could only imagine how good other things could be with him. "Oh."

"But this"—he motioned between the two of them—"would screw everything up."

The sexual fantasies trying to weave in her head blinked out. "I like you, Eli."

She frowned, her brain starting to wrest control back from her hormones and focus on his words. "I like you, too."

"I think we could have a really cool friendship, and I've learned those are hard to come by." He rubbed a hand along his jaw. "I don't want to mess this up—and I would—if I let what just happened go any further. I would hurt you. Disappoint you."

"You don't know that." The words were out before she could stop them. *Hormones: 1. Logical brain: 0.*

"I do," he said grimly. "If we start this, I already know where it'll end. And you don't want that kind of ending. You're looking for things I can't and will never be able to give you—or anyone else for that matter. I like living alone. I'm not looking for a relationship. I don't even believe in the concept of marriage. I'm much better as a friend than someone's boyfriend, believe me. This would be a dead-end road. *I'm* a dead-end road."

She opened her mouth to protest that no one can know the future, that he was young, but something about his tone and the look on his face stopped her. There was a resignation there, like something had already been grieved and accepted. This wasn't some speech from a twenty-five-year-old guy who just wanted to hook up with as many people as possible. This was something deeper, some kind of trauma that had left its mark on him.

She wanted to ask a thousand questions, wanted to tell him that his fate wasn't sealed, that the past didn't have to dictate the future, but she was also smart enough to know that if she even put a toe on that let-me-play-therapist path, he'd slam the door in her face and she'd lose their budding friendship along with anything else. So instead, she took a breath and nodded. He was not her client. He wasn't asking for her help, only her understanding. "Okay."

"Okay?" A look of gratitude crossed his face—gratitude and relief. He nodded. "Okay." After a moment, he put his hands on his hips and released a long breath. "That was a great fucking kiss, though. *Damn*, Eli."

She laughed at the break in tension and leaned her head back against the column. "So good."

"Thank God I didn't kiss you in front of the group," he said. "You know how long my friends would've teased me about getting a hard-on during a game of Spin the Bottle?"

She pressed her lips together to stanch her laugh. "Eons."

"Into the afterlife probably," he agreed. "I can't believe I lost control like that." He crossed his arms and gave her a stern look. "Honestly, if this friendship is going to have any chance, I really need you to work on being less hot."

She snorted and put her hand to her chest. "Oh, so this is my fault? Blame the woman. That's how it always goes."

"Kidding." He put out his arm so she could hook hers with his. She joined him. "But really, I'm sure there are absolutely disgusting things about you. I need you to share those with me immediately."

"I eat peanut butter and pickle sandwiches," she offered as they made their way back to the door to the house arm in arm.

He grimaced. "Yes, like that. Gross. What is *wrong* with you?"

She laughed. "Sometimes I add hot sauce to that."

He made a gagging sound. "You're a monster, Eli. I don't

know if we can be friends now that I know that. Maybe we should just fuck after all and call it a day."

She unhooked her arm from his and shoved him playfully when they reached the door. "Get over yourself. You didn't even bother to wonder if I would say yes if you asked. You assumed I'd just fall into your bed and thank you for the privilege."

He stayed facing her as he walked backward through the door. That smug, pretentious smile she was beginning to think of as endearing lit his face. "Oh, Eli, you showed your cards way too early to play poker with me now." He pulled up his sleeve. "Exhibit one: *The lady wants to lick my tattoos.*"

She narrowed her eyes—and very pointedly tried not to look at his really bitable shoulder. "I. Was. Drunk."

"Keep telling yourself that, Eli." He reached out and pulled her gently through the doorway. When he didn't stop tugging her hands, she ended up closer to him than she'd planned. He bent forward and kissed her cheek. Then his lips brushed her ear. "I like that you want me. Evens the playing field, you know? Means we'll both have to fight for this friendship." He leaned back and smiled. "It will keep things…"

"Interesting," she said with a sigh.

"Exactly."

He left her standing there, watching him leave, her head spinning and her body still thrumming with lost opportunity.

After saying a quick goodbye to Khuyen and Trinity, Eliza found Andi downstairs a few minutes later. Andi had been chatting with Jayleigh, who'd been manning the door, but she came over to Eliza when she saw her. She gave Eliza an up-and-down look. "Whoa, what happened to you?"

"What?"

"You look, I don't know, disheveled." Andi waved her hand in front of her.

Eliza straightened her pajama top and smoothed her hair. "I was out on the back porch. There was a breeze."

She handed Eliza her newly freed phone. "Did you find Beckham?"

"Uh-huh."

Andi tilted her head. "And?"

Eliza made a show of unlocking her screen and making sure there were no messages so that she didn't have to look at her too-observant friend. "And it was interesting."

"Hmm, I sense a story," Andi said, sounding all too happy about that fact. "I expect details on the way home."

Eliza made a noncommittal sound as they headed to the car. Even though she was usually happy to dish with Andi about things, she didn't think she'd share what had happened on the porch quite yet. For one, she didn't have the energy to analyze it, which Andi would inevitably want to do. But also, for some reason, the moment shared on the porch with Beckham seemed fragile in some way, easily shattered, like if too many people looked at it, it would crumble under the scrutiny. Like those ancient artworks that disintegrated a little each time they were exposed to light.

For now, she wanted to keep it protected, for her eyes only. Private.

When they reached the car and Eliza walked in front of her to get to the driver's side, Andi sniffed the air. "Do you smell that?"

"What?" Eliza asked, startled from her thoughts.

"That smell." Andi's face was tipped up like she was still trying to catch the scent. "Is that *watermelon*?"

Eliza rolled her lips together, trying not to smile, and opened the car door. "No idea."

chapter **fourteen**

BECKHAM GRABBED A BOX OFF A HIGH SHELF LABELED *Round metallic purple, 7mm.* He plunked it onto the flat pushcart dolly that Will had parked in the middle of the store's wide aisle.

"How many is that?" Will asked as he eyed a box of mini stuffed New Orleans Saints footballs with a furrow in his brow.

Beckham grabbed another box, this time of long, green throw beads instead of purple. He eyed the cart and did the math quickly in his head. "Seven hundred and twenty."

"Get a few more cases of those," Will said. "The group said no short beads. We have a reputation to protect."

Beckham grabbed a box of gold-colored beads and added it to the haul. "You sure that's not just the guys guaranteeing they get a lot of shirt-lifters?"

Beckham hadn't grown up with Mardi Gras. Even if he had grown up in New Orleans instead of Arizona, he wouldn't have been allowed to go to a celebration that had ties to both Catholicism and paganism. But he'd picked up the traditions pretty quickly since he'd moved here. And he knew that the longest, most unique plastic bead necklaces were often held out as bait at parades to get women to lift their shirts. It wasn't his favorite tradition. After his strict upbringing, he was mostly a live-and-let-live kind of person, but it felt a little weird to have women flashing breasts while people's kids were nearby just trying to get some beads.

Will smirked. "That's definitely some people's motivation, but even the women don't want the cheap stuff. Plus, we're riding in Metairie this year and not in the city, so it will be more family-friendly." He held up one of the footballs. "You think I should get these? Might be fun to throw."

Beckham shrugged. "Sure. It's not my money."

Will grabbed a box of them and stacked it on top of the cases of loot already on the cart. "This is going to be fun. I know you've been to the parades, but it's a whole different experience riding on a float."

"I appreciate the invite. Seems like a New Orleans bucket-list item," he said.

Will had asked Beckham a few weeks ago if he'd wanted to ride with his coworkers because they'd had a few spots open. Normally, Beckham wouldn't do anything that would put him in front of the public, but they'd be wearing masks so he decided to give it a shot.

"Yeah, man, no problem," Will said. "I owe you anyway."

Beckham picked up a tiny stuffed duckling in a purple, green, and gold jester hat, checking the price and then putting it back. "For what?"

Will pushed the big cart slowly down the aisle as they walked. "For introducing me to your friend Eliza. We're going to dinner this week. We had a really good time at the party."

"Oh." Beckham forced himself not to grimace. "That's cool. Glad you two hit it off."

"We did. She's really easy to talk to. Smart, too." Will stopped and picked up a bag of gold doubloons, testing their weight in his hands, and then glanced back at Beckham over his shoulder. "Plus, I mean, wow."

Will tossed the bag of doubloons his way. Beckham caught them on instinct, the coins clinking together. "Wow what?"

"Don't give me that," Will said, grabbing more bags. "I know you two are coworkers and she's not your type or whatever, but you have to acknowledge she's smokin'. Fire emojis all the way."

Fire. Those minutes on the porch came back to Beckham in a rush—the feel of Eliza against him, her response as hungry as his, her mouth sweet and hot and tasting of sugar. Her hands squeezing his tight, like she was having to fight not to touch him in other places. The sounds she'd made...*fuck.* He'd had actual sex that hadn't felt as visceral and erotic as that kiss had. If they had... *Stop.* That kiss had been a huge mistake, and he needed to stop thinking about it.

He dodged Will's question and tried to shove the memory from his head. "What do you mean, not my type?"

Will gave him a come-on-now look. "I'm not saying that like it's a bad thing. She's just more...refined than the women I've seen you go for. Established, you know? Like she knows how to be in her own skin, knows what she wants, that kind of thing."

"So I go for the unrefined? She's the expensive wine and I'm hooking up with wine coolers?" Beckham asked, annoyed.

Will laughed, his chest-deep chuckle carrying down the aisle of the store. "Don't get your nuts in a twist, man. I'm not saying that. You're just younger than I am and have a type to go with that. You like women who are still in their freewheeling phase, experimenting, ones who want to have fun and not get into anything heavy. You're the guy friend they'd call if they want to try out a threesome and need a third."

"Fuck you," Beckham said grumpily as he tossed the bag of doubloons onto the cart. "I'm not the threesome guy. They'd call Khuyen for that."

Will smirked. "Yeah, you're probably right. You don't like

strangers." He grabbed the cart and started pushing again. "But am I reading this wrong? Are you into Eliza? Because if you're into her, I won't overstep and—"

"No," Beckham said quickly. *Too quickly.* "It's fine. We're just friends. Coworkers. That's why I didn't kiss her in the game. I brought her to the party to meet people. That was the whole point. I'm glad you two got along."

Will smiled, his brown skin glowing like he was lit from the inside. "Sweet. Because I'm really looking forward to the date."

"Great." Beckham's teeth pressed together, his jaw flexing as he tried to regain his goddamned sense. "And you're right, about her knowing what she wants. Fair warning, she's not looking for hookups. She's met a lot of assholes on dating apps and is over it."

Will shrugged like that was no big deal. "That's cool. I'm taking her out to get to know her. I'm open to wherever that leads." He reached out and patted Beckham's shoulder. "You don't have to stress, man. I'll be good to your friend. I wouldn't disrespect her."

Beckham sighed. He *knew* that. Knew Will was a really good guy. Goofy as hell sometimes but solid and smart and decent. He should be happy Will was taking Eliza out. She deserved a guy like Will and vice versa. But *goddammit it all*, he wanted to lift each box of beads off that cart and throw them, watch things bust up and spill out.

That kiss with Eliza had been a major error in judgment. It had triggered something inside him. Something that was making him feel what he never felt about women—*possessive.* That urge right there was reason enough to squash this thing with Eliza. Any feeling that put him even remotely in the ballpark with his father was a five-alarm fire. Whispers of his dad's sermons drifted into his head about how wives were supposed to honor and obey their husbands, how the man was the head of the household, how the woman's role was to serve the family. He remembered how his dad would have final veto on which friends his mother could spend time with, how he'd get in her face when she'd have an innocent conversation with a male member of the church, regularly accusing her of affairs. Possessive. Sneakily abusive.

Beckham had no right to feel anything about who Eliza did and didn't date. He *would not* be that guy.

He could handle this. After all, he had a lot of experience dealing with temptation. Every day, he got up and chose to stay sober. He walked through parties like NoPho surrounded by alcohol and didn't have to have some long, internal debate anymore. He knew how to choose the smart route now. And each time he did, it made it a little more automatic.

He needed to do the same with Eliza. This was just simple attraction. Biology. Hormones. Nothing groundbreaking. He could learn to be around her like he'd learned to be around bourbon. He simply needed to keep putting himself in the challenging situation until he grew accustomed to its effects.

He would fix this.

After he helped Will load up his SUV and got into his own car, Beckham picked up his phone and tapped a contact. Eliza answered on the third ring. "Hey."

"Hey," he said, angling his AC vent toward him. "You busy?"

He could hear something clicking on her end—a pen, maybe. "No, just finished up my last appointment of the day. What's up?"

"I have this weird thing that if I watch the first movie of a franchise, even if I've seen it before, I need to watch the series through again," he said, a true fact but also a convenient one for this purpose. "So I was wondering if you're up for a little *Empire Strikes Back*."

The pen stopped clicking. "Like another co-watch on the phone?"

He leaned his head back against the headrest. "Or maybe hang out in person? I could pick up takeout. My place isn't far from work."

The pause on the other end of the line had so much weight to it that he felt the phone get heavier. He was freaking her out. This sounded like a date. It was not a date. *This is not a date.*

"If you're busy or not up to it, that's fine," he said quickly. "I was just hanging out with Will and he said y'all are going out later this week, so I thought maybe I'd catch you on an open night. Save you from the risk of being bored and tempted to go back to your social media." *There. See! I know you're going out with someone else. This is not a date.*

She cleared her throat. "Um, you know what? Sure. It's been a long day and a movie night sounds good. But can we do it at my place?"

"Your place?"

"Yeah, I don't want to leave Mabel alone all evening," she explained. "She's a good girl, but if she doesn't get some playtime at night, she gets anxious and starts barking nonstop and bothering the neighbors."

"Oh." He let out a breath. "Yeah, sure, that's fine. Trent gets pissy if I *don't* give him alone time."

"Perfect."

He pulled his seat belt across his chest. "I feel like I just invited myself over. Feel free to tell me to fuck off."

She laughed. "I do feel free to tell you that, but I don't want to. Just don't expect a perfectly clean house, and bring something good to eat because I'm starving."

He pressed the button to start his car. "Feelings on étouffée? I know a place that makes a good one."

"Pro-étouffée."

"Shrimp or crawfish?" he asked. "And over rice or over potato salad?"

"Rice for sure. And I like both so pick whatever."

"On it," he said, smiling despite the fact that he was setting himself up for a white-knuckle mission. "I have to run by my condo to feed Trent and tell him how amazing he is and that no other cat will ever compare, then I'll head over."

"Of course. Priorities."

"Sevenish work for you?"

"Yep. Sounds good." She paused. "And Beck?"

"Yeah?"

"Thanks for not making it weird after what happened this weekend. I really liked hanging out with you and your friends."

"Even with ridiculous slumber-party games?"

"Even with that," she said, a smile in her voice. "This experiment is making me realize how small I let my world get. And how boring, really. Being online all the time makes you feel like you're connected to so many people, but really, I've worked so much for so long that I let a lot of connections fall away. I only have a small handful who are the true definition of a friend, people I can trust. I'm glad... Well, I'm just glad that now I can add you to that list and that I'm meeting more people out in the real world who may join that circle."

Great. If that didn't make him feel like a damn hypocrite, he didn't know what would. A true friend. Someone she could trust. She didn't even know his real name. And she definitely didn't know that his purposes tonight were selfish.

He closed his eyes, breathed. Vowed to do better. She was telling him what she needed—a good friend. He could do that, be that. Well, at least he could try.

"I'm glad too, Eli," he said softly. "See you soon."

....

"Mabel," Eliza said patiently but firmly. "*Boundaries.*"

Beckham laughed and lifted his Styrofoam container of shrimp étouffée out of Mabel's reach. Mabel had jumped onto the couch and sat on Beckham's lap, facing him and stretching for his food.

"Sorry, pups," Beckham said, running a hand down Mabel's back. "I don't have any left. And your mom said no table food."

Mabel panted and her tail thumped the couch cushion as if Beckham had said she was gorgeous and definitely deserved all of his dinner.

Eliza smiled and reached for Mabel's collar. "Come on, girlie, give the guy some space."

Mabel did a half huff/half sneeze, which was her version of frustration, and hopped back down to the floor.

Eliza crouched down to her level and scratched Mabel behind her ears. "All right. Go lay down. Bedtime."

They'd been working on this command for a while, and blessedly Mabel trotted off to her kennel. At first, Eliza had been reluctant to have Mabel sleep in one, but the shelter had said that it would help her feel secure. Mabel did seem to like it, so Eliza had let go of her guilt.

"Wow," Beckham said after Mabel had disappeared into the other room. "I wish Trent would listen like that. He's the one who tells *me* when it's time to go to bed. He plops in the middle of my bed and yowls like he's dying until I come into the room."

Eliza laughed. "Trent missed his calling in theater. So dramatic."

"One hundred percent." Beckham put out his hand to take Eliza's empty food container. "Here, I'll go throw these away."

Beckham disappeared into her kitchen for a minute, and she got up to grab the blanket she used when it got cold in this part of the house. They'd made it through half the movie so far but had paused it when Mabel started getting in their face about dinner.

Eliza had been more than a little surprised when Beckham called her with the invite this afternoon. They'd talked at work since the party, and everything had seemed fine, but she'd secretly wondered if the kiss had changed things, if they were *acting* like everything was fine when it really wasn't. But she should've known better. Beckham had told her early on that his hookups tended to be with friends. He was obviously used to navigating that tricky space where you've shared some intimate moments with someone but there's nothing romantic there. He was a compartmentalizing master it seemed. She was new to that kind of dynamic but working on it.

She hadn't known what to expect, how tonight would feel for her, but so far, this had been nice. When she made herself put the physical attraction stuff to the side—wrapped it up in a nice little box in her brain—only to be opened in private, she realized that she just straight up liked hanging out with Beckham. He made her laugh. He made her comfortable.

Normally, if someone new was coming over, she would've curated every damn thing. What her place looked like, what books she had out, what outfit she wore, how she fixed her makeup and hair. And multiply that times a hundred if it was a cute guy coming over. When the knee-jerk instinct to do that had hit her this afternoon, she'd rushed home to prepare before Beckham came over. But halfway into picking an outfit, she'd frozen and recognized what she was doing for what it was. *A performance.*

Beckham had been right about her tendency to do that. She hated that it was her go-to behavior. When had everything become a show? A dance to impress other people? It made her wonder if for all the work she'd done on herself, maybe she'd never quite grown out of that ostracized seventh grader who obsessed about having the right shoes, outfit, everything to try to get an in with the people at her new school.

It was a thought she needed to sit with.

But at least she'd been able to recognize her behavior this time and stop herself. She'd halted her outfit perusal and had gone against her instincts. She'd walked into her bathroom, washed her makeup off like she would've done after work on a normal day, put on yoga pants and a tank top, and pulled her hair up into a messy bun. The only adjustment she'd made to her normal nightly routine was keeping her bra on.

She'd welcomed Beckham as a friend and as herself. That had felt liberating. And he'd seemingly done the same, showing up in black joggers, a soft-looking gray T-shirt, and his Vans.

Beckham came back from the kitchen and took his spot on the other end of the couch. He draped his arm out along the back of the couch, making his T-shirt stretch and the couch cushions squeak. Goose bumps prickled the tattoos on his arms. "Ready for the second half or do you need to get some sleep? You can kick me out at any time, you know?"

She smiled. "I'm good. I'm worried for the rebels." She reached for the lamp next to her and clicked the light off. Now that they didn't need to navigate food, they could watch the movie in proper darkness. She kicked her foot out, shifting part of the quilt his way. "You can share my blanket if you want. I know this room gets cold. Old house. Drafty."

He eyed the quilt and then cleared his throat. "I'm fine."

"Oh really, tough guy?" She cocked a brow at him. "You have goose bumps."

He glanced down at his arm. "I'll live."

Without allowing herself to think too hard about it, she got up and went to his side of the couch. "Stop being ridiculous." She plopped down next to him and pulled the quilt over them both. "I'm capable of sharing as long as you don't mind me in your personal space. You did once have your tongue in my mouth. I think we can probably manage our arms touching without catching each other's cooties."

Ha. See, she could compartmentalize, too. *Look how totally fine with what happened I am!*

He snorted. "Trying to cuddle with me, Eli?"

She pulled the blanket up to her neck and tucked her legs up onto the couch. "You wish, hacker."

He chuckled under his breath and then reached for the remote, starting the movie again.

Before long, she could feel his body relax next to her. His arm ended up on the back of the couch again, only this time, it was right behind her.

She wasn't cold anymore.

Damn. She really needed to put a padlock on that box in her brain.

chapter **fifteen**

BECKHAM HAD PLANNED FOR TONIGHT TO BE THE equivalent of sitting in a bar during those first months sober. He did not plan for it to be sitting in a bar with a bottle of high-end bourbon pressed into his hand with the bartender saying, *It's on the house.* That was what this felt like. Eliza next to him under a blanket, his arm almost around her.

The clean scent of her hair was wafting into his nose and her barefaced casualness was bringing to mind what she'd look like in bed. This was all too much. His mind kept drifting to how easy it would be to lean over and kiss her again, to put his arm fully around her, to slide his hand beneath her—

"Will said he's really looking forward to the date," he blurted out, even though he was generally opposed to talking during movies.

She glanced over at him, eyebrows up. "He said that?"

On-screen, Princess Leia said, *I have a bad feeling about this.*

"Yeah. He, uh, mentioned it while we were getting Mardi Gras supplies," Beckham said.

"Huh." She turned to him slightly, tone careful. "He usually talks to you about his dates?"

Beckham grabbed the remote and lowered the sound on the

movie. "I mean, he'll mention them sometimes. Not like a play-by-play or anything. But I think he was just saying it to me since I introduced you two."

"Oh." Her lips pursed a little with the word, her lower lip pushing out. He wanted to bite it.

"He won't, like, kiss and tell if that's what you're worried about," Beckham added, feeling like he was rambling now, but he needed to distract himself from the dirtier thoughts trying to push past his good sense. *The devil inside*, his dad would've said. Beckham didn't believe in the devil anymore, but that reckless part of himself could be loud sometimes.

"That's good." She nodded, almost to herself. "I mean, that'd be weird. Him telling you about our dates."

"Definitely." He gave her a smile that felt too tight. "Not something I want to hear. I already had to watch him kiss you. That was more than enough."

A line appeared between her brows, and she squared her body fully toward him, her legs tucked beneath her. "What do you mean, more than enough?"

Fuck. Had he said that out loud? "Nothing, it's just, you know, you don't want to know that much about your friends' sex lives, especially if you're friends with both people."

"Afraid you'll accidentally picture us doing naked, dirty things and will be traumatized?" she teased.

He grimaced. "Well, I definitely don't want to picture *Will* doing naked, dirty things."

Her brows lifted right as he realized what his statement had implied. The glaring omission.

"Or me, right?" she asked, tone tentative.

He cleared his throat and tried to play it off. "Come on, Eli, you have to know that ship has already sailed. I pictured all kinds of things during that kiss. I'm human and male. But that's not the point. There is no point. I don't even know how we got into this conversation. Go out with Will. Do dirty things. I don't care. Back to Star Wars?"

"Wait, do you *not* want me to go out with Will?" she asked, a perplexed look on her face.

"Huh?" Panic alarms were going off in Beckham's head, but he kept his expression nonchalant. "Why are you even asking? I basically set you two up."

She gave him the look that she probably gave her clients when they were withholding information. "That wasn't my question."

He was stupid. So freaking stupid. He was better at lying than this. He'd created a whole new identity, a whole new life, goddammit. But somehow this woman turned him into a witness bumbling on the stand. He clenched his jaw, tried to center himself, but the truth came out anyway. "I *do* want you to go out with Will. I think you two would hit it off." He met her gaze. "But I also have some weird primal urge to mark you with my scent and tell other guys to go fuck off."

Her eyes widened.

"Yeah. I know. I'm a dick." He scrubbed a hand over his face. "So right now I'm living somewhere in the space between those two things, trying to not be the aforementioned dick."

"Beck..."

"I know. I'll go." He flicked the blanket off his legs so he could get up.

But Eliza put a hand on his arm. "Wait."

He stayed where he was. "Eli..."

"I've pictured you naked, too," she said, her gaze steady on him. "Like a lot. Like if thought crimes were a thing, you could press charges over all the things I've imagined."

The admission had his breath getting stuck in his throat and a bolt of heat flashing through him. What exactly had she pictured? He wanted every last detail. With demonstrations.

"So thank you for telling me that you're there with me because, I don't know, that makes it feel...right."

"Makes what feel right?"

"Since that first day," she said, her gaze dipping down for a moment, "we've been able to say things to each other that we normally wouldn't say to a casual friend. It's kind of our thing." She glanced up and sent him a little smile. "Confession friends."

He smirked at the term.

"I like that," she went on. "It feels...safe. In a good way." She dragged her teeth over her bottom lip like she was trying to find the right words. "In a sexy way." She lifted her gaze to his. "I think I'd like to make another confession."

His throat was tight. "What's that?"

"I want you to stay."

His shoulders sagged and he turned fully to her, pulling his bent leg on the couch so he could face her. "God, Eli. You know I want to say yes to that, but we've already had this conversation. You know why this would be a bad idea."

"I know. You can't be what I want. I can't be what you want. But maybe that doesn't matter right now." Resolve filled her brown eyes. "I trust myself enough to handle it. I know what it would be and what it won't be."

He frowned. "But I don't want to hurt you. That's literally the last thing I want to do."

She poked him gently in the shoulder with her index finger. "I appreciate that, but Beck, I'm not some delicate flower. I've been through a helluva lot more in my life than some guy sleeping with me and not wanting to stay with me forever. You think you're going to be *soooo* good in bed that I'm just going to die if you won't tell me you love me and propose on the spot?"

His eyebrows shot up.

She gave him a wry look. "Like I said the other night, *get over yourself*. You're twenty-five. You may not even *know* how to be good in bed yet."

He opened his mouth to protest, but before he could defend himself, she pressed her fingers gently over his lips.

"Kidding. And yes, I would like a relationship. I'm aiming for that. And yes, I'm over hookups. But I also understand that you're not that guy—in either case. You're not the guy who's going to want to be my boyfriend, but you're also not the guy who's just looking to get laid and ghost me. You're my friend. And I hope that if we walk into my bedroom right now and get naked, that afterward you'll still be my friend."

He stared at her, properly stunned into silence.

"Well?" she asked, lowering her hand.

He frowned. "Of course I'd still be your friend."

"Then maybe this—whatever this is between us—is exactly what I need," she said, open honesty in her voice. "I don't plan on sleeping with any dates anytime soon. My goal is to take things slow, to really get to know guys first. But that doesn't mean I don't still think about sex, that I don't still want it sometimes. And since we had that kiss, I kind of want it a lot. With you."

"Eli..." The temptation was glittering, blinding. He wasn't strong enough to resist this. He didn't want to be.

In the background, Yoda warned Luke to beware of the dark side.

When Beckham didn't say anything more, Eliza shifted on the couch, put her hands on his shoulders, and straddled his lower thighs. He was already half-hard and the sight of her on his lap was too fucking much.

"I think there's only one way this friendship is going to work," she said softly. "We need to get this part out of our system. You're making it hard to concentrate on Star Wars, and that just won't do."

The ropes he'd tied himself up with gave way. He couldn't, wouldn't, fight this anymore. He lifted his hands and cupped her jaw. "No, that won't do at all."

"So?"

"Come 'ere, Eli." He guided her down to him. "Just come here."

And then he kissed her and stopped worrying about all of it.

Maybe some temptations weren't meant to be avoided. Maybe Eli was the kind he needed to get absolutely wrecked on before he could move on.

Maybe he needed to drown.

....

Eliza didn't know where the streak of boldness had come from. This was the opposite of the plan she'd had tonight. She'd been firmly focused on reestablishing the friend vibes. But the way Beckham had looked at her when he'd said *I pictured all kinds of things during that kiss...* It'd done her in. The heat that had zipped through her had burned up all her best intentions. His words hadn't been romantic in tone. He'd used the word *primal* and that felt right to her. The two of them hooking up didn't make sense for so many reasons, but there was just something undeniably... magnetic between them. It made it hard to concentrate.

Since the night of the kiss, her secret thoughts about Beckham had gone from vaguely sexy to downright filthy. Some of the fantasies that had floated through her head the last few nights before falling asleep... If she still went to confession, she'd probably give the priest a heart attack. If she didn't do something about this, she and Beckham wouldn't last as friends anyway. They'd always be working hard to avoid the electricity humming in the room.

"Come 'ere, Eli," he said, his blue-green eyes silver in the light from the TV. "Just come here." Then he guided her down to him and put his mouth to hers.

Instead of going straight for the kind of kiss they'd shared the other night, he took her bottom lip between his teeth, lightly scraping and sending tendrils of awareness snaking down her spine. Her fingers curled into his T-shirt. Then he kissed the corner of her mouth and the bow of her lips, cupping her jaw and taking his time. Her heartbeat hammered, his deliberate pace making her ache.

He slid his hands down to her neck and tipped her head back, exposing her throat. His lips brushed against the hollow there. "Were you trying to kill me with this outfit?"

She scoffed, though the sound came out a little strangled. "You think I tried to impress you with yoga pants and no makeup?"

He kissed her collarbone and shifted his hands down to her hips. "These pants hug every part of you. It's seriously distracting. There's almost nothing between...you and me."

He ran his palm over her thigh and then pressed the hot heel of his hand against the most sensitive part of her, applying pressure. She made a sharp sound and her body shuddered. *Oh God.* How long had it been since she'd been touched by someone other than herself? She didn't want to count the months.

Beckham groaned. "See. Barely anything. I bet I could make you come without even taking them off."

"So cocky," she said, trying to tease, but the words came out too breathy for her to pull off the sarcasm.

He dragged his thumbnail gently over the center of her, that little bundle of nerves, slow and wickedly precise. Her thighs tightened, her sensitivity dialed to high, and she gripped his shoulders.

"Take off your bra," he said, voice quiet but full of authority.

His firm tone gave her a hot shiver. He might be younger than she was, but he didn't lack for confidence. That streak of bossiness would piss her off in other arenas, but in bed, *yes please.*

She reached for her tank top.

"No. Just the bra for now."

She wet her lips. His gaze was heavy on hers. His thumb dragged across the seam of her pants again, making sensation radiate upward, the eye contact only enhancing the effect. She reached behind her, unhooking her bra, and then slipped it off and tossed it aside. The relief she usually got from taking off her bra at night—that whole body sigh—was an entirely different experience watching Beckham watch her. Nothing was relaxing about this. Every part of her was humming like a power line. His attention dropped to her breasts, which were now easily visible through her pale-pink tank top, her nipples hard and sensitive against the soft cotton.

"You're gorgeous, Eli," he said, the little catch in his voice belying how cool and calm he seemed on the outside. He reached up with his free hand and cupped her breast. His thumb traced over her nipple through the shirt. "You want to lick my tattoos? Well, I've wanted to lick some parts of you, too."

"I approve of this plan," she said, closing her eyes at the feel of him touching her.

"Lace your fingers behind your back," he said, his thumb stroking, stroking, stroking.

Her eyelids fluttered open. "Why?"

He looked at her. "Trust me?"

She swallowed past the tightness in her throat, doing a gut check and finding no worry there. She did trust Beckham. She felt...safe with him. "Okay."

The smile he gave her warmed her blood.

She laced her fingers together behind her back, which pushed her chest out toward him. Before she could prepare herself further, Beckham leaned forward and put his mouth on her breast, keeping the thin layer of cotton between them, but dragging his tongue over her in a way that made that little layer of abrasion send sparks of sensation along her skin.

She moaned softly and goose bumps chased up her body.

Beckham took his time, sucking and nibbling, cupping her in his hand and making it hard not to writhe against him. Not being able to touch him amped up the feeling, her senses honed in only on what he was doing to her. Her body was tightening, hovering at the edge of something bigger. But then he started to stroke her between her legs at the same time. She was damp there now, hot, the thin stretchy material of her pants and panties doing nothing to protect her from the pressure of his fingers. She rocked against his touch, needing more and feeling like it was too much at the same time.

"Go on. Come for me, Eli," he said before pulling down the neckline of her tank top and taking her into his mouth. The hot, wet heat of his tongue and the expert stroke of his fingers was all she could take. Her head tipped back and her nails bit into the tops of her clasped hands as she cried out, orgasm crashing over her like a thunderstorm.

Beckham *mmm*ed against her skin, his reaction sending her higher. He held her and touched her through it, keeping her riding the peak for long, delicious moments.

"Beck," she begged, not sure what she was begging for. "*Beck.*"

"Fuck, Eli," he said, pressing his forehead to her shoulder, his breath warm and quick against her skin. "God."

He rocked the heel of his hand against her clit until he'd wrung out every last bit of pleasure and she gasped, her fingers coming unlinked. She braced her hands on his shoulders, tipping forward, spent and breathing like she'd run a marathon. He gathered her against him. His erection pressed thick and hard against her, but he simply held her, letting her bury her face into the crook of his neck and coast her way down from the high.

He stroked her back gently, his heart beating fast against her chest.

After a few moments, she whispered. "I take it back."

He dragged his hand down her spine. "What's that?"

"You might know what you're doing."

He laughed, but it sounded a little pained. "Don't be too impressed yet. If we stay in this position much longer, I might go off in my pants like a teenager and ruin the street cred I just earned."

She started to giggle, this ridiculous sound that she couldn't control. The orgasm had made her goofy.

"Not. Helping," he teased.

"Sorry, sorry," she said, trying to wrangle the laugher, and scooted back a little. She glanced down at the very obvious state of his arousal. "We should probably take care of that."

"No pressure. Honestly. We can stop here if you want. I know how to take care of things if need be."

She lifted her head to look at him. "Shut up. I've been promised tattoo tasting. Don't hold out on me now, hacker. Unless *you* want to stop."

He laughed. "I really, *really* don't want to stop. I'm just trying to be a decent guy."

In the background, Han Solo told Leia that Lando was a scoundrel and she'd like him.

Eliza arched a brow. "I think I'm more in the market for a scoundrel."

Beckham's grin was slow and wide. A scoundrel's smile indeed.

Eliza started laughing again. "Bedroom?"

"'Yes, Your Highness*ness*,'" he said, quoting a line from the movie.

"This is the nerdiest dirty talk I've ever had." She climbed off of him and put out her hand. "And I'm so here for it."

So here for *him*.

chapter **sixteen**

BECKHAM FOLLOWED ELIZA INTO HER BEDROOM, AND SHE shut the door so Mabel wouldn't wander in and be scandalized. Eliza hadn't even considered the possibility that she and Beckham would end up here, so her room was as she'd left it this morning— bed unmade, stack of romance novels on her nightstand, her black sleep mask sitting on top of the pile. "Sorry it's kind of messy…"

Beckham smirked and wrapped his arms around her waist. "You think I care if your bedroom's ready for an Instagram shoot?"

She looped her arms around his neck. "I'm thinking no."

"I'm thinking you're right." His palm slipped beneath her shirt, his fingers spreading against her tailbone. The hard part of him was pressing against the soft part of her. "I don't need the glossy version, Eli. The therapist who has all the answers. This thing we have, this…heat. I think it's because we've been messy with each other from the start."

Lord, wasn't that the truth. Alone at Christmas. Drunk after a date. A public shaming. She'd never been so…*not* put together in front of guy as she had with Beckham. "You haven't been messy."

He snorted softly. "Are you kidding? I'm a disaster. I *own a cat* now. I freaked out in a game of Spin the Bottle. And I'm about to take my friend's date to bed, breaking every guy code out there."

She bit her lip, smiling.

"You have no idea," he said, guiding her to the edge of the bed, his hands slipping down and cupping her backside, "how far outside my lines I'm coloring right now. I'm completely off the page."

The words made her belly tighten in the best way. She pushed up on her toes and kissed him. That was all it took to break the restraint he'd been showing.

He groaned into her mouth, and his hands went to the hem of her shirt. He broke the kiss only to tug her tank top over her head. He tossed it over his shoulder, the fabric hooking on her desk chair, and he looked down at her. His gaze was like a heat brand marking her skin. He lifted his hand, cupping her and dragging his thumb around her nipple, making it perk to attention. "So damn sexy. Every part of you."

She shivered under the attention and then reached out and plucked the front of his shirt. "Your turn. I've been promised ink licking."

"As you wish." He grinned and reached for the back neckline of his shirt and yanked it over his head in one swift movement. The fabric hit the floor, and her tongue pressed to the roof of her mouth as she took in the new view. *Hot damn.* She must have had good karma built up or something to be having this night with this guy. Beckham's colorful tattoos continued from his arms to the front of his shoulders, making him look like art. But that was just the start. He had a dusting of dark chest hair that trailed down to a flat, lean stomach, and one nipple was pierced with a little silver hoop. Every part of him was better than the fantasy she'd created in her head.

"This is not even fair," she said, tracing a finger over a line of tattooed text. The Latin words snaked around a tattoo of a compass rose. "I mean, *look at you.*"

He smirked. "You sound offended."

"*I am*. How am I supposed to act like a rational person when you look like this?" She huffed. "I want to, like…bite you. I don't even know who I am right now. Not a biter normally, I'll tell you that."

A full belly laugh escaped him then. "Eli, you're a special snowflake." He pulled her close again, her breasts pressing up against the warmth of his chest, his coarse hair tickling her. He touched his forehead to hers. "And biting is definitely allowed—as long as I can bite back. Acting rational is not required." He slipped his hands beneath the back band of her yoga pants. "In fact, I forbid it."

The humor evaporated in an instant, his eyes intense, and he hooked his thumbs in her waistband, dragging her pants and panties down. The cool air of her bedroom drifted over her, kissing her skin with goose bumps.

He'd crouched down in front of her and helped her get clear of her clothes, pulling the pants off and tossing them to the side. He groaned and then looked up at her from his position on the floor. She slid her fingers into his hair, the blond strands tickling her knuckles. He turned his head, kissing her palm, and then he leaned forward and pressed his mouth to her inner thigh. Her grip on his hair tightened.

He worked his way up, sending shivers through her, and finally kissing her at her very center. He flicked his tongue against her. Her knees wobbled and she let out a soft groan. "I'll never last on my feet."

He dragged his tongue along her one more time and then rose to his feet and kissed her lightly on the lips. "Then let's get you on your back, Eli."

She flipped her comforter flat and lay back on the bed. Beckham stood to the side, watching her. He ran a hand over the back of his head. "I'm in trouble. I'm never going to get any work done ever again." He reached for the waistband of his joggers. "I'm going to have to move offices. Every time I see you, I'm going to remember you like this."

She swallowed hard as she watched him push his pants and boxers down and off. She shouldn't have been surprised, but still, the view made her suck in a breath. The guy was gorgeous everywhere, and when he straightened and took himself in his hand, giving himself a casual stroke, she was ready to form his fan club and become the president. "Same. You're...wow."

And she meant it. She was no virgin and she'd been with attractive guys before, but there was something so unapologetically raw about Beckham's sexuality, a lack of any hint of shame or subtext or ulterior motive that felt new to her.

Even when she'd had good sex, she was usually in her head about it. The questions and analysis were right there at the surface. *Does this mean something? Is this guy going to ghost me? Am I doing this right? Is he having a good time? Am I having a good time? Do I look weird in this light?*

None of that was running through her head right now. She and Beckham were friends who were going to do this because it was fun, because it'd feel good. The simplicity of that was its own kind of freedom. She felt like she could say anything, ask for anything. But she asked for the most obvious first. "Condoms are in my drawer."

Beckham sat on the edge of the bed and reached for something on the floor—his wallet. He pulled out a packet and tossed it onto the bed next to her. "I've got it."

"And I've got an IUD," she added. "So we don't have to worry about...anything."

He stretched out next to her, both of them propped up on one elbow, facing each other. He trailed his hand along her hip. "Tell me how it's best for you."

The request startled her for a moment. It was something no

guy had ever asked her. Then she realized how ludicrous that was—that no guy had ever thought to ask. What the hell had she been tolerating? She reached down between them, giving in to the urge to touch him.

He closed his eyes, a soft gasp passing his lips as she wrapped her fingers around him. "How about I show you?"

....

When Eliza climbed on top of him, Beckham worried that he really was going to have an embarrassing moment. Every bit of control he usually had in these situations was shot right now. Eliza was beautiful, sure, but he'd already known that. No, the thing that was killing him was how responsive she was. Every touch, every taste came with a big reward. A shudder. A sigh. A hungry look that made him weak in the knees. It made him want to show her every fun way he could make her feel good. He wanted to eat up her reactions like candy.

Eliza braced her hands on the bed, leaning over him, and pressed her lips together in mock concentration. "Hmm, where to start? Where to start?"

He smiled and reached up to tug her hair free from the bun. It tumbled down, the ends tickling his chest like the light touch of fingernails. His cock flexed against her and she smiled, looking enormously pleased with his reaction.

"I promise not to make you wait much longer," she said, not sounding at all apologetic.

"Take your time, Eli. I'm not exactly suffering here."

"Then I'm not doing my job." She leaned down to kiss him, and he put his hand to the nape of her neck, deepening the kiss. The feel of her tongue against his sent fire burning through his veins again, but right when he was about to lose his mind, she broke away and shifted her attention.

The second her teeth touched his shoulder, he nearly lost it. His head pressed back into the pillow, a deep groan escaping him. He hadn't known if she'd been joking about biting him, but he was all for her making good on the promise. He hadn't ended up with all this ink without some appreciation for a little pain. He threaded his fingers in her hair and gripped, letting her still lead the way, but liking the idea of giving her a little taste of roughness back. She made a rumbly sound in the back of her throat, letting him know she approved, and then she ran her tongue along the Marcus Aurelius quote burned into his shoulder: *The best revenge is to not be like your enemy.*

"Eli." He murmured her name like a prayer.

But she was only just getting started. She traced his ink with her tongue, her hair tickling his skin like a hundred feathers as she worked her way down, waking up every nerve ending along the way and making his cock ache like it'd never been touched before. Eli was nothing if not thorough and detail-oriented—or maybe she just thoroughly enjoyed torturing him—but he was a happy victim. There were worse ways to die.

She sucked his nipple piercing into the hot cavern of her mouth, tracing his ribs with her fingernails, and then dipped down to circle his navel with the tip of her tongue. He used every ounce of willpower he had to stay still, to let her do whatever she liked, but when she dragged her teeth along the vee of his pelvic bone, the tip of her nose tracing a cool line against sensitive skin, his body lit on fire. He automatically reached down, squeezing the base of his cock, keeping himself in check. No way was he losing it before he had a chance to be inside Eliza.

She lifted her head, her eyes sparkling in the low light as if she'd accomplished exactly what she set out to do, and handed him the condom. "Don't make me wait any longer."

He quickly tore the packet open and reached down to roll it

on, loving the way that Eliza watched him. He gripped her hips and guided her upward, loving the way her hair spilled around her shoulders, the way her breasts rose and fell with quick breaths. This image would be burned into his brain. He wasn't sure exactly how they'd landed here in this moment but he was so glad it was now. Eliza lowered herself, slow and deliberate, and the snug, sweet heat of her body enveloped him one delicious inch at a time, stealing his breath when he was finally seated deep.

Sweet fucking hell. Did it usually feel this good?

He wasn't going to last long. Not this time. He hadn't realized how long he'd secretly been fantasizing about this, and the fantasy paled next to the reality. But he damn sure was going to make sure she came again and then next time... *Next time.* Right then he knew there would be a next time if Eliza was game. Because this wasn't going to be enough for him. One night of this was only going to make him want her more.

Figuring out all the ways he could make her moan was going to take a while. He looked forward to working his way through that scavenger hunt. What sound does she make when I bite her here? What noise will she make if I lick her there?

They started to move together, the rhythm of their bodies falling into perfect sync. He held eye contact, loving the dark look in her eyes, the smoky heat there. He reached out to stroke her where their bodies met, relishing the way her thighs instantly clenched around him. She gasped his name and tipped her head forward, bracing her hands against his shoulders and rolling her hips in a way that made him almost choke on his tongue.

"Fuck. Eli..." His words sounded strangled.

"*Beck.*"

Her body tightened around him like a fist and her nails dug into his shoulders. She cried out, her orgasm sweeping her under, and he closed his eyes and lost himself to her. *Eli. Eli. Eli.*

Later, when Eliza was stretched out next to him, their bodies both sapped and the buzz of orgasm starting to fade into sleepiness, the panic began to creep in to take the place of all those good things he'd been feeling. He didn't want to be like the guys who'd ghosted her, didn't want to give her even a hint of that kind of rejection, but he also knew he couldn't stay over. He didn't do that. With anyone. Ever.

"Eli…" he said into the darkness, trying to figure out how to say it.

"Want to finish the movie before you go home?" she asked. "I have ice cream."

He closed his eyes. He didn't know if she'd saved him from the conversation on purpose or by chance, but he wanted to kiss her all over again. "That sounds perfect."

"Good." She rolled onto her side and patted his chest, sending him a little smile. "That was a lot of fun. You're not so bad at this sex thing, Beckham Carter."

He laughed and tugged a lock of her hair. "Not so bad? Gee, thanks. Your enthusiastic endorsement is overwhelming."

She rolled her eyes. "I think I made my level of enthusiasm pretty clear."

"True." He gave her a look of mock seriousness. "Mabel did howl back at you at one point."

She smacked his chest, half-laughing. "I did not *howl*."

"I thought you were going to transform into a wolf there for a minute," he went on. "I mean, it was a possibility. There's a sexy werewolf book on your nightstand, and you *do* bite."

"Shut up." She was fully laughing now and tried to playfully hit him again, but he grabbed her hand and kissed her knuckles.

"The whole thing was hot as hell, Eli," he said, sitting up. "You can bite me anytime. But right now, it's ice cream o'clock."

After they both got dressed, he followed her out to the kitchen where she procured two pints of cookie-dough ice cream. She handed him one of the pints and a spoon.

"Straight from the container. I like your style, Eli."

"I'm no amateur. Plus, I'm not sharing." She hugged the pint to her chest.

They settled back on the couch, the blanket over both of them, and watched the rest of the movie, gorging on ice cream.

When it was time to leave, she walked him to the door and gave him a hug. Friend zone reinstated. "Tonight was…great."

"It was," he agreed. "I told you we could friend with benefit the hell out of each other."

She laughed softly. "We certainly did that."

"Thanks…for everything." He leaned over and gave her a quick kiss on the cheek. "I'll see you tomorrow."

"Okay." She opened her lips and then shut them again.

He narrowed his gaze. "What?"

She tilted her head, all innocence. "What what?"

"Don't give me that. You want to say something else." He cocked his chin at her. "Go 'head."

She sighed and crossed her arms. "I guess I just need to know what the rules are here."

"Rules?" he asked, wary. He'd never been a big fan of those.

"Well, first, I assume this might happen again. If the opportunity presents itself," she said in an almost businesslike tone.

He smiled. "I am definitely open to that if you are."

"Right. I am, but then how do we…handle it with your friends and such?" Her forehead wrinkled. "Do we, like, hide that this happened? That it may happen again?"

"From Will, you mean," he said, finally catching her meaning.

She dipped her head a little. "Yeah, I guess so. And with your other friends if I go to more get-togethers or whatever."

Beckham sighed and scrubbed a hand through his hair.

"Normally, I'd say feel free to be an open book. My friends aren't the judgy type about relationships or hookups or anything in between. But I've never done *this*...not with someone who was going to go on a date with one of them. It's a...unique situation."

"So...a secret." Her tone was careful, like she was weighing the words to see how they felt.

He sighed, not loving adding another secret to his list but not seeing a better path forward. "For now, I think that's for the best. If things go well with Will, then...we won't...do this."

She nodded and hugged her elbows like she'd caught a chill. "Yeah, if things get serious with anyone—with Will or anyone else I may go on dates with through this analog experiment—this will need to stop. Us hooking up would be...counterproductive, I think."

"Agreed." He really, really didn't want to think about her sleeping with other guys. Especially his friend. Selfish thought, sure. But it was what it was and it wasn't going away. "How about this? If you think things are moving into the physical place with a new guy, you tell me, we stop. And I–I won't sleep with anyone else while we're doing this."

Her brows arched. "I wasn't asking you to be exclusive."

He leaned forward as if telling her a secret. "News flash, Eli, I'm asking *you* to be exclusive. I'm only returning the favor."

She blinked. "Oh."

He stepped closer to her again and leaned down to kiss her on the mouth this time. "Even if we're just friends, my guess is you don't want to think about me sleeping with other women right now either."

Her nose wrinkled. "I don't."

"Well, same here." He shrugged. "Plus, I need to save up my energy. I have a feeling you're going to put me through my paces."

She rolled her eyes.

He stepped back, feeling buoyed by the plan. "We good?"

She nodded, a little smile there. "We're good."

"G'night, Eli."

"Night."

He drove home feeling better than he had in a long damn time.

chapter **seventeen**

Untitled Book Because Titles Are Hard
By Eliza Catalano

Chapter 4
The *When Harry Met Sally* Dilemma

We all know the premise of the movie *When Harry Met Sally*. Harry believes that (straight) men and women can't be friends without the sex stuff getting in the way. Sally believes that's ridiculous and that, of course, they can be friends.

I've always been a Sally in this debate. I've had guy friends throughout my life. I could be friends with them, think they were objectively attractive, and not have any interest in sleeping with them or making the relationship into something more. Honestly, it didn't even seem like a debate to me. However, a few weeks into this off-line dating experiment, I find myself considering this issue from a different angle.

What of the friends-with-benefits setup?

This dynamic has been around forever. It's not something new or a concept I'd never heard of. I hadn't personally gone down the friends-with-benefits road with anyone—hadn't ever been tempted to, honestly. But I've had friends who have, and clients as well. I thought I had no judgment about it. However, recently, when I started to look more closely at this idea, I realized I had some preconceived notions.

Maybe because I've watched too many rom-coms in my life, I assumed that in the friends-with-benefits dynamic, at least one person was secretly in love with the other and was using the agreement as a guise, hoping the relationship would turn into more. Embarrassingly, I also had a bias that it was usually the woman who had these feelings. *Hey there, internalized misogyny, how you doin', girl?*

I think this is part of the reason why I never considered trying this kind of relationship myself. I didn't want to be that hopeless woman in love while some guy friend just saw me as a convenient way to get laid. This seemed like a particularly painful way to get your heart broken because you can't even blame the other person when it ends. You signed up for it. You just didn't hold up your end of the deal.

Recently, however, as I dropped the online dating and instituted the three-dates-before-intimacy rule that I mentioned in the previous chapter, this friends-with-benefits option has taken on a different light. A friend of mine, one who's helping me with this project, mentioned the possibility early on—that we could hook up as friends if we ever wanted to. At first, it seemed like a ludicrous idea. Why would I sleep with someone who wasn't a possible long-term partner when my very project is about finding a real relationship?

Then we had a movie night...

Eliza stopped typing, her fingers hovering over the keyboard as a smoke signal of guilt moved through her. *Poof.* Guilt. Should she be writing about this? She wasn't using Beckham's name, but he'd know it was him if this book ever saw the light of day.

"Ugh." The grunt of disgust was loud in the quiet of her office.

She didn't want to *not* write about it either. After her movie night with Beckham, she'd realized what a great—sexy, amazing, mind-blowing—option the friends-with-benefits thing could be in someone's dating life. You could keep active in the dating world, exploring the possibilities, searching for something long-term, but you could take the sex part out of it up front. If you had a friend to satisfy that physical urge already, at least until you were ready to take it to the next level with someone new, you could avoid rushing things. You wouldn't be tempted to go home with someone too soon just because your hormones were raging.

Like tonight, she was going out with Will. She was looking forward to it, but it was also a huge relief to know that she wouldn't have to have the should we/shouldn't we debate with herself at the end of the date. She'd already made that decision. Three dates minimum first. And if she got the urge to do anything before that, she could call Beckham.

Beck. She sighed and leaned back in her chair, staring at her blinking cursor. She needed to think about this harder, whether she was going to write about him. She hit Save and exited the doc.

A knock on her door had her looking up. She'd left it ajar since she wasn't in session. "Come in," she called out.

Andi poked her head in, her hair in bouncy curls today. "You busy?"

"Nope, finished for the day." Eliza closed her laptop. "Just killing time before my date with Will tonight. What's up?"

Andi slipped inside the door and nearly pranced over to Eliza's couch. "So hey!"

Eliza laughed. "Wow, someone's had a lot of coffee today. Hey."

Andi's knees were bouncing. "Are you excited about your date?"

Eliza gave her a careful look, afraid Andi might burst into a cloud of caffeine or something. "Suuure."

"Cool. Guess what?" But she didn't give Eliza a chance to respond. "The wedding is happening!"

Eliza blinked. "What? Whose?"

"Mine!" Andi declared, a big, goofy grin on her face. She popped up like a jack-in-the-box.

"Oh my God!" Eliza stood and came around the desk to give Andi a hug. "That's great!"

"Right?" Andi released her and plopped back down on the couch, her curls bouncing. "I mean, it's not going to be like a *wedding* wedding. Our original plan was to elope, you know, just go off one weekend to some place cool and do it, but..." She flattened her hand to her chest. "When I thought about doing it with no friends around, it just didn't feel right. Hill called me out on it. He'd figured out that it was why I was dragging my feet about picking a place."

"Smart guy, that one," Eliza said, sitting on the edge of her desk.

"He is. So, once he said he was totally open to whatever I wanted to do—big wedding, small wedding, elope, hire a marching band, ride in on camels, whatever—it just felt like this huge relief." She took a breath, possibly her first one since entering the office. "And all of a sudden, all I wanted to do was plan it like *right now*. I'm so freaking ready to marry this dude."

"Oh, honey, I'm so happy for you guys," Eliza said, her chest squeezing tight, her friend's happiness like a sugar rush. "What are y'all going to do? Please tell me camels aren't really an option. You know they spit, right?"

Andi laughed. "No camels and nothing big. I still don't want that. But I do want friends there. That's what I'm here about," she said, bracing her hands on her knees. "Do you have any weekends you're going to be unavailable in May?"

"May? I—" Eliza scanned her mental calendar. "I don't think I have anything, at least nothing important that couldn't be canceled."

"Perfect. We want to have a little outdoor ceremony in the park before it gets too hot. Nothing fancy. I'm thinking like barefoot and prairie skirts and wildflower bouquets. Kind of a nature theme. Just a handful of guests."

"That sounds beautiful," Eliza said a little wistfully.

"Will you be a bridesmaid? I swear there will be no ugly dresses."

Eliza pressed her hand over her heart. "Of course. I'd love that. And I'd wear an ugly dress for you."

"Yay!" Andi did a little clap. "Hollyn's going to be one, too. She agreed as long as she doesn't have to get up and give any speeches or toasts. She said she used to have nightmares about botching a wedding toast. Jasper, on the other hand, offered to do an interpretive dance and comedy sketch if need be."

Eliza smiled. Hollyn had come a long way from the socially anxious woman Eliza had first met a few years ago. Hollyn had met Jasper, her improv-actor husband, here at WorkAround and had worked really hard with him and her therapist to improve her anxiety. But Eliza appreciated that the woman knew where to draw her lines. Wedding toasts were a hard no.

"I can't believe this. I'm so happy for you," Eliza said.

"I'm happy for me, too." Andi beamed. "And of course, you can bring a date. Maybe Mr. Tiger Lawyer if things go well tonight."

Eliza laughed. "Let's never call him that again. But, yeah, we'll see. Someone has to really like you to do the wedding date thing. That's a big ask."

"Hey, my wedding is going to be an awesome good time for all," Andi said, tipping her chin up. "A downright privilege to be present."

"I have no doubt."

Andi stood, still bouncing a little on the balls of her feet. "Well, I know you've got to get your game face on for your date. I just couldn't hold in the news for a minute longer." She gave her another hug. "Thank you for being a bridesmaid."

"Can't wait."

Andi let her go and gave her a little wave before hurrying out the office. Eliza had a feeling that the whole of WorkAround, whether they knew Andi or not, were soon going to know she was getting married.

Eliza headed to her door to shut it so she could change from her work clothes into something a little more date appropriate, but Beckham stepped into the doorway before she could. He had a coffee cup in his hand and a perplexed look on his face. "Everything okay with Andi?"

Eliza grinned. "Why?"

"She just told me hi, spontaneously hugged me, and then strolled down the hall like it hadn't happened."

Eliza laughed. "She just set a wedding month, May. She's hyped on love and romance...and probably lots and lots of caffeine."

His brows arched. "May? That's pretty soon."

"It's a long time coming. She and Hill have been engaged for a while. If it'd been up to him, he would've married her the day he proposed, but I think he was waiting for her to figure out how she wanted to do it. Apparently the answer is in the park in peasant skirts with flowers in our hair."

"Our?"

"I've been awarded the honor of bridesmaid." She curtsied.

His expression darkened for a moment. "My condolences."

She made a sour face. "Why do you say that? She's not going to pick ugly dresses."

"It's not about the dress thing." He shrugged a shoulder. "I just think it's an antiquated tradition."

"Antiquated," she said, unimpressed.

He sipped his coffee. "Yes. Do you know why bridesmaids exist?"

She put her hand on her hip and struck a pose. "To look super fly in matching dresses?"

"No, they used to travel with the bride on the way to the wedding, dressed like her, so that if any other dudes wanted to kidnap the bride, they'd get confused and steal a bridesmaid instead."

Eliza scoffed, slightly horrified. "That cannot be true."

"I kid you not." He tossed his empty coffee cup in the little trash bin in the hallway. "Same with the best-man thing. That's the dude who's the 'best' in a sword fight if some kidnapper shows up to steal his friend's property, his prized virgin bride." He leaned against her doorjamb, arms and ankles crossed. "When you dig into the details, the whole marriage and wedding thing was based on some pretty messed-up stuff. Not love."

"Your romantic streak is truly inspiring," she said, pressing her hands to her heart. "You should write sonnets."

"I didn't make up the history."

She sighed. "Should I even ask how you know all this stuff? Late-night Wikipedia surfing? Plans to go on *Jeopardy!*?"

He considered her for a moment, and she thought he was going to give her some throwaway answer, but then he said, "My parents were—*are*—very fundamentalist in their religious beliefs.

When I was old enough to realize that not everyone was that way, I made it my business to find out everything I could about where those beliefs came from, the origin, the reasons, so I could figure out what it was that *I* believed."

"Wow, that takes guts, to push back against what you've been taught," she said, another piece of the Beckham puzzle shifting into place. This guy was all still waters, but every now and then he gave her a glimpse of what was beneath. "Is that why you and your parents don't get together on Christmas?"

"That's why we don't get together ever."

She frowned. "I'm sorry."

"I'm not." He pushed up from the doorjamb, straightening. "And damn, how'd we end up in this conversation?" He laughed a little stiffly. "I think you just used your therapist magic on me."

"No. Just being a friend, wanting to know more about you," she said. "But I'll respectfully disagree with you about the marriage thing. I think marriage is whatever the two people who are in it make of it. Sometimes that's a bad thing and it doesn't work out. Sometimes that's a beautiful thing that becomes a lifelong commitment. Sometimes it falls somewhere in between. Andi and Hill? They're going to be great together. They're the forever kind."

He nodded. "I wish them nothing but the best, honestly. And hopefully no marauding kidnappers come to sweep you away during the ceremony."

She sniffed. "Hill's a former firefighter. I think he and his firefighter friends will be able to keep the guests safe from marauders. Maybe I'll make sure my date brings a sword just in case."

"Glad to know you'll be safe." He glanced down the hallway. "Speaking of dates, I chatted with Will earlier because he's lending me a book. He said he was going to meet you here tonight, so he could drop it off to me."

"Yeah, he should be here soon. We're going out to dinner. I was about to get changed," she said, this conversation feeling slightly surreal. A few days ago, Beckham had been naked beneath her. Now they were casually chatting about the guy she was about to go out with.

"Cool." He stepped backward into the hallway. "I'll leave you to it."

"Thanks."

She shut her door and grabbed her bag from under her desk. She still had about twenty minutes before Will was supposed to get here, but she wanted to be ready to go. She changed out of her gray pantsuit and into pair of black skinny jeans and an off-the-shoulder pink top. Casual and comfortable but still dressy enough for a date. She was just swiping on a fresh coat of lipstick when her phone buzzed.

Beckham: Will's here in my office. Head over when ready.

She stared at the message. God, this was bizarre. She could write a whole chapter in her book about this moment.

She texted him back, took another minute or two to finish touching up her makeup, and then she headed out. When she stepped into Beckham's office, Will turned her way and smiled. "Hey."

She returned the smile. "Hi." Will looked downright dashing out of his tiger onesie. He'd worn dark jeans and a light-blue button-down shirt untucked. He'd rolled up the sleeves a little, exposing his well-muscled forearms and a stylish gold watch that caught the light. His whole vibe was casual but with a refined and expensive edge. She could see him making an argument in a courtroom and wooing jurors to his side.

He came over and gave her a quick peck on the cheek. "You look great."

"Thanks, you too," she said and then glanced at Beckham,

who was behind his desk, feet propped up on it and arms crossed, his vintage Pearl Jam T-shirt stretched along his chest.

Beckham gave her a mischievous look. "No one's going to tell me how great I look? I'm hurt."

Will snorted.

Eliza bit her lips together because frankly, Beckham did look hot. His T-shirt had ridden up a little above his jeans and she couldn't not look at the sliver of exposed skin.

"You ready to go?" Will asked. "I know I'm a little early. I had to drop something off to Mr. Ego over here."

"Yeah, I'm good," she said, looking back to Will and trying to get herself focused on this date.

Beckham lifted a hand. "Y'all have fun."

The words were casual and light, but Eliza detected a hint of something else there. Beckham wasn't as comfortable with this as he was pretending to be. There was a twinge of annoyance. But she wasn't going to read too much into it. If Beckham had been leaving with a date in front of her, she'd probably feel a little prickly about it, too.

They were only friends with benefits, but they were also human.

"Thanks, man," Will said. He put his hand lightly on Eliza's elbow to guide her out.

She glanced back once to tell Beckham bye, but he'd already dropped his feet to the floor and turned back to his computer. They'd been dismissed.

chapter **eighteen**

BECKHAM GLANCED AT THE CLOCK FOR THE FIRST TIME IN hours. He'd buried himself in his video-game project to get his mind off the way he'd felt watching Will and Eliza together. The irritation that had bubbled up, the jealousy, had been like acid in his mouth. He refused to let that shit eat at him. Eliza going out with Will was a good thing.

Tonight, Eliza had doubled down on her feelings about marriage. The wistful look she'd gotten on her face talking about Andi's relationship had been undeniable. Eliza wanted that for herself. The love story, the wedding, a guy who could give her the happily-ever-after—if there was such a thing. He had a hard time believing anyone could be truly happy trapped in something that took a set of lawyers and a pile of money to get extracted from.

He'd caught himself giving Eliza his speech about the origins of marriage and had spilled details about his family that he never shared with anyone. He never slipped up like that, but afterward he'd realized why he'd done it. He'd wanted to win her to his side. He'd wanted her to realize that marriage was a trap and drop her search for 'til death do us part altogether, to step outside the matrix and see it for what it was. He wanted her to get it, to get *him*.

He was such a dumbass. Awards could be given for how stupid he was being. He was making the same mistake he'd made years ago. Of course Eliza wasn't going to magically change her entire worldview just because they'd had a great night in bed. He was delusional if he thought that would make any difference at all. He was only a temporary fix for her. A stopgap. Will and guys like Will were the endgame.

He couldn't be.

The clock was inching past eleven, and Beckham's brain was too tired to keep working on the project. He closed out the screen and then opened his browser. Like he did every few months, he typed in a web address he had memorized.

The page for his dad's church came up, the happy shining faces of his parents and the rest of his family filling the screen. His dad looked cocky and proud, dark hair slicked back, blue eyes sparkling. His mom had that beatific smile of hers that made her look like a mannequin, and then his six siblings—one boy, five girls—were lined up in front of his parents by age order. He hadn't even met his youngest sister. She'd been born after he'd left.

That gave him a pang. He missed his brother and sisters, but even if he tried to reach out to them, they wouldn't be allowed to speak to him. Daniel, his older brother, would probably outright threaten him if he tried to come near. Beckham's siblings all believed what they'd been told about him. That he was a lost cause, a threat to their pristine lifestyle, a nasty smudge on all that shine they projected to their followers.

They probably also blamed him for the TV show's cancellation, which had happened a year after he'd left. *Seven on Sunday* didn't work as well when the Laketon brood had become six. They no longer had their black sheep to keep the drama going and the audience interested. His dad still broadcast his sermons and gave updates on the church's web channel, but that audience was limited to those who believed his father's teachings—a niche group at best.

On the website, the donation box was prominent in the top corner of the screen—money always at the heart of anything his dad did. Even with the show canceled, there were still options for donations, branded merchandise, a book about raising kids, a set of children's bedtime story books, homeschooling curriculums, and public appearance requests with speaking fees listed. Beckham clicked on the Sign In link and typed in the fake credentials he used to get in to the protected pages. He'd set up this system for the family originally when they'd seen that the only thing that got him excited was technology, and though they'd changed up their security features, he could still get in without even blinking.

He got to the screen he needed. Through that, he could access his dad's files, the drafts of his sermons, the business plans, even the secret emails he sent to one of the church widows, a woman he'd been having an affair with for a number of years. Beckham liked knowing he had dirt on his dad if he ever needed it to protect himself.

Even though he knew what he'd find, he clicked on the Family Profiles page. His name was still on there—Matthew Joseph Laketon—but the photo was of him at seventeen, dark-haired and not smiling. They couldn't erase him. *Seven on Sunday* had followed his family throughout his childhood, so his existence couldn't be denied. But they'd done their best to minimize his presence. Under his name it said *Age: 25 Occupation: Unknown About: Some of God's children fall off the path. The Laketons are praying that their son Matthew will atone for the things he has done and seek God's love and forgiveness.*

"Don't hold your breath," Beckham muttered.

The last thing under his name was *Spouse: Jessica Laketon.*

Seeing that added line of text always made his stomach turn, brought him back to those horrible few months when that label had been real. Of course, in the church, it was *still* real. The annulment in the Arizona state files made no difference to the church. Divorce wasn't an option in his dad's permutation of religion.

Jess's name was a hyperlink to her entry in the church member directory. Beckham clicked on it. Her profile came up, her photo updated, her occupation listed as *homeschool aide*. He stared at the photo, trying to find a hint of the feisty girl he'd first met when he was fifteen, but the blond woman on the page looked like a stranger.

Every time he went in and checked, he hoped that she wouldn't still be there, that she'd left the church. But he knew that the more years that went by, the more unlikely it was that she'd ever leave. Jess had been raised in the church and bought into what his dad was selling—or, more likely, was too scared to question it. Eternal damnation was quite a threat. Or maybe they'd convinced her that because of the leaked video, she'd be seen as nothing but a slut in the outside world. That the church was the only place that would have her. Whatever the reason was, she stayed.

Beckham clicked deeper into her file and then opened another screen alongside it. Within a few seconds, he'd transferred money from an anonymous account into hers. He'd never forgive himself for what he'd done to Jess, the hurt he'd caused her, how publicly he'd destroyed her reputation, but sending her money every few months so that she didn't have to depend on the church or someone else made him at least feel like he was doing *something*.

Jess knew where the money was coming from, and she was the only one from his old life whom he'd sent his contact info to. He wanted her to know she had a friend in the outside world that she could come to if she wanted to bail. But she'd never reached out or even acknowledged that she'd received the money.

He closed out the windows and shut down his computer,

weariness pressing down on him. He rubbed his hands over his face, trying and failing to wipe away his grim mood, and then packed up his stuff. WorkAround was mostly empty as he made his way through the bottom floor, but the clicking keyboards of those who rented the hot desks at night provided the soundtrack.

Most were people starting their second shift of the day, coming here to put time into a side hustle after a long day at a pay-the-bills job. The coffee bar was still open, a perk of working in a twenty-four-hour operation. His stomach rumbled, reminding him he'd skipped dinner, but he didn't want any of the prepackaged offerings they had at night. He'd roll through a drive-thru on the way home—get some proper late-night food.

The air was cool but humid when he stepped into the parking garage, the weather trying to figure out if it wanted to be winter or spring, and the scent of car exhaust filled his nose. He was digging in his backpack for his keys when a flash of pink caught his eye. He paused and turned his head in that direction. A few yards away, Eliza was standing near her car with Will. Her car door was open, Will was leaning his arm along the top, and they were both in profile as they talked, smiles on their faces.

Beckham was in the shadow of the stairwell where they wouldn't notice him, but he shrank back a step to make sure he'd be fully out of view. He still could see them through the space between two concrete columns. He knew he shouldn't be spying—*hello, creeper*—but he forced himself to watch. He needed to see this, to keep his head on straight.

Will laughed at something, his head dipping low and his shoulders shaking, the sound echoing in the cavernous space. Eliza put her hand on his arm, smiling at whatever the joke was, looking sexy as hell even in the washed-out glare of the garage's fluorescent lights. Will lifted his head.

Cold awareness went through Beckham.

He's going to kiss her. Beckham recognized Will's body language, how he was looking at her, the way he'd shifted the space between them. Beckham's hand tightened on the strap of his backpack.

Will dipped down.

....

He's going to kiss me. The thought hit Eliza with one hundred percent assurance. She could feel the air shift as Will leaned in a little closer. The date had been a lot of fun. Will was sharp and funny, easy to talk to. Handsome. She hadn't had such an enjoyable date in a really long time. A kiss seemed like the appropriate way to end it.

But for some reason, a little snap of hesitation went through her at the thought.

Beck.

She didn't know why he came into her head in that moment, but he did, and it threw her off. *No. Stop that.*

She couldn't feel guilty about Beckham. They weren't dating. She was supposed to be exploring things with other guys. That was the whole point of this. And the only way to test the chemistry with Will was to see how she felt if things got a little physical.

Will's hand went up, gently cupped the side of her neck, and he dipped down. His lips touched hers, a gentle press, one that left the option for more, but she found herself pulling away before it could go any further.

She rolled her lips together and glanced up, feeling uncharacteristically shy. "Thanks for a nice night."

Will smiled, seemingly unperturbed by her abrupt end to the kiss. "Me too. We should do it again."

"I'd like that," she said, meaning it, but also feeling a little off-kilter. Even though she believed in a woman's right to date around, to sleep with whomever she wanted, to not owe any guy any explanation about it if there was no commitment, she realized she'd never actually juggled multiple guys. Even when she wasn't in an official relationship, she'd always been a serial monogamist.

Her father had told her when she was young that her laser-like ability to focus on a goal was her superpower. But now she realized it'd also been how she'd handled her dating life. Singularly focused.

Right now it felt like the opposite of a superpower. It felt like a fatal flaw.

"I'll give you a call, okay?" Will said, stepping back and holding her door open.

"Sounds great." She lowered herself into her car. "Drive safe."

"You too." Will shut the door when she was safely inside. He headed off to his SUV and gave her a wave as he pulled out of the garage and drove off. Once he was out of sight, she leaned her head back and closed her eyes. Why did she feel so damn exhausted? It was just a date. A *good* date, at that. Shouldn't she feel energized? Hopeful?

She didn't know how long she'd been sitting there when a light knock on her window had her jumping. She yelped, her eyes flying open, and on autopilot, grabbed for her purse where she kept her pepper spray. But when she turned her head, she let out a breath. Beckham was peering in with an apologetic look on his face.

"Sorry," he mouthed.

She put her hand to her chest. "Jesus." She grabbed the door handle and opened the door. "What the hell, man? You scared the shit out of me."

"Sorry about that." He hiked his backpack higher on his shoulder. "I just thought I'd point out that dark parking garages late at night aren't the safest places for naps."

She swung her legs out, facing him. "I wasn't napping. I've only been here for…a few minutes. I was about to leave."

"Is everything okay?"

"Yeah, it's fine. Just a little tired." She adjusted the neckline of her top, the off-the-shoulder part getting a little too close to an off-the-body top.

He braced a hand on her car door, and his gaze swept over her as if checking to see if she was really okay. "How was the date?"

"Great!" she said quickly, her voice full of forced cheerleader pep. *Ready? O-kay! Date was great! Boy, it's late!* "Will's nice."

He nodded. "I know."

"He kissed me," she blurted out and then inwardly cringed. *Shut up.*

Beckham glanced away, eyes narrowing like he was looking at something in the distance. "I saw."

"You *saw*?" Heat filled her cheeks. "Stalk much?"

"Pure chance. I worked late and was about to head home." He looked back to her. "I'm glad y'all had a good time."

She stared up at him, something feeling off. The normal spark in his eyes wasn't there. No mischief, no smugness, not even a hint of pretentiousness. He just looked...flat. "Hey, are *you* okay?"

"Me?" He frowned. "Yeah, I'm fine. Just a little tired and a lot hungry. Got too caught up in a project and forgot to eat."

The words made sense, but her spidey sense didn't buy it. She'd been a therapist long enough to spot a dodge when she saw it. "Want to grab something at that late-night burger bar down the street?"

His brows arched. "Didn't you just get back from a dinner date?"

She smirked. "I did, but he took me to this really nice tapas place. Everything was one bite so, quantity wise, not so filling. Plus, I was nervous because—first dates—so I barely ate. I was going to pick up something on the way home. I could literally bury my face in a plate of fries right now."

Beckham chuckled, some of the humor coming back into his eyes. "Poor Will. Tried to impress you and left you starving."

"Don't you dare say anything. The one bites were delicious." She pinched her fingers together. "Just teeny tiny."

He laughed again. "All right, well then I'll happily take you up on the burger. Can I leave my backpack in your car?"

"Yep." She climbed out of the car and took his bag from him, tossed it in her back seat, and then grabbed her purse.

He cocked his head toward the exit to the street. "Come on. Let's find you something more substantial. Can't have you wasting away, Eli."

They headed out side by side, but when they got to the street and the green Walk sign started to blink, he grabbed her hand so they could hurry across. He didn't let go when they reached the other side.

She tried to ignore how that simple handhold felt more intense than her entire date night had.

Freaking hell. She wanted to pull that part of her psyche aside and give it a good talking-to. She could not, *would not*, develop a crush on an unavailable man, a dude who'd made it abundantly clear that he wasn't seeking something romantic. She was smarter than that. *She* was the person who counseled *other people* not to do those kinds of self-destructive things.

She slipped her hand out of his and balled it into a fist.

chapter **nineteen**

ELIZA GROANED AS SHE LEANED BACK IN THE BOOTH, HER mac-and-cheese-topped burger half-eaten and her fries mostly gone. "Okay, so maybe I overestimated how big of a burger I could take down. Or maybe I should've skipped the strawberry cheesecake shake."

Beckham sipped his own shake and then gave her a surely-you-can't-be-serious look. "But they're only on the menu one night a week. Skipping this cheesecake shake when available would be a cry for help. Why else would anyone do that?"

"True. It really was our duty to get them." She grabbed a napkin to clean the grease from her fingertips. "I've been meaning to try this place. My friend Hollyn reviewed it a while back and gave it good marks." She glanced around. The restaurant had originally been a diner and retained some of that retro-kitsch look with the black vinyl booth seating and the long counter at the back, but the new owners had turned it hip, lowering the lighting with Edison bulbs and painting the walls a deep forest green. And they'd elevated the diner favorites on the menu, keeping the prices affordable but the creations unique. "It's a cool vibe in here."

"Agreed." He jabbed his straw in his shake, stirring it. "Perfect for second dinner at midnight."

"Obviously." She glanced out the front windows to the dark street outside and then scanned the handful of other diners in the restaurant. Two silver-haired ladies from a few booths over were looking their way. A familiar image popped into her brain. "You know what it reminds me of?"

Beckham tipped his chin up in silent question as he bit a fry.

"*When Harry Met Sally*, the famous scene in the diner...or was it a deli?" She frowned. She'd been writing about the movie for her book but realized she hadn't seen it in a while. She needed to add it to her list to rewatch.

"Haven't seen it," Beckham said.

"Wait, seriously?"

He shrugged. "Nope. Have heard of it. It has a funny sex scene or something, right? But I haven't seen it."

She tilted her head, processing that. "How is that possible?"

"Remember what I said about my parents? I had to sneak in movies when I was growing up. If it wasn't PG *and* reviewed by them first, it was a no-go. Anything with cussing, sexual tension, nudity, or violence was out. So I had to be selective when I got the chance to watch something I wasn't supposed to. A rom-com wouldn't have been something I went through the trouble for, especially at that age." He grabbed a napkin and wiped his mouth. "I've watched a lot of things since, but I'm still playing catch-up on some pop culture stuff."

She stirred her straw in her almost empty shake, considering him. That was the second time he'd mentioned something about how strict his parents had been. She'd known from the start there was some issue there, an estrangement, but she got the feeling he was sharing things he normally kept to himself. She didn't push for more, knowing it could spook him, but part of her ached to know all the things about him.

"Well, it's a movie worth watching. But the famous scene you mentioned is Meg Ryan faking an orgasm in a restaurant after Billy Crystal basically says he'd know if a woman was faking." She smiled. "She sets out to prove him wrong."

He leaned back and stretched his arm along the booth seat. "Maybe I should've sought the movie out. Fifteen-year-old me probably would've really appreciated watching that scene."

"Meg Ryan nailed it," she said with a nod. "Plus, Carrie Fisher plays her friend, so you would've gotten a little Princess Leia fix, too."

"I'll add it to my list," he said, pushing his food to the side. "So, have you ever Meg Ryan-ed it?"

"Faked an orgasm in public?" she asked, a teasing note in her voice. "No, but I definitely wouldn't be above embarrassing myself in public if it meant I got to prove a know-it-all wrong like Sally did in that scene. I *really* like to be right."

He gave her a wry look. "We have that in common. But I meant, have you ever faked one in general?"

"Ah." She gave him a wouldn't-you-like-to-know look. "I didn't with you, if that's what you're asking."

"Eli," he said, leaning forward on his elbows. "That is *not* what I'm asking. Did I mention the howling? You kind of showed your cards with that. No poker face at all."

She playfully flipped him off and he laughed.

"Faked *with anyone*," he clarified.

She sipped the last of her shake and then shrugged. "Sure. Sometimes."

He frowned, clearly taken aback. "Really?"

"Don't look so shocked. Remember?" She pressed a finger to her chest. "Bad dating history."

A line appeared in his forehead, and she couldn't tell if he was confused or annoyed. "Yeah, but what's the point of doing that? Like why not say, *Hey, this isn't working, let's try something else?*

I would imagine most guys would want to know so they can make it better."

He made it sound so simple, but it wasn't. At least not for her. She stared at him as she sifted through possible answers in her head and then finally settled on the truth. "I don't know. I guess sometimes it's just...easier. Guys want to feel like they're good in bed. Most want to know that I've had an orgasm, too. But I can get really in my head sometimes, and once that happens, it makes it challenging to get to where I need to go. I can still enjoy the event without having the big finale, though. Plus, I know how to take care of myself if need be after they leave."

Beckham's frown had deepened. "That's bullshit, Eli."

She bristled, the previous humor of the conversation falling to pieces on the floor. "Not asking for your opinion, *Beck*."

"Sorry, I didn't mean it like that. I just mean...you shouldn't have to perform for the sake of protecting some guy's ego." He leaned back. "That really kind of screws you both. You don't get what you need, and he walks away thinking that what he did worked, which means he'll do it again. Sets you both up for failure and isn't fair to either side."

She released a breath, letting go of the righteous indignation that had been building. Great, yet another area where she'd been performing for someone else. Or maybe it hadn't been for the guy's sake at all. Maybe she just phoned it in sometimes because it was easier than digging deeper into why the sex wasn't working for her. The realization rankled. "I guess so."

"Believe me," he said, tone grim. "I've been on the other side of that equation and it fucking sucks."

Now it was her turn to be surprised. "Of someone faking it?"

"Yeah." He swirled his straw in his shake, a little muscle in his jaw twitching. "With my first girlfriend. I was seventeen and had no idea what the hell I was doing. It's not like someone had sat me down and given me any kind of sex talk beyond *Don't do it before you're married or you'll burn in hell* and *Its only purpose is to make babies*. So when we started having sex, I thought, *Great, this must be how it's done. I'm sure as hell enjoying it.* Turns out, she was hating every minute. Didn't tell me until much, much later after we'd slept together many more times."

Eliza gasped softly. "Oh wow. That's..."

"Yeah." He made a humorless sound. "She was only tolerating it to please me. Hadn't wanted to lose her virginity at all, in fact, but hadn't wanted to say no because she thought I'd break up with her." He glanced up. "I wouldn't have, for the record. I just thought she was on the same page with my screw-the-rules, let's-piss-off-our-parents rebellion. Not the case." His gaze looked faraway for a moment, his posture tense. "When I found out how she really felt, it made me feel like a monster, like a date rapist."

Eliza frowned. His tone of voice was breaking her heart a little. This wasn't some minor adolescent fumble. This was something that had left a mark on him. Those early sexual experiences could really impact a person if they went badly. She'd seen it time and again with her clients. "That sounds awful, Beck. But unless you're leaving stuff out of the story, that's not date rape or being a monster. Not to get therapisty but..."

He narrowed his eyes in warning.

"*But* the words we use to label things," she pressed on, "especially about ourselves and our experiences are really important. Can make something feel like a truth when it's really a funhouse-mirror reflection of it. So we have to be careful. What happened with your girlfriend sounds like an unfortunate situation due to bad communication between two kids who weren't prepared to have an adult relationship, not you trying to take advantage of someone."

He didn't answer for a moment, and she worried she'd gone

too far with her counselor-speak. It was something she was always on guard for with friends. But finally, he blew out a breath and ran a hand over the back of his head, a humorless smirk touching his lips. "Wow, how the hell did we end up talking about this? Midnight milkshakes with you are dangerous. Next we'll be analyzing my dreams."

She recognized a retreat when she saw it. She let him have it. "Well, for what it's worth, I promise I'll never fake with you." She gave him a little smile, hoping to bring the conversation back to a lighter, safer place for them both. "Not that I'd have to, based on the other night. But if I have an off night, I promise I'll tell you."

He stretched his arm along the back of the booth again, taking up space, a wicked look in his eyes. "If you have an off night, Eli, then you won't have to wait until I leave. I'll just stick around and watch you take care of yourself. Fun times will be had by all."

Her skin warmed, and she swallowed past the sudden parched state of her throat. She was glad they'd picked a booth out of earshot of anyone else. "Only if you afford the same invitation to me."

His dimple appeared, his lips hitching at one corner. "To watch me get off? That'd do it for you?"

"It wouldn't *not* do it for me," she said, working hard not to picture that scene in vivid erotic detail, Beckham wrapping his hand around himself, showing her how he gets himself off when alone. She didn't want to burn into ashes right there in the diner.

He smiled fully then, wolfish. "You're a super-fun friend, Eli."

She laughed. "Stop flirting. I have early appointments tomorrow and am already out way past my bedtime. I cannot be tempted tonight."

That wasn't entirely true. But really, she couldn't quite bring herself to go on a date, kiss *that* guy, and then go home with his friend the same night. No matter how enticing that sounded right now. This time with Beckham was starting to feel a little too...

everything. She needed to be careful. Not let the lines she'd drawn around this relationship get blurry.

He pointedly looked down at her plate and then back to her. "Don't worry. I know better than to proposition anyone who just put away *that* much food."

She let out a how-dare-you gasp and then threw a french fry at him.

He dodged it and laughed. "Kidding." He pulled out his wallet and dropped a few bills on the table. "Come on, let's get you back to your car."

"You don't have to pay," she said, reaching for her purse. "We're friends, remember? Friends split the check."

"Next time. I was the one who hadn't eaten and guilted you into dinner."

"You did not guilt me." She unzipped her purse. "But you pay every time. That adds up and—"

"Eli." He stood and put out his hand to help her up. "Put away your money. It's fine."

She zipped up her bag, consternation making her lips press together, and took his hand.

When she was standing in front of him, he gave her a patient look. "Are you worried you're going drain the poor twenty-five-year old's bank account?"

"I—" She huffed a breath and looped her purse over her shoulder, not knowing how to finish the sentence. She actually *did* worry about that, but when he put it that way, it sounded condescending and insulting.

"Can I tell you a little secret?" When she didn't answer, he went on. "I'm one of the best at what I do. You know what means?"

She crossed her arms in challenge. "That you're cocky?"

He leaned close to her ear. "That people pay me a lot of fucking money to do it. I may wear thrift-store T-shirts and drive a used car, but that's by choice. I can buy a lot of burgers, Eli. Give me another year or two, and I could probably buy the restaurant."

Her eyes widened as he straightened and looked down at her. "Oh."

He squeezed her shoulder. "So let me pay for your burger, all right? You can treat next time if you want."

She wet her lips, processing that. "Okay. Thanks."

He shrugged. "None needed."

They headed out into the cool evening and walked back to WorkAround, a comfortable silence falling between them as Eliza quietly processed the night. Before long, they were back in the parking garage. Their footsteps echoed. The lights hummed. Her heart quickened. When they reached her car, déjà vu hit her smack in the face. Not even two hours ago, she'd stood here with another guy in the same position.

Beckham opened her door for her, his body close enough for her to smell the sweet berry scent of the shake he'd had.

Was Beckham going to kiss her, too?

She had no idea what she wanted the answer to that question to be. Warring factions took up arms in her head. *No, we're just friends! Yes, but we're sleeping together! No, you've already kissed someone! Yes, but you're not committed to anyone and are a grown woman who can kiss whomever you want!*

The indecision left her frozen. Nerves filled her as he cupped her face and leaned down, but his lips landed on the top of her head instead of her lips. The contact sent a hot shiver through her.

"Text me when you get home," he said, leaning past her and grabbing his backpack from her seat. "So I know you made it safely."

She swallowed past the constriction in her throat. "Will do. Thanks again for the second dinner."

He looped his backpack over his shoulder. "Thanks for the company."

He gave her one last smile and then walked away—toward a perfectly practical Nissan Maxima. *I'm one of the best at what I do.*

An electric spark moved through her at the memory of how he'd said it, making her hyperaware of every inch of her body. *Dammit.* She got into her car and pushed the ignition to start it. If confidence in a guy was a turn-on for her, she should've gotten this feeling with Will. Will's whole vibe landed in that sweet spot where he was self-assured but not full of himself. But she hadn't felt that flutter with him like she had tonight with Beckham.

Beckham pushed her buttons. All. Of. Them.

The warring factions in her head put down their weapons and started sewing white flags.

She was in so much damn trouble.

chapter **twenty**

BECKHAM WAS IN SO MUCH DAMN TROUBLE. WHAT WAS *wrong* with him? For being someone whose job was privacy and security, he couldn't seem to keep his mouth shut around Eliza. All that careful work he'd done since escaping his old life, all those privacy layers he'd put in place, all the alternate history he'd concocted for his new existence were apparently obliterated from his mind when he got into a conversation with Eliza. And he couldn't even blame booze for his loose lips.

Eliza simply gave him that look that said she really wanted to *understand* him, and then he...couldn't fucking lie. She was like truth serum. He'd never told anyone in his new life about being forbidden from mainstream movies or about his relationship with Jess or how he'd felt like he'd violated Jess even though she'd been saying yes—the way that memory still sat on his chest like an elephant.

Maybe it was because Eliza was a therapist. She'd been trained to draw out people's secrets and shames, to channel empathy and safety. But he suspected it was more than that. Something about her, the way she was so open with him, made him want to give her the same back. He didn't want to be the guy lying to her—about anything. He wanted to tell her who he was. He wanted to not have to be careful about what he said. He wanted to tell her…that it'd bothered him to see her kiss Will tonight.

He groaned aloud as he closed the door to his condo behind him. He resisted the urge to bang his head against it. This was not how this thing with Eliza was supposed to work. This was supposed to be fun and casual. He should not be feeling…what was this? Jealousy? Angst? Oh God, was this *angst*? *Fucking hell.* She was turning him into a teenager again.

He tossed his bag next to the couch and headed to his bedroom. Maybe he was just exhausted. He needed sleep. This would make sense when he was more clearheaded.

He went into his bathroom, stripped down to his boxers, and went through his nightly routine as quickly as possible. When he climbed into bed a few minutes later, he reached for the remote so he could watch TV for a little while, but his phone buzzed on the nightstand. He left the remote alone and grabbed his phone instead.

Eli: Made it home. U?

He propped a pillow behind his head and thumb-typed.

Beckham: Yep. Just got in bed.
Eli: Me too. Tonight was fun.

He hesitated. Did she mean with him or on her date with Will?

Eli: Though I think you implied that I'm a pig at one point, so I'm still stewing over that. 😔

He chuckled softly and hit the call button.

As soon as she answered, he said, "Don't put words in my

mouth, Eli. All I meant was sex is a little like swimming. You might want to wait an hour after you eat before you jump in."

She laughed, the sound quiet, almost husky at this time of night. "Noted."

He leaned his head back against his pillow. "Well, I know you're tired…"

"I'm not that tired," she said. "I mean, I am, but I'm not one of those people who can come home and go straight to sleep. I'll probably read something for a while."

"Oh." He thought of that stack of colorful romance novels he'd seen on her bedside table. "What'cha gonna read?"

"Dickens," she said resolutely. "Or maybe Proust."

Proust? He burst into a laugh. "And you're a damn liar. I saw your stack, Eli. It's going to be something with a shirtless guy on the cover, isn't it?"

"Those really are the best books," she said, a smile in her voice. "So probably. And not all romances have shirtless guys, for the record. Sometimes there are illustrations. Or a duke in a cravat, if you're really lucky."

Her easy tone sent a ripple of warmth through him. He tapped his fingers along his breastbone, not wanting to let her go quite yet. "Read one to me?"

She made a sound that was half laugh, half disbelief. "What? So you can tease me about them? Come on, Beck."

"No, not to tease. I'm honestly curious," he said, meaning it. He wanted to know what Eliza liked. "Plus, I'm not sleepy yet either. Hearing about some dashing duke sweeping away some sexy peasant girl sounds soothing."

She snorted. "Have fantasies about dashing dukes?"

"Doesn't everyone?"

"True," she conceded. "But let me see if I have a historical in this stack. Most of these are contemporaries."

"Read whichever kind you want," he said, enormously pleased she was playing along. He liked that Eliza didn't take herself too seriously and seemed to be game for most anything. He never would've expected a therapist to have such a playful, silly side.

He could hear her shifting around on her end, the squeak of her mattress. "Ooh, here's one. Not a duke and a peasant girl but a viscount and a lady."

"I don't know..." he said, dragging out the words like he was really debating. "A viscount sounds like a discounted duke. I may need a hero with a higher rank than that, but we'll see if he can win me over."

"The viscount is highly insulted, I'll have you know." She paused. "You really want me to read to you?"

He nestled back against his pillow, his hand sliding to his stomach, the sound of her voice cozy against his ear. "Only if you're game."

Sheets rustled on her end, a soft *swoosh, swoosh*. "Yeah, okay. But I might feel a little weird reading aloud to an empty room."

"Hold on, how about this?" He grabbed another pillow and arranged it next to him, then he propped up his phone against it and hit another button.

He wasn't sure if she'd answer, but it was only a second before the screen changed and the video call kicked in. Eliza's face appeared on the screen, her hair loose and her face clean of makeup, a little shine to it like she'd rubbed cream on it. His gut tightened, the sight of her in bed bringing back visceral memories.

"Well, hi," she said. "Long time no see."

He smiled. "Maybe this will make it less awkward? No more empty room."

"Maybe." She bit her lip, considering him, and the screen bounced a little. "Hold on."

She sat up, the video jumping and blurring, and then situated her phone off to the side, probably setting it against a pillow like he had. Now he could see her at an angle in the lamplight of her room.

"Does that work?" she asked. "Can you hear me okay?"

"Yeah, and the view ain't bad either."

She was sitting up, propped against her headboard with pillows, her knees pulled up under the covers and a book in her hands. Her T-shirt looked to be a man's white undershirt, the fabric thin and revealing the shadows of what was beneath.

The front of his boxers twitched. Welp, so much for any hope of him concentrating on the book she was going to read to him.

She gave him a sly smile. "I'm not the one with my shirt off. You're downright indecent over there."

"Want me to put a shirt on, Eli?" he teased. "To not offend your delicate sensibilities?"

"Of course not. Romance story-time and a shirtless guy go well together." She shrugged. "I mean, it's not a cravat, but…it'll do."

He laughed. "Next time I'll be better prepared."

"All right. Here we go," she said, lifting the book and opening it. She cleared her throat. "*London, 1820. Sebastian St. Clair had never detested the taste of tea so much. From behind her teacup, the mother of the four unmarried Lancaster sisters stared at him with the predatory smile of a tiger, a tiger fixated on getting all of her young swiftly out of the den and off her hands.*

"*The woman had prattled on for ten minutes about how skilled the third sister was at the pianoforte, as if musical skill were the missing factor that would send Sebastian rushing to make a proposal. He wished to tell Lady Lancaster that he was there only because his own mother had insisted he accept the invitation and that he had absolutely no intention of wedding any of her offspring. But the gossip that would stir in the ton would not be worth the headache.*"

Beckham settled in, watching Eliza as she read, her voice smooth and soft.

"So he drank tea and ate the offered biscuits. And smiled politely. And tried not to count the minutes. Beatrix, the oldest of the brood, a girl who had once been his childhood friend, had not said more than a few polite words thus far. But the way Bea was looking at him, the little smile that curved her lips, made him think she was thoroughly enjoying his torture. He wanted to throw a biscuit at her."

Beckham chuckled. "Uh-oh. Biscuit-throwing is definitely foreplay."

"One hundred percent," Eliza agreed. "And looks like we're going to have a feisty heroine on our hands."

"Excellent. Feisty is hot."

"As are grumpy viscounts," she said with a nod.

She went back to reading, and he tucked his arm behind his head, the tight tension he'd been carrying inside him all day loosening. This was...*nice.* He'd never had a problem sleeping alone. He preferred it that way—liked his space, liked the clear boundaries of parting ways after sex. But lying there with Eliza, even in a virtual way, felt cozy and comfortable and *sexy.* He wished he could just reach through the phone and pull her next to him, curl her back against his front, let her read while he could feel her pressed against him.

His boxers twitched again, his cock hardening at the thought, the images. He shifted a little to hide the evidence, and a soft grunt escaped him as the fabric brushed across his body. He cleared his throat, trying to cover it.

Eliza stopped reading, too perceptive to miss it. "You okay?"

"I'm good."

She flattened the open book against her chest and gave him a look. "Are you trying to stop yourself from making jokes about my romance novels?"

He laughed. "No, Eli."

She tilted her head in a skeptical-prosecuting-attorney kind of way. "Then what?"

"If you must know, my lady," he said, feigning a British accent to go with their reading material, "I had an impure thought about you in that bed and got...stiff. So I'm trying to be a proper gentleman and be discreet about it."

Her gaze flicked downward even though he doubted she could see much in the low light of his room. "Oh."

"Sorry about that." He flicked his hand at the screen. "Go on."

But she didn't pick up the book. Her teeth pressed into her bottom lip. "Can I see?"

"See—" His blood heated. *See.* She wanted to see that he'd gotten hard. This wasn't what he'd intended by telling her, but he wasn't hating this turn of events. "Think I'm lying?"

She shrugged a shoulder, the move coy. "You could be."

He reached out and switched on his lamp to the low setting, bathing the room in warm light, and then rolled fully onto his back again. He dragged the covers down, maybe taking a little more time than necessary, and watched Eliza watch him. When he moved the covers down to his thighs, revealing the now fully tented boxers, Eliza let out a sharp little breath.

"Not lying," she said, her voice carrying a little grit.

He wrapped his hand around himself, fabric pressing against sensitive skin, and a shudder went through him. *Hell.* His own hand shouldn't feel so erotic, but knowing Eliza was watching seemed to turn his hand into hers in his mind. "Not lying. I have no self-control apparently. Viscounts really do it for me."

She laughed, a low, musical sound. "To hell with viscounts. *This* is really doing it for me."

The words were like static electricity against his skin. "Yeah?"

She nodded.

He gave himself a lazy stroke. "Show me."

She rolled her lips together and put the book aside, jostling the phone. "I want to," she said when she turned back to the screen. "Like I *really* want to, and I feel like I can trust you, but having been burned by a video recently, I don't think I'd be able to relax enough to do anything R-rated on camera."

The words rang clear, cutting through the haze in his brain. Fucking hell, she was right. The privacy expert was about to have video phone sex on an unsecured connection. Being around Eliza turned him stupid sometimes. He dropped his hand to his side. "You're right. I wasn't thinking."

"You're thinking with something," she teased.

He snorted.

She considered him for a moment, her eyes narrowing. "Turn off your video and put your phone next to you."

The words caught him off guard. "What?"

"Put it next to you. I'll do that, too." The video turned off. "We can lie next to each other and…listen."

"Oh." *Oh.* "You sure?"

"Turn off your camera," she said, voice soft. "And take off those boxers."

A rush of pure, hungry heat went through him. He reached out and clicked off his camera. "You're my new favorite friend, Eli. Have I told you that?"

"Ditto," she said, her voice drifting into his bedroom. "Now it's your turn to tell me a story. Tell me exactly what you're doing…"

He reached down. "I'm sliding my boxers off." He balled up the fabric and tossed it to the floor and then opened his bedside table's drawer. "I'm getting what I need to make things nice and slick." He grabbed the little bottle of lube he kept in there, and then stretched out on the bed, taking himself in his hand and closing his eyes. "And I'm thinking of you."

Lately, that was all he'd been doing.

Her breathing got a little more audible on her end, and he could tell she was getting undressed too, could picture how unbelievably sexy she would look putting her hands on herself, showing him exactly where she most liked to be touched. He'd never wished more that teleportation was possible.

"Tell me what you're doing, Eli..." he said, his own breath hitching as he tightened his grip.

And she did. In wonderful, vivid detail until every part of him was ready to explode.

"Tell me what I'd see right now, Beck..." she whispered after he'd made a pained sound.

"I'm sliding my fist faster now," he said, voice strained. "Squeezing tighter, getting slippery from more than lube. I'm imagining you here. Your hands on me. Your mouth..."

"Tell me everything you're doing," she said, her words barely a whisper now, her breathing turning choppy. "Please don't stop."

He replied with filthy words and detailed description, losing himself to the sounds of her pleasure, because he couldn't tell her the real answer to that question. *What am I doing?*

Getting too close.

Enjoying this too much.

Breaking every damn rule in my book.

This thing with Eliza was supposed to be fun, and it *was*, but it wasn't supposed to feel like this. It wasn't supposed to matter.

chapter **twenty-one**

Field Notes and Book Research

Analog ways to meet potential dates:

Join a club that matches an interest you have but that also
allows for conversation with others.

Create your own NoPho group.

Go old-school and go out with friends to a bar.

Join a class to learn a new skill. Pick something that would
attract both genders.

Ask friends if they know anyone you should meet.

Dig deeper into your own interests and find the places where
people with those interests gather.

Say yes to getting together with a group of your coworkers
after work.

Go to the conferences for your profession, attend the mixers.

~~Befriend a hot coworker, then sleep with him for months and
forget you were supposed to be doing an experiment at
all.~~

"Ugh." Eliza scratched out what she'd written and stared at the words, her mind turning, turning, turning like a wind turbine.

Her book had come to a screeching halt over the last few weeks, and she could see why. She was back to giving advice that she wasn't taking herself. This six-month experiment was supposed to be about going analog and experiencing the dating world that way. She was supposed to be putting herself out there, meeting new people, going on dates. She pulled out her day planner and flipped through the pages.

The proof of her failure to do so was right in front of her. She hadn't been on a date since Valentine's Day. Not an official one at least. She couldn't call what she and Beckham were doing— watching movies, eating together, and hooking up—dates. That wasn't a label allowed in their whatever-they-were-doing arrangement. But those nights had certainly filled up most of her calendar. Every night that they were together, she drew a little B in the bottom corner of that day in her planner. She told herself she was keeping the record for research purposes, but now she didn't like what she was seeing.

It was obvious when the shift had happened. The night she had read to Beckham on the phone had changed things. The B's started showing up two and three times a week after that. She hadn't realized it at the time, but weeks later, she could see that it had been the start of her journey down a really dangerous path.

After that ridiculously hot phone sex that she still couldn't believe she'd had, they'd stayed on the phone talking—about life, about movies, about random things—until deep into the night. She'd woken up the next morning with her phone dead on the bed next to her, having fallen asleep without ending the call.

She wasn't experienced at this kind of friends-with-benefits setup, but things like all-night phone conversations had seemed… not so casual. Thoughts of Beckham began invading her mind during the quiet parts of her day—and every night. She found herself texting him when she had a random idea or thought just to hear what he had to say on the topic. And he'd come over to her place at least twice a week. They'd fallen into an easy rhythm of hanging out and hooking up. And even though he never stayed over, it never felt like a booty call. It felt like...a relationship.

Yet, when Valentine's Day rolled around, Beckham had said he had to work, and she'd found herself on a date with Will. The dinner had been great. The conversation lively. But when he'd tried to kiss her, she'd given him her cheek. She'd wanted to call Beckham.

This was not how this was supposed to work.

She couldn't write her book because she wasn't doing what she was supposed to be doing. This book wasn't about how to develop a crush on your unavailable friend. That would be a super-shitty book. With a terrible ending.

And this week was driving home the problem with a heavy hammer. When Beckham was coming over all the time, she could distract herself from the fact that she had wandered way off course from her plan. Who needed to think about books and projects and long-term life goals when she had a smoking-hot friend who could screw her up against the wall of her kitchen and make her forget her own name? Time with him had become some version of a drug.

But like a drug, when it was taken away, she felt the loss on all levels.

She stared at the current week in her day planner. There were no B's to be found. Beckham had been out on a remote job this week, working on some computer breach at a company in Baton Rouge. So there'd been no visits. No hookups. They'd exchanged a phone call and a few texts, but he'd been busy and it'd just been casual conversation. Beckham fell back into that easy, friendly vibe with seemingly no problem navigating blurry lines. He seemed to be adept at turning the intimacy dial up and down with ease.

Eliza, on the other hand, had a dial that was getting stuck on high volume. The reality of that had hit her this morning. She'd walked into work, looked at his locked door, and her chest had hurt. She realized with dread that she freaking *missed* him. Not like a casual *Oh, I wish he was around to hang out.* Not even a physical ache of missing him in her bed. But like really, really missing him. In a way that felt bone deep. She possibly was…pining.

And *that* was a big problem.

When she'd agreed to this arrangement with Beckham, it'd seemed like a good solution—a practical one, too. A no-strings-attached fun affair while she went on dates with guys with real partner potential. But that was not what this had turned into for her. Her brain apparently only had a set amount of designated space for male companionship, and right now that space was filled up to the rafters with Beckham Carter. No other guy had a chance at wedging the door open and getting into her head, much less her bed or her heart. She'd already put off Will twice since Valentine's Day, claiming schedule conflicts when he'd tried to set up another date.

And she definitely hadn't done a damn thing on this list of suggestions she'd made for her book.

She sighed, ripped out the page from her notebook, and tossed it toward the trash can, missing it completely. She leaned back in her desk chair, cold nausea moving through her. She knew the answer. Hated it. But knew it.

She spent her days trying to help her clients make the healthy choice, not the easy choice. There was a clear healthy choice in this situation.

She was going to have to end this thing with Beckham.

Self-defeating behavior was not her jam, and this was feeling like a classic case of it. If her goal was a loving, long-term romantic relationship, catching the feels for a guy who didn't believe in that was asking for pain. She needed a healthy dating diet, and Beckham was all chocolate fudge sundaes and whipped cream—delicious but destined to lead to trouble in the long run. She needed to make space for men who wanted something more instead of indulging with a guy who'd told her from the start he couldn't *be* the guy.

She was her young client falling for the married college professor. She was that middle school version of herself getting a crush on a guy who had no interest in being her boyfriend.

She couldn't let herself fall in love with Beckham. It would hurt too much.

After a fortifying breath and an internal pep talk, she picked up her phone, and texted him.

Eliza: U busy?

He responded within a minute.

Beckham: Wrapped up a few minutes ago. What's up?
Eliza: Need to chat

Three dots appeared, then disappeared. Her phone rang.

She startled at the noise and put the phone to her ear. "Hey."

"Hey," he said, a murmur of conversation and clicking keyboards in the background. "One sec. I'm walking out of the office and am about to be in my car."

The sounds changed—wind, then his car door opening and closing, the engine coming to life. The radio blasted.

"Sonofabitch," he said, turning the blaring music down. "All right, sorry about that. Everything okay?"

Eliza turned in her chair, looking out her office window, wondering if she should've waited to call when she had her thoughts more put together. That was another problem with Beckham—she was impulsive around him. Messy. "Um, I'm okay."

"*She said in the least convincing tone ever,*" he said in a movie narrator's voice. "Come on, Eli, what's up?"

"I like you too much." *What? No.* That wasn't what she'd meant to say. "I mean…" *Fuuuuck.*

Beckham chuckled a little, but it was a confused chuckle. "Uh, I think you're neat, too?"

She cringed and pressed her fingers to the spot between her eyes, trying to regain her composure. "No, I mean, I've been thinking, since you left and, uh, I've had some space to think about it, and I think our…arrangement is, um, turning out to be counterproductive."

Brilliant speech, Eli. Your college education was really worth that price tag.

There was a pause on his end. "Counterproductive."

She swallowed hard. "Yes."

He cleared his throat. "Is this your way of telling me you want to sleep with Will so now we have to stop? Because I'm a big boy. You can just tell me that straight up if you guys are getting to that point."

"What? No. I don't want to sleep with Will at all," she said, too quickly—*way, way* too quickly.

"Wait." Another pause. "You don't?"

God. She tipped her head back against the chair, realizing the confession was true. "No. Will's great, but…I'm not interested in him that way. It's just a…friend vibe."

"Oh." Beckham seemed to be processing that. "Okay, then… what do you mean 'counterproductive' then? It's been a long day and I might not be tracking fully here."

She wet her lips, nerves surfacing again, and straightened her spine, trying to find her courage. She often told her clients to act the feeling first even if they weren't feeling it yet. Then the emotion would often follow the action. Act calm. Calmness would come. Act confident. Confidence would show up. *Act confident.*

"This friends-with-benefits thing was an experiment for me, and I'm finding that I'm not cut out for casual. Turns out I can't really separate the physical stuff from the feelings stuff, and well, I'm starting to like you too much. I've missed you this week. And that's a problem. It's making me not want to go find other people to date—which is pretty much the opposite of what this experiment was supposed to accomplish."

"You don't want to date other people," he stated, his tone unreadable.

"No. Have you met you? You're at my house a few nights a week and are kind of distracting," she said, attempting to lighten the conversation. "Makes it hard to consider other options. Go on an awkward date with a stranger, or hang out and get naked with the hot friend I'm already sleeping with? No contest."

He was quiet for a long moment, and her face grew warm. She hated, *hated* being this vulnerable. She was the therapist, dammit, the cool-under-pressure one. Right now she felt like her preteen self about to get crushed by her crush.

"Why do you like me?" he asked finally.

"Oh my God," she said, throwing a hand up in exasperation. "Seriously, Beck? I lay out an embarrassing I-can't-handle-the-arrangement declaration and you want me to stroke your ego?"

He made a frustrated sound. "It's not about my ego. I just... want to know what you mean."

She groaned and got up from her desk chair so she could pace off the anxious energy coursing through her. "I mean that I thought this would be about sex—and that part has been great, really great—but the other part is the problematic part."

"The other part?"

"Yes, there's like this...comfort level I feel when I'm with you.

Like all these years I've been going on these dates, and no matter the guy, there's a layer of pretense there—on both sides. It always feels like I'm starring in a play I didn't audition for. Like after dates with Will, I look back on the night and think, *Who was that woman on the date with him? It certainly wasn't me.* But with you, maybe because we started out how we did, I don't have the urge to put a shine on myself. I'm just the me I am when I'm with my friends. Except unlike with my other friends, I'm sleeping with you."

"And that's a problem," he said, tone flat.

"Yes. Because I love my friends," she said, putting her hand to her chest. "But I'm not allowed to love the friend I'm sleeping with. Because then it's no longer a friendship—it's a heartbreak waiting to happen. I have to stop this before it gets to that point. I'm not a masochist. And I shouldn't be missing you like this. It's a sign. A bad one."

He was quiet for a long moment, and she started to wonder if the call had dropped, but then his voice cut through the silence. "What are you doing tonight?"

His words startled her. "What?"

"Are you going out? Home? What?"

She rubbed her forehead, a headache brewing. "Home."

"We shouldn't have this conversation over the phone," he said, sounding a little rushed. "I'm heading back to the city and have to stop at home first, but I can be at your place by seven. I'll bring food. Is that okay?"

Awkward conversation in person, even better. *Hurrah.* But she found herself nodding. She was a grown woman. They should talk about it in person. "All right."

"Okay. It's a plan then. And Eliza," he said softly.

"Yeah?"

"I've missed you, too."

Then he hung up.

chapter **twenty-two**

MABEL BOUNCED AROUND BECKHAM'S FEET AS HE CARRIED a bag of takeout and a carrier full of needy cat through Eliza's front door. "Whoa, there," he said, being careful not to step on the overexcited pup. Her tail was wagging so hard, he feared she'd tip herself over with the momentum. Trent meowed from his carrier. "I'd take this welcome as a compliment," he told Mabel, "but I think you're much more excited about the shrimp po'boys and Trent than you are about seeing me."

Mabel whined, confirming his suspicion, and nudged her nose against the bag, declaring po'boys more interesting than cat.

Eliza reached down to take Mabel's collar before the dog took off with their dinner. "That bag does smell exceptionally tasty," she said. "I can't blame her. Mabel, sit." She nodded toward the carrier. "Um, what's up with Trent?"

Beckham bumped the door shut with his foot as Mabel reluctantly sat. "Long story. Do you mind? He can stay in the carrier. I picked him up from the cat sitter and brought him home, but after being gone a week, he...would not let me leave again. The yowling he did was like a knife to the heart. So I took him to the pet store for treats and supplies, then brought him here. He's a needy cat. Sorry."

Eliza laughed a little and stroked Mabel's head. "It's fine. You can let him out if you want. Mabel is friendly with cats."

"I'm not sure Trent will be friendly to Mabel, but we can see how they do. I'd also need to get that bag of kitty litter out of the car. Do you have a box or something I could put some in? I don't want Trent christening your house."

"Yeah, I have a cardboard box that could work. Go ahead and grab the litter. Just meet me in the kitchen," she said, taking the carrier and bag of food from him. "If we eat at the counter, Mabel won't be able to bother us too much. And I can give her some dinner to distract her."

Beckham hurried back out to the car, grabbing the bag of litter, and then headed to the kitchen. Mabel was giving Trent's carrier a curious sniff when he walked in. Trent meowed, but Beckham couldn't tell if it was a *Hey, what's up, doggo?* meow or a *Get the hell out of my face, canine scum* meow. Mabel didn't seem to be deterred either way.

Eliza went to the pantry to get Mabel's food while Beckham unloaded the sandwiches, the mayo already leaking through the butcher paper they were wrapped in. He grabbed napkins and two bottles of water from the fridge, setting everything up in front of the barstools at her counter. Then he fetched the Tabasco sauce from her cabinet by the stove. He realized how comfortable he'd gotten navigating her space over the last few weeks. He'd never known where any other woman he'd slept with kept her hot sauce.

No wonder she wanted to talk.

"Who's hungry?" Eliza said in an animated voice as she shook Mabel's bowl at her. "Who's a pretty girl?"

Mabel hurried over and whined, hopping up on her back paws. Beckham smiled, the warmth on Eliza's face hard to look away from. No matter how tonight turned out, he was happy he'd said yes to Eliza on Christmas. She and Mabel were a match meant to be. And he and Trent…well, they'd come to an understanding in their stalker/stalkee relationship—the understanding being that Beckham allowed himself to be stalked.

Eliza made Mabel sit and then put her bowl of food in front of her. The dog buried her face in it, sending the bowl skidding along as she ate. Eliza shook her head, smiling, and then disappeared into her laundry room. When she came back out, she handed him a low-sided cardboard box. "Will this work? You can let Trent out and see how he does, if you want."

"Should be good. Thanks." He poured some litter into the box, set it by her back door, and then washed his hands. Beckham leaned down and unlatched the cat carrier. "Want to be social, dude?"

One lone paw stretched out of the carrier as if testing the air temperature and wind speed. After a long moment, Trent sauntered out, tail flicking with judgment. Mabel hurried over to see what new friend was here, and Beckham stood guard, ready to intervene. But to his surprise, Trent allowed Mabel a sniff, and then he flopped on his side to start cleaning himself. Mabel quickly lost interest and went back to her food.

"Well then," Eliza said with a shrug, "I guess they're both equally unimpressed with each other."

"So it seems."

She looked over to him, her smile no longer there. "Thanks for picking up food."

"No problem. Thanks for letting me come over." He sat on one of the stools, hating the stiff turn in the conversation.

She stayed on the other side of the counter, her hands gripping the edge. "Yes, just what I wanted after my awkward confession on the phone. A face-to-face come-to-Jesus meeting."

His brows lifted. "You could've said no."

She wrinkled her nose. "I'm trying to be a grown-up."

The distasteful way she'd said it almost made him smile, but he kept his reaction in check. "For what it's worth, I think you're one of the most grown-up people I've ever met."

She snorted. "Sure. Let's press that age-difference button for some added fun." She made a pointed motion with her index finger. "Poke. Poke."

"I'm not talking about that. You know I don't give a shit about our age difference." He leaned his forearms on the counter, trying to find the right words. "To be honest, I'm in fucking awe about how straightforward you are. That phone call today?"

She narrowed her eyes, as if bracing herself.

"It was the work of a stone-cold, badass grown-up. You don't play games or tiptoe around stuff. I don't have to guess at what you're thinking." He cleared his throat. "It's…one of my favorite things about you."

Her suspicious expression softened. "Oh."

"So I came here to do the same. To return the favor."

She tipped her head a little. "Of being straightforward?"

"Yeah. And talking about what you brought up on the phone." He patted the stool next to him. "But let's eat first. Neither of us are good when we're hungry."

She gave him a wary look but then glanced down at the po'boys. "All right. Those do look good and I'm starving."

He smirked. "Come on. We'll leave the adult conversation for after dinner. For now, let me tell you what Trent did to my cat sitter…"

He went on to tell her about the hell Trent had put the cat sitter through, rounding it out with the finale of Trent knocking the poor woman's bowl of Froot Loops into her lap and then freaking out at the noise and climbing—and tearing down—her new curtains. He and Eliza were both laughing, and Eliza was near tears by the time he finished his story and they'd polished off their food.

Eliza dabbed at the corners of her eyes. "That poor girl is going to have to find a new profession. She's going to have nightmares."

"Yeah, she's never going to watch Trent again for sure," Beckham said, grinning and balling up the butcher paper so he could throw it away. "I think it's all part of Trent's evil plan to always be at my side every moment of the day."

Eliza looked to Trent, who'd commandeered the dog bed in the corner of the kitchen. "And he looks so innocent."

Beckham tossed the trash in the garbage can. "Smoke and mirrors."

A few beats of silence passed between them, the distraction of Trent fading and the reason Beckham was here roaring back to life with a stench of awkwardness.

"So…" she said.

"So." He took a breath and walked back to the counter, grabbing the bag he'd brought the sandwiches in. He handed it to her. "I brought this."

"Dessert?"

He shook his head.

She peeked into the bag, brow knitted. "Oh." She pulled out his special edition *The Rise of Skywalker* DVD and then gave him a curious look. "I thought this was have-a-serious-conversation night, not movie night."

He rocked back on his heels, his thumbs hooked in his jean pockets. "I was hoping the two might not be mutually exclusive."

"Meaning?"

"Meaning, on the phone, you told me we have to stop the physical part of our relationship." Even saying the words left a sour taste in his mouth and a vague feeling of panic rippling through him. Not being able to touch her was going to be a special kind of torture, but he also understood and was trying to do the right thing. The grown-up thing. He'd known that part was temporary.

They'd stated that from the start. "But does that also mean you don't want to be friends anymore?"

"I—" Her lips clamped back together like she didn't know what to say.

"Because if that's what you need, I understand, but like I said on the phone, I missed you, too, Eli." He leaned back against her counter, wanting to be honest but also walking a fine line. "These last few months have been more fun than I've had in a long time. And I'm not just talking about the sex, though that has obviously been fantastic. I like just hanging out with you. If no one's bothered to tell you lately, you're kind of a kick-ass human."

She blinked, her lips parting slightly.

"You're smart as hell, keep me on my toes, make me laugh, have great taste in movies and food. And…" He cleared his throat. "You talked about how on dates, you can't be yourself? Well, I feel like that with…pretty much everyone on some level."

She frowned, her fingers curling around the DVD case.

"But with you, I find myself telling you things I haven't told my other friends. I…*trust you* in this weird, almost instinctual way. Maybe it's the therapist thing, but I think it's more than that." He ran a hand over the back of his head, trying to find the right words. "I think we…get each other and that's not an easy thing to find. So I'm not real excited to just walk away from you. Not having you in my life would kind of suck." He grimaced. "No, not kind of. It would absolutely suck. A lot. You've basically become my favorite person. I want to call you first. For everything."

Eliza stared at him, her teeth digging into her bottom lip. Then her eyes went shiny.

"Oh shit," he said, pushing off the counter and going over to her. "What'd I say? I'm sorry, I—"

She shook her head and stood, her fingers coming up to press against his lips. "Shut up, Beck."

He tried to say her name, but she shook her head again, silencing him.

"Just listen for a minute," she said, her voice soft. "You said I'm a grown-up, and I think you're right. I've always wanted to make the right choices, the mature ones. I wanted to know *how to do life the correct way*. Like there was some official test with an answer key. That's probably why I became a therapist. Part of me thought I'd get to learn all the secret rules, avoid the pain of mistakes."

He lifted his brows in response. She lowered her hand, but he could tell she wasn't done.

"I've had my life plan written down since I was ten. I've known what I wanted to be, where I wanted to live, when I wanted to get married, what my husband should be like, how many kids I wanted to have, down to their gender and names. I've vision-boarded the ever-loving hell out of my life." She shook her head, a look of chagrin on her face. "I've imagined being the recipient of romantic declarations and grand gestures."

He frowned.

"But what you just said, about me being a friend, was the most romantic thing anyone has said to me in my life," she stated flatly.

The words hit him in the gut. "Eli…"

"Sometimes I get so frustrated with my clients. What they've been doing isn't working, yet they keep doing it, the path too well worn to step off of. But that's what I'm doing, isn't it?" She put her hand to her chest. "I like you. You like me. We miss each other when we're apart. We're having all this fun, are cool not sleeping with other people. I've been feeling happier than I have in a long time, but you don't fit into my life plan. You're not"—she made air quotes—"'marriage material.' You aren't a neat and tidy pin on that vision board of mine. So I called you to end it today even though I'm actually...happy being with you. How much sense does that make?"

His chest felt tight. Part of him wished he could give her everything she wanted, but even the words *marriage material* sent anxiety welling up in him, that trapped feeling he'd felt in his previous marriage pinging through him, that weight of responsibility, of expectation, how easily he'd crumbled beneath it. How completely he'd failed.

When his whole life had blown up, when he'd ruined things for Jess so publicly, he'd thought marriage would fix it. He thought it was the answer, but he'd learned it only made things worse.

"I should know from what happened with my parents that no one is guaranteed a future," she went on. "My mom and dad thought they had time. They'd worked all their life to get to retirement and only got a few months to enjoy it." She snapped her fingers. "*Boom.* One drunk driver and they were gone. All of their future, gone." She waved a hand in front of her. "We can make all these plans, but all we get is today. That's the only thing we can count on. So I can spend my days trying to find a hypothetical someone for my future, or I can spend my *right nows* with someone who makes me happy *today*." She looked up at him, a vulnerability there. "I've really liked my *right nows* since I've met you. I don't want this to be over either. I just got scared today."

The words were what he wanted to hear. He'd felt shredded when he'd gotten off the phone with her earlier today. He didn't want to end this thing either. But what she'd said also made him wary. He put his hands on her shoulders. "Eli, I don't want you to give up what you want to accommodate me. I know I'm a little—or a lot—fucked up about relationships. What you want is normal. I'm the one with the issue. You don't have to bend yourself to that."

She stepped into his space and put her hands on his chest. "Maybe normal is overrated."

He let his arms wrap around her, but his body remained tense.

"If you honestly want to be with me *exclusively*," she said, "I don't need a label beyond that. This whole analog experiment has been about dropping the performance. Labeling a relationship is its own kind of performance. It's for the sake of other people so they can categorize your situation, so that we can check a relationship status on our Facebook. I don't need to put on that show. We can just be...together without a label. Friends. Lovers. Both. Exist in the in-between space."

Something tangled inside him unwound a little, his heart picking up speed. *The in-between space.* With Eliza. It sounded like everything he wanted wrapped up and handed to him as a gift. "You're truly okay with that?"

She nodded, her gaze meeting his. "Right now, I am. If that changes in the future, I'll let you know. All I want is a promise that you're not sleeping with other people. I do need that."

"You already had that," he said softly. "That part's easy."

A slow smile lifted her lips. "I know. I'm super good in bed."

He laughed and slid his arms down to her waist, a buoyant feeling filling him. "You're not wrong."

"So?" She looped her arms around his neck.

He touched his forehead to hers. "So I guess we're watching Skywalker rise tonight?"

"The outlook is good."

Yes. Yes, it is. For so many things. He leaned down to kiss her, their mouths at first meeting in a soft press, but soon her lips were parting and his hands were sliding beneath the hem of her T-shirt, the connection turning heated and hungry. She moaned in to his mouth and he broke away from the kiss. "Or maybe the movie can wait."

chapter **twenty-three**

"HELL YES, IT CAN WAIT," ELIZA SAID, HER ARMS AROUND Beckham's neck. "Or as Yoda would say, *Wait, it can.*"

Beckham laughed and cupped her face. "Hot *and* nerdy. How am I supposed to resist?"

She could say the same to him. Earlier, she'd called him to end this. She'd told herself it was the wise decision, the mature one. But the minute he'd started telling her all those things he liked about her, all those wonderful things that no guy had ever said to her, she'd been done for. Maybe wise was overrated. She was tired of waiting for the fairy tale. She just wanted to be happy right now.

"You're not supposed to resist," she said with a smile. "That's kind of the point."

"Agreed." He slid his hands behind her thighs and lifted her off her feet. She yelped in surprise. Mabel barked. Trent ignored them. "Come on, let's not traumatize the kids."

She laughed and he carried her into her bedroom, kicking the door shut behind them. He flipped a switch by the door, which turned on her bedside lamp. Her bed was unmade and she had a bra hanging over the back of a chair. She hadn't expected to have bedroom company, but at the moment, she didn't care about the state of disarray. Beckham wasn't looking at her messy bedroom. He was looking only at her, and the promise in his eyes sent shivers straight to her toes.

He set her on her feet and tugged off her T-shirt. She wiggled out of her jeans, leaving her in just a pair of black cotton panties and a pink bra.

He tossed her T-shirt aside and guided the two of them to the bed, his gaze tracking over her. He propped himself up on his elbow next to her and drew a fingertip along her sternum, through the valley between her breasts, and then lower to the triangle of fabric between her legs. The tip of his finger traced lazily down the center of her and then circled the little bundle of nerves that was now growing very, very aware. "I've spent my whole week imagining you just like this. Since I left, I haven't been able to think about much else." He traced the edge of her panties, the crease of her thigh. "I was tempted every night to call you from the hotel and have a repeat of the night you read to me. The way you sounded when you came that night...I can hear it still. Makes me hard every time I think about it."

She shivered beneath his touch and the words. "I never knew phone sex could be like that," she confessed. "I thought it'd be weird or cheesy but...you made me a believer. You have a sex voice."

He chuckled, the sound warm and husky. "A sex voice?"

She turned her head to meet his gaze. He had a lazy, languid expression on his face, like he could tease her all night. "Yeah, when you get turned on and you switch from friend mode to...this mode, your voice turns into...I don't know, warm syrup on a hot biscuit. And I'm the biscuit."

His eyelids went hooded and he teased a finger along the band of her panties. "I like that image. Sounds delicious. And sweet."

She opened her mouth to respond, but before she could, he

shifted his body down and off the foot of the bed. He kneeled there and grabbed her behind the knees, gently dragging her toward him. Before she could gather her thoughts, he'd tugged her panties off, exposing her to the cool air of the bedroom.

"Beckham," she whispered, not sure if she was asking a question or begging for the obvious answer.

"Shh," he said, the warm air of his breath cascading over her. He slid his palm beneath her thigh, bending her leg and exposing her fully to him. "I've been waiting all week to hear you make those sounds you make and to get your taste on my tongue."

Her belly clenched in anticipation, but there was nothing she could do to prepare for that jolt of electric bliss when Beckham put his mouth on her. *Oh. God.* Unlike the wham-bam-thank-you-ma'am hookups she'd had over the past few years, Beckham Carter was never in a hurry. He didn't try to get her to orgasm as quickly as possible so he could get on with the activities. No, he liked exploring, taking his sweet time. His tongue traced her curves and his lips pressed kisses along the tender flesh, sucking gently, tasting every bit of her body and then making these pleased, humming sounds that vibrated through her like a low-grade earthquake.

She was a volcano, ready to explode. *Boom.* Done. There would only be a black, singed outline of her body on the mattress by the end of this.

He dragged his tongue along her clit and slid two fingers inside her, knowing exactly where she liked to be touched most. Her heels dug into the mattress, and her back lifted like she was trying out for a new version of *The Exorcist*. She let out a sharp whimper and grabbed a fistful of blanket, afraid she'd launch herself right off the bed. *The power of Beckham compels you.*

"That's the sound," Beckham said, slowly moving his fingers inside her, and then he gently bit the inside of her thigh. "Fucking gorgeous, Eli. I could spend all night right here, tasting you, listening to you."

"I won't survive the night," she gasped, arching again when he curled his fingers a little. "Spontaneous combustion exists."

He pressed his lips against her pubic bone and she could feel him smile against her. He lifted his head and drew his tongue along the crease of her leg, making her nipples tighten against her bra. "Ask me for what you want, Eli, and maybe I'll give it to you."

"You want me to beg?" She lifted her head to look down at him, intending to be sassy, to be stern, but seeing him there, mouth inches above her, desire in his eyes, she lost all train of thought. She reached out and grabbed two fistfuls of his hair. Heat flared in his gaze. "Please, Beck. Make me come."

He didn't smile or joke or tease this time. Instead he held the eye contact and let her guide him down, her grip on his hair tightening. She couldn't look away from those blue-green eyes as he put his mouth on her.

The sensation rocketed up her legs and made her stomach tighten, but she didn't look away. She watched him watching her. The feel of his lips and tongue and fingers drove her to the brink, but what put her over the edge was that connection—the unapologetic eye lock—that held her in thrall. She'd never felt such a deeply visceral attraction to someone, a magnetic pull that she'd been fighting since day one with Beckham, like her atoms were inexorably drawn to his. Her whole body seemed to hum like a power line. Then he curved his fingers just right, and all thought blinked out of her mind.

Her orgasm crashed over her like hard rain, waking up every inch of her with sensation. Her head tipped back and her eyes finally closed. She made noises he'd tease her about later, but she didn't care. For now, she just let all that feeling soak into her skin.

When she was still panting, Beckham pulled away. She blinked her eyes open in the dim lamp light, catching sight of him tugging off his T-shirt and then unzipping his jeans. He smiled down at her, his hair a complete mess, his tattooed arms like art. "Full confession...I'm taking really dirty mental pictures of this moment right now."

"Are you now?" She smiled back and reached behind herself to unhook her bra. She slipped it off and tossed it aside. "Might as well get full-frontal mental photos."

"Agreed."

"But you definitely have too many clothes on."

"My deepest apologies." He shucked his jeans and boxers, and her gaze dipped lower, relishing the view. He took himself in his hand, gripping himself with that sexy casual way he had. "Taking your own photos?"

"Hell yes, I am. But I'd rather take a topographical survey. Come 'ere." She reached out and took his hand, then guided him onto the bed with her. He braced himself above her, and she curled her hand around his neck, bringing him in for a kiss. He tasted of salt and sex and her, and the feel of him hard against her thigh only stoked the embers again.

She lifted her hips against him, wanting, needing him, but he put a steadying hand on her hip. He broke the kiss and looked down at her. "Where are the condoms you said you had? I forgot to replace the last one in my wallet. I didn't...plan for this tonight."

She wet her lips, staring up at him. "When was the last time you were tested?"

"Um." It seemed to take him a second to register the question. "I had a checkup around Thanksgiving, and I've been with no one except you since, but—"

"I'm good too," she said. "Tested since my last and have an IUD. But it's up to you. The condoms are in my drawer."

He brushed her hair away from her face, a line appearing

between his brows. "Give me a sec." He rolled away and got a condom out of her drawer. After rolling it on, he came back to her and pressed a kiss to her mouth. "I trust you. I just...would rather use one."

"No problem," she said, meaning it. She smiled up at him, drawing him against her body. "Where were we?"

His smile was slow and sexy. "I believe we were right here." He dipped his hand between them, finding the place where she was slick and aching for him, and he coaxed her back up the hill as they kissed and explored each other, taking their time, knowing there was no rush.

When he finally pushed deep inside her, she knew she'd made the right decision tonight. All she could think about was this man in this moment. She was living in the now.

She'd worry about the future another day.

A while later, they were lying next to each other under the covers, curled up, sapped of energy, and debating whether they wanted to try to make it through the movie.

"We could always watch it another night," Beckham said with a yawn. "Or take a nap first."

"Mmm-hmmm," she murmured, curling deeper into the crook of his arm. "Naps are good."

Something scratched against the door.

Then there was a meow.

"Uh-oh," Beckham said.

Eliza lifted her head. "I think we have company."

"I've got it." Beckham slipped from beneath the covers and headed to the door.

Eliza sat up, pulling the sheets over herself and enjoying the view of Beckham's bare backside.

He opened the door and laughed. "Well, hello. Guess you two became friends."

Mabel bounded in past him and then jumped onto the bed. Trent sauntered in and hopped up on the chair where her bra was hanging. He gave it a cursory sniff and then batted it with his paw.

Beckham turned, smirking. "Sure, come on in, you guys. Don't wait 'til we're decent or anything."

Mabel trotted along the bed and licked Eliza's face. She laughed and gently nudged the dog away. "Wow, no boundaries, either of you. Mabel, down. You know you're not supposed to be up here."

Mabel plopped down atop the covers, tongue lolling out.

"Welp, guess sexy cuddling time is over," Beckham said, humor in his voice. He grabbed his boxers and pulled them on. "They must want to watch the movie, too."

"Far be it from us to deny them movie night." Eliza glanced at her TV. "Want to watch in here?"

"Sure. I'll grab the movie."

Eliza tugged on a T-shirt and panties as Beckham got everything set up and then they both slipped back under the covers. But less than an hour into the movie, Eliza heard a soft snore next to her. She turned, finding Beckham with his eyes closed and his chest rising and falling with deep breaths. Trent was curled on the pillow next to him, pressed against the top of Beckham's head.

She propped herself on her elbow to look at the two of them, wanting to brush the hair out of Beckham's eyes, knowing she should wake him up, but she couldn't bring herself to do it. They both looked so peaceful.

But the night had been a roller-coaster ride and her own adrenaline hadn't worn off fully yet. Nervous energy was making her restless, and there was no way she could fall asleep right now. She grabbed the remote, lowered the volume a bit, and then gingerly got out of bed.

She padded into the kitchen, got a glass of water, and then sat down at her desk with her laptop. She shuffled papers out of the way to make room, peeked over her shoulder, and then opened a fresh document.

Untitled Book Because Titles Are Hard
By Eliza Catalano

Chapter 8
The "Oprah Is a Badass" Consideration

When I was in graduate school and brainstorming what my research project should be for my master's thesis, one of the hardest first steps was knowing the right question to ask. What specifically did I want to know? Until I could pin that down, I couldn't fashion a study to measure it.

With this life experiment, I'm starting to wonder if I'm asking the wrong question. Conceivably, I'm asking, how does one find long-lasting love in the modern world without the aid of the internet? But really, it's much more basic than that. At the root, I went into this looking for the traditional happily-ever-after—love, then marriage. That's the desired result. But maybe I'm missing a more important question. The *why*.

Why is this the goal I'm seeking? Why has marriage become the brass ring for me? My friends-with-benefits guy is staunchly anti-marriage. When he first laid out his arguments to me, I won't lie, I rolled my eyes and chalked it up to a guy wanting to get laid without the bother of a commitment. But lately, I've been thinking more about it. Why did I feel so defensive when he took a shot at matrimony?

Is it simply because that's what I've been taught—by my

parents, by society, by the movies? Is it because I think that marriage offers some guarantee that the relationship will last? Even if I ignored the divorce rate, I have miserable couples who come into my practice every week to prove that guarantee false. No, the more I think about it, the more I wonder if the heart of this is that I haven't felt like *enough* on my own.

Which gets me to the real question: Why can't I be a badass like Oprah or Goldie Hawn? Those two women have found love but have purposely held on to their unmarried status. Together with their partners but independent of the label. Strong and confident women who have successful careers and life partners. They and their partners choose *every day* to stay together. There's something, well, *romantic* about that, isn't there?

I'm not going to apologize for wanting love in my life. Love and belonging are right there in Maslow's hierarchy of needs, so I know I'm not alone in that desire. But perhaps, marriage is more about the performance of it all for me.

I'm learning through this going off-line process that I've fixated on my outward-facing persona more than I care to admit. I wanted to have those Instagram pics showing off the elaborate wedding proposal my boyfriend pulled off. I wanted to flash the ring at the camera. I wanted to have those smiling, just-hitched photos. But why? To prove to others I'm worthy of love? To prove I'm capable of counseling other people about their relationships? To be envied?

I'm not liking my answers to those questions. Self-examination is ugly, y'all. Necessary but ugly. It's time to figure out what I really want.

And maybe what I want is *him*. Labels, be damned.

chapter **twenty-four**

BECKHAM AWOKE WITH A START, COMING OUT OF A DREAM where he'd been falling. He grabbed a fistful of sheets to ground himself, his heartbeat pounding in his ears.

He blinked in the darkness, trying to clear his head and make sense of his surroundings. Something warm shifted against his head. That part was familiar. Trent had a bad habit of sleeping on Beckham's pillow with him. But everything else felt off. The scent was different, the sounds. His eyesight adjusted slowly, the dark breaking just a little, and then awareness dawned. *Eli.* He was at Eliza's place. In her bed.

Shit.

He'd fallen asleep. He turned his head. Eliza was facing him, lying on her side, her hand tucked under her cheek, her breathing slow and steady. The sight stalled him for a second. Goddamn, she was beautiful. She looked so peaceful and tousled in the best way. He had the urge to reach out and touch her, to trace the curves of her face with his fingertip, to kiss her eyelids, but he didn't want to wake her. He lifted his head gingerly, working hard not to jostle her, and peered at the clock on her side of the bed.

6:17 a.m.

It was morning. *Morning.* He'd slept over.

He hadn't done that with anyone since he'd been married to Jess. He had a rule. No overnights—hard stop. Sleepovers made things too blurry. They crossed the just-friends line in a big way. There was nothing more intimate than sharing morning breath. He let his head fall back to the pillow, his thoughts whirling. *Okay, it's fine. Breathe. Not something to freak out about.*

He was in new but not necessarily dangerous territory. He and Eliza had been clear and honest with each other. Last night, she'd come over to his side of seeing things. They were going to keep this going without pressure or labels. They were both happy being with each other right now and that was what mattered. Sleeping over didn't change anything. In fact, maybe it was a rule he could break with her. He could trust Eliza. And fuck, he'd missed her while he was in Baton Rouge. He was glad to be next to her now instead of alone in his own bed or that hotel. But it still felt...foreign.

Trent stretched and hopped off the bed, apparently sensing that Beckham was awake. Beckham rubbed a hand over his face and tried to settle back down. But his brain started going and he realized it was a lost cause. Plus, Trent would probably be angling for breakfast and would get noisy if denied.

After one more glance at Eliza to make sure she was sleeping soundly, he eased the covers off himself and quietly climbed out of the bed, careful not to bounce the mattress. Eliza murmured in her sleep but otherwise didn't move.

He let out a breath and found his clothes in the dark, tugging them on, then quietly headed out of the room. He wasn't going to bail—that would be a dick move—but he couldn't lie there for hours with his thoughts circling like a buzzard. No thanks.

He closed her door, made a pit stop in her guest bathroom, blessedly finding some mouthwash, and then headed into the kitchen. He found her coffee supplies and got a pot going, and then he headed out to his car to get a can of cat food from the pet-store bag. He set out food and water for Trent and then poked around in Eliza's fridge and pantry. Making breakfast would give him something to concentrate on.

When he'd left home, he hadn't known how to cook much of anything. In his family, the women were taught the domestic stuff, not the boys. And when he'd gotten married, Jess had shared that belief, that she should cook for him. The thought made his stomach turn now because at the time, he'd thought, well, obviously the wife should be the one who cooks.

He'd worked hard to deprogram himself from his upbringing, but sometimes he still worried that there were misguided beliefs buried in his subconscious somewhere. He was constantly on guard for that. One way he'd tackled the domestic one was to make sure he knew how to cook some simple things for himself. Bingeing episodes of *America's Test Kitchen* had helped him in that quest, and then Khuyen had given him a few lessons once Beckham had the basics down.

Eliza had a bag of frozen hash browns and the rest of the ingredients he needed to make a hash-brown casserole. He put the hash browns out to thaw, set the oven to preheat, and started gathering what he needed. He had a little trouble finding her baking dish, but soon he had everything ready to go. He mixed everything up and popped it into the oven.

Trent hopped up on a little desk Eliza had in the corner of the room and gave Beckham a questioning look. He walked over and scratched the top of Trent's head. "I know, buddy. I didn't mean for us to stay the night."

Trent ducked his head into the rub, seemingly willing to forgive the transgression as long as the petting continued.

"And you really shouldn't be up here on Eli's stuff." He gave Trent one last scratch behind the ear and then patted his side. "Come on, dude. Get down."

Trent went reluctantly, and when he jumped, he sent a file folder sliding off the desk and papers skidding across the floor.

"You see," Beckham said with a sigh. "Look what you've done now."

Trent sauntered off, tail in the air, as if to say, *That mess is your problem. Clean it up, peasant.*

Beckham crouched down to gather the papers, doing his best to keep them unwrinkled. He'd tucked most back into the folder, but one page had escaped under her desk. He reached for it and shook off a dust bunny. He wasn't trying to look at what was on the page but a line caught his eye: *The* When Harry Met Sally *Dilemma.*

He frowned, his conversation from the diner with Eliza coming into his head, and scanned the top of the page.

Untitled Book Because Titles Are Hard
By Eliza Catalano

Chapter 4
The *When Harry Met Sally* Dilemma

"What the hell?" he said under his breath. He stood up and begin reading. At first, he was confused, and then awareness begin to dawn, a sinking feeling filling him.

Recently, however, as I dropped the online dating and instituted the three-dates-before-intimacy rule that I mentioned in the previous chapter, this friends-with-benefits option has taken on a different light. A friend of mine, one who's helping me with this project, mentioned the possibility early on—that we could hook up as friends if we ever wanted to. At first, it seemed like a ludicrous idea. Why would I sleep with someone who wasn't a possible long-term partner when my very project is about finding a real relationship?

Then we had a movie night...

An icy, sharp feeling filled him, frost moving through his veins. He wanted to disbelieve what he was seeing, but as he read more, the truth was staring him in the face. Eliza was writing a book about her experiment—and about *him*. And not in a private journal kind of way but in a going-to-show-it-to-the-public way. He tried to breathe through the anger, to think. This was an old doc, the chapter referencing a night from early on. Maybe she'd stopped when things got more involved between them.

He eyed her laptop, and without evaluating the ethics of it, he opened it. Her lock screen came up, asking for the password, but it only took him a minute to get past the barrier. The screen opened up to her last document.

The "Oprah Is a Badass" Consideration

His eyes skimmed the first few lines and then clicked into the document info.

Last saved 3:12 a.m.

This morning.

"What. The. Fuck?"

They'd had this great night, had opened up to each other, made relationship-type decisions. Had been building something. And right after they'd fucked, she'd gotten up to write all about it *in her book*?

The betrayal was a metallic taste on his tongue, everything going bitter and getting colored in completely different shades. She'd told him she wouldn't use this experiment as a show. He'd told her he wasn't down for helping her with that, but here it was in black and white. This was...a stunt. This whole thing. What they were doing. *He* was a stunt. Reading about their first movie night had made him sick to his stomach, old buttons being jabbed. He couldn't even bear to look at what she'd written about last night. Had she rated him on his goddamned bedroom skills?

Flashbacks to the video of him and Jess going viral flashed through his mind, and all the feelings came rushing back. That crushing feeling of his privacy being violated, the trauma of such personal details of his life and body out there for public consumption, the public derision. People commenting on him like he was some character from a TV show and not a human being. When this ended between him and Eliza, would she write about that, too? That he was good for sex but not much else? Tell the world how he let her down? Use him as an example of yet another man who wouldn't commit?

He stared at her screen, wishing he wasn't seeing what he was seeing. Last night, he'd finally let himself believe that maybe, maybe he could have something good with Eliza, that they were on the same page, that maybe he could feel safe with someone, but...

"Morning, sunshine."

He looked up, startled. He had no idea how long he'd been standing there, but the scent of roasting onion was drifting from the oven.

Eliza was in the doorway in just a long T-shirt and panties. She crossed her arms and smiled his way. "Is that breakfast I smell? How you found anything to cook in here is a wonder."

He didn't answer.

"Beck?" A little line appeared between her brows. "Everything okay?"

He forced himself to keep his voice calm. He picked up a page from her desk. "Trent knocked over your papers."

"Oh." Her gaze flicked to the pages he was holding and then

to her open laptop. He could see when she processed that the screen was on. "You opened my computer?"

His jaw flexed. "I hacked into it actually."

"You *what*?"

He lifted the page in his hand. "You're writing a fucking book, Eliza."

The words came out like an arrow—sharp, pointed.

She stepped into the kitchen, her arms dropping to her sides, a look of mild panic on her face. "I—"

"About us. About what we're doing." He threw the page on the desk. "How long after we fucked last night did you wait before coming in here to write all about it?"

She winced. "It's not like that. It's not... I was going to tell you when and if there was something worth telling. It's just...a draft, ideas, me processing my thoughts. I know I said I wouldn't blog about it or whatever, but you don't get a say in whether I write a book or not. My career is my mine and—"

"I'm *in it*," he said, voice hardening. "Private details about what we've done together. I didn't agree to that. We made a deal."

"I'm not using your name," she said, her words rushed.

He scoffed. "Oh, right, that's a real guarantee of privacy." He slammed her laptop closed. "You know what happens if you get a book deal and this gets published? You know how long it would take some armchair internet sleuth to deduce who this guy you worked next door to is? Come on, Eliza. It'd take five minutes."

"Okay, I get that. I'm sorry about that part." She stepped closer but then halted. "But would that be that big of a deal? I mean, if people knew it was you I was with? I've said nothing bad about you."

He made a sound of disbelief and put his hands out to his sides. "*Have you met me?*"

She winced.

"I have no social media or internet presence. I'm part of a group that has parties without phones," he said. "Have you ever considered that I protect my privacy for a reason? That it might be vitally important to me?"

She frowned as if no, that thought really hadn't occurred to her. "I thought it was just because of what you see at your job. Is there something else?" Her eyes widened a little. "Oh shit, are you hiding from the law or something?"

He shook his head and ran a hand over his face, feeling really, really tired all of a sudden. "You know, part of me wondered why you agreed to this. Why last night you were all of a sudden okay with me not being open to marriage or kids, why you changed course on what kind of guy you wanted in your life." He looked at her, the door that had opened for her inside him now slamming shut. "But now I get it. It's material. *I'm* material. This is just some kind of fucked-up experiment. A way to get a book deal and some attention and maybe get laid every now and then, too."

She reared back like he'd hit her, hurt flashing in her eyes. "Are you being serious? You think I'm with you as an act?"

His fists clenched at his sides. "Sure looks that way. It all makes sense now. Why else would you agree to this?"

"Beck," she said, exasperation in her voice. "Yesterday, I called you to break it off. What good would that have been for the book?"

"A nice dramatic chapter."

"Oh, come on," she said, anger leaking into her voice now. "I get that you're upset—and yes, I should've told you—but do you think I'd put myself through this for a damn book?"

"Put yourself through this," he said flatly. "Sorry it's been such a trial."

"You don't get it, do you?" she said, lobbing the words at him like a missile. "I've turned *my whole plan* upside down because of you. Look at how stupid I'm being. You're twenty-five and have no interest in pursuing something long-term. If it were one of my clients telling me this story, I'd tell her to run. *I know better* than this. But I put myself out there last night anyway, *knowing* you're going to break my heart, *knowing* that I already feel too much for you. But doing it anyway because—"

"Because it makes for a good story," he said, a bitter edge in his voice.

Her fists balled, her eyes getting shiny, and she looked away. "No. Because I'm falling in love with you, and I thought maybe it'd be better to have that experience in my life, even if it's brief, than never feeling like that for anyone ever. Because at least then I'll know how it feels to get that excited just to simply be around someone, to feel that fire in my chest. Because I've never felt with anyone else what I feel with you."

I'm falling in love with you. Her words tore at him with claws, but his anger was too hot, too fresh, to accept them. "Guess I'm fulfilling the role you assigned me then. This will make a great entry in the book. How the younger guy who can't commit let you down."

The vulnerable look on her face disappeared in a flash, a hardness coming into her still teary eyes. "I didn't assign you that role, Beckham. You gave yourself that label because it keeps you safe. You've convinced yourself that you're *so* alternative. That it's philosophical for you." She swiped roughly at her cheek where a tear had escaped. "Oh, you don't believe in marriage or kids because blah, blah, blah. You know, I bought that for a while, thought maybe there were some genuine reasons you felt that way, but that's not it, is it? At the end of the day, you're just like any other dude who wants the benefit of having a woman around but not the hard, emotional work of a genuine relationship. You don't want to actually put out effort for it. You're not edgy, Beckham. You're just immature and scared."

Angry heat rushed through him, shades of his last fight with Jess surfacing, her words echoing. *Be a man. Be a man and take care of me.*

Eliza flicked her hand toward her desk. "And no, I shouldn't have written about you without your permission. I'm genuinely sorry about that. But we could've talked about it, hashed it out, addressed the issue like adults. Instead, you hack my goddamned computer, get mean, and pick a fight, which means you want an out. You slept on it and changed your mind about what you said last night and are looking for a reason to justify backing out. Well,"—she swept her arm out in front of her—"don't let me stop you on your way out the door. I deserve to be with someone who will give me the benefit of the doubt, who will ask questions before accusing me of things. I was willing to bend a lot to be with you, but I'm not bending on that. I deserve more than that."

What he heard was *I deserve more than you.* He couldn't agree with her more. He'd been in over his head with Eliza from the start. He'd been fooling himself to think they could find some happy spot in the middle. *Live in the space between*—what a joke.

"Yeah, I guess you do. And I deserve someone who doesn't see me as a fun project to write about," he said. "That's all I've been this whole time, isn't it?"

She opened her mouth, but he beat her to it.

"You know why you don't know my reasons behind why I don't want marriage and a family?"

She crossed her arms as he stepped closer.

He bent down and met her gaze. "Because *you never really wanted to know.* You think you're falling in love with me?" He shook his head, straightening. "You don't even *know* me. The therapist, the woman who knows all the ways to get someone to open up, didn't push *at all* because you'd already created the image of who I was in your head, the role I would play in your story, and you didn't want anything to mess with that narrative. You liked the *idea* of me. The twentysomething commitment-phobe is such a neat, easy stereotype. That's all I ever really was to you—a project."

"Beckham."

"You ever considered that it's you who's scared?" he asked. "I bet every date you've gone on, you've already decided who the guy was by the end of it and how he would let you down. You expect people to disappoint you. To leave you."

Her eyes shone with tears even though her stance stayed closed and angry.

"And if they don't, you push them away first. You tried to get rid of me last night." He pointed at her desk. "And you wrote up an insurance policy just in case. Because you're smart, Eliza. And you knew *exactly* how I'd feel about that book. You wrote our end from the start, guaranteeing the demise not just of our relationship but of our friendship. That way you can prove you're right. People always let you down or leave you. The guys you've dated. Your parents. You're the victim. Unlucky in love and life. That's the story you hang your hat on."

Tears tracked down both her cheeks now, but her jaw was clenched and her arms were crossed so tight, her knuckles were white.

Seeing her like that made his chest hurt, but he needed to get the words out. "I don't believe in marriage because I've already had one that failed spectacularly."

A look of shock crossed her face.

"But you're the one who's actually scared of it." He stepped around her and scooped up Trent, tucking him under one arm and grabbing the cat carrier with the other. He turned to her. "Why else would you have connected so fast with someone like me? Why would I be so appealing? If you really feel how you say you feel about me, then you don't want what you think you want. And if you *do* really want that, then the only reason you were with me was for a snarky, *aren't men the worst?* story to tell in your book."

"Beck," she said finally, her voice raw.

"Which one is it, Eliza?"

She shook her head, tears flowing now. "I...don't know."

"Yeah, neither do I," he said, exhaustion filling him. "I can't do this. I've already been someone's show pony. I won't be yours. Goodbye, Eliza."

As he walked out of the kitchen, the oven beeped.

Breakfast was ready.

And they were done.

chapter **twenty-five**

ELIZA STROKED MABEL'S HEAD, THE SOUND OF *GILMORE Girls* playing on low volume in the background and her phone in her hand. She scrolled through her Instagram for the first time in months. She'd thought the distraction would help, would take her mind off what had happened with Beckham, but the endless well-lit photos of people's lives blurred together.

She found herself clicking on her own profile. She dragged her thumb across her screen, her posts sliding by. Seeing her smiling face, her quippy wellness suggestions, her upbeat stories...it was like scrolling a stranger's feed. Who was that person? Was she *ever* that person?

People's comments on her posts were full of thank-you's and compliments.

Yasss, girl!
So pretty!
#LoveThis
This is a great tip! #SelfcareFTW

These strangers thought she had it together, thought the

Instagram therapist had it all figured out. She made a disgusted sound in the back of her throat. She was a damn fraud. She knew nothing. Absolutely goddamned nothing about how to do life. This whole feed was all a show.

Hell, maybe her whole freaking life was a show. Had she ever done anything without a little part of her thinking, *What would they think of me now?* That chip on her shoulder that had been chiseled deep during her adolescence was still there, unable to be satisfied. She always needed to prove herself just a little bit more. She wanted her old classmates and anyone else who'd doubted her in her life to open up her Facebook or Twitter or Instagram and be like, *Oh wow, Eliza Catalano really became someone. Look how wrong we were. Look how successful and happy she is. Great job. Big following. Hot husband. Smart kids.*

Or *bestselling book…*

"God," she said, groaning aloud. "Insecure, much?"

Mabel glanced up, her doggy eyebrows twitching. She must've decided Eliza looked distressed enough because she laid a big, wet lick along Eliza's cheek and nose.

Eliza smiled despite herself and kissed Mabel on her head. "Thanks, sweetheart."

Mabel laid her head down on Eliza's lap, and Eliza went over her argument with Beckham for the hundredth time. Part of her was still so angry with him. The things he'd said to her had ripped pieces of flesh from her, the accusations barbed and painful. But was that because some of them were true?

She was still reeling from the knowledge that he had been married before. He'd said she'd never asked him why he felt how he felt, which was true, but he also hadn't volunteered it. He could've opened up to her. That miss wasn't solely on her.

But it had made her realize that she still didn't know much about his past. She knew he'd grown up in a strict household of some sort, his parents restricting movies. She knew he'd had a friend who'd had a leaked sex video. She knew he was estranged from his parents for some reason. There was more story there, but she hadn't dug.

Why hadn't she dug?

That was normally her nature—to be nosy. To delve into people's stories. That was her actual job. Yet with Beckham, she'd settled for living in the moment. Why?

Because it felt like a fairy tale.

The answer came to her as if from outside herself.

Being with Beckham had held a magical quality from the start, and she hadn't wanted to mar it with reality. She'd been so tired of overanalyzing every date, being let down by every guy, that just being with Beckham had felt like a break. She hadn't had to impress him or put on some image. She hadn't had to evaluate every aspect of his personality to see if he was long-term material. Their start as friends had let him sneak into the back door of her subconscious, not triggering her "must be perfect Eliza" instinct or the "must be the perfect guy" expectation.

It'd felt like taking a huge, much-needed breath of cool, clean air.

She'd felt free with him. Light.

He was this young, gorgeous, interesting guy who'd laid no expectations on her. Maybe she hadn't wanted to ask too many questions because then she'd have to see past that, to face his flaws. Because of course he'd have them. He was a human, after all.

Oh God. Oh God. Oh Gaaawd.

Maybe she *had* fallen in love with *the idea of him*.

Without thinking, she woke her phone screen and hit a button, her heartbeat racing up to the speed of a panic attack.

Andi answered on the second ring. "Hey, you, what's up?"

"I am a completely horrible person," she declared. "A selfish, self-centered asshole."

"Um, first of all, don't you dare talk about my friend that

way," Andi said. "And second of all, where are you, where should I meet you, and how much alcohol should I bring?"

Eliza closed her eyes, her chest squeezing tight. She loved her friends more than life. "I'm home. I need food more than liquor. Can Hollyn come, too?"

"I'll check," Andi said, all business now. "Either way, I'll be there soon with carbs."

"I love you."

"Same, girl, same. Sit tight."

Less than an hour later, Andi and Hollyn were on her doorstep. Hollyn lifted a takeout bag, her cheek twitching from a facial tic. "I brought chips, queso, and tacos."

Andi had a Tupperware container and a grocery bag. "And I brought Hill's fresh-baked chocolate chip cookies, a gallon of ice cream, and a big-ass bottle of hot fudge. There's also tequila if things take a turn."

Eliza stared at her two friends and then burst into tears.

"Oh, honey," Hollyn said, rushing forward and putting an arm around her. "Come on, let's get you inside."

Andi took all the food and shut the door behind them. "I'll be right back."

"I've got her," Hollyn said, guiding Eliza to the couch.

Mabel trotted behind Andi and the scent of tacos. Eliza let Hollyn lead her to the couch. She sat down in a heap, sniffling like a little kid. *God*, she hated crying.

Hollyn gently rubbed her back, supporting Eliza in that quiet, solid way she had.

Andi was back a minute later. She sat on the chair next to the couch, handed Eliza a cookie and a tissue, and then said, "Who did this to you, and how slowly should we murder them?"

That made Eliza laugh, a choked snort-cry sound, and she took the cookie. "Shouldn't we have dinner first?"

"Oh no," Hollyn said. "With crying like this, cookies first is the protocol."

Eliza dabbed her eyes with the tissue, already feeling a little better now that her friends were here. "There's no one to murder. I'm the asshole." She took a big bite of the cookie and kept talking, the words coming out more garbled. "And I'm going to die alone because I don't fall in love with real people. I fall in love with the idea of a person and then use them for my own selfish purposes."

Andi gave her a patient but pointed look. "You're not going to die alone. You have us. We are going to *Golden Girls* the shit out of our future decades whether there are dudes in our lives or not. That's already decided. But what the hell are you talking about? Who did you fall in love with and use? Is this about that guy Will?"

"No," she said miserably. "Beckham."

"Wait, *what*?" Andi said, looking altogether confused. "You're in love with *Beckham*?"

"Wasn't he supposed to be helping you meet guys?" Hollyn asked.

Eliza wiped her nose with the tissue. "No, I'm in love with the *idea of him*—as he so harshly pointed out."

"What does that even mean?" Andi asked. "And when did you have time to fall in love with him—or the idea of him?"

"We've been sleeping together for months."

"Oh. Wow." Andi nodded as if impressed. "Nice."

"No, not nice. Bad idea. Bad, bad idea," Eliza declared between aggressive bites of cookie.

Hollyn and Andi exchanged a look. Andi arched an eyebrow. Hollyn bit down on what looked to be an almost smile.

Eliza glanced between the two of them. "What? What is that look for?"

"No look," Hollyn said, but her nose wrinkled and her cheek twitched, giving her away. Her Tourette's did not make for a successful liar.

Andi flicked her dark-red bangs away from her forehead. "It's nothing. It's just...I'm thinking this is less about the *idea* of a guy and more about, you know, the actual guy. I haven't ever seen you this distressed about...anyone. Usually you just tell colorful stories about the bad dates. The dominant emotion is usually annoyance, not tears."

"We were just supposed to be friends with benefits," Eliza started. "It was supposed to be simple."

"Oh Lord," Hollyn said with a little laugh. "Been there, girl. I'm married to my former let's-keep-it-casual guy."

"Well, I'm not going to be marrying this one. He's anti-marriage," Eliza said.

Andi snorted. "Fun. One of those."

"Yes. Or no. I don't know," Eliza said. "Apparently it's because he's been married before and it went badly, but I didn't know that because...I never asked him why he felt that way. And that's the problem. I was afraid to dig too deep on anything with him because I knew it wouldn't last. It was fun, and I didn't want to taint that with reality."

"That's understandable. It was new. You wanted to keep it low-key," Andi said reassuringly.

Eliza swallowed another bite of cookie. "He said I cast guys in roles. That I expect them to let me down, to leave."

"That's not fair," Hollyn said. "You've just learned from experience. Guys have let you down."

"But *he* didn't. He didn't lead me on. I agreed to what we were doing. I knew where he stood. I signed up to be hurt in the end," she said, looking back and forth between her two friends. "Why would I do that? Am I that desperate? It's not like I don't know that I can handle life on my own. I already do. Have for a long time. I don't need a guy."

"Of course you don't," Hollyn said, giving Eliza's arm a little squeeze. "But that doesn't mean it's a bad thing to want love and a relationship."

"And signing up for that kind of relationship doesn't make you desperate," Andi said. "It just means that you thought he was worth it. Something about him made you willing to take the risk. Would you have agreed to that kind of situation with someone else? If Will had offered some friends-with-benefits goodness, would you have done it?"

Eliza frowned. "No."

"So that tells you something," Andi said with a nod.

"It means you should follow the crazy," Hollyn added.

Eliza looked to Hollyn. "What?"

Hollyn tucked her mane of curly hair behind her ears. "The way I could tell Jasper was someone special to me was because I was willing to do crazy things I would've never considered under any other circumstance. God himself could've asked me to do improv, and I would've told him no. But Jasper got me to try it. He coaxed me out of my comfort zone one painstaking step at a time, but I wanted to go there. Because he was there, holding my hand through it."

Eliza's heart squeezed.

"Same with Hill," Andi said. "There was this trust there with him that I never felt with anyone else. Made me feel like I'd go anywhere with him."

"That's not what this is," Eliza said with a headshake. "I don't even know him. Not really. I was too self-centered to even ask him the most basic questions about his family or history."

"That can come later," Hollyn said, waving a hand as if to brush away that point entirely. "Those are details. How do you feel when you're with him? What's it like when you're just hanging out and having a meal? Or chatting at work?"

Eliza leaned back on the couch and rubbed her hands over her face, trying to really think through the question, check her gut. "It feels...easy. Fun. Like I could say or do anything. Like if I made a weird joke, he'd totally get it. I feel with him like how I feel with you guys...except that I also want to lick all parts of his body."

Her friends both smiled.

"What?" Eliza asked, giving them a suspicious look.

"You're screwed," Andi said, her smile turning knowing. "Completely and totally fucked."

Hollyn reached out and patted her knee. "What she means to say is that you may not know his family history or have asked all the questions, but you know *him*. On some intuitive level, you get him, and it sounds like he gets you."

"And I hate to break it to you but that, sugar plum, means you probably love more than the idea of him," Andi said, tilting her head like she was delivering a death sentence. "So now we have to figure out what you want to do about it."

"There is nothing to do about it," Eliza said, letting that reality wash over her. "He's pissed at me because he found out I was writing the book and that he's in it. I can apologize again for that, but that's only going to go so far because I'm also not quitting the book just because he said so. I'll conceal his identity more, but he doesn't get to make that call for me. It's a project I feel invested in. I've worked hard on it."

Hollyn nodded. "Agreed. Not his call. You have the right to write about your own experiences."

"And even if I could get him on my side about that," Eliza said, "it doesn't change that he doesn't want the same things I want." She rubbed her forehead where a crying headache was forming. "To be honest, I'm not even sure what I want anymore."

"What do you mean?" Andi asked.

"I mean, he wasn't wrong that I go in expecting guys to let me down. Some genuinely do, but sometimes I think I'm setting up a self-fulfilling prophecy. Look at Will," she said, flicking her hand as if he were standing right in front of them. "Good-looking guy, smart, funny, easy to get along with. There were literally no red flags. He's going to be a great husband to someone one day. But send him on a date with me and I just...wasn't feeling it."

"You can't account for chemistry," Hollyn said. "Sometimes people that make sense on paper just don't click with each other."

"Sure, but I think it's more than that. I think I like the idea of marriage and family. I love the thought of having something like my parents did, but some other part inside me must not be convinced. I find a reason to disqualify every guy I meet, and the one I did develop feelings for...disqualified that possibility from the start."

"You know," Andi said. "There's no rule that you have to get married or have kids or any of that stuff. I mean, I know you know that intellectually, but do you, like, *know* that?"

Eliza frowned.

"I'm marrying Hill because it feels right for me, but I don't know yet if I want kids. I kind of like the idea of it just being us and maybe some pets. And if we don't have an official marriage ceremony and get a piece of paper to say we're married, I wouldn't feel any differently about him. All I know for sure is I want to be with him forever and he feels the same. That's good enough for me," Andi said. "Have you ever considered that you like being single? That you love the freedom of it?"

"I..." Eliza started but then pressed her lips together, not knowing what to say.

"You have a great career. You have super-fabulous friends who love you like family. Your own house. An adorable dog. You don't need some guy to come in and complete you or whatever. You've already got your shit together, girl," Andi went on. "So maybe you haven't settled with anyone because you're happy on your own. And maybe you just want some fun and intimacy with a guy who isn't asking for anything from you but to be who you are already."

Eliza stared at Andi, the words seeping in like beams of light into her foggy brain.

"And maybe that's why you're feeling things for Beckham," Hollyn added. "Part of you senses he can give you that. He fits into the happy life you already have and adds to it. The world tells you that the biological clock is ticking, that you need a husband, kids, smiling family Facebook photos, whatever, but maybe what would really make you happy is a sexy best friend who's down for sleepovers."

Eliza let out a long breath. "But I'm the romantic one in the group. I'm a marriage counselor, for God's sake. And all those movies I watch, all the books I read...a best friend with benefits doesn't sound like a happy ending. Shouldn't I want a happy ending?"

"Honey," Andi said with a little laugh, "a happy ending is the one that makes *you* happy. The hard part is figuring out what that is. I know you look to your parents' marriage as a touchstone, but didn't your mom give up her career to follow your dad's job?"

Eliza swallowed past the dryness in her throat. Her mom had given up a tenured professorship. "She did."

"Maybe part of you is scared that you'll have to give up major things, too," Andi suggested.

The words landed solidly. That was probably why she'd reacted so strongly to Beckham not wanting her to write the book. Any hint that she'd not have control over her own career moves had pushed her buttons hard. Her mom had chosen to give up her career, but Eliza had always wondered if her mom had regretted it. All that hard work just to walk away from it...for love. "Oh God," she said, shaking her head. "Who's the therapist in the room again?"

Hollyn smirked and shrugged. "We all have our blind spots."

Eliza's head was spinning. She didn't say anything for a solid minute, trying to process her thoughts.

"You know what you need?" Hollyn said, breaking Eliza from her whirlwind thoughts.

She looked up. "What?"

"Queso," Hollyn declared. "Come on. Everything will better after that."

"Amen, sister," Andi said, getting up and putting out her hand to Eliza. "And maybe just a wee bit of tequila."

Eliza took Andi's hand and laughed. "I love you guys."

"Don't blame ya," Andi said. "We're frawesome."

Eliza got to her feet and lifted a brow. "Frawesome?"

"Fucking awesome," she said with a shrug. "I'm trying it out. Like froyo only with swear words."

"Keep workshopping that one, writer lady," Eliza teased.

Andi snorted and flipped her off.

But Eliza felt better already. Maybe her friends were right. Maybe this wasn't a character flaw, being single and bad at dating at thirty-two. Maybe it was a feature and not a defect. Because the one thing she'd never, ever considered before had been the most obvious question of all...*was she already happy?*

That wasn't a question single women in their thirties were taught to ask.

She was supposed to have a hole in her life. And after her parents had died, that feeling of something missing had grown wider and deeper. She'd felt near desperate to re-create what they'd had, the stability of a marriage, that assuredness that she wouldn't be alone.

But maybe what she had wasn't a marriage-shaped hole at all. Maybe it was simply...*grief*. The kind she had to walk *through*, not *around*. Nothing was going to replace the spot her parents had filled. She no longer had the safe space that her mom's hugs and long talks provided. Or the feeling of her dad always looking out for her future with his overly detailed but well-intentioned advice. No love could be *that* love. Finding a guy wasn't going to patch that.

But that didn't mean she didn't have additional space for other kinds of love. The love of her friends filled her with joy. The sweet doggie kisses from Mabel lit her up with delight. The passion for her job filled her with purpose. She had so much.

And maybe one day she'd find a guy who added to those wonderful things, but she was no longer interested in forcing it or worrying about it or bending over backward to fit into some guy's detailed relationship rules. Beckham's issues were his to own and deal with. She cared about him, maybe even loved him, but she wasn't his therapist. It wasn't her job to fix him, especially when he didn't want to be fixed.

She also didn't need him to fix something in *her* life. She was fine all on her own.

No. More than that.

She was frawesome.

She followed her friends into the kitchen, passing the couch where she and Beckham had first curled up together to watch Star Wars. She glanced at the ghost image of the two of them, mentally releasing her grip on the hope that they had something special, and she let him go.

Goodbye, Beckham Carter. May the force be with you.

chapter **twenty-six**

AFTER ANOTHER LONG DAY OF WORK, BECKHAM FOUND himself venting to Trent about a particularly challenging computer security issue he'd faced today. Trent, for his part, seemed to listen but offered no helpful advice on how to tackle the newest virus that had invaded one of Beckham's client's systems. Instead, he meowed, demanding dinner.

"I'm working on it, buddy." Beckham grabbed the container of cat food from the pantry, autopiloting through his new nightly routine. He'd been going in late and leaving late for the last two weeks, making sure to avoid the times Eliza was usually in the hallway. It was juvenile, but he just didn't want to deal with any of it right now. He didn't know what to say or even who was right or wrong anymore. Maybe neither. Maybe both. All he knew was that the situation sucked. A lot.

So he worked and worked and then came home to Trent, going through the soothing motions of feeding him, getting him water, putting out fresh litter, and giving him cuddle time. Beckham just needed to keep moving. The minute he let his mind wander, he got pissed all over again and then hurt and then back to pissed.

And that anger was mostly directed at himself. He'd known better than to do this. Since everything with Jess and then getting sober, he'd been an expert at keeping things chill. Easy, low-key relationships with friends. Full control at his job. No-drama dates with women who didn't want any more from him than a fun night. Stress had been a cancer in his life, one that had triggered addiction and dangerous behavior. His father had told Beckham when he was a teenager that he had a weak personality, one that couldn't handle hard things. He'd told his father he had a dick personality, but his dad's words had buried under Beckham's skin just the same. Because the truth was, when the video had been leaked and things had gotten intense for him and Jess, he had collapsed under the weight of it. He'd drowned himself in alcohol, and when that didn't work, he'd run away.

Since then, he'd done everything he could to get stress out of his life so he wouldn't find himself in that kind of death spiral again. Leaving his family, his marriage, and the belief system he'd grown up with. Shedding his old identity so the media couldn't seek him out. Starting a new life with clear rules. He wasn't cold, but he didn't get his feelings involved in anything. No one could crush you if you didn't give them access to the fragile parts of yourself.

Then Eliza had happened.

Beckham had thought he'd played it smart with her. What they'd had was different from what he'd had with women before, but he'd been up front about what he could and could not do. He'd allowed himself to feel…affection for her, but thought he hadn't let it go beyond that. What a delusion that had turned out to be. If that had been true, seeing her writing that book shouldn't have torn him up like it did. The fact that she'd lied to him shouldn't have felt so soul-destroying.

The truth was he'd let his guard down. He'd let himself get too attached, left himself open. He felt…too much for her. And hearing her throw the *love* word around, well, he didn't believe she really felt that way—she wouldn't if she truly knew him—but the ache it had sent through him had been unacceptable. He shouldn't want that from her. It was selfish, for one. Eliza deserved to get what she wanted—the fairy-tale guy with the fancy wedding and the two-point-five kids and whatever else she imagined for her life. He couldn't be that guy. But it also scared the hell out of him that he didn't want to imagine her getting back on those dating apps or going out with anyone else.

That jealousy was new and foreign to him. He'd never had that, not even with Jess. He'd always thought that the possessive posturing guys did was ridiculous. He wasn't a caveman trying to secure a female for his genetic line's survival or whatever. But goddammit, when he'd seen Eliza kiss Will, he'd wanted to stomp around like a Neanderthal.

Which was all the sign he needed. He had to go cold turkey with Eliza. Just like the booze. He didn't want anything or anyone in his life to have that kind of pull on him.

Trent meowed, breaking Beckham from his tornadic thoughts, and then knocked his water bowl over. He skittered backward and yowled when he got wet.

"Dude," Beckham said with a sigh. "If you put both paws in it, you're going to get wet."

Trent looked at him as if Beckham had personally doused him and therefore offended him on a deep level.

Beckham dropped a kitchen towel on the floor to mop up the puddle and then grabbed the bowl and went back to the sink to refill it. As he was setting it on the floor, the doorbell rang. He frowned, wiped his wet hands on his jeans, and then went to the door. Khuyen had said he might stop by for a little while to play video games—another mindless activity Beckham had leaned into lately—but usually Khuyen texted when he was on his way up.

Beckham pulled his phone from his pocket to see if he'd missed a text as he made his way to the door. Seeing nothing, he bent a little and checked the peephole. The person standing on the other side had long blond hair, her back turned to him.

Ah, someone had the wrong condo. He quickly unlocked the door and swung it open.

He cleared his throat. "I'm sorry. I think you might have the wrong—"

The woman turned around, familiar blue eyes meeting his.

His stomach dropped, the rest of his sentence falling away. He blinked, not believing what he was seeing for a moment. Maybe he'd fallen asleep on the couch with Trent. Maybe he was dr—

"Hi, Matt." The soft, familiar voice was like hearing a ghost whisper in his ear.

All his breath left him, goose bumps pricking his arms, and his old world came crashing back into focus.

"*Jess.*"

....

"Beckham's backed out because he's going through one of his workaholic phases, but you should totally come. We have two open spots now. It's going to be a blast."

Eliza smiled and tucked her phone against her ear so she could fold the clothes she'd dumped onto her bed. This was the second time Will had called her in a week, and she found she enjoyed chatting with him when there wasn't any pressure of a date surrounding it. When she'd admitted to him that she felt more of a friend vibe than a dating vibe with him, he'd easily accepted the news and said he was happy to have a new friend. "I'm sure it will be, and I appreciate the invite, but Beckham will probably change his mind."

"So?" he said, and she could almost hear him shrug. "That means there will still be one more spot."

She wrinkled her nose at the thought. Trapped on a Mardi Gras float with Beckham for hours, everyone shoulder to shoulder and nowhere to escape? *Hello, torture.* "Beckham and I... aren't really talking right now. Stupid work argument. So it'd be awkward if we both end up on the same float."

"Work argument?" Will sniffed. "Uh-huh."

She paused in folding a pair of pajama pants. "What?"

"You're a therapist, and he's a computer security specialist," he pointed out. "What work thing would you have to argue about? Who gets to use the coffee machine first?"

"We don't have a coffee machine. There's a coffee bar," she said, dodging the question and tossing the pants onto the bed in a messy heap.

"Come on. What happened?" Will asked, a genial tone in his voice. "Is this because you two won't admit you have a hard-on for each other?"

She stiffened. "What? I—"

Will laughed. "Oh, don't give me that shocked routine. I'm not blind. We had fun when we went out, but it was real obvious why the friend zone was our destiny."

"What was real obvious?" She grabbed the phone so it wouldn't slide off her shoulder and sat on the bed.

"That I wasn't the guy you wanted to be out with on Valentine's Day. You talked about Beckham for half our date. And his stealth mode wasn't any better. He always got uptight when I talked about liking you or going out with you—and Beck can be an intense guy but he isn't an uptight one. Plus," he said conspiratorially, "Trinity saw you making out on the porch the night of the NoPho party. She didn't tell me until after I told her about our Valentine's date, but she said y'all looked pretty into it."

Eliza sighed, liking Will even more for his easy candidness. He really was a terrific guy. Why couldn't she have fallen for *him*? Her heart had terrible taste. "I'm sorry. I wasn't trying to lead you on. I really do think you're great and wanted to go on those dates, but I was distracted. Beckham and I had a thing that wasn't supposed to be an actual thing. But it...got complicated and didn't work out."

"Because Beck screwed it up?" he guessed.

She grabbed a balled-up pair of socks and squeezed them like a stress ball. She would not get emotional, dammit. She'd moved on. Was looking at her potential dating life with brand-new eyes after her epiphany of not needing a guy to have a full and happy life. "No, it just...wasn't meant to be."

At first, she'd hoped maybe there was a chance she and Beckham could still be friends after he had cooled off about the book and they could talk it through, but he'd avoided her completely for the last couple of weeks at work. Once she'd seen him coming down the hall with his lunch, and when he'd noticed her, he'd literally turned on his heel and gone back the other way. She had no time for that kind of nonsense. If he couldn't even talk things out, then there really was no hope. Even in a friend, she needed a guy mature enough to have an adult conversation. She wasn't going to play high school games.

"That sucks. I'm sorry," Will said, sounding genuine. "But that shouldn't stop you from being friends with me and the rest of the group. Beckham will get over himself. In the meantime, you could have a killer Mardi Gras. Come and get drunk on the power of being the distributor of the beads," he said with dramatic flair. "The crowds will beg for your attention. People will scream at you like you're a rock star."

She laughed and bit her lip, considering it. She really did like the group and the whole NoPho concept. Plus, she'd never ridden on a float during Mardi Gras, and that seemed like a bucket-list item that'd be fun to check off. "Well, maybe I could—" Her phone beeped. She frowned. "Hey, can you hold on a sec?"

"Yeah, sure."

"Thanks." She pulled the phone away from her ear to see who was calling and to make sure it wasn't the emergency answering service for work. But it wasn't a client. Beckham's name lit the screen. Her heart gave a little leap and then she inwardly groaned at that reaction. She put the phone back to her ear. "Hey, Will, sorry, can I call you back?"

"No problem. Just give Mardi Gras some thought. I'll hold the spot for you for now."

"Thanks. I'll let you know." They ended the call, and she clicked over to the other line. "Hello?"

"Eliza."

Eliza. Not Eli. A pang of loss went through her.

"Yeah. Hi. What's—"

"I need you," he said, cutting her off, his words rushed. "Are you... Can you come over?"

I need you. The words short-circuited her brain for a second.

"Come over?" She looked down at her yoga pants and old Tulane T-shirt. "Are you serious?"

After all this silent treatment, was he making *a booty call*? Because he had another thing coming if he thought he could treat her like he had and just call her up and—

"Yes, I'm sorry. I know it's late and that we haven't... I haven't...talked to you. But I have a friend here and...I need your help. She does," he clarified. "Your professional help."

"Oh." *Oh.* That came out of left field, sending Eliza's thoughts scattering like marbles, but the distress in his voice made her instincts kick into gear before her brain caught up. "Is the friend in immediate danger? To herself or to others?"

"I... Not *immediate* immediate. I don't think so at least. But, I just...need you here."

His vulnerable tone sent worry through her. Any thought of

the conflict between them fell away for the moment, and she went into professional mode. "Let me change my clothes, and I'll be right there."

"Thanks, Eli. I really appreciate it."

Eli. She closed her eyes, pushing away the feelings that drummed up. *Focus.* She needed to focus. He wasn't calling because he needed her, the friend. He was calling because he needed Eliza, the therapist. She needed to keep her head on straight about that.

When she arrived at Beckham's a half an hour later, he opened the door looking as worried as she'd ever seen him. His blond hair was sticking up like he'd run his hands through it too many times and his skin was washed out, but what really had her catching her breath was the look in his eyes. There was no trace of the spark he always carried. That playful sarcasm, that innate *him*ness that always seemed to convey he contained multitudes—none of it was there. He looked hollow and…freaked out.

"Hey," she said when he didn't say anything. "What's going on?"

He glanced over his shoulder and his Adam's apple bobbed. He looked back to her. "There's a lot to explain, and I'll say up front that I'm sorry I didn't…share this part of my past with you. I don't share it with anyone, but I'll tell you whatever you want to know after. For right now, I need help talking her down."

His words raised a thousand questions for her, but she needed to hone in on the only one that mattered. "Talking *who* down?"

Beckham opened the door wider and let her in. Eliza walked inside, her tennis shoes squeaking on the pale wooden floor of Beckham's modern condo as she followed him through the small foyer. He stopped at the entryway to his living room. A young blond woman was sitting on his navy-blue couch, a throw pillow hugged to her chest, and her ankle-length denim skirt draped across her folded legs. Her eyes were puffy and her cheeks tearstained.

Eliza looked back to Beckham, her brain scanning through possibilities and coming up empty.

"Eli," Beckham said, his voice quiet and calm, like he was trying not to spook the woman. "This is Jess. My—"

"His wife," the woman said, cutting him off and giving him a wounded look.

The words hit Eliza like a throat punch, but years of training kept her expression smooth. "Okay."

"My *ex*-wife," Beckham corrected, his tone patient but firm. "Jess and I were married when we were teenagers. I had it annulled."

"You married me in the church in front of God," Jess said, swiping a tear away from her cheek and looking to Beckham like Eliza wasn't even in the room. "We promised ourselves to each other. That's supposed to be forever, Matt. And you just...left me there."

"Matt?" Eliza looked to Beckham, no longer hiding her what-the-hell-is-going-on expression.

He cleared his throat. "I changed my name when I left the church." He gave Eliza a look. "When I left *the cult*."

Whoa. Eliza's lips parted slightly, and she took another look at Jess. The conservative clothes, the lack of makeup. Beckham had said he'd grown up in a strict household, but she hadn't realized he'd meant...this.

"Don't call the church that," Jess said and then turned to offer Eliza a far from welcoming look. "And who are you?"

Feeling defensive and off balance, Eliza wanted to cross her arms and give Jess a haughty look, but she forced herself to keep her posture open, nonthreatening. "I'm Eliza, Beckham's...uh, Matt's friend."

"She's a counselor, Jess," Beckham said, coming closer to stand beside Eliza. "I think you should talk to her. I think she could help."

"I don't need her help," she said, dismissing Eliza. "I just need you to come back with me. It's time. You've had your chance to sow your oats. I get that you needed to do that. Now it's time to come back, pray for forgiveness, and fulfill your duty as a husband. It's wrong to make me keep waiting. It's time to start our family—and I can't do that alone. My birthday is next week, and I refuse to have another one pass without my husband. I want a life."

Fulfill his duty as a husband? Eliza balked inwardly. She'd apparently stepped into the twilight zone.

"And you should have those things if that's what you want," Beckham agreed. "But I'm not the one who's keeping you from them. My father and this belief system he's hammered into you and everyone else is what's keeping you from those things. It's a prison." His voice was rising, his frustration evident. "*Leave the church,* Jess. No one in the mainstream world is going to judge you for being divorced or shame you for sleeping with me before we were married. You can have whatever kind of life you want. You can find someone new to love and have your family. Make your own choices."

Jess nailed him with a pointed look. "I'm married *to you.*"

Eliza touched Beckham's elbow, sensing he was losing hold of his calm. She needed to assess the situation before emotions went off the rails. "Can I talk to you in the other room for a sec?"

He gave Jess another glance and let out a breath. "Yeah, sure. Jess, give us a minute."

Beckham led Eliza out of the living room and into his bedroom. He shut the door and turned to her, leaning back against the door like it was the only thing holding him up.

"I'm sorry," he said, closing his eyes briefly and scrubbing his hands over his face. "I meant to handle that better. I just—"

"Tell me what's going on, Beck," she said, keeping her voice gentle. "I'm good at puzzles, but I can't help if I don't know what

I'm working with. What I've got so far is that you were raised in some sort of conservative religious sect, got married young, and left. Your ex wants you back. But why am I here?"

Beckham lowered his hands, looking worn out. "Have you ever heard of the show *Seven on Sunday*?"

The non sequitur threw her off for a second. "Uh...yeah, I think so. Is that the one with the family with all the kids?"

"Yeah." He lifted a hand like he was taking an oath. "Meet one of the seven."

Her breath whooshed out of her. "Oh my God, seriously?"

He lowered his hand. "My whole childhood was on TV. Every mistake. Every embarrassing moment. And that sex tape I mentioned to you way back when?"

She nodded. Dominoes were falling into place in her head. *Clack. Clack. Clack.*

"That was a tape of me and Jess's first time. Someone filmed us and leaked it, wanting to expose my family as frauds. Look at Matthew Laketon caught with his pants down, divesting his sweet, naive girlfriend of her virginity no less, and using all the dirty words he wasn't allowed to use on TV. We'd broken the biggest rule in the church besides murder—sex before marriage. The internet went nuts for it. Everyone loves a public shaming of a hypocrite."

Eliza winced. The thought of anyone's first time being captured and put out for public consumption made her stomach hurt. The damage that could inflict on a psyche...especially a tender teenage one. "God, Beck."

"It was bad for me, but it was worse for Jess. That video was proof of sin. Premarital sex was frowned upon for guys but life-ruining for a woman in the church. She got an instant label—a modern-day scarlet letter. Her future was gone. No guy would want to date her, and the women would consider her a bad influence so would avoid her." His gaze was far off like he was looking at a movie of his old life.

"We had to get married to give her any chance at a respectable life there, but...I couldn't handle it. I didn't want to be married. I didn't want to be in my dad's church. Or on the show. I had already been planning to leave when I turned eighteen. I'd been secretly researching colleges and learning all I could about coding and hacking. But then when the marriage happened, I felt trapped. I was angry all the time. I started drinking to try to get through it. I thought about driving my car off a bridge."

Eliza pressed her fingers to her lips, the pain in his voice carving little gashes on her heart.

"And I felt so alone. Jess, who'd always been my ride-or-die up until that point, thought the marriage was a great solution. She bought into the hype that her highest purpose would be as a mother and wife and all that jazz. She thought it'd be fun to be part of the show. I couldn't get through to her. So one day, I snuck off and called my uncle. Uncle Darren is gay, and Dad had forbidden the whole family to have contact. But I found his number in my dad's files. Uncle Darren hadn't seen me since I was seven, but he told me that if I wanted to leave, he'd give me a place to stay. Just like that. No questions asked. He and his husband saved me. I tried to get Jess to leave with me, but she wasn't interested. So I ran as far and fast as I could."

Eliza shook her head, her heart breaking for the kid he'd been. "I'm so sorry. I can't even imagine. I was raised Catholic and sex before marriage was a no-no, but if you broke that rule, you could be forgiven. To put so much pressure on two young kids... Your dad's church sounds—"

"It's a cult," he said bluntly. "TV liked to paint it as a novelty, as a harmless sideshow, but it's not just some garden-variety conservative church. It's a carefully controlled system where the men get to keep all the control and the women and kids have to fall in line. But when you're raised in it, it's hard to see a way out. Jess needs help."

"Why is she here now?" she asked.

"Because I think I led her on without meaning to." He lowered his head and sighed, his shoulder hunching. "She's the only one I ever told about my new name and where I was. And I've sent her money since I left because I wanted her to have a way out if she wanted it. I thought when I opened my door and saw her there, that this was the moment, that she was finally going to leave, but...she's seen this all differently."

"Meaning?"

"She took all that as a sign that I was still taking care of her, doing my duty as a husband or whatever, and would come back one day. That I just needed time to work through my crisis of faith. But I guess it's been one too many birthdays of waiting for her, and now she's going to force the issue. Most of the women in the church have children very young, usually in that first year of marriage."

Eliza sat on the edge of his bed, all the information a lot to process. "Oh, wow."

"Yeah, and I was ready to set her right on that misguided notion and send her back to where she apparently wants to stay, but then she told me that if I didn't come with her, she was going to take a bottle of pills and end things." He looked over at Eliza, heartbreak in his eyes. "That without a family, she had no purpose or reason to be around."

Eliza sucked in a breath, sympathy for Jess rolling through her. To grow up thinking your only worth was as someone else's wife or mother. To think you were nothing without that...

"That's when I called you," he said. "That scared me. I'm out of my depth here. I don't know if she's being serious or not, but

I don't want to take any chances." He raked a hand through his hair, his whole body tense. "I don't want to be married to Jess, but I still care about her. She used to be this whip-smart, funny girl, and it's killing me to see her like this. She could've been anything she wanted to be. And I ruined things for her."

Eliza frowned and got up. She went to him and put her hand on his arm, getting him to look at her. "You didn't ruin things, Beck. You were both children. The blame falls on the oppressive system you were raised in." She pressed her lips together, anger welling. "I'm not anti-religion. Religion can be a great comfort and support system for people, but in the wrong hands, it can be twisted into something ugly. And it can brainwash even the smartest people. Jess isn't going to be able to see your side easily at this point. She's in too deep."

His forehead crinkled with frustration. "So what do I do? I don't know how to help her."

Eliza straightened and looked in the direction of the living room. "Let me talk to her. I'll assess whether her threat of self-harm is a true risk or if this is more a last-ditch effort to try to get your attention. If she truly has a plan and the means to harm herself, then, legally, I'll have to intervene and report it. She'll need a stay in the hospital for an evaluation."

"And if not?" he asked.

"Then I have someone I can recommend. I have a colleague who specializes in exit counseling, which can help people who are in these situations to break free." Eliza met his gaze, trying to couch his expectations. "But Jess would have to be open to that. She'd have to want the help. If she doesn't want to leave, you can't make her."

A defeated look crossed his face. "She's never going to agree to that. She didn't drive all those hours from Arizona to get here and hop into therapy."

"You never know," Eliza said, trying to be hopeful. "Maybe her upcoming birthday triggered her to find you now, but maybe there's also more to it. It was a risk to come here. Maybe some little part of her wants out. Sometimes people cry for help without realizing they're doing it."

"Right." Beckham lowered his hand, lacing his fingers behind his neck as if the truth was just too heavy to hold.

"I promise I'll do everything I can," she said gently.

Beckham looked up, meeting her gaze, and then he stepped forward. Before she knew what was happening, he'd wrapped his arms around her. He hugged her close and pressed a kiss to the top of her head. "Thanks, Eli."

"Of course," she whispered, the hug feeling like too much and not enough all at once. "Let me see what I can do."

When they returned to the living room, Jess was still on the couch, but was holding a digital photo frame. From Eliza's angle behind Jess, she could see the pictures that were scrolling across the screen. Trent fighting with a plant. Trent sleeping on a chair. Beckham laughing with his friends at a restaurant. Eliza and Mabel on the couch at Eliza's house. A Beckham selfie with Trent curled around his head.

Beckham cleared his throat, alerting Jess to their presence. She quickly put the frame back on the side table. Eliza walked around the couch to sit in one of the chairs and saw that Jess had been crying again. Jess swiped at her cheeks and peered at Beckham. Her voice was a whisper when it came out. "You've built a whole new life. Without me."

Beckham's gaze filled with a stark sadness. "I'm sorry, Jess. I'm not coming back. My life is...good here. Stable. Even happy sometimes." He glanced at Eliza and then back to Jess. "I want that for you, too, but I can't be the one to give you that."

"Jess," Eliza said, voice soft.

Jess turned her head and gave Eliza a look full of suspicion, but she didn't say anything.

Eliza pressed her hands to the top of her knees, centering herself. One wrong move and she could send Jess running. This was outside of her specialty, but if she could just make sure the girl was safe in the short-term, she could get her to someone more qualified for the long-term. "Jess, I know you don't know me and have no reason to trust me, but I can see you're in pain and I'd like to help if you're willing to let me. Beck—*Matt* would like to help, too."

"I don't need help. I need my husband back," Jess said, her voice breaking a little at the end. She pulled the throw pillow back into her lap.

"I understand. Sometimes when our pain is really intense, when it feels like it's pushing on us from every side, it makes our vision narrow down to a pinpoint where we can only see one, maybe two ways out of the pain," Eliza said, keeping her tone. "Would you say getting Matt back feels like one of those solutions?"

Jess glanced at Beckham. "It is the solution."

Eliza nodded. "I know it feels that way. But Matt—Beckham—has chosen a different life for himself, and he has the right to do that. He is a healthier person because of that choice. Leaving the church was an act of self-care for him, and as someone who knows him in this life, I can tell you he's become a really kind and amazing man." She peeked at Beckham, and the way he was looking at her made her chest tighten. She looked back to Jess, trying to catch her gaze. "We all have that right—to choose the path where we can be our healthiest and happiest."

Jess held the eye contact for a second before looking down and picking at the piping of the throw pillow.

Eliza tread carefully. "If you feel like your life will be happiest in the church, it's your right to stay there." Beckham gave her a what-the-hell look but she ignored it. "Just like Beckham made his choice, you can make yours. But if you're not fully happy there, if you're not finding comfort and peace, if you feel like you don't have freedom to be the person you want to be, then you have more options than you might be able to see right now."

Jess shook her head. "I don't have options. I have no husband and no one else will take me as their wife. I don't have my own money. I didn't go to college." Tears slipped down her cheeks. "I cry all the time. I just want it to stop. I've thought about...pills."

Beckham sat next to Jess and put his arm around her.

Eliza's heart broke for the girl. "Do you have access to pills?"

She nodded, crying again. "In my purse."

Beckham sent Eliza a worried look.

A means and a plan. Eliza didn't have a choice now, but she hoped to get Jess where she needed to go willingly. "I'm so sorry you're going through this, Jess. That pain is a lot to carry. You've been through trauma, and your body and mind haven't been given the tools to process it. The depression is telling you there are no options, but it lies. That's what it does. But I promise you there are people who can help you through this. You won't always have to feel this way."

"And if you need money, Jess," Beckham said, "I can help you. I can help you get a place, get on your feet."

"We want you to be safe, first and foremost," Eliza said, appreciating Beckham's generous spirit, but knowing that Jess wasn't in a stable enough state to just leave the cult and strike out on her own. There was a lot of work to be done first. "And you don't have to make any decisions about the church. All that's important right now is that we get you some help for the pain, okay? We can take you to a doctor. Get some help."

Jess lifted her head and looked to Beckham, a cornered-animal expression on her face. "Matt."

"It's okay," Beckham said, his tone reassuring. "Eliza is one of the smartest and most kindhearted people I know. I trust her completely and so can you. If she says she can help, she can."

His words and unequivocal vote of confidence made Eliza's eyes burn.

Jess looked to Eliza, her gaze evaluating.

Eliza was already calculating how quickly she could grab her phone and call 911 if Jess tried to run. But finally, Jess's shoulders sagged and she nodded. "Okay. What do I need to do?"

chapter **twenty-seven**

"You think she's going to be okay?"

Eliza looked over at Beckham, a shaft of light from the streetlamp putting his face half in darkness. He'd driven her back to his place from the hospital so she could pick up her car, but neither had wanted to go home yet. They'd decided to take a walk and had found themselves strolling the path along the Mississippi River. "I think it's a good sign that Jess checked herself in willingly."

Beckham looked out at the black water of the river, his hands shoved deep in the pockets of his jacket and his blond hair dancing in the breeze coming off the water. "That was because of you. The way you talked with her…" He peered over at her. "You're really good at what you do."

"Thanks." She gave him a little smile and tucked a hair that had escaped her ponytail behind her ear. "Guess those student loans were worth it."

"It's more than therapy skills," he said. "You're kind of magical, Eli. You make people want to open up to you because… people sense that you'll accept them just as they are."

The words warmed her. "I do accept them. If you don't meet someone where they're at, you'll never really meet them." She kept her gaze forward, the lights on the Crescent City Connection bridge sparkling in the distance. "They'll just give you the front they give everyone else. I wasn't going to change Jess's mind about her beliefs tonight. But I could tell she was scared and feeling alone, that she didn't feel safe. I could give her options to help with that."

He made a sound in the back of his throat. "That's what you did with me, too, isn't it?"

She glanced over at him, the sharpness in his tone catching her off guard. "What?"

"Accepted me where I was at." He was only giving her his profile, his jaw muscle flexing, his hands still stuffed in his pockets. "Spending time with me despite all my fucking hang-ups and stupid philosophies. You must have a really high tolerance for bullshit."

She frowned, halting her step, and put her hand on his arm. "Hey, what are you talking about?"

He stopped and turned, his shoulders hunched against the wind. "When you were talking with Jess tonight...I had the thought, *God, how horrible for Jess that her whole life is defined by my dad's screwed-up beliefs. That she has to be deprogrammed like some virus-ridden computer. I'm so glad I got out when I did. Wow, ain't I smart?*" He scoffed. "And then I looked at you and thought about what had happened between us and it hit me. I've got the same damn computer virus. It's just a reverse image of hers. My father is just as in control of me as he ever was."

Eliza crossed her arms, the wind becoming more biting, but she didn't want to distract Beckham from whatever he needed to get off his chest. "What do you mean?"

"My brilliant life plan to give a big fuck-you to my dad was to do the opposite of what he'd want me to do," he said, bitterness edging his words. "He wanted me to wait for sex until

I was married, so I slept with my girlfriend before she was really ready and screwed up her life. He forbade alcohol, so I became an addict. He wanted me to be on a TV show, so I went off the grid. He thought tattoos were defacing what God gave you, so I inked up as soon as I could. He wanted me to follow every rule, so I became a hacker."

The self-disgust in Beckham's voice was breaking her heart a little. "Rebellion is a natural reaction to all that restriction."

"Every decision I've made has had a piece of him in it, and I hate that." He shook his head. "I'm...screwing everything up."

"You're not screwing everything up, Beck. Don't think—"

"*I am.*" He met her gaze, sadness there. "Look what I did to you. Instead of *asking* you about the book when I found those pages, I jumped straight to nuclear bomb mode. I broke into your computer—me, the privacy guy—broke all my rules and violated your trust. I turned you into the enemy when it was really him I was mad at. I couldn't just...let myself be happy. I had to blow it up. How fucked up is that?"

"Beck—"

"And he wins anyway," he scoffed. "He wanted me to be a husband and a father, and I was so, so determined not to give him the satisfaction that when someone amazing walked into my life, I did everything I could to push her away and let her down."

Eliza's therapeutic response died on her lips and her throat tightened.

"So yeah," he said, voice softening. "I'm screwing everything up. I lost the woman I'm in love with because I didn't know what to do with that kind of happiness when it finally came my way. I couldn't even recognize how beautiful and precious it was. How beautiful and precious *you* are. I'm so, so sorry, Eli."

Her breath and her ability to form coherent thoughts left her. "You're...in love with me?"

A tentative smile touched his lips. "Don't tell Trent."

A choked laugh escaped her, but she still couldn't process everything he'd said. She found herself reaching her hands out to him, the need to touch him in some way necessary in that moment.

Beckham stepped closer and took her cold hands, lacing his warm fingers with hers. "I'm messed up, Eli. I realized tonight that I've...got work to do. I probably could use some of the same therapy Jess needs. I don't know where the real me is between who I was raised to be and who I've become in response to it. But I don't want you to accept me as I am. I don't want you to let me get away with it anymore. I want to be the kind of guy you could fall in love with for real. I want to be better. For you. *With* you." He looked down at their joined hands. "If you'll give me another chance when I'm done."

The bridge lights wavered in her vision, her eyes filling with tears. She squeezed his hands and touched her forehead to his, trying to find her voice. "I'm sorry, Beck. I can't do that."

He sucked in a breath and lifted his head. His hands tried to break away from hers and she could see his expression closing off.

But she held on and smiled at him. "I'm not waiting for all that. Because I *already* love you. Right here. Now. How you are this minute. I never stopped. I'll love you before therapy and after therapy." As the words came out, her chest filled up with the rightness of them, of how good it felt to speak the truth. "We're in this together. And you can't change my mind on that. Don't even try. I'm really hardheaded."

A startled look crossed his face. "Wait. You *still love me*? Even after what I did?"

"You told me that day in the kitchen that I don't know you. And for a while, I believed you. That I'd fallen for the idea of you. That I just wanted *someone*. But..." She brought their joined hands to her heart, pulling him close. "I don't need to know your life story to know the man. I know by your actions. You're Beckham Carter, the guy who would adopt a difficult cat because he knew that cat wouldn't find a home otherwise. Beckham, who dropped everything and broke the law for a near stranger to help her get rid of an embarrassing video."

She held his gaze even when tears escaped down her cheeks. "Beck, the man who wouldn't let his coworker spend Christmas alone because he somehow sensed that she needed a friend more than anything else in that moment and he chose to be that." She pressed her lips to their joined hands. "You have the biggest, purest heart of any guy I know, Beck. I love that guy."

His eyes were tender now, glittering. "Eli... God, what am I going to do with you?"

"Lots of things, I hope," she said with a little smile. "And I'm sorry, too. I should've told you about the book. We should've discussed it like grown-ups. I didn't handle that well either."

He nodded. "No more secrets for either of us, okay? We're smart and love each other. Let's trust ourselves to talk things out."

She smiled. "Deal."

He released her hands and then tucked a stubborn lock of hair behind her ear. "God, I've hated every single moment we've been apart these last few weeks. I've been...lost without you."

"Same," she whispered, her vocal cords tightening with emotion.

He held her gaze. "You're the most beautiful person I've ever met. Inside and out. From the start, you've made me want to break every rule in my book." He frowned. "No, not just break them. I'm ready to throw the whole damn rule book in a pit and kill it with fire." His hands slid up her arms and cupped her face. "I love you so goddamned much, Eli. I've always been so afraid of that word, but now I just want to say it over and over again. I don't want to be with anyone else. I don't want you to be with anyone else. I want all the fucking labels with you. Tattoo your goddamned name across my heart and call it yours if you want. You've got me."

A hum was moving through her, every part of her feeling more alive. She swallowed past the lump in her throat. "You've got me, too. I'm done for, Beck."

"Thank God," he said, releasing a relieved breath. He leaned close, his nose touching hers. "I'm going to kiss you now."

She shivered in his hold. "I'm going to let you."

He brought his mouth down to hers, and any chill she'd felt from the breeze off the river dissipated in an instant. The kiss was gentle at first, but their restraint didn't last long. It felt like years since they'd been able to touch. She wrapped her arms around his neck, their bodies pressing close, and their lips parted.

Their tongues tangled, and she groaned deep in her throat. His hands moved to her hips and then the backs of her thighs. He lifted her off her feet and she wrapped her legs around his waist. He pressed her against a streetlamp and kissed her long and slow, all the feelings they were now allowing themselves to admit pouring into the kiss.

"I love you," he murmured against her lips and then kissed her jaw, the sensitive spot behind her ear, the curve of her neck. Her skin burned hot. "Want you."

"I love you back," she said, breathless, her fingers gripping his hair. "Want you back."

His tongue grazed the curve of her shoulder and she moaned, but then a bright light lit up the back of her eyelids.

She winced at the shock and Beckham cursed, breaking away from the kiss but still holding her up.

"What the hell?" he said.

Eliza opened her eyes, and the light disappeared. Spots of color danced in her vision.

"What do you kids think you're doing out here?" a firm female voice said. "It's three in the morning."

Beckham set Eliza down on her feet, and her vision cleared. A dark-haired police officer was standing a few feet away, a long flashlight in her hand.

"Uh, sorry, officer," Eliza said, straightening her shirt, her face heating. "We were just, um…"

"Declaring our undying love for each other, Officer," Beckham said matter-of-factly. "No offense, but you kind of interrupted the moment. The closing song and make-out montage were about to start."

The officer gave him a dry look, but Eliza caught a hint of humor in the hitch of the woman's lips. "Have your montage somewhere else. This part of the Riverwalk is closed to visitors at this hour."

Beckham smiled and draped his arm over Eliza's shoulders. "Sorry, we didn't know. We'll get out of your way."

"Have a good night, Officer." Eliza gave her one more polite smile. The last thing she and Beckham needed to commemorate their happy moment was a ticket for trespassing.

They turned to walk in the other direction.

"What song would it be?"

The question came from behind them.

She and Beckham halted and turned. "Excuse me?"

The officer shrugged at Eliza's question, a slightly chagrined look on her face. "You said the closing song was about to play. What song would it be?"

"Oh." Eliza glanced at Beckham.

"I'd say…" Beckham smiled down at her. "'It Had to Be You.'"

Eliza stared at him, his answer pinging through her and settling in just the right spot.

The officer pointed her darkened flashlight at them and nodded. "Solid choice. You two have a good night."

The officer turned to walk away, but Eliza was still staring at Beckham. "'It Had to Be You.'"

He lifted a brow. "You approve?"

"You watched *When Harry Met Sally*," she said, delighted.

"I've watched it three times in the last two weeks. That Nora Ephron was a genius."

For some reason, that felt like the most romantic thing he'd said all night. When he'd been ignoring her at work, he'd been watching one of her favorite movies. He'd been thinking about her as much as she had thought about him.

She leaned in to him, putting her head on his shoulder, a feeling of contentment moving through her. She didn't need a man to be happy.

But she'd found the right person to be happy with. "It had to be you."

He hummed a few bars of the song and then tightened his arm around her and kissed the top of her head. "You and no one else, Eli."

They took a slow walk back into the city and found their way to the same diner where they'd first talked about the movie.

They had a strawberry cheesecake shake to share.

And a life to start.

chapter **twenty-eight**

THE SUNLIGHT CUTTING THROUGH THE CURTAINS BURNED with an intensity that had Beckham groaning and rolling over. Trent meowed, protesting the movement, and hopped down to the floor. The patter of his feet disappeared as he left the bedroom.

The clicking of doggy nails followed swiftly behind.

Beckham smiled and curled his body around the soft, warm body next to him. Eliza reached back to grab his arm, bringing it around her. "Do we have to get up yet?"

Beckham kissed the curve where her neck met her shoulder. "I think it's almost lunchtime."

"When you go to bed at five in the morning, lunchtime is way too early," she said. "Are the children fed?"

He laughed softly. "They're good. I put out food before we came to bed, and they're both out there now."

Last night after the diner visit, they'd swung by Eliza's place to pick up Mabel and bring her to Beckham's place. Even though he and Eliza had both been fall-on-their-faces exhausted after the emotional day, the thought of sleeping without her hadn't appealed.

"Good. They can keep each other busy." Eliza wiggled a little, nestling closer, her backside pressing against his quickly awakening front.

All she'd worn to bed was one of his T-shirts and a pair of panties, and it had taken every ounce of restraint he had to not touch her beyond cuddling before going to sleep. He loved her and she loved him, and that knowledge was the sexiest damn aphrodisiac he could think of. They were free to be with each other. No games. No angst. Just... him and Eliza feeling what they wanted, being how they wanted, and loving how they wanted. He'd never slept with a woman without that layer of *just friends* keeping the interaction at a certain level.

He didn't have to have that pretense with Eliza anymore. The thought made him want to do all the things, find all the ways to make her feel good.

He was glad he'd waited last night and not rushed it when they were exhausted. A sleep-soft Eliza was well worth the wait. He slipped his hand beneath the hem of her T-shirt and dragged his hand across her belly. Her skin was like silk beneath his fingertips.

She *mmm*ed quietly and her belly dipped beneath his touch. "Well, good morning to you, too."

He smiled, knowing she could feel him growing hard against the curve of her butt. "This waking up together thing is a pretty sweet gig. I open my eyes and *bam*, a beautiful, sexy Eli is right within my reach."

"Agreed," she said, arching against him and dragging the soft cotton of his boxers against his cock and making him tighten all over. "Now when I have filthy sex dreams about you, I can just roll over and have you here to help me out with that."

He'd been dragging his hand up and down her stomach, his pinkie teasing at the waistband of her panties, but her words had him pausing. "Hold up, you have filthy sex dreams about me?"

"You have no idea." He could hear the smile in her voice. "You've been haunting my dreams since we met."

He grinned. This was the best news he'd ever heard in his life. He propped his head up with his other arm, so he could see her. Her eyes were still closed, but there was a smile playing on her lips. "You're going to have to tell me one now."

She laughed and opened her eyes, turning her head to look up at him. "I do not."

"Oh, come on. You can't give a guy that kind of gift and then not let him open the present." He tugged a lock of her hair. "Give me a peek inside that dirty brain of yours."

She pressed her lips together, narrowing her eyes, but then relented. "Fine." She turned her head, leaving him with her profile. "I may have had one where we were at another NoPho party but we were playing a version of Blindman's Bluff. The one where the person blindfolded has to feel the person they caught and identify them in order to win."

"You were blindfolded?" Because he would totally be down for that game.

"No, *you* were," she said. "But you had this uncanny ability to track me. No matter where I ran or hid, you were right on my tail. When you finally caught me out on the deck, you turned me around, and I had to be quiet because I didn't want to give away who I was. You whispered against my ear that you knew how to get me to make noise. You made me hold on to the railing. Then you dropped to your knees and pushed my dress up. I wasn't wearing anything underneath." She peeked an eye open and smirked. "I really, really lost the game."

All his blood rushed downward at the image. He could picture her there on that deck, the breeze in her hair, her dress rucked up and her hands gripping the railing, her beautiful legs spread for him and the taste of her on his tongue.

"Now I know which game to suggest for the next party." He dragged his hand beneath the band of her panties, groaning when he found her hot and slick against his touch. "But no one else gets to play."

She gasped softly, rocking against his hand.

"I've dreamt about you, too," he said as he drew circles with his finger, stroking her close to where he knew she'd need it most, but taking his time getting there, enjoying this too much. "But they've all been waking dreams. You've driven me to distraction at work. The suits really do it for me."

She laughed, though it sounded a little breathless. "No one. Is turned on. By boring skirt suits."

"Eli, have you seen yourself?" he asked and kissed her neck, working his fingers along the softest part of her. "The way the skirts hug your ass. The V-neck blouses that give me just a hint of what's beneath. The heels? Come on. I've unbuttoned those suits and did bad things to you on your desk a thousand times in my head."

She shuddered against him, moving to the rhythm of his touch. "I can make that happen, you know. I do make my own schedule, and my door has a lock."

He pressed his teeth gently into her shoulder, the offer enough to drive him mad. "There goes my productivity."

She laughed and he couldn't take it any longer. He needed her. All of her.

He shifted on the bed, getting ahold of her T-shirt and pulling it up and off her. He took care of the panties next, tossed the bedcovers onto the floor, and then dragged her underwear down her hips with his teeth.

He got rid of his boxers and then crawled up the bed. She lay on her back beneath him. Her hair was a wild dark mess and her eyes were eating him up. She was so beautiful it hurt. He kissed her gently. "I'm in love with you, Eli."

She reached up and ran her fingers along his stubble. "I don't think I'll ever get tired of hearing that. I'm in love with you back."

He grabbed the T-shirt she'd been wearing and smiled. "I hope you trust me, too." He twisted the fabric and then draped it over her eyes. She exhaled sharply. "Lift your head."

She did as he asked and he knotted the T-shirt behind her head.

He put his mouth close to her ear and whispered, "Now. Don't make a sound."

....

Eliza swallowed hard, her heartbeat picking up speed. She'd told Beckham about the dream but hadn't expected him to take it to heart. She wasn't complaining, though, because every nerve in her body seemed to report for duty.

Beckham traced a finger down her sternum, taking his time, and then drew a spiral along her breast, making her nipple tighten.

"If you stay quiet," he said in that low, sexy voice of his. "I'll make you pancakes." He flicked his tongue along the underside of her breast, making her heels dig into the bed. "If you don't, you have to make *me* breakfast." He kissed the spot between her breasts. "Understand?"

She nodded, unsure if she was allowed to talk or not.

"Good girl," he said and she could hear the smile in his voice.

Normally, she'd take umbrage to being told she was a good girl. If some other dude had said that to her in bed, he'd get a lecture. But the way Beckham said it pushed some button she wasn't going to question. When you trusted someone, the sex world didn't have to be like the real world. You could play, try on different roles, feel safe to just be turned on by whatever turned you on as long as both people were into it.

Beckham took her nipple into his mouth, tugging gently and sending sensation straight downward. She tipped her head back, refusing to make noise, and gripped his shoulders. She didn't just want to play this game, she wanted to win. But he was playing dirty. He rocked his hips, dragging his cock over the slick, aching part of her. Her back curved and she bit her lip, catching a moan before it could escape.

"You feel so good, Eli," he said, canting his hips, changing angles so that little bundle of nerves was getting a full-frontal massage with every rock. The pressure was building, her body tiptoeing on the edge. "I bet we could both come just like this. Would you like that?"

Yes. Please. Yes. Her nails dug into his shoulder muscles. She nodded emphatically.

He laughed softly. "What's that? Can't hear you. Guess it's not working."

He lifted his hips away.

She wanted to scream. Her fist hit the bed.

"So frustrated," he said, obviously enjoying this. "Maybe you need a break."

She was about to give in and protest, but then his hand was bending her knee and the hot wet heat of his mouth was on her. The shock of it, of not being able to see it about to happen, heightened the feel. An audible breath escaped her, but he didn't call her on it.

Beckham had already learned her personal sweet spots, and he used that to his full advantage. He slipped his fingers inside her, finding the place that made her toes curl, and then he devoured her one stroke at a time with his tongue.

She reached blindly for his hair, got a grip on him and then channeled every ounce of her willpower to stay quiet. Her breaths were pants now, and the sound of him tasting her, that deep rumble of pleasure in the back of his throat, was one of the most erotic sounds she'd ever heard. With her vision gone, every other sense had become hyperaware. The sounds he was making, the cool feel of the sheets, the scent of his shampoo and her arousal. She was lost to all of it, her hips rocking against him, her fingers tight in his hair, keeping him where she needed him most.

Beck. Beck. Beck.

As if hearing her silent plea, he moved his fingers to exactly the right place, and she broke into a thousand pieces. Her palms planted on the bed with a hard slap, and her back lifted. The sharp, intense sound of her inhale was like someone coming back to life. Beckham groaned against her, riding the orgasm with her, and then pulling away when she finally, finally cried out.

He shifted away, giving her a reprieve, and the bed bounced as he made his way back up to her. He pulled off her blindfold, and the light created stars in her vision for a moment. When it cleared, he was staring down at her, his eyes full of fire.

"That was the hottest thing I've ever heard," he said, his voice hoarse with need.

"I couldn't stay quiet," she said, still breathless.

"You get all the pancakes." He bent down and kissed her long and deep. His cock pressed against her thigh and she reached for it.

He grunted when her hand wrapped around him.

"We're not done," she said, giving him a stroke that made him shudder. "Want to get some practice for that bending-me-over-the-desk thing?"

Heat filled his gaze. "Roll over, Eli."

"Where are your condoms?" she asked. "I can put one on for you."

His expression flickered with surprise, like the thought hadn't occurred to him. He glanced at his bedside table and then back to her. He smiled. "Roll over, Eli. A fun bonus of having a girlfriend. All we need is us. I want to feel every bit of you."

Girlfriend. The word probably shouldn't have given her such a thrill. Labels weren't important. She'd even gotten on her proverbial soapbox about it. But to hell with it. She liked hearing it on his lips.

She flipped over onto her hands and knees, her hair falling forward, and the heat of her *boyfriend* pressing against her back. He kissed her shoulder. "We're going to have so much fun together, Eli."

Yes. Yes, we are.

A lifetime of fun. She knew that without a shred of doubt coloring it.

He pushed inside her, slowly, deeply, filling her body...and filling her heart. This was new. This wouldn't always be easy. Relationships took work. But for the first time in her life, she was thankful for every terrible date she'd ever been on. Those painful, awkward, and weird experiences had taught her not to settle. They'd shown her what she didn't want. They'd given her a clear vision, so that when Beckham had walked into her life, some quiet part of her had known.

There he is. My person.

As they lay next to each other a while later, satisfied and spent and staring at the ceiling in blissed-out wonder, she took his hand.

"What are you thinking about?" he asked her, his voice soft and sleepy.

She turned to him and smiled. "That I can't wait to go on our first date."

epilogue

One Day Later

ALIGNED Dating Profile

Eliza C.
Age: 32
Location: New Orleans
Occupation: Therapist
Likes: Retro movies, chips and queso, and people who can
make her laugh
Account Status: Closed

Two Months Later

Receipt from NOLA Blue Tattoo shop

Customer—B. Carter
Description: The word Eli, upper left chest
Price: $200
Paid in full

Four Months Later

ENTERTAINMENT NEWS WITH MIZ POPPY

EXCLUSIVE: Leaving Sunday Behind

Matthew Joseph Laketon, former cast member of reality show *Seven on Sunday*, speaks out about why he left the show and his father's church, and discusses issues of children's consent on reality TV. *Click for full story*

Six Months Later

Instagram Profile

Eliza Catalano
Therapist and Future Published Author

Posts: 4015 Followers: 9542 Following: 1203
Latest posts:
#1
Photo of Eliza signing a contract

Caption: The *Dating It, Hating It* book is happening, you guys! (Tentative title because titles are hard.) The story of some really, REALLY bad online dates. A friend who challenged me to go analog and what happened next. Plus, look for a bonus chapter of great tips on how to go analog from my very pretentious, no-social-media beau. ;) Look for copies out in the world early next year!

#2

Photo of Eliza and Hollyn in flowing prairie dresses with Andi smiling in the middle with a bouquet of wildflowers.

Caption: Congratulations to two of my favorite people, author Andi Lockley and chef Hill Dawson! Their wedding registry was the best I've ever seen. We each were asked to bring one book recommendation we thought Andi would love and one recipe we thought Hill should try.

#3

Photo of Eliza, Beckham, Will, Khuyen, Trinity, and Hannah waving from a Mardi Gras float while wearing jester hats and gold eye masks.

Caption: #FlashbackFriday A NoPho party is the best kind of party but sometimes pics are nice. Flashback to that time we had the best Mardi Gras float ever and the worst costumes. Life tip: Never wear a hat with bells on it. My ears are still ringing.

#4

Photo of tiny baby socks

Caption: I'm not a mom, but seeing all these itty-bitty adorable things at my friend Hollyn's baby shower (y'all know her as Miz Poppy) is making my uterus quiver. I mean…the socks, y'all.

#5

Selfie of Eliza and Beckham on their couch. Mabel the dog is half in frame licking Eliza's face. A black cat paw is visible in the top right corner of the frame as if batting at the camera.

Caption: When you try to take a selfie with your dude to celebrate moving in together and the kids get jealous.

One Year Later

Items in Beckham's backpack

1. An early review copy of *Dating It, Hating It* signed by the author
2. A receipt for his final exit-counseling therapy session
3. A contract for the rights to his latest video game
4. A receipt from a sandwich shop where he and Eliza met up with Jess who was on her lunch break from her classes at the community college
5. A bottle of water
6. A chocolate chip LaraBar
7. Two plane tickets to Florida and the keys for his friend's beach house tucked into an envelope labeled: *You won the bet*
8. A little black box with a big shiny ring

Dedication on the opening pages
of *Dating It Hating It*

*To Harry, thank you for understanding why I needed to share this story and for being my biggest cheerleader when the writing got hard. *spoiler alert* This story has a happy ending. Never mind, you know that. You were there. I love you.—Sally*

Two Years Later

Eliza's CVS receipt

Snickers Bar $0.99

Family-size bag of Lay's potato chips $3.99

Purina One Cat Food $10.29

Pup-Peroni $4.99

Prenatal vitamins $24.99

Five Years Later

Instagram Profile

Eliza Catalano-Carter

Occupation: Therapist and Bestselling Author

Posts: 10k Followers: 31k Following: 3212
Latest posts:
#1

Photo of a group under a large oak in Eliza and Beckham's backyard. Hill with his arm around Andi and a set of cooking tongs in his other hand. Hollyn and Jasper smiling and leaning in to each other, her with a very pregnant belly and him holding the hand of their little girl, Giselle, whose curly hair has gone wild in the wind. Eliza and Beckham laughing at something and looking right at each other, their little boy, Harrison, at their feet, holding a bored Trent and wearing a Yoda T-shirt. Mabel is off to the side, breaking into a pack of hot dogs she's stolen from the bag by the barbecue pit.

Caption: Family.

#2

Photo of Eliza, Beckham, and Harrison wearing Santa hats and standing in front of the animal shelter. Eliza is holding up a sign that reads *Want to get a puppy with me?* Beckham's reads *Or a grumpy cat?* Harrison is cuddling a one-eyed calico cat that just won't leave him alone.

    Caption: Happy Gotcha Day, Solo. We show up to volunteer for pet adoption day, and the kid gets adopted by a new cat. Merry Christmas, y'all! :)

Eliza hit the button to post the photo and then she turned her phone off. Even though she'd gotten back onto social media after her initial experiment with Beckham, she only dipped in once a day and turned it off on weekends. Moderation seemed to be the sweet spot for her. Beckham still happily abstained, and they continued attending NoPho parties, but now the parties were mostly rowdy dinners at one of their friends' houses with everyone's kids running around and playing analog games.

But now it was time for a longer digital break, her annual phone break that always started on Christmas—her favorite day of the year. She tossed her phone on the coffee table and smiled as Beckham sauntered in from the hallway, looking like the best kind of Christmas present in his plaid pajama bottoms and black Grinch Stole Christmas T-shirt.

"Harrison give you any trouble?" she asked, flipping the knit blanket off her legs so she could get up.

"Nah." Beckham wrapped his arms around her and pulled her close. "He said he was going to stay up to wait for Santa, but I was only two pages into his bedtime story before he was out. Solo refused to leave. I gave up and put his cat bed in there."

Eliza laughed. "He's got your genes. Difficult felines are just drawn to him."

"It's a gift," Beckham said with a smirk. "Difficult felines and…"

He gave her an up-and-down look.

She lifted a brow. "Watch it."

"And beautiful, sexy, wildly interesting ladies," he finished and kissed the tip of her nose. "Well, one at least. The perfect number I need."

She glanced at their tree, the lights sparkling. Once upon a time, she'd never felt so alone on this holiday. But tomorrow they were going to Hill and Andi's for brunch and would spend the day with the people they loved. And tonight she and Beckham had the whole night ahead of them. "We should probably put the presents out."

Beckham's hands slid down to her waist. "Or…we can have movie night first."

She grinned up at him and looped her arms around his neck. "*Or* sounds so much better. Think we'll actually make it through a movie this time?"

"Not a chance, Eli." He lifted her up. She wrapped her legs around his waist. And he carried her off to bed.

The TV stayed dark all night.

Santa was late the next morning.

Merry, merry Christmas.

Acknowledgments

First, thank you to my readers for trusting me with your precious time and for always being so enthusiastic and kind. Hearing from you is the best part of my job.

To Donnie and Marsh, I love you the most.

To Dawn Alexander, thank you for believing that I could write this book even when I was banging my head on my desk and declaring that I definitely could not, that my writing brain was broken. (Writers can be SO dramatic.)

To my mom, for reading every book I write, and to my dad, for *not* reading them. ;)

To my editors, Mary Altman and Phuoc Le, for helping me wrestle this book into shape, and to the rest of the team at Sourcebooks for all their hard work.

To my agent, Sara Megibow, I'm so glad to have had you in my corner from the very start.

And finally, thanks to Cal Newport, author of *Deep Work* and *Digital Minimalism*, who will probably never know he's mentioned in a romance novel but whose ideas about the internet and our brains gave me the initial inspiration for a story about a woman who was in desperate need of a digital detox.

About the Author

Roni wrote her first romance novel at age fifteen when she discovered writing about boys was way easier than actually talking to them. Since then, her flirting skills haven't improved, but she likes to think her storytelling ability has. She holds a master's degree in social work and spent years as a mental health counselor, but now she writes full time from her cozy office in North Texas where she puts her characters on the therapy couch instead. She is a two-time RITA Award winner and a *New York Times* and *USA Today* bestselling author.

YES & I LOVE YOU

First in the emotionally compelling Say Everything series.

Everyone knows Miz Poppy, the vibrant reviewer whose commentary brightens the New Orleans nightlife. But no one knows Hollyn, the real face behind the media star…or the fear that keeps her isolated. When her boss tells her she needs to add video to her blog or lose her job, she's forced to rely on an unexpected source to help face her fears.

When aspiring actor Jasper Deares finds out the shy woman who orders coffee every day is actually Miz Poppy, he realizes he has a golden opportunity to get the media attention his acting career needs. All he has to do is help Hollyn come out of her shell… and through their growing connection, finally find her voice.

"Absolutely unputdownable!"
—Colleen Hoover, #1 *New York Times* bestselling author, for *The One You Can't Forget*

For more info about Sourcebooks's books and authors, visit:
sourcebooks.com

WHAT IF YOU & ME

Second in the emotionally compelling Say Everything series.

The world can be a scary place. At least, that's what Andi Lockley's anxiety wants her to believe. It doesn't help that she narrowly escaped a dangerous man years ago, or that every relationship since has been colored with that lingering fear. But things are better now—she's channeling everything into her career as a horror novelist and true-crime podcaster, and her next book may be the breakthrough she needs. If only her grumpy new neighbor would stop stomping around at all hours of the night.

Former firefighter Hill Dawson can't sleep. After losing part of his leg in a rescue gone wrong, he's now stuck in limbo. He needs to figure out what he's supposed to do with his life, and he can't let himself get distracted by the pretty redhead next door. But when someone breaks into Andi's place, Hill can't stop himself from rushing in to play the hero. Soon, a tentative bond forms between the unlikely pair. But what starts out as a neighborly exchange quickly turns into the chance for so much more...if Andi can learn to put aside her fear and trust in herself—and love—again.

For more info about Sourcebooks's books and authors, visit:

sourcebooks.com

THE ONES WHO GOT AWAY

Only a few survived the Long Acre High School shooting. Twelve years later, the kids once called The Ones Who Got Away are back...and ready to claim the lives they never truly got to live in this emotional and steamy series by *New York Times* bestselling author Roni Loren.

The Ones Who Got Away

Olivia Arias is ready to end the decade-long riff between her and Finn Dorsey and move on. But when her attempt at closure turns into a kiss that reignites their old flame, moving on proves tougher than either of them thought...

The One You Can't Forget

Chef Wes Garrett is trying to get back on his feet after losing his dream restaurant, his money, and his mind in a vicious divorce. But when he intervenes in a mugging and finds he's saved Rebecca Lindt, the divorce attorney who helped his ex-wife, his simple life gets a lot more complicated.

The One You Fight For

Shaw Miller and Taryn Landry weren't meant to meet each other. They weren't meant to fall in love. Now they're left grappling with undeniable feelings, both of them wondering: When the world defines you by a tragedy, how do you find your own happy ending?

The One for You

For Ashton Isaacs, Kincaid Breslin is the one who got away. For Kincaid, Ash is the one for her...she just doesn't know it yet. When fate throws them together, they'll have to deal with the ghosts of the past and decide who they are to each other now... and whether they can forge a future together.

"Absolutely unputdownable, delivers all of the feels! Roni Loren is a new favorite."

—Colleen Hoover, #1 *New York Times* bestselling author, for *The One You Can't Forget*

For more info about Sourcebooks's books and authors, visit:

sourcebooks.com

Also by Roni Loren